DYNASTY CODES

DARK TIDES

DYNASTY CODES

DARK TIDES

SARAH CAELAN

Dynasty Codes 2: Dark Tides
by Sarah Caelan

Paperback ISBN: 978-1-7644815-2-6
eBook ISBN: 978-1-7644815-4-0

First edition: October 2023
This edition: February 2026

A catalogue record for this book is available from the National Library of Australia

Editors: Chloe Cran and Jason Martin
Cover Art: Florianne Briffaut
Cover Format: Donika Mishineva
Map Artwork: Giulia Calligola. <lunarmorriganarts.com>
Typeset: Kristine Joy Magno

To the readers.

I'm so happy you're here to walk The Wilds with me.

This is a global tale, so we have a way to go yet before the next warm hearth and rest stop.

Lace up your boots, grab a rain jacket, and bring a flask of your favourite hot, comforting drink.

There's sea monsters around.

I C E
THE
NORTH
North by West
North North East
THE
UNKNOWN
BEYOND
East to South
East South East
South East to East
WEST

ANDS
SEA WITCH
ND
IRE
TAIHEYO
OCEAN
ITA
HIZEN
OECLA
ISHIL
DERING
ABYSS
SHON WA
CENTRAL
SEA
SOUTHERN OCEAN
WALL
OF ICE

HIÉ REGION
Aoyama Prefecture
Shogo Prefecture
SHRINE
ABANDONED FARMHOUSE
YAMAMOTO VILLAGE
GARDEN
FARMERS' HOUSE
HIÉ TOWN
HARBOUR
SECRET HARBOUR

Contents

World Map vi

Hié Region Map viii

Prologue xi

Dark Tides 1

Epilogue: And Beyond 473

Noble Blood Teaser 478

Glossary 485

Acknowledgements 489

About Sarah Caelan 492

Prologue

The boy was young when he was stolen from his home. He could never remember how old he'd been, just that he wasn't old enough to have become an apprentice. Where the boy came from, all children became an apprentice in a trade when they turned eleven. He never made it.

He grew up by the sea, in a land known as Eire to the world of trade. He just called it home. Back then, the boy never cared what his country or even his village was called. Had he known then he'd one day be taken from it, he may have paid closer attention. After all, how could the lad have known then how big the world was? Or how he'd never be able to find his way back?

The boy was taken in the dead of night. Boots thudded over the straw-covered mud that made the floor of the stone house more bearable to walk on. He startled awake as rough hands grabbed at his head and forced his mouth shut. A sack was shoved over his head, blinding him, and he was pulled from his parents' house before he could make a sound. He stumbled along at the fast pace of his captors, tripping over something beneath his bare feet. He heard the rush of the wind and the crash of the ocean against the cliffs, he smelt the sea air, he stumbled in the sand. Then he heard footsteps thudding on wood, his soles scraping against the rough grain. When they finally uncovered the boy's face, he saw the inside of a ship. That's all he saw for a couple of days, other than two other children stowed away with him. Not from his village, but he thought he recognised the boy from the next village along the cliffs. The girl, he'd never seen before.

The children weren't allowed on deck until the ship was long out at sea. There was no hope of squinting into the distance and recognising the shape of the land to one day identify it as their long-lost home.

Only a few days after they'd been taken, the girl was pulled from their stowing place and taken elsewhere on the ship. She died, screaming. She screamed a lot that night. Sometimes it was muffled, sometimes not. The boy didn't know how or why or where at the time. He could just hear the screams. It would scar him forever. When the screaming stopped suddenly, the lad held his breath and waited. A splash. He knew her body had been thrown overboard.

A soul for the great sea witch.

The other boy died days afterwards. He went pale and grey and thin like the ghouls from the scary folk tales the people from the lad's village tried to scare children with to get them to behave. He tried not to think about those scary stories. Instead, he guessed the other boy hadn't taken to the conditions of life on the ship or had eaten bad food. He knew some folks didn't handle change well, especially when the change had been that forced. Years later, he'd learn the other boy's condition had been more like the scary folk tales.

Another soul for the great sea witch.

He didn't ask what had happened to either of the other kids. He learned early on that if you ask questions, you get beaten. He'd learned that the hard way—the same way he learned scars never faded, that they acted as lessons for the future.

The young boy slaved on the pirate ship for so long that he lost track of how much time had passed. The days were strange out at sea, and sometimes he didn't even go up into the light or into the dark, depending on shifts. Like that, a long time passed. His body grew less frail and weak. It became less easy to manhandle, and the pirates knew that. It was time to move him on—to sell him, get the money, and start again.

The boy, likely well into his teen years then, was moved onto a different ship. One just as vile and from the same pirate group. This one had room for a lad his age, and they were just as ready to beat submission into him and make sure the questions were kept beaten out of him. They'd killed the previous youngster this way—too fierce with a punishment. Someone died, you got them replaced. He knew it would be the same if he died. He'd just be another soul sent to the sea witch. So, he refused to die. The lad knew within days on that godforsaken ship that he wouldn't die on it, just like he knew he wouldn't die on the last one.

His soul was his.

Among these villainous pirates, he plotted his escape. He planned and imagined it as he worked and as he lay in his stinking hammock at night, plotting until it became impossible to fail. It was just a matter of timing. The lad waited until their crawling eyes stopped observing him as much. He let them believe he'd resigned himself to the ship. He got older. The lad became one of the crew who killed and stole from merchants. He became one of the crew who crept onto land and into homes and stole other children from their beds. He saw them kill and attack the children, never learning why they bothered kidnapping the children if they were just going to kill them anyway.

He wondered why they'd never killed him.

The lad learned what happened when the pirates stole girls. And the weak boys, too. Lots of screaming, sometimes muffled, then finally a silence and a splash as the corpse was thrown overboard.

Another soul for the great sea witch.

Sometimes, they made him watch, wouldn't let him cover his ears with his hands or turn away to stop from seeing. They smirked and laughed and told him to join in. The boy threw up each time, and they laughed harder, pushing him out of the way and saying he didn't deserve to join in if he would act like that. He didn't want to. He never wanted to. He learned how to tune inwards, to see but to become blind. The lad ran through his escape in his head instead, trying to ignore the screams.

When the time came for his escape, all the boy knew was how to sail, steal, and kill. And drink. They got him into drinking pretty early, which he grew to be glad for. That way, he could hide the things he couldn't stand. As tough as the lad got physically, he was still the young boy from Eire, the land of magic, old tales, laughing people, and music, and the place people worked hard to make an honest, modest living. Somehow, this boy from the land of magic managed to survive the rough months and years on the streets of a shitty port and on just as shitty ships until he slowly made his way far to the east. He hoped they'd never find him there. The years passed as he worked a boring but honest life aboard simple ships, hauling cargo and supplies and delivering them. Eventually, he found a land he wanted to stop at. Hizen, in a region called Hié. There, he became a hunter and a workman, doing chores and physical work for people in return for payment. Less money and less drink, but it was enough for him. By this time, he'd become a man. And all he wanted was to be the man he could have been if he hadn't been stolen.

Another soul for the great sea witch …

1

A New Mission

The ship lurched beneath Gora's feet, and icy spray spotted across his face. No matter how often it happened, it still made him wince. Here, at the bow of the three-masted galleon his daimyō Ii Yoshiko had entrusted him with when she made him captain of her new navy, headed by his ship, the *Sea Guardian*, Gora could see the forever that was the ocean. Miles and miles of nothing but the boredom of the wide sea. He almost didn't care what ocean it was. They were all the same when you were sailing in them. Each just as temperamental as the other and all relying on the mood of the moon. And, until people could control the mood of a giant object that lived in the sky, the oceans would do as they wanted. Today, that meant tossing Gora and his crew about like a drunk bastard carrying a basket of eggs.

'Captain!'

Gora turned towards the voice, using his fingers to roughly comb back his soaked auburn hair to get it out of his eyes enough to see a young Hizen lad skid across the deck towards him. They both scrunched up their faces as more icy water crashed against the hull and over the gunwale. The boy's name was Miyoshi Yūki, but many of the crew on Gora's ship called the lad by his given name, Yūki, as a nod to his youth and their affection. Miyoshi's gentle name and features and how he tied his long hair back in the traditional ponytail of his countrymen meant he was often mistaken for and treated like a young girl. Here, the crew liked to play on that, too. As for Gora, he treated the boy like anyone of his crew—calling him by his last name, as was fitting in the captain–crew relationship.

He took his new role from Yoshiko seriously.

'What is it, Miyoshi?' Gora's frustration at the cold spray forced his words out more like a growl than he intended, and the lad's eyes flashed for a moment with indignation.

'Shingo wanted you to see something.'

Gora took one more resigned look out into the great stretch of grey-blue liquid hills that crashed around them. There was nothing more to see here for now, anyway. His eyes lingered on the figurehead for a moment—a beautifully carved dragon lady: woman in body, but with the scales and regalia of a dragon— before he grunted for the lad to take him to Shingo, Gora's first mate. Sprightly as ever, Miyoshi slipped and skipped across the deck, stopping regularly to look back at his captain with wide eyes and to bow apologetically for running too far ahead.

Just like a puppy. Gora sighed, wondering why he didn't just slow down and walk.

'Be careful when the seas are rough, lad,' Gora said as he caught up and pulled the lad in closer, guiding him by the shoulder.

They met Shingo holed up in his quarters, which offered him blissful privacy from their crew, which, stuck on a ship in the middle of the great expanse of nothing for weeks on end, meant luxury, even if the small wooden cabin was sparse, with little but a hammock, a chest, and a desk where a greying, stocky Hizen man gave a quick nod of his head as his captain crashed into the room.

'Shingo.' Gora strode over to join Shingo at his desk, wondering if his black hair was peppered with more greys than when they first met. 'You've been admiring that there map, now, since we left port. What more can you see in it that we've not already?'

Gora had stared at that map so much he was sure he could see it perfectly in his sleep. But Shingo, as precise and diligent as ever, couldn't drop it. It was as if he was memorising every route in the section of the world that had been inked onto that parchment.

'Captain.' Shingo stood, grunting lightly at the effort. He gestured towards the map with his hand as he spoke. 'I'm concerned about chasing pirates through their own domain. This part of the ocean is riddled with dangers, and our crew don't know it well enough. You said yourself it's been years since you sailed these waters regularly. What if something changed?'

'There's no doubt it *has* changed,' Gora stressed, shoving a cold hand into his pocket for warmth, hoping to bring back the feeling to it. 'The ocean always changes. If we were to sail back home to Hizen tomorrow, we'd meet a different sea to the one we came in.'

'*That* I can agree with. But more changes in ten years than you may think. New ports are built, rock forms break and form ribs in the sea for ships to crash upon, pirate towns move out and sea monsters move in.'

Miyoshi, still standing behind them, made a high-pitched noise at the mention of sea monsters. The two older men pretended not to hear it.

'Shingo'—Gora ran a hand through his dark red hair in disbelief—'you still believe in sea monsters? Have you ever seen one? Because I haven't. And I've even sailed the cursed black lagoon of Sagros, known for unearthly dangers.' His hand dropped to rub the stubble on his cheek. They'd been at sea roughly two weeks by this point, and he couldn't be bothered with the effort of regularly shaving on a rocking ship.

'Captain, our daimyō can turn into a dragon. I'm not ruling out sea monsters just because no-one has seen them.' When he frowned and narrowed his thin, black eyes like that, Shingo's weathered face showed his worry clearly. Too clearly. Gora would have to address that with the man in private to ensure he could shield his concerns from the crew.

'That's because everyone who sees them dies,' Miyoshi muttered. The two older men wheeled around to see the lad wide-eyed and squeezing his mouth together to say no more. 'Sorry, sirs!' He bowed and didn't look up until Gora growled at him to 'stand up straight, already'.

Their dark eyes searched Gora's for an answer. He sighed again. Until recently, he'd have scoffed at all mentions of the mysterious and magical and laughed at those superstitious enough to believe in them. He'd had enough of superstitious idiocies from his time stuck sailing with pirates—damned overly superstitious bunch of sea slugs. Ridiculous considering they were the scariest and most brutal creatures *he'd* met on the oceans. But, after he'd worked last year with the exiled noble Yoshiko, his view of things had changed. The girl had turned out to be from an ancient line of matriarchs blessed—or cursed, no-one quite knew which—by the wind and ocean dragon spirits, gaining enhanced senses and abilities. Their strong bloodline mixed with sheer determination, rage, and need to create the first daughter in generations who could transform into a dragon in the image of the spirits themselves.

After that, Gora started believing more in the supernatural. Still, he wasn't sure whether he was ready to believe in every supernatural or magical monster from all the tales of the world.

'I understand your concerns.' He let out a soft breath as he thought. 'But we have our mission, and we knew what it involved when we took it. You can't combat piracy and slavery at sea without running dangerous routes. Pirates hide in notoriously rough seas to make it difficult for them to be followed, but I'm sure even they won't hide where sea monsters live. It would make it too risky each time they tried to return. Can't live on top of a sea monster, now, can you?'

Neither Shingo nor young Miyoshi looked convinced. The lad had paled at having to deal with pirates again, and more so at the mention of sea monsters. Gora couldn't blame him.

Roughing up Miyoshi's dark hair to comfort him, Gora remembered his own experience of being stolen by pirates as a child, and he wasn't thrilled to be dealing with them again, either. But that was why he was here. If the mission would stop more children from being taken and killed, then he'd see it done—sea monsters or no.

He tried to lighten the mood a little. 'You never know. If our ship is blessed by the daimyō, who is blessed by the spirits of the wind and ocean, the sea monsters may leave us be. She's practically related to them!'

Shingo's face remained impressively stony, and the lad looked like he was about to keel over. Gora clenched his mouth shut to prevent himself from saying more.

A particularly strong spray of waves and the howl of the wind buffeting the tiny window in Shingo's cabin made the three glance outside beyond the glass. Gora scratched the back of his head, as he always did when he thought hard about something, and hummed in thought.

'She's looking angry outside. And it'll only get worse over the next couple of days. If we can hold out tonight, we can pull into a nearby port for a little more safety to last out the storm.' He looked at Shingo, hoping the man would know which one he meant without Gora having to say it with Miyoshi in the room.

'You wouldn't be planning on pulling into Shon Wa, would you?' Shingo growled.

Gora winced and snapped his head to look at Miyoshi, who shot in: 'Shon Wa? Isn't that the sketchy pirate port we pulled into before?'

The lad paled, and for good reason. The last time Gora's crew pulled into Shon Wa port, Miyoshi had accompanied him to the port to see it for himself, refusing Gora's warnings. Many of the lowlifes in the port on their last visit had mistaken Miyoshi for a girl, with his youthful, clear face and long hair, and Gora had needed to protect him from all sorts of grabbing hands.

'It's the nearest place we can call a port to shelter from the storm. And we need answers. We'll not find out where old Frewin is hiding if we head to a government harbour. If we can bring the ship into a cove here'—he pointed on the map at a little indent by Shon Wa port—'then we won't be in the thick of the pirates. I can then go on land and nose about a bit to find out where that old sea slug is while the crew stays aboard.'

Shingo huffed through his nose and bent over the map once more, trying to find the little nook Gora pointed out. Miyoshi waited, bouncing on his toes.

Then Shingo sighed. 'I'll follow you, captain. We knew our mission was hunting pirates. We knew what it would involve, and we can't hide from them forever, and that there port *is* the closest to hide from the storm in.'

As if to prove a point, the ship lurched on a particularly high wave, and strained cries could be heard from their fellow sailors on deck trying to keep the *Sea Guardian* steady. They nodded to one another and ran up to join them, immediately met by heavy cold spray in their faces. Jelani, a tall, sun-blessed southerner from Qecla, padded barefooted towards Gora.

When Jelani reached Gora's side, Shingo darted off to delegate the bringing about of the ship to turn towards Shon Wa.

'Captain?' Jelani roared over the noise of the growing storm, despite standing next to Gora. Standing beside him, Gora always gave a double-take at how tall Jelani was, all lanky arms and legs. Gora was fairly tall—or so he believed—but Jelani, lean like a blue-crested crane of Hizen, stood a whole head taller. So now Gora looked up into the man's giant brown eyes and serious face, immediately sensing the worry on the man's face.

'Aye?'

'There's a ship off our port bow. Can't see the details yet, sir.' Jelani's Hizen was getting good after being with the crew for so long, spoken with the clipped accent of the Qeclan people.

The storm was bringing all pirates in the area into Shon Wa, seeking shelter. Thinking it unlikely they'd attack the *Sea Guardian* when hunting for a place to dock, but knowing it wouldn't do to be reckless, Gora squinted up the mainmast to check who was in the crow's nest. Quinni.

'Tell Quinni to keep it under observation and let us know anything further,' Gora decided. 'Once you've relayed the message to him, go check the cannons and the gun port. Take Taro and Kyo with you, won't you?' Jelani nodded and bound for the shrouds. Even in a storm, he climbed them better than a chipmunk up a tree. Gora's attention turned to Miyoshi, who was slinking past. 'Lad, pass the message to the others to keep an eye out for pirates, now. There's a ship ahead we need to watch.'

The lad frowned but nodded, already rushing on to his next duty as Gora strode to join his helmswoman Yonemura at the helm.

Like most of the *Sea Guardian's* crew, who were mostly from Hizen fishing families or local merchant sailors, Yonemura was born to the seas around Hizen. The small woman, soft-faced despite being in her fortieth years, was almost as well respected and high ranking as Hizen coast-folk came. She'd lost her family to the Acrein slave raids and managed to escape Acrein with Gora and Yoshiko, becoming a crucial part of their journey home thanks to her skill in navigating and ship handling. Afterwards, not wanting to return to an empty house, she'd vowed to Yoshiko she'd use her skills and knowledge of sailing to help the cause. Yoshiko had rewarded Yonemura well and given her one of the top positions on the *Sea Guardian*—second mate and helmswoman. Gora was glad of it. Yonemura was the most skilled crew member at the helm and could navigate through any danger. This moment was no exception. He could see Yonemura grimace as she hefted the great helm by the spokes and held it steady, her small frame holding the galleon's weight with ease. The route ahead was no problem; her charcoal-coloured eyes pierced the waters ahead as if she could see through the waves.

'Yonemura!' Gora cried over the rising wind as he got closer. She bowed her head and caught his eye briefly but kept her focus ahead. 'Shingo told you the headings?'

'Yessir. The cove's still a little way off. And there's a ship ahead.'

She gestured her head to the side slightly and Gora followed, nodding. 'Jelani said too. He's checking cannons in case we need to fire a warning. But I don't think they'll trouble us. They'll be heading for shelter too. And drinks. Lots of them.'

Yonemura smirked. 'Good job the daimyō gave us an incon-spicuous ship. Can't tell who we are.' Her higher voice cut through the low howl of the wind like a blade.

Gora agreed, and for a moment, they made proud talk of the ship Yoshiko had given them. It had been fixed and refurbished after being taken as a prize for beating Acrein, now a high-class warship galleon with all the glories of both Acrein and Hizen. The black lacquered body and red lacquer trimmings gave it quite the impact. It was the perfect disguise for going undercover to go after pirates and slave traders without being traced back to Hizen.

Yonemura yelled across the deck for the crew to brace themselves, and she pulled the ship into a rough starboard turn at the peak of a wave. With the bow searching out shallower waters beyond a series of rocks ahead, Gora was sure he could already smell the stench of a pirate settlement.

Just imagining it, he growled to himself, crossing his arms over his chest as his crew ran about and worked the ship without orders.

Yonemura tugged at the helm again to avoid a rock formation ahead, and the ship slid down the roots of a wave in answer. Finally, they hit the calmer waters behind the boundary of the rock formation.

'Hurry! Get her past that cliff before the other ship reaches the rocks,' Gora bellowed out over the noise of the ocean beyond the rocks. On gentler waters, though still not home and dry, the crew darted more easily across the deck and pulled at the rigging. Yonemura wove between upcuts of rock, her eyes darting like a hawk's, navigating the ship around rocks before Gora even knew they were there. He left her at the helm and ran to get a better view of the stern side, leaning on the gunwale and squinting his eyes to watch the distance. Just as the crew pulled into calm waters beyond the cliffs, the pirate vessel behind them cut past the rock formation. The crew of the *Sea Guardian* held their breath for a moment, staring at the following ship.

It sailed on, deeper into Shon Wa waters, straight towards the main port.

'Are they avoiding us, sir?' Miyoshi piped up from behind Gora, his dark hair appearing by Gora's elbow as the lad leaned on the gunwale, copying his captain.

'Looks like it. More focused on getting to port at this point. They know we're here, but I don't think they'll bother coming out in this weather.' *Not when there's drink and bad sex waiting for them,* he added to himself.

Miyoshi pulled a face, still watching the other ship with wary eyes.

'Don't worry, lad. We'll be staying here. At least, you will be.'

'You're going to land?'

'I need to find out about our old friends,' he said as he turned away, smiled reassuringly to the young lad, and then paced across the deck and watched Shingo handle the dropping of the anchor. Gora checked their position. 'She'll be good here, Shingo,' he called.

Shingo nodded. Quinni was scaling the shrouds with the same ease Jelani had—despite his much broader, larger physique—and jumped beside them with little sound. If Gora hadn't seen the man coming, he'd have leapt out of his skin. Instead, he clapped his hands on the man's great back and smiled.

'Jelani's below deck sorting out the cannons and resources. Go check on him. We may need them yet. We'll be here tonight.' Gora grimaced at the thought as he watched Quinni disappear below the deck in long, loping strides. As he stood there, a huge gust of icy wind hit him, and the realisation of having to stay here through the storm—here, of all places—sank in just as quickly as the anchor they'd just dropped.

Shit, Shon Wa, the fuckin' mess of a place the sea scum of the oceans wash up at to drink, dick about, then drown in debts they collected from it all. And to think I'd once vowed I'd ne'er return. Here I am again. Twice in one year!

As a cabin boy to the pirate captain Foy, and then under Frewin's command, Gora had visited Shon Wa many times. One of the more infamous of the free ports, it was one of the few places safe for pirates to dock. There'd be no merchants or military sniffing about there. It was free for the worst of the people to do as they wished. There were only a few other places like it in all the oceans. The problem was, being a safe landing spot for sea scum and pirates meant it was also infamous for being one of the least safe places in all the oceans.

Gora looked about the deck to see who of his crew looked remotely scary enough to join him on his trip to the port and back.

No-one. No-one really looked the part.

Previously, he'd taken Jelani, another Hizen man who'd not joined them on this journey, and Miyoshi, who had insisted on seeing the strange place. Miyoshi had attracted too much of the wrong attention from all the foul men of the sea for his young, feminine looks. Though the people who washed up here didn't care for gender. Anyone vaguely pretty made it onto their list. Here, Miyoshi would be like a gift from the spirits. Quinni was probably the closest to being the sort of person to take to port. He was tall, well built, and knew his way around a fight. But Gora wondered if he'd be ready for a trip to Shon Wa. There was a softness in him that wouldn't sit well there. Quinni was simply too kind, and it would be easy for the pirates to read that from his face.

Instead, Gora wondered who else.

Ikeda hopped up onto the deck from helping Jelani check the cannon deck. As a Hién guard, he'd know his way around a fight and easily handle the pirates. Plus, Ikeda had fought alongside Yoshiko, and Gora knew he came with great recommendation, though Gora still grumbled that the lad should have stayed back in Hié as Yoshiko's personal guard and not abandoned her like he himself had to chase ugly pirates halfway around the world.

But he's too pretty, Gora growled to himself, looking over Ikeda's flawless skin and long hair, which was pulled back in a tie away from his face. He'd cause more of a fuss than Miyoshi did. *They'd ruin him. Partly from jealousy and partly from lust over anything even remotely beautiful—a need for treasure.* Pirates, he knew, took anything beautiful they could get their rough, sea scum hands on.

Not Ikeda, then. He can guard the ship.

'Daiki, I'd like you to join me to port.' Gora called one of the more rugged-looking Hizen men over. Daiki, Ikeda's mentor, had been a high guard of Hizen for many years and was recommended by Yoshiko. He'd been one of the guards loyal to her father, the philosopher and poet Hitoshi, the husband of the previous daimyō, and had been blackmailed during the takeover when the noble family went missing. This meant his family had been taken to

Acrein on the first ship, leaving Daiki behind, forced to work hard in the hopes the traitorous council would stick to their word and bring his family back. They never did. Daiki had shaved his head, losing the traditional long hair of the Hizen warriors, and vowed to avenge his family. He joined Gora's quest to combat slavery and piracy on Yoshiko's suggestion. He'd be the perfect person to join Gora at Shon Wa.

Miyoshi ran past, skidding in front of a bulky Hizen man—Sakai, the newest of his crew, hired just before they left Hizen. The lad chatted happily, and Sakai turned to face him, too. He nodded at his captain politely.

Of course! Gora had his man.

Gora didn't know much about Sakai—the man kept his past to himself—but Gora had managed to get a bit out of him before he hired him, said he couldn't let him on the ship without knowing the basics. Had to keep his crew safe.

Sakai had understood. He'd spoken to Gora in private, explaining he was from a different domain and had run to Hié to escape his past—a dangerous one he'd been forced to join due to poverty, and one that he was now determined to leave.

'Just want a simple life now, sir. A good one.' Sakai's heavy-set face showed the shadows of his past, and Gora immediately related. 'Honest work, you know.'

Gora *did* know.

He'd stressed their mission and its danger, but Sakai didn't seem to care. Said it would be good to earn some good karma under his name. Gora had hired him—he certainly needed as many people as he could find. The crew was still too small to face the threat he knew he was up against. And while he still had his doubts about Sakai, he knew months of being in close quarters on a ship would give plenty of opportunities to dig up more of the man's past.

Taking Sakai to Shon Wa with him would be the perfect opportunity. And Sakai's more dangerous history would make him an ideal candidate for being on guard in that scummy place.

Trio decided, there was no time to waste. The drinkhouses of Shon Wa were calling, and it was time to hunt.

Quinni and Ikeda stood guard by the rope that led over the side of the ship towards the rowing boat they'd lowered into the cove for the three heading to Shon Wa. They nodded silently to the solemn trio as they climbed over the side and into the bobbing vessel. Even from this far, Gora could see the concern in Ikeda's eyes as his mentor went and he couldn't follow. The lad had been keeping an eye on his mentor ever since Daiki had lost his family. Gora was sure this was the first time they'd been separated since.

'Shingo?' Gora roared up at them. Shingo peered over the edge. 'Don't come after us. No matter what. We'll find a way to get back. This ship, and anyone on it, must not enter Shon Wa. If we don't make it back, you know what to do.'

Shingo nodded and clapped a frowning Ikeda on the shoulder. 'Yessir!' he bellowed back over the roar of the storm, giving the young samurai a stern look that clearly said, *That's how it will be.*

Aye, that's how it'll be, now. But Gora knew he'd be damned if he'd be stranded on Shon Wa, even if it meant swimming back through a storm. Or dying trying.

2

Into Shon Wa

The little boat bobbed recklessly through the rising waves towards Shon Wa port, the rising storm even roughing the sea in this protected harbour. The ships loomed like giants, their masts reaching up to scrape the heavy black clouds as Gora and his companions wove through the labyrinth of stinking pirate hulls, narrowly missing a schooner as it pitched on a wave that rocked the dockings. As Gora muttered under his breath, Gora, Daiki, and Sakai leapt up onto the ancient, creaking wooden jetty, and Gora shoved a coin into a port-slave's hand to tie the boat up and watch it well. Even then, he still half-expected they'd have to swim back or steal a return vessel. Daiki and Sakai stiffened and fell in behind their captain, glancing about darkly, curling and uncurling their fists with an all-too-clear agitation that made Gora nervous. Daiki's eyes flitted about as he took in the sights that were so unfamiliar, curling his lips and nose in disapproval of the rancid smell of too many drunk bodies gathered in one place—and the crew hadn't even hit the main drinkhouse street yet.

'I hate this place already,' the old samurai muttered, fiddling with his sword hilt.

'It's like the underbelly of Kioto,' Sakai muttered, causing Gora and Daiki to whip their heads to look at him. The stocky man shrugged. 'Don't get me wrong, it's nice on the surface, but ain't if you end up in the wrong crowd.'

He fell silent there, and neither of the others pushed any further. Instead, they stomped across the mostly worn planks of the extended port town, breath hitching at any hint of creaking or cracking beneath their boots, wondering at the many buildings and stools resting on the very planks the port was built on. Each time Gora visited, he became more and more amazed the place didn't collapse under the weight. To their side, two pirates scuffled and tumbled to the ground. As they fell, the thunderous crash reverberated through the planks beneath their feet, rattling their bones and seemingly every drinkhouse in the row, judging by the sound of tinkling metal and wooden tankards tumbling into one another. Gora swore the whole place was ready to collapse in on itself. But, somehow, by the fate of the world's curses and the stickiness of spilled spirits, the wooden boards held together.

Thank fuck for that.

Their destination lurked ahead: a popular tavern known as the Kraken's Belly in Traders' language. Traders' was a linguistic stew, with words and phrases from every corner of the world simmering together, a language that every international trader, merchant, sailor, and pirate had to know if they wanted to do any kind of business. The Kraken's Belly was meant to be a place where pirates could drink and eat their fill, but Gora would never call what they served 'food'. Better than the slop most pirate ships served up, though, particularly on the deep mission where you could be at sea for months on end. And as he, Daiki, and Sakai wouldn't be eating here, he didn't need to worry about the bout of food sickness that always followed eating in such places.

'All we're here for is news of Frewin,' he told the other two, keeping his voice low but struggling to compete with the raucous laughter and bellowed curses all around them. 'Don't eat or drink anything anyone offers you. If he pulled into Shon Wa at any point, this'll be the place he'll have been. He always comes here. Bet there's something in it for him. If not, they'll still have news.' The two nodded, faces serious and eyes darting about.

'Oy, 'keep,' Gora called out in Traders' as they got to the grimy bar. He leant his elbows on it, instantly regretting it as he felt a liquid seeping through his shirt sleeves.

The tavern keeper—or 'keep, as everyone called them— grunted back at Gora, eyeing him up warily, wiping his nose as he glared. Daiki looked personally offended at the lack of manners, but, used to it, Gora shrugged and held his gaze. When it looked like the man was listening, Gora called out again.

'We're lookin' for Frewin. Ain't seen him about, have ye?'

The 'keep glared. 'Woss it to ya?' There was something wrong with his eye, Gora decided. It was just stuck in one place. And he wasn't a Shon Wa local; his skin was too pale, like he was from a north-western country. Gora realised he must've turned off a ship here.

'Need t' chat. We made a deal a few months back.' Gora slouched a little where he stood, hooking his thumbs into the waist of his slacks. He and the other two had chosen their most casual and least conspicuous clothes. Simple sailor garb. And Gora had left his Hizen captain's jacket behind. No-one needed to know who he was. Here, he was just a simple sailor. For added emphasis, Gora looked lazily about the tavern, filled to the brim with noisy, drunken, rowdy sea slugs crashing into one another and spilling their drinks as they clumsily bumbled about between the bar and their stools.

The 'keep sniggered, and Gora saw the man had lost half his teeth, the others soon to follow judging by their ill colour. 'Wotcha makin' deals with Old Frewin fer? Stupid fing t' do.'

Gora shrugged and leant back against the bar, looking boredly out to the drinking and fighting ahead. Daiki and Sakai were trying too hard, standing as stiff as wrestlers trying to prove themselves: fists curled, faces in full frown. Gora frowned too. They'd attract more attention that way.

'Relax a little, you two,' he said to them in Hizen. 'You'll bring the fight to us, lookin' like that.' Then he turned to face half on to the 'keep, flashed a grin, and continued in Traders', 'S'fine. Used t' sail with him. Go waaay back. The old codger practically raised me.'

The 'keep scrunched up his face as he scrutinised Gora again. 'Don't look like a pirate, lad.'

Gora shrugged again. 'Can't help that I'm pretty,' he teased and flashed his most charming grin before letting his face quickly fall blank again. 'Anywho, he been around lately? Need t' pay him back, ya know. Maybe you'll get a share of it … if you help us out.'

The mention of payment perked the man at the bar up. Gora immediately knew he'd won. The 'keep pretended to wipe down the bar with a cloth that only seemed to add more grime to it, and Gora thought he heard the *shlopping* noise as it pulled away from decades of spilt spirits. Really, the 'keep was more interested than ever, and Gora could read the forced focus on the man's face as he tried to hide the greedy look in his eyes. All pirates and their associates were the same. It was easy to spot.

'Woz 'ere las' week, or woz it more?' The 'keep decided he knew something after all. He stood up straighter, puffed out his chest, and grinned his toothless smile as if he had something really juicy to tell now money was on the table. 'Over'eard summat about Ishil. By the sea witch's great tits, did he look rough. All red and scarred and burned, like. Like 'e'd just been boiled. Wouldn't happen t' know wot happened to 'im, would ya?'

Gora's eyes widened. *That would've been Yoshiko*, he realised. To the 'keep, Gora just swore. 'Sounds rough. Last I met him, he was just as wrinkly and normal as ever. Nothin' red abou' him but his big sunburnt nose.'

The 'keep roared with laughter, drawing the attention of some drinking sea scum nearby. Gora felt his body tighten and tried not to make eye contact. 'Well, not just 'is nose, now.' The 'keep leaned over the grimy bar and rubbed his fingers together. Gora rolled his eyes and slapped a couple of coins in the 'keep's hand before his eyes bulged further and he drooled even more. Shon Wa accepted any currency if you handed over enough of it. There were enough people sailing anywhere that anything could work.

Gora had handed him a couple of shiny Acrein coins he'd taken from the ships after the invasion. There was no way he wanted to be giving them any clues they'd come from Hizen. They didn't need anyone else turning up with ships and cannons on the coasts.

The 'keep eyed the coins as much as Gora knew he would— new and shiny, straight from the Acrein warships. 'Di'n't peg ya for an Acrein, lad.'

'I'm not. Just had a bit of fun with one of their ships recently.' He wasn't exactly lying.

The 'keep's eyes flew open in amazement; clearly, he believed Gora about knowing Frewin from the past a little more. 'Not easy ships to raid, them. Not bad, lad. And 'ere woz me lookin' at your lads there, thinkin' you woz all a bunch of flounders!'

Sakai and Daiki had relaxed into lounging positions by the bar, staring in opposite directions, Sakai with his arms folded over his chest, muttering at Daiki. They looked more the part now, but Gora could easily imagine what the 'keep meant. Even Sakai with his gang-lifestyle past appeared only half as intimidating as these sea slug folks. Gora shrugged, and not wanting to hang around to attract any more conversation or attention, Gora muttered something to the 'keep about needing a good whore or two and strode off, calling Sakai and Daiki to follow.

He'd never seen them move quicker.

'Did you get the information you needed, captain?' Daiki asked, eyes scouring their left flank like the military man he was. He still moved too stiffly. Gora made a note to pull him up on the fact he wasn't officially a well-esteemed man of the royal guard anymore. He had to pretend to be a mercenary now.

'I did. Tell you on the ship.'

'I'm amazed such a person could tell you anything of use,' the guard continued, turning back to look at the tavern for a moment, lip curling again.

'The underworld knows everything,' Sakai said, his voice low, dangerous.

Gora nodded in agreement, scratching at his arm. He always felt itchy in such places. Like the dirt of others was rubbing off on him even as he passed them. *Probably is—fleas.* He shuddered and distracted himself.

'Well, you'd be amazed at how much people who sell alcohol for a living in a pirate port know about everything,' Gora said. 'You just need to pay them enough to loosen their tongues.'

They were interrupted by Sakai jumping as something rushed at them from the right. A man crashed into them, narrowly missing taking Sakai down with him. Instead, the old mercenary had jumped out of the way, surprisingly nimble for his bulk, letting the pirate collapse in a heap on the port boards. Daiki instantly drew his sword and leaned over the man, glaring at him with a dare to even move. Noticing movement from the place the pirate came from—the pirate who was now squirming on the floor and squinting up at Daiki's blade in his face—Gora saw the red and snarling face of a tavern maid. She'd just kicked the man out, he realised, literally. Without waiting any longer, she simply turned on her heels and marched back between the tables, grabbing orders and empty mugs as she went. Gora snorted as the sorry-looking sap beneath them slithered off to find another tavern.

So, that's how it had been.

Workers here knew the drill.

'Let's get out of here,' Gora said, urging them through the drunken crowds and chairs. 'It stinks.'

At this, Daiki sheathed his blade, but his hand never left the grip until they were pushing back out in their little rowboat to return to the ship. Even then, he watched the port with narrowed eyes until they rounded the cliff and Shon Wa disappeared. The three men pushed the boat against the strong winds towards the *Sea Guardian,* muscles aching to heave the tiny vessel over the growing crests. They were pleased to see Quinni hailing them from above and calling the others to lower the rope ladder. Night was falling. Gora didn't want to waste any more time in such a place. When evening fell, the chance of passing through Shon Wa without attack was close to zero, and navigating the ship through a labyrinth of rocks back to the open ocean in the dark would be just as dangerous. Not even Yonemura's keen eyes and skilful steering could get them through into the open ocean. And with a storm raging, there was no hope out at sea. Instead, they'd have to stay the night in their little nook, hoping the pirates in Shon Wa were too content with drink and bad sex to come out in the storm. Gora knew it would be foolish to slack. By dark, he'd set a strong watch at points around the ship. No-one would be getting close.

3

Mapping The Route

Shingo, Yonemura, Daiki, Jelani, and Sakai gathered with Gora in his large captain's quarters at the aft of the ship, below the poop deck, to hear the report. Though Daiki and Sakai had been there, their minimal knowledge of Traders' would have meant they didn't understand what had been said. Jelani was the strongest at Traders' in the crew, but even his ability was limited to mostly ship commands.

'We're heading for Ishil. Remember the pirate, Frewin, that followed us from Acrein into battle then tried to steal those three kids?' Everyone but Daiki and Sakai nodded and muttered something of disapproval. 'Apparently, he's there. Been this side of the world since we saw him, so he's our first target. We can try to get information from him, too.'

'We're not teaming up with him again, are we, captain?' Shingo looked rightfully concerned.

Yonemura cursed at the thought, and everyone looked at her in surprise. It wasn't the sort of language to expect from a respectable Hizen woman. Gora grinned, knowing his language was influencing her, then continued, 'Not ever again. You know we only did last time because they forced themselves on our ship. The daimyō gave us the mission to take down the pirate and slavery circles. This time, we're finishing what she started. That ship and its crew will not be sailing again.'

The four faces around him looked confused. Gora relayed what he heard from the 'keep.

'Frewin's hurt. After he took the Hizen children and Yoshiko went after him, he's badly burned. He'll be weak. We know he's on one of the ships that deals with child kidnapping and slavery, so let's get him and then hit the next ship.' Gora gritted his teeth, trying not to remember the time he'd been sold to Frewin. He wondered if he could remember the location of that old pirate slave-trading town, the place all the kids that survived were sold onto the next ship.

'What's the name of their ship, captain?' Daiki asked.

'The *Cutter*,' he replied in Traders', then translated the rough meaning of it for them in Hizen. 'And the name fits them—the damned sea scum cut down anyone and anything in their path. Ship's captained by Frewin; he bought me from the old son-of-an-ogre Foy who kidnapped me as a child. He's right in the thick of everything and happy to be there. If we can take him down, it'll be a big hit for the pirate and slave circles. Piece of sea scum.'

The others fell silent, staring at the small wooden desk between them all. They'd had to know to be able to sail with him on this mission. His crew had a reason of their own to leave their lives in Hizen. Most had been captured as slaves by the Acrein slave traders, had their families taken, or had been blackmailed by the corrupt council and had their families threatened, or a combination of the three. Everyone here had a strong motive to be against the pirates. It wasn't the sort of mission Yoshiko and Gora had wanted people to go on without the personal drive, as it put her citizens in danger. Everyone had to have the motive to fight.

Even the lad, Miyoshi. He'd been taken as a child with his mother to Acrein. They both managed to find each other again on the ship after the escape. Since then, Miyoshi had been eager to stay with Gora on the ship and use his experience from fishing boats to help Gora's crew. It had taken a lot of persuading to his mother to let him come on the ship. But Miyoshi had been determined. Yoshiko and Gora had to vow Gora would do whatever he could to keep Miyoshi safe.

The room was silent except for the squeaking of the shifting woodwork as the vessel pitched and rocked in its mooring.

'So, Ishil.' Shingo brought Gora and the others back into the room. He tapped his finger on the map to bring their attention to the sprawling coastal lines. Everyone scooted closer. 'If the weather is good and we maintain a steady pace of between ten and twelve knots, we can be there in between nine and eleven days. It's on the other side of that continent'—he prodded a rough finger on the map—'so we'll have to go around that leg there. Looks like the best route is just right round the central sea and up the coast. No point cutting through.'

'Any sea monsters known to dwell in those waters?' Gora teased, losing his grin as Shingo gave him his best old fisherman glare. Say what you want about pirates and mercenaries; the put-out and hardworking folks who knew true hardship gave the best rough looks.

'We'll find out by dangling you by your feet over the bowsprit, captain,' Shingo warned. 'There's plenty of rigging strong enough.'

Jelani sniggered. Gora knew he had lost and, not allowing them to see the first mate dominating the captain, threw his hands in the air with raised eyebrows and feigned surrender. 'Alright, ol' man. I'm just kidding, now. I've heard nothin' of sea monsters in those parts. Our crew's safe—from that at least.'

Gora's gaze met Yonemura's across the table. She used a simple *kanzashi* to pin back a section of her black hair, leaning over the map. 'Yonemura, study the map during the storm. Get your bearings. You can stay here while I'm on deck.'

Yonemura nodded.

Gora turned to Daiki next. 'Continue training the crew. They've improved, but we need more. Pirates are reckless. Fighting with honour won't work. Teach them to play dirty.'

Daiki bowed, promising daily reports.

'Sakai.' Gora's heart skipped a beat as he locked eyes with the man. Shadows from the flickering lantern danced on Sakai's hardened face, reminding Gora of the underworld he had emerged from. 'Join Daiki in teaching the crew how to fight. Your street fighting is well needed.'

Gora looked at Sakai meaningfully. He wasn't going to reveal Sakai's dark past—wasn't his place. That was the man's own business to tell people if he wanted. But he wasn't going to lose the opportunity to have the crew—his honest, honourable crew—learn from the only man on board who'd had experience with the rough side of the world.

Sakai nodded solemnly, and he bowed his head next at Daiki, who observed the man with curiosity. *Let's hope it helps him open up a bit. Get to know the crew more.*

Jelani stepped forward. 'And me, sir?'

'Jelani, you understand a bit of Traders', right?'

'Basic, sir. Orders only,' Jelani replied, and Gora saw the man's face drop for a moment as he reminisced about his time as a slave, toiling on Acrein ships in the local ports and river routes.

'Think you can teach the crew some basic phrases?'

Jelani's grin returned, revealing gleaming teeth, and he seemed thrilled to take on a guiding role. 'Yes, sir.'

'Good. We all need to understand Traders' to understand the people we're up against. It's impractical for me to translate all the time. Everyone sailing and dealing internationally should know it. I'll teach you more, and together, we'll ensure the crew learns. From now on, this ship speaks both languages.'

Jelani nodded, and they dispersed. Only Yonemura was left, bent over the map with a compass and a frown, tucking a stray lock of her hair behind her ear to keep it out of her way.

4

Killing Time on the Way to Ishil

They left with the storm. While the pirates and sea scum of Shon Wa were nursing their hangovers and peeling themselves from the damp beds of whores or the floors of taverns, the crew of the *Sea Guardian* set sail before the first ray of the sun's light had inched over the horizon.

The *Sea Guardian* made the slow and steady pace of a ship that had a decent wind behind it and a sea that had got over its tantrum under it. Gora was happy the sea witch had calmed her moods; the next few days were easy sailing. Easy and boring. Gora felt the mind-numbing nothingness of being out at sea.

To combat the tedium, the crew drilled weapons and fighting with Daiki and Sakai, and Jelani taught them how to understand and respond to orders in Traders'. Others diligently worked on the ship, their gazes filled with envy as they watched Yonemura kick Miyoshi's behind in training. Raucous laughter pealed over the ship as the crew playfully taunted the lad for losing to a woman in her middling years. Indignant, Yonemura sought her revenge by skilfully defeating those who had laughed at her expense.

With things to learn and keep themselves occupied with, the crew were less bored and rowdy and had something to focus on. Gora, on the other hand, well, Gora was as bored as an ice siren sitting in the vast waters of the Penrath Expanse—a supposedly cursed region of the Southern Ocean. Few dared to sail there. The combination of icy waters, tumultuous storms, and the ghost of the previous sea witch who had been sunk there by terrified pirates meant few went in. For, when the foolish few went in, the bored ice sirens took full effort to steal their prey, glad to finally have something to do. That was exactly how Gora felt. He'd run all the ship's numbers countless times and checked on the ship, the crew, the routes, and the seas. Now, there was nothing to do but watch with envy as his crew clashed wooden staves, and he battled his position and wondered whether it would be acceptable to join in. What did a captain do when it came to spare hours? He couldn't remember.

His decision was interrupted as Miyoshi appeared beside him, wrestling with a tangled ponytail after being roughed up by Yonemura. Out at sea where rougher winds blew salt water, Miyoshi was forever trying to untangle his hair.

'Need a hand, kid?' Gora asked after watching Miyoshi scrunch his face up with effort for a moment.

'What you gunna do?'

'I was thinking of braiding it for you. Most sea-faring folk do. Keeps it easier to handle.'

'What's a braid?'

Gora thought for a moment. 'Remember some girls back in Hizen had part of their hair in a style that went down the side of their head like a little crown? Or like Yonemura has now, twisted up in a spiral behind her head?'

Miyoshi narrowed his eyes, wondering if this was going to be another joke about how feminine he looked. Gora hurried to explain further.

'Well, that's a braid. People of all genders do it all over the world. In different ways. It looks good and it's easy to look after.'

'Is it a girls' thing?'

'No. Sailors, pirates, warriors, and anyone really, do it, too. I've seen some warriors from the north put little braids down the sides of their heads and in their beards, with rune-beads as talismans for luck and protection. And remember when those pirates came to Hizen?'

He nodded.

'Did'ya see any pirates with their hair tied back in one of those braids?'

The boy thought for a moment. 'Oh, yeah. I saw a couple. Didn't look great though. All slimy.'

'That's because they don't take good care of it. But, if you clean it as much as you can while we're on the ship, comb it, and braid it, then it'll be fine. Like Yonemura's. Hers looks nice, right? You won't have to untangle it as much as you are doing now, too.'

'Why don't you have a braid then? You used to be a pirate, right?'

'*Used* to be,' Gora stressed, feeling a pang in his chest at being associated with those sea scum. 'Not all pirates have them, just some. But I admit I did used to have one. I cut it when I ran away. I prefer it short, like my dad used to have.'

'Did he have red hair, too?'

'You bet, kid. It was even more red than mine.'

'No way!'

'It's true. Now, want that braid?' Gora suggested, hoping the lad would accept.

Miyoshi nodded and spun around so Gora could reach his hair. Gora leaned back against the gunwale and took the comb the boy had been impatiently tugging through his long, black hair.

'How'd you know how to untangle it like that?'

'Years of practice. I hated having long hair. Mine's wavier than yours, so it got tangled all the time. I got it in a right mess once when I combed it like you were, starting from the top and just tugging and tugging, hoping the knots would come out. It just made a huge ball of messy, knotted curls that wouldn't come out, no matter what. I nearly hacked it all off. But I tried working from the bottom, getting rid of the tangles bit by bit. It hurt less and worked, so I just started doing it like that all the time.'

'It's how my mum does it, too. But I get too impatient. It was never a problem until recently. The wind out here is really strong.'

Gora hummed in agreement and finally tugged all the knots out to reveal Miyoshi's long, naturally straight hair. Then he split the boy's hair into three sections and passed the comb back.

'Usually, people split their hair into three parts for a braid. You can do more if you want to be fancy, but that's for rich people with too much time on their hands. Or fancy occasions like weddings. Three will be fine.'

'Okay.'

'First, you bring an outside piece over the middle one and hold it there. Then the opposite outside piece over the new middle one. Then another outer piece over the new middle one. Can you see where I'm going with it now?'

'Not really.'

'Point is, always work to bring an outside piece over the middle one and hold it in its new place. Left, right, left, right, choosing a new piece every time. Do that all the way to the bottom.'

He nodded, but Gora wasn't sure the lad fully understood.

'Good; pass me that ribbon, lad.' Miyoshi passed back the blue fabric he tied his hair up with, and Gora wound it round and round a few times before tying it off. 'Awh, I forgot to do the pretty bow,' he teased.

Miyoshi whirled around and glared at Gora, who just threw his hands up innocently and laughed. The boy pulled his braid around to inspect it, just in case. There was no bow. 'Thanks, captain. Can you show me how to do it on someone else so I can see what you did?'

'I'm not sure how Yonemura would feel about me braiding her hair for her, sorry. And I doubt Nishimura or Kyo would let me, either. They tend to just tie or knot it up and deal with it.' *On second thoughts*, Gora wondered, *Nishimura might*. Nishimura Gin had incredible, long hair that he regularly took good care of. Perhaps it would be best to pass the boy over to him for seafarers' long-hair care.

'But then I can't learn how to do it myself.' Miyoshi seemed disappointed.

'Try Nishimura,' Gora voiced his thoughts. 'He's on the night rotation now, but it won't be long until he's back in the morning one. Ask him. If he doesn't know braids, see if he'll let Yonemura or Moori model it for you on his hair.'

Miyoshi nodded and then turned as he heard his name being called by Daiki further down the ship.

'Yūki, you're up again.' They both looked at Gora, waiting for him to dismiss Miyoshi to return to his training.

'Off ya go, lad. You need to learn how to look after yourself. Next time a pirate tries to make you his woman, you'll know how to hurt him.'

The lad scowled and bound off, leaving Gora looking for something to do. Daiki spotted Gora hovering a moment and hollered over at him, too. 'You free for a moment, captain?' When Gora nodded, he looked pleased. 'I heard you're quite the fighter. Fancy giving us a demonstration?'

Now, that's more like it!

Gora tried to hide an excited grin by focusing on rolling and loosening his shoulders as he strode over. 'I think I can spare a few minutes,' he lied. 'Me versus you, oh great and loyal warrior of Hizen?' He glanced at Ikeda working in the shrouds further down the deck. 'That is, if your loyal guard doesn't destroy me if I'm too close to winning!'

5

Strange Sightings in the Forest

Yoshiko escaped the governance hall, taking a quick turn around the building and hurrying on what she hoped would be the quietest path, finally free of the morning-long governance meeting. Since the rebuild of Hié, she'd had to sit through countless hours of them, fixing issues and meeting people to discuss what needed to be done to both rebuild and reform the domain. Yoshiko loved the rebuild element of it, but listening to grown adults moaning about things they thought were problems when they could just easily solve them themselves was something that chipped away at her. Making a new goal to ease them into autonomy, Yoshiko planned to create a council with elders in each industry. That way, they could discuss issues within their capabilities and bring some responsibility to those who had the knowledge. Anything they couldn't solve, or anything governmental, could then just stay in the meetings she attended.

Yoshiko took a great inhalation of the fresh air, feeling it refresh her drowsy soul.

I used to respect Mother for her wit in the governance. They're so dull. How did she do it?

Forget sharp wit. Yoshiko's brain felt like it was wading through a bog.

Some of the requests and discussions she found interesting, particularly when it was meeting the local craftsfolk and citizens in the rebuild. But other times, with the politics, she really wished she could leave and stroll the town instead, watching how the domain was doing and speaking with the people.

And to think I used to want to be a diplomat, travelling to other places and sitting in their discussions. Would she just have had to sit through countless of those, veiling her words dealing with other leaders and daimyō far more egotistical than her mother had been?

'Lady Yoshiko!'

Ah, she found me already. She knew that voice and those footsteps, the soft clanking of body armour that the woman wore nearly all the time, even if she didn't need to. Still, Yoshiko continued, ignoring the pursuer, knowing she could catch up.

'Lady Yoshiko?'

'Yes, Chisaka?'

Chisaka was her new bodyguard—Gora had enforced the rule that she needed one, and with Ikeda, who had been his first choice, gone with Gora on the cause to stop the pirates, Chisaka Reina was the next choice. She was young, energetic, and very skilled at fighting, high up in the guard ranks but not so high that ego and age got to her. Gora had felt more comfortable knowing that a woman was looking after Yoshiko, and Yoshiko felt happy knowing that Chisaka had known Masa well. And as Masa's death still haunted Yoshiko, having that common connection reassured her, giving her someone to talk to.

The trouble was, Chisaka was a stickler for the rules and enforced them on Yoshiko too. Between her and Suki—who was fitting in well with Yoshiko's house as her new lead maid—Yoshiko was forced to do things more properly than she would have liked. And just when she thought she could get away with strolling the town freely or escaping whenever she liked.

Perhaps she could learn more from her mother and their escape climbing down the *tenshu* walls after all.

Perhaps that's even why she was so good at escaping the compound.

Now, Chisaka walked easily beside Yoshiko, hand casually resting to attention on her katana's handle, long, waist-length black hair pulled back impeccably into a ponytail, narrowing her eyes at Yoshiko as she caught Chisaka's gaze to acknowledge her arrival.

'How often must I tell you not to wander off without me?' the older woman nagged. 'Last year, you were kidnapped and taken halfway around the world.'

Yoshiko raised a brow, looking away with a huff. 'How often must I tell you that Gora and I got caught on purpose?'

'Be that as it may, it happened, and before that, you were nearly taken from your bedroom—by an insider, no less!'

Yoshiko had to grimace then. It was true. Had her mother not come for her first, scaling the *tenshu* walls and climbing to Yoshiko's bedroom window to lead her to their escape, Chinen— their closest ally turned traitor—and his followers would have succeeded in killing her.

'I knew you'd catch up,' was her lame excuse for now, and she ignored the point about the events of last year. 'I just wanted to get away before anyone tried to keep talking to me.'

'Are you talking in particular about that diplomat from Naga who keeps sending you marriage proposals and ridiculous gifts?' Chisaka looked boredly behind them. 'I thought I saw his face in the crowd.'

Yoshiko scrunched her nose up. 'Did you know the last thing he sent via that messenger was a jar of makeup? *To cover up those unfortunate scales*, the note said.' She ran a finger down the scales on her jawline, wondering if they really looked that unfortunate.

'You've told me.' Then Chisaka let out a smile, and Yoshiko couldn't help but think her guard looked a little like a fox spirit when she did. 'And I already sent someone to return it along with a threat of a lost finger.'

Yoshiko couldn't help but smile back. 'Now that's a bit much.'

'Not really,' Chisaka said, returning to business with a huff and a glare in her dark eyes. 'You're the daimyō now. They can't suggest such things.' Then the woman tossed her long ponytail back over her shoulder importantly. 'I won't allow it. Feel happy I didn't threaten to gouge out his eyes.'

Yoshiko snorted, and the pair fell into a comfortable silence as they made their way down the bustling steps to the first layer of the castle compound. With the sky as clear as it was, Yoshiko wanted to walk the town, to stretch her legs after a morning of governance, and to see if there was any news from Gora. The *Sea Guardian* had been away for months, with no news. She knew their first stop had been Shon Wa, the place Gora described as the hovel the scum of the earth hid in on this side of the world, and things were only going to get worse from there.

But still, he'd agreed to send word when they stayed in their first official government port—wherever that might have been. Did that mean they'd not arrived at one yet?

She nibbled at her nails again.

Though she had not been one for biting her nails in the past, since her curse had started showing on her body, her nails had started to grow more quickly. A combination of being irritated by them and worried about Gora and her comrades had started this habit, and Suki was forever nagging at her for it. How bold her maid had become since they'd first met and Suki had hardly said a word to her.

Yoshiko glanced sidelong at Chisaka again. She'd grown bold, too. Even now, while her mind was wandering, the older woman was nagging her over something.

Did Mother ever get this with her court?

She stared unseeing as they walked, knowing there wouldn't be time today to go to town. Besides, if there was news, it would be brought immediately to her. It was just her nerves and curiosity getting the best of her.

I should have gone with Gora after all ... It would have been much better than waiting here, wondering. And the adventure, no matter how dangerous, would have been worth it. Some of her closest allies had gone with him, and Yoshiko was realising that an uneasiness she'd been feeling this whole time might just be envy.

Gora, Ikeda, Daiki, Moori—a noble daughter she'd once hunted with—and a couple of people they'd escaped from Acrein with. People she'd grown close to and considered her friends. Now, they were all on that ship, and she was here.

But she knew she was needed here. How could she go off gallivanting on adventures around the world when her domain was in such a state?

Chisaka was saying something again.

'What?'

Chisaka looked at her blankly, stopping mid-sentence.

'Say that again,' she asked, more nicely this time, remembering she wasn't around Gora or Nubia anymore and had to speak more formally.

Her loneliness panged again. Nubia. Oh, she missed her. Where was she now? Had she got home and found her husband?

She managed to catch what Chisaka was saying this time. The shogun wanted to visit next month to review the ship-building progress. Yoshiko nodded vaguely, eyes meandering over the castle compound. Samurai in her family's indigo colours marched freely, bowing as they passed her, and diplomats in an array of colourful kimonos argued amongst one other. Workers dashed about in their trousers and tied jackets—all in different shades of navy and indigo—making sure the castle operated smoothly and was safe and kept clean. A scraping noise turned her head upwards, and she stopped walking, watching as a craftsworker crouched on the edge of a roof, replacing gable tiles to ensure they held for the next few winters. The woman's apprentice was calling up at her from below, holding a bound bamboo ladder against the side of the whitewashed walls. Yoshiko couldn't help but smile. Life seemed so much friendlier these days, with the bustle of life returning to the castle.

Or was she just more open to it, now she wandered freely and could speak with whoever she wanted?

She turned back to Chisaka. 'I always love the shine of the fresh roof tiles,' she explained at her guard's quizzical expression. 'Shogun Kazuhito will bring a great host of people to join him. We must be ready to accommodate them. And let's visit the shipyards tomorrow to prepare them for his visit. He is supporting our new position building ships for international trade, knowing it will bring new income to all of Hizen, but he will still want to monitor it closely. He will be critical, and the craftsfolk should be prepared. Send a messenger to Shogo confirming his visit, and another to the shipyards.'

Chisaka bowed. 'And what of today?'

'Were you hoping I would forget?' Yoshiko grinned, feeling a rush of energy. 'I waited all through the governance for this. We're going hunting, remember?'

* * *

A wild energy within her soared as the wind thrashed at Yoshiko's face, and she turned in her saddle to grin back at Chisaka, who rode not far behind on a young, sandy gelding. Since returning to Hizen and the Hié keep, Yoshiko had taken up the care of her father's gorgeous black mare—Yukako—who had thankfully been kept alive after her father's assassination.

Even Chinen couldn't kill this horse. She's too valuable. Yoshiko watched the mare fondly as the horse's ears twitched.

Yukako had been found at Chinen's holdings near the western border, and Yoshiko had nearly cried she'd been so overcome with happiness at their reunion. Now, she rode Yukako whenever she could, enjoying the quicker trip to the forest than her arduous journeys by foot the year before.

'I get that you're sentimental, but I don't understand why we have to come all the way out here to hunt rather than going to the forest just north of the compound,' Chisaka grumbled yet again as her gelding caught up and matched Yukako's pace.

'It's as you said,' Yoshiko called back. 'I'm sentimental. Plus, it's quieter out here.'

She didn't want to run into any hopeful nobles trying to *conveniently* bump into her in the forest. That was another part of daimyō life she'd not expected—all the people trying to curry their favour with her. She knew it had happened to her mother, but her mother had been excellent at shutting it down. Yoshiko, on the other hand, felt inadequately equipped to deal with it and often relied on Chisaka butting in with some kind of interruption or excuse for her.

The guard nodded, eyes showing understanding—finally. Or was it that Yoshiko had finally admitted she was just hiding out here? Feeling suddenly embarrassed and like a failure of a leader, she clicked her tongue and drove Yukako faster, relieved when the forest finally loomed over them and the horses slowed to a trot as the great green expanse swallowed them whole.

'I'll add that this *is* a nice part of the forest, far as it is,' Chisaka said eventually as they dismounted their horses and continued on foot, guiding the horses by the bridles. 'As you say, quiet. Though I'm not sure I could handle camping here too long.'

Her dark eyes analysed Yoshiko, her face serious. Back when Chisaka had first become her guard and confidant, she'd felt uncomfortable with the older woman's seemingly mind-reading gaze. But it had proven helpful, with how Chisaka could read situations and set them up in ways that could best advantage Yoshiko—particularly escaping from overbearing nobles and diplomats—and Yoshiko realised it was just part of Chisaka and how she took her role very seriously.

'I won't pretend it was easy, as if I were some child of the forest,' Yoshiko admitted, fiddling with Yukako's reins. It had taken her ages to open up to Chisaka about her time away from the keep, but she'd needed someone to talk to about it. And if Chisaka was going to be her confidant, Chisaka had reminded her at the time, she needed to know *some* parts of Yoshiko's history to know what not to tread on. 'I don't really remember much of it. I was in a weird place.'

As expected of the guard, she followed on fluently, translating Yoshiko's hidden thoughts and replying. 'And will we visit the Lady Asumi's grave while we are here today?'

Yoshiko nodded, clenching her teeth. 'Always.' Then she finally met her guard's firm gaze. 'But only after the hunt. We can't visit her without an offering, of course. And what would she love more than freshly hunted meat?'

That and the little decorated rice sweet Yoshiko had brought in her pack to share with her mother.

Another flash of wild energy surged through her, and Yoshiko's sombre mood was burned away. Since returning from Acrein, her body had begun to change, influenced by the curse in ways her mother had warned her. But it wasn't just visible changes, with scales flecking her skin in areas, but in temperament, too. Increasingly, Yoshiko found herself holding back a burning energy that she felt had to be released lest it burst forth like those times in Acrein.

Not wanting to burn Hié to the ground, instead she released the energy regularly, training or hunting.

Now I know why Mama was always so active.

'Let's go,' she said, trying to hurry Chisaka, tapping her fingers on Yukako's reins and looking into the trees to spot their first catch.

And, as expected of Chisaka, she understood, immediately tying the bridle of her gelding to a tree and jumping forward to do the same for Yukako as Yoshiko fumbled to string her bow with fingers that felt full of lightning.

'Can I go on ahead?' Yoshiko asked, not needing permission but knowing how much Chisaka would nag if Yoshiko just ran off. The guard nodded.

'You know how to find me when you're ready,' was the woman's simple reply. 'I'll set up camp here.'

Grateful, Yoshiko darted off, immediately feeling the relief from the burning power inside. It was a daily struggle now, keeping it back. The daily exercises kept it at bay, but it was only when she could run free in the forest that it lowered enough to keep her feeling free. But their forest visits were few and far between— weekly at best.

Mother's solo trips to the surface when we'd been in the caves make more sense now, Yoshiko reflected as she ran, pinning her katana to her hip, bow in her other hand. *Though I still don't condone it.* It had been a fast fall to her declining mental state, and Yoshiko knew her mother had put herself at risk too much, burning energy or not.

Tears stung her eyes, and Yoshiko refused to think about it. Today, she was here for her own freedom, not to dwell in the past. She succumbed to her wild side, letting her senses take over, drawing an arrow from her quiver and letting her cursed hearing and eyesight find the first catch. Her body followed instinctively.

She grinned at the following screech and heavy thud.

When she did return to the camp, armed with a large wild boar resting over her shoulders, Chisaka had got a fire going. She looked up and eyed Yoshiko's catch.

'Had fun?'

'Immensely. Perfect for easing the stress of listening to Governor Endo for so long this morning.'

Chisaka let out a snort. 'He did go on.' Then she stood up, brushed her *hakama* off, and tied back her long hair once again, this time twisting it up into a knot to keep it out of the way, staring at the boar. 'The only thing we can do with this today is make a soup or stew and take the rest back to the compound. Roasting it will take too long.'

Yoshiko plonked herself down. 'That's fine.' She rested her cheek on her fist as she watched Chisaka prepare their meal. Before Gora had left, he'd told Chisaka never to let Yoshiko prepare food. Chisaka had listened all too readily. Now, no matter how often Yoshiko asked to help, bored with sitting idle, Chisaka's answer of 'I don't want to die today' was the same every time.

She pouted as Chisaka rolled up her kimono sleeves and cut into the carcass, focused, and Yoshiko lay back on the leafy forest floor and gazed at the world above, time passing only by the noise of the cooking and the deepening of the smells. Chisaka didn't bother speaking to her. She knew the woman was just letting her be, and it wasn't long before Yoshiko had dozed off. Eventually, the guard's voice broke the spell of the forest, and it wasn't to tell her the food was ready, much to her stomach's disappointment.

'Your friends?'

Yoshiko stirred at her low, quiet voice and opened one eye lazily. If it wasn't food, she wasn't getting up. Gone were days she felt she had to stand on ceremony and act her position around Chisaka when no-one else was around. She needed somewhere to relax, and Chisaka had learned to cope with her 'disappointing lack of propriety'.

Or so she'd put it.

Friends? No-one was around that she could sense, so, confused, Yoshiko sat up and looked around, following the woman's gaze.

It took a moment to see what Chisaka was referring to.

On a tree root just ahead of Chisaka, Yoshiko laid eyes on an unexpected and tiny creature. It was green, its face almost leaflike, with a small body not unlike a young child's but many times smaller, and it glowed just slightly in the shadowy forest. Large, round eyes—rich green or brown, Yoshiko couldn't tell, perhaps somewhere in between—watched them silently. There was no mouth that she could see, so she wondered how it ate or communicated.

'No,' she finally replied with a whisper. She'd never seen a creature like this before.

The trees about them rustled, but there was no wind. Skin pricking, Yoshiko looked about, noticing Chisaka do the same, her eyebrows furrowing and hand reaching by her crossed legs for her cooking knife.

'Don't,' Yoshiko said, not knowing why.

Leaves fell about them from above, but the pair startled as, upon landing, they stood back up, and more of the creatures— of greens and reds and yellows, of all colours—surrounded them, watching with those large eyes, silent.

Yoshiko shivered, instincts quelling the urge to fight. Voice failing, her breath caught. Glancing at Chisaka, Yoshiko saw the pallor on the woman's face and realised they both shared the same predicament.

Another rustle went up, and the creatures swayed in a non-existent breeze, and Yoshiko realised *this* was how they communicated.

Tiny bare feet barely made a sound as they padded over tree roots and skipped over the fallen leaves, easing closer to the two sitting by the campfire. One that appeared like a rusty orange-brown leaf skipped over to Yoshiko, stopping right by her side, staring up at her and locking her gaze.

She felt a bead of sweat trickle down her back and tried not to shudder.

'*Kodama?*'

Chisaka's quiet voice broke the spell Yoshiko felt under, and Yoshiko tore her gaze from those small round eyes and turned to her guard.

'Huh?'

'*Kodama.* Tree spirits. Do you think that's what they are?'

Yoshiko looked back down at the little leaf-faced creatures. She'd read about *kodama* in folktales and poetry, of course, but with few people ever having seen them, their descriptions were vague and few. With little to go by, Yoshiko figured that if such spirits existed, they would likely look something like this. And if these were *kodama*, no wonder people didn't report sighting them often. They'd be mistaken as leaves, with people thinking they were going crazy to think they had little bodies.

She nodded and turned back to the creature by her side, only to realise it had disappeared. Blinking, confused, she searched for it, noticing they had all disappeared without so much as a breath of wind to carry them or a rustle to signal their departure.

Mouth dry, Yoshiko looked back at Chisaka, and a silent communication confirmed what both women felt.

Quickly eat food and leave.

6

Taking the Night Rotation

Since the day Gora had joined that training group, it had become something of a regular occurrence. He and Daiki sparred a few times for each of the different training groups, modelling the differences between the Hizen and mercenary fighting styles.

Sakai had surprised him, and Gora saw a different side to Hizen fighting—the rough and dirty kind with blades, wrestling, and the foul play of the underworld. And if anyone guessed Sakai's past from it, no-one complained or treated him any differently. Out here, they were all the mercenaries.

And everyone needs as much training as they can get. Can't moan about who they learn it from.

Out here, Sakai wasn't his past. He could be whoever he wanted. Just part of the *Sea Guardian* crew.

Over time, Gora became pleased to see the growth of his crew. Daiki and Ikeda's fighting loosened up, Sakai became more sociable and less guarded, and the rest of the crew grew in skill quickly. Jelani and Quinni even showcased the distinct styles of their homeland. The weapons were different, and their movements were more fluid and animalistic. Gora wondered if the Qeclan people had observed how the wild cats and birds of prey attacked and tried to copy it. Each time Quinni fought, Gora was reminded of the predator animals. Miyoshi had been in awe and embraced their teachings, eagerly learning from the two Qeclans, seeking their guidance even during his off-duty hours. Gora marvelled at the lad's boundless energy, questioning whether he was too light on the boy.

After several days of this new routine, Gora sat with some of the day crew in the galley for an evening meal before his upcoming night shift. Miyoshi, as lively as ever, bombarded Shingo and Yonemura with a barrage of questions. Suddenly, the boy turned his attention to Gora, who was sipping his soup directly from the bowl.

'Captain, if you can beat Daiki in a fight, who would win if it was you versus the daimyō?'

Shingo laughed and clapped Gora—who was spluttering his soup in surprise—on the shoulder. 'Your turn to get bombarded with questions, captain!'

'Yūki's at his weird questioning again.' Yonemura looked across at the boy with a sad fondness. Gora knew she missed her own children every day. 'It's the age.'

Six members of the day crew huddled around the galley table, joined by Kimura, the young and attractive son of a famous restaurant owner in Hié and *Sea Guardian's* cook. Kimura leaned casually against the cupboards and joined the merriment, enjoying a momentary break with a cup of steaming green tea. It would be Gora's last meal with the day crew for a while, since he would be joining the night crew. This meant he would have to temporarily stop participating in the fight training sessions that took place during the day. Aware of the limited time they had, the crew bombarded Gora with questions while they still could.

'How I'd love to see Daiki's face if he was here to hear this!' Kimura flashed a devilish smile, watching Gora through his long fringe as he waited for an answer. 'It'd be the daimyō, of course, eh, captain?'

A couple of others chimed in, expressing their agreement and suggesting they should bet on the outcome. Gora felt the need to defend both himself and Daiki.

'Firstly, I beat Daiki because I fight dirty.' Gora seized the opportunity to impart a lesson. 'He's more skilled, but skill doesn't always matter in a fight. It's about what you're willing to do. If you use tactics and your surroundings to your advantage, it doesn't matter who you're up against.' The others teased him for avoiding the question. 'And, I'd like to point out that Yoshiko had proper training by the dragon daimyō Asumi herself! *And* the finest tutor recommended by the daimyō. All that before she went rogue and learned the art of fighting dirty from yours truly.'

'That means she'd win.' Kimura winked at Miyoshi, and Yonemura agreed while she playfully elbowed Miyoshi. Gora glared at them both as the others roared with laughter. No matter how much he defended himself, he had to admit the truth. Yoshiko was one of the most skilled fighters he had ever encountered, despite her reluctance towards it.

Quinni grinned as he drank the last of his soup. 'That's great news for little Yūki. Fight with determination, and you will become as strong as the daimyō!' He laughed and tried to dodge Miyoshi's indignant flails, his long limbs flying about the small room.

Gora chuckled, rising from the table and returning his bowl with thanks to Kimura. In the background, he heard Miyoshi's constant protesting of being called a girl, fading away as Gora stomped up towards the darkness of the night rotation in the vast ocean.

* * *

The night shift was a stark contrast to the bustling activity of the day. In the cold darkness, a skeleton crew performed their duties, their movements muted and their surroundings barely illuminated by their lanterns. It was a solitary existence, away from the liveliness of the main crew. But the ocean never slept, and a ship needed to continue ploughing through the ocean or would find itself washed up to a different location by the waves. And there always needed to be a watch. A sleeping ship was easy prey. Gora and Shingo, as captain and first mate, understood their duty to take turns overseeing the night shift.

'Tomioka,' Gora called out to a man faintly lit by the glow of a flame-lit lamp ahead of him. The man turned, features barely visible in the dark save for his characteristic wavy black hair and kind expression.

'Yes, captain?' Tomioka Jiro was the leader of this rotation. Gora had split his crew into three main groups, each with a skilled sailor as their leader. The groups rotated between morning, afternoon, and night shifts, with a slight overlap of time in between. They also ate and slept at the same time. Any problems within the groups would be relayed to the leader, who would then relay it to Shingo or Gora.

'We're not long to Ishil. We need to be on a tighter lookout for trouble as we reach the place Frewin was reported to be. I've added a couple extra crew from the morning rotation to your group to give the night shift a hand. They start tomorrow evening. Any problems, let me know.'

'Yessir.'

Tomioka continued to relay news to Gora about the last few night shifts. So far, there were no issues. Just the usual issues of crew missing the day shifts with the training, and some slacking off with speaking the orders in Traders'. Sakai, Tomioka said, was slower at learning the new language than the others. He requested extra attention be given to help the man remember the orders. Gora agreed, and the two parted ways to continue their duties.

That night, Gora paced the deck and checked the ship was in good shape. He watched as Ikeda checked the ropes and polished salt water from the side to keep the wood and lacquer in good health. Gora was pleased with how his crew were meticulous and proud of their roles. Even this young samurai, who'd never worked a ship before, picked up the duties on the ship, guided by the more experienced sailors, and learned to perform them well.

Next, Gora dashed up to the forecastle and padded towards the figurehead, his favourite place on the ship. No matter how he strained his eyes, he couldn't see it in the darkness. Even when he extended his lantern out, the light wouldn't get close enough. Craftsmen of Hizen had carved a dragon lady and fitted her to the front of the ship in honour of their daimyō. That way, she could adventure with them, even though she stayed behind in Hizen to run the domain. The craftsmen had carved the dragon lady so well that it was as if an extra crew member took watch from the front of the ship. Gora tried to imagine the dragon lady figurehead staring into the deep black ahead and wondered if she could see anything. Yoshiko, the only true dragon lady he'd ever know, could see in the dark. Her dragon-blood had given her enhanced senses and abilities, including seeing the world in darkness. Would the figurehead be like her, too?

Sometimes, when he knew he was alone, Gora liked to stand on the forecastle and speak with the figurehead. He knew Yoshiko would have loved to join him and the crew on this mission, so he told her of everything that happened: the way the crew teased Miyoshi, how well Daiki was fitting in and how his fighting style was changing, how Jelani and Quinni like to play pranks on Yonemura and the other more seasoned sailors, and how Yonemura and Moori were fitting in well with the lads. He also admitted how much he wished Yoshiko could have come with them, though he knew she couldn't. The figurehead didn't look anything like Yoshiko, but it made him feel less lonely. After all his years of hating pirate life and everyone around him, and then hiding himself from society in Hizen in fear they'd discover who he was and hate him, he never expected to make such a close friend.

Did he miss her? Of course he did.

He stared out into the darkness where he knew the dragon lady figurehead would be. She'd be staring into the black beyond, her strong, lightly scaled arms crossed with her hands resting in the kimono sleeve of her other arm. Very few knew what those hidden hands held within the carved kimono sleeves. But, in mere days when they reached Ishil, the crew of the *Sea Guardian* and their target, Frewin, would soon discover what this dragon lady could do.

7

Funayūrei

Miyoshi never worked the night rotation. One of the only members of the crew who didn't, Miyoshi never experienced the utter swallowing darkness of the night at sea that the others spoke about.

Not that he minded. He liked the daylight. When all his chores were done, he could nose about and watch the horizon for the pirates they were hunting, imagining the huge part he'd play in their success. And if there was a ship dealing with human trade, Gora had said they'd get them, too.

He remembered the death ship too well. His mother had said he'd likely never forget it, and Gora, who'd also still got harsh memories from his time as a captive, confirmed it. Miyoshi didn't want to remember it, but he knew he'd have to. The least he could do was make sure he could stop others from experiencing the same thing—that's why he was here on this journey with Gora. To stop those who steal others.

Miyoshi had been one of the lucky ones. Both he and his mother had survived and come back to his father in Hizen. While they'd been separated in Acrein, they'd both been in the main port town that the ship Gora and the daimyō Yoshiko had taken for the escape had been in. Pure chance, and they'd both taken it. Others hadn't been so lucky. Miyoshi heard that many people had been killed after they'd left, and the survivors had to wait for a ship home after the battle at Hizen port.

Escaping his owner in the town had been terrifying.

Sneaking through that crowded port onto the escape ship had been terrifying.

But it had been worth it.

And now, Miyoshi knew this mission would be terrifying too, but he was determined to make it worth it. To give himself a new life, away from fishing like all his family before him, doing something more honourable and exciting by helping others—like a samurai guard, but on the sea. Doing what he was good at— sailing—and protecting people with it.

Not just catching fish.

Each day since they'd left Shon Wa, he vowed to keep watch, to be the one to spot the pirate ship. So, each day, when he wasn't doing his chores, Miyoshi stared out into the endless horizon, face set, mission set.

He'd be the one who saw it first.

That's where he was now, leaning against the gunwale, staring out over the dark waters ahead one evening after finishing his rotation, debating heading down to the galley to join the fun of the evening now it was too dark to see into the distance.

Can't see a ship in the black of night.

But still. What if?

'The *Cutter*.' He tried the sounds, playing with each phoneme, wanting to get the Traders' right. He squished his cheek against the lacquered wood, feeling defeated for the day. 'What's "cutter"?'

A glow in the abyss ahead of him made him raise his head again. It wasn't a star—too low—nor was it the orange glow of a flame lantern. He furrowed his brows and looked harder. It was a soft, white glow, misty looking.

'A ghost?'

He'd heard stories of ghosts. Hizen folktales were full of them. Miyoshi's heart pounded at the thought of them.

The lad watched as the glow grew, the mists swirling around it more obvious. It was moving fast for a ship, and the boy knew then it had to be something from the stories.

Urgently, he searched for someone else on deck to clarify his thought. That he wasn't seeing things. The peaceful, long-haired Nishimura was at the helm, looking almost as if he was meditating, though Miyoshi knew he was focused on navigating. Couldn't be interrupted.

Next he saw the scary, stony-faced man from another region. Sakai. Miyoshi knew that even if he looked big and scary, Sakai was actually very quiet and gentle to speak with. Miyoshi liked Sakai and often spent time with the man. He was the one to talk to.

The boy ran up to Sakai and tapped him on the arm. He ushered the stocky man to the gunwale and pointed at the glowing in the distance. Except, even in the short time he'd run across the deck and back, it had got closer. Much closer.

Miyoshi and Sakai stared up at what was easily visible as a glowing ship, silent and ghostly and moving fast as if on a hidden breeze and blessed by the sea dragons themselves to sail. Aboard, similarly glowing pale figures went about the deck idly—as if the ship didn't even need labour to sail—and in a movement that the boy could only describe as wafting.

One of the ghostly figures turned to face them, and Miyoshi took an intake of breath.

'Sakai, what are they?'

But the other man was silent, and when Miyoshi turned to look up at him, the man's stony face was awash with fear, wide-eyed, jaw clenched.

The misty figure leapt from the ghostly ship, landing noiselessly directly on the water, and ran across the waves without trouble.

Miyoshi grabbed Sakai's *haori* sleeve. 'Sakai!' He couldn't tear his eyes away.

Once the figure reached the hull of the *Sea Guardian,* they launched themself at it, and with light, effortless movements, they scrambled up the giant hull.

Miyoshi's heart roared, and his breath came in short, sharp intakes.

A rough hand grabbed Miyoshi's arm and pulled him away from the ship's edge, breaking the trance. Miyoshi looked away from the glowing white figure clambering up the ship and into the dark, anxious eyes of Sakai.

'Go, lad,' the man growled.

'Where?'

'There's a bucket with a hole in it in the cleaning room. Remember it? Go get it.'

Miyoshi stared at the older man, unable to believe what he was hearing. *What does he need a bucket with a hole for?* Anyway, he was unable to go get it, even if he wanted. His body still felt the freeze of fear.

'Now!'

Miyoshi flinched. Something in the man's gravelly voice and urging eyes told him he couldn't falter here. And besides, didn't he want to prove himself?

He forced himself to move, racing away from the gunwale, and crashed down the steps towards the storeroom Sakai was talking about.

The bucket with a hole in it. *Why the one with a hole?* he grumbled, still confused.

By the time he returned to Sakai, the ghostly figure was standing on the gunwale, towering over the stocky man, both figures locked in eye contact.

There was a wild screeching noise.

Is that the ghost making the noise?

'I said the lad's getting it,' Miyoshi heard Sakai growl back.

The boy ran up to them and held the bucket out to Sakai, wondering what he was going to do with a bucket with a hole in.

The older man nodded towards the glowing figure. 'Give it to *him.*'

Miyoshi puckered his face, looking at Sakai strangely, but slowly handed the bucket to the figure on the gunwale. Unable to help it, Miyoshi looked into the ghostly face.

Human. They looked human, but there was something gruesome about their expression. Something suffering. Horrified, the boy froze, holding the bucket out.

The ghostly human snatched the bucket and shrieked again at the two sailors, leaping back down into the night.

Heart pounding, arms still raised, Miyoshi tried to find his voice.

The ghostly ship had gone, taking its odd crew with it.

Finally, he summoned his legs, and he slowly edged away from the gunwale, turning to trudge down to the galley to beg Kimura for something that would ease him of this experience. As he did, he saw everyone on deck had stopped what they were doing and were watching Miyoshi and Sakai, mouths open, expressions as horrified as he felt.

So, it *had* happened.

Beside him, Sakai stirred too, stomping away from the ship's edge and, hand clutching Miyoshi's shoulder, pulling the lad with him.

The boy felt relieved to be away from the edge. The night seemed too thick, too dangerous. What else was hiding out there?

'Funayūrei?'

Miyoshi followed the voice to Nishimura, who had his hands resting on the spokes of the helm lightly but was watching the two by the gunwale. His face—even *his* face—was serious, where normally it was peaceful and contented.

Miyoshi, unable to answer, implored Sakai for an answer, but the quiet man just nodded gravely, and there were groans from the others around them.

Funayūrei? He'd heard of that before. Where?

'I've never seen them before,' Moori said, her voice almost too quiet to hear. 'Do you see them often on the ships?'

Miyoshi watched as others on the deck shook their heads, and he shook his own.

Moori was a noble and had never been on a boat before, he recalled. But, even he, who had been raised on boats, had never seen anything like that.

Funayūrei. Boat spirits, he thought. The ghosts of people who had died at sea and haunted fellow sailors, trying to bring them down with them.

So that's why Sakai had needed the bucket.

He'd heard of stories of the *funayūrei* demanding buckets so they could fill vessels with water and drown them.

An icy wind blew, sending shudders and prickles all over the boy's body. He imagined those ghostly figures standing all over their ship, pouring water over them, their own giant, pale vessel lurking soundlessly nearby.

'Sakai?' Miyoshi tugged at the man's sleeve, bidding the vision from his mind. Sakai looked down and met his gaze. 'Why did you give him the bucket with a hole?'

'Can't drown us with a holey bucket. Water falls out.'

The boy almost couldn't believe the genius of it, and when he told the older man, Sakai shrugged.

'Tomioka told me.' Then the man sniffed. 'C'mon, lad. Let's get a drink. See what Kimura can come up with help to us.' He paused and looked warily back to the edge of the ship, eyes narrowing as he hunted about. Miyoshi saw a flash of relief cross the man's face, realising they must be safe. 'Hopefully something strong.'

And, needing no further persuasion, Miyoshi scampered after Sakai towards the galley, eager to bring warmth and light back to his world, even if it did involve listening to Kimura teasing him.

8

A Merchant Ship in Trouble

While the crew recovered from their horror, Gora's days of the night rotation passed uneventfully and with his nose pressed so close to the ship's ledgers that he could smell the ink and the rice paper. He didn't like handling the inventory. It was too many numbers for a man who liked to work with his hands, but it was a regular part of his role that he'd had to embrace. Coming into his new role as captain, he'd expected calculating the finances and resources to be hard, but they were easier than he had expected. Despite that, in this light and after a whole night of prowling the deck and checking on his night rotation, the black, squiggling lines were heavy on his eyes. Gora glanced out of the small cabin windows at the rising sun. All he needed to do now was brief Shingo and then he could head to his bunk.

* * *

'Captain!' A cry came with pounding steps in the wooden corridor beyond his quarters, followed by a thumping on his door. 'Captain!'

Gora rubbed his stubbled cheek and heaved himself out of his bunk, eyes bleary and thick with sleep after finally being able to retire for the day. It couldn't have been long since he'd returned to his cabin after briefing Shingo for the day rotation, surely?

56

He opened the door, not caring how ragged he looked, grunting at a stunned Miyoshi. The look on the boy's face made Gora feel uncomfortable. He didn't look that rough, now, could he? And his undershirt was long enough to cover his manhood, even if he'd slept without his slacks. He wondered what was shocking the poor lad.

He grunted again, signalling for the boy to hurry up.

'Captain, Shingo's called for your urgent attention at the bow!'

Gora sighed, muttered for the lad to wait, and pulled on his slacks and boots, tucking in his undershirt as he followed the lad up to the deck. As he stepped onto the deck and into the cold air, he wished he'd thrown on a *haori* or overcoat. The winter was coming in, and it always hit the oceans before it hit land. He rubbed his arms and strode to meet Shingo at the bow, leaving Miyoshi to run off to his next duty.

'What's the trouble, Shingo?'

The older man turned to bow slightly as Gora caught up. The lines at the corners of Shingo's eyes deepened as he and Quinni stared into the distance with furrowed brows. Gora followed their gaze to see a ship, still too far off to recognise what kind with the naked eye.

'That ship appeared on the horizon after dawn. We've been observing since. She's getting closer.' Shingo handed Gora his spyglass, black lacquer with painted designs, a gift from Yoshiko. Gora had foolishly left his in his cabin when Miyoshi ran to get him. 'We think it's a merchant vessel but can't be sure yet.'

Gora scrunched up his eyes as he peered through the spyglass. 'It's big in the hull. Seems to be a merchant. But what's the urgency over that, now?' Merchant vessels were rarely a problem.

'Look to the starboard of it, captain. Just a bit,' Quinni said, pointing with his finger.

Gora moved the spyglass slowly to the starboard side. He passed a dot on the horizon and went back. 'Another ship?'

'Ishil port's that way. How often do you see two merchant ships leaving the same port and going in the same direction?' Shingo asked.

'Rarely,' Gora responded, squinting his eyes to get a better look at the second ship.

'We thought it might be pirates,' Quinni said. Gora admired how quickly his Hizen was improving.

Shingo nodded and looked at Gora, waiting his assessment.

'Could be a pirate or mercenary vessel giving chase. Ishil's popular. Plenty of merchant ships go there for the unique and quality goods. And this huge stretch of ocean provides plenty of places for a mercenary vessel to hide and catch traders unawares.'

Shingo nodded. 'That's what we thought. What're your orders, captain?'

Gora thought back to the map and the port of Ishil ahead. They'd made it in good time and would be near Ishil port soon. If Frewin was heading for Ishil, he'd be in this area.

He looked through the glass again, frowning. *Is it him?*

From this distance, he couldn't identify the ship.

'Quinni, keep watch of the second ship. Send Miyoshi with any news. It could be Frewin, but it may not be. There's plenty of pirates in these parts that would be eager to ambush a merchant vessel with Ishillian goods. They've the best silks and spices around, I've heard. Quite the luxury.' Gora raised his eyebrows at the tall Qeclan and clapped a hand on the man's shoulder, receiving a nod in answer and an affirmation in Traders'.

Then, with suspected action to come, Shingo was sent to rouse extra crew from the afternoon rotation to help early on deck, and Gora went to get suitably changed for his role. It wouldn't do to have a leader marching around half-dressed.

* * *

Miyoshi returned when they were first able to identify details on both ships. By then, Shingo and Gora were meeting Kimura in the galley to discuss the rations, planning to pull into the port of Ishil to restock food supplies. Kimura was in the middle of explaining some of the goods he wanted to find in Ishil when Miyoshi burst through the door.

'The ship looks the same, captain!' the boy cried as he crashed into the room, freezing as he saw everyone staring at him and remembered his manners. He stopped, ran back to the door, knocked, bowed, and waited. Shingo and Gora burst from their seats, making the lad jump.

'Can we resume this later, Kimura?' Gora asked the young chef, who rested his chin in his hand and smiled in response.

'Of course, captain.'

Gora prompted the boy further as he and Shingo followed the lad back up to the deck. 'The same as …?'

'That old pirate, Frewin. Quinni and I remembered what his ship looked like. You can see it in the spyglass. It's the same. He's chasing that merchant ship.' The boy started to jog to keep up as Gora and Shingo strode full speed to the bow.

'Are you certain?' Shingo asked the lad. His face echoed Gora's, both wondering if it would be that easy to find the pirate ship they were looking for. Something felt wrong.

'Yessir!'

Quinni handed Gora the spyglass he'd lent them to keep an eye on the ship. He peered through it.

'Well, whatcha know? They're right. I'd recognise that ship anywhere.' Gora lowered the spyglass and frowned.

The merchant vessel looked as if it had sped up to outsail the pirates, and, as they had expected, it was an Ishillian trader with a streaming orange flag. Gora was watching it absentmindedly, trying to think about what they'd do next, when he noticed the vessel had turned. Gora realised the *Sea Guardian* crew were still sailing flagless. Unable to identify them, the Ishillian merchants must have thought them pirates or mercenaries and turned from their route to avoid a second trouble.

'Raise the flag!' Gora roared down the deck. This wasn't the time to be unidentifiable.

The crew rushed to raise the Hizen flag: white with a blue dragon curled in the middle. Hopefully after spotting this, the trade vessel would pull closer to their original route and pass them. If they did, it would be easier for Gora and his crew to cut Frewin's ship off and catch them. Moori raised the flag, shouting back across the deck when it was up, and Gora saw the Ishillian vessel turn back towards its original route.

Good, he thought. They probably thought it was the safer option; with two ships against the pirates, they'd have a better chance.

'Jelani, Quinni, Ikeda, Sakai, raise the gunports on the starboard bow and the starboard side and prepare to fire. Miyoshi, run the flame powder from the armoury to the gun decks.' Next, Gora ran to meet Yonemura at the helm. 'Yonemura, take us portside. We'll cut them off and ready a warning shot, if needed.'

She nodded, and both squinted into the distance to see the Ishillian trade vessel turning closer. Unfortunately, Frewin's ship was faster and closing in.

Frewin always chose speed over bulk. It's how he caught his prey.

'Nishimura, call Satou and tighten sails. We need to go faster.'

They'd woken the whole crew by now, and everyone from the night rotation was on deck and trying to look lively after so little rest. Gora called to Moori again, asking her to ready a signal flag for communication. He planned to raise it and catch the attention of the pirates. Frewin could decide from there whether he would take it calmly or not, or keep chasing the Ishillian merchant ship.

Well, if they choose to attack, we'll be ready, Gora hoped. Daiki padded up to him as if he'd read his captain's mind.

'Captain, the crew is armed, and the armoury is ready. Miyoshi is running the flame powder well, and the gunports are ready to arm. Waiting for your command.'

Gora was impressed. This man really didn't need to be told what to do when it came to battle.

'Are the crew ready for a close fight?' he asked of their skill, whether Daiki thought their training had helped.

'I'd always ask for more time, but ready enough. The crew are learning well, but against pirates, I'd rather not risk it. Ikeda, of course, has trained with me for many years. He's a prodigy. He'll keep us safe. And, of the rest of the crew, I'd recommend Yonemura, Nishimura, Sakai, Jelani, Quinni, and Satou to be the ones you call upon to fight first. Satou might be a craftsman, but he's lethal with sharp tools. Moori is good with aim. Put her in a long-range position. Maybe get her to use *that.*' Daiki nodded his head towards their trump card at the figurehead, and Gora immediately knew what he meant. 'She seems to be quite attached to using guns, too.'

'Moori is one of the few to know how to operate the one at the figurehead anyway, other than Satou, who knows how to repair and maintain it. She was there when it was tested and loaded, such is her position in Hié.' Gora thought back to the conversations he'd had with the craftsfolk and Yoshiko about it. 'Thanks for your recommendations. I'll do what I can to avoid a fight, but we may not be able to help it. I intend to communicate with Frewin first, but I can't promise they won't try anything dirty. Keep an eye out. Everywhere. They'll sneak aboard from anywhere. Do whatever is needed to protect the ship and crew. Our goal is to destroy them, after all.'

'With such a small crew, I wonder if that's even possible.' Daiki sighed as they walked together on the deck, watching the full crew run about to prepare.

'Aye. But with the rebuild of Hié, we couldn't get many more to join the mission. Yoshiko was concerned, but I convinced her I'd hire more crew when we pulled into a respectable port.'

'Can I recommend we hire fighters, captain? Training the crew is well and all, but we need more experienced fighters.'

'That's the plan,' Gora agreed again. 'We left knowing this would be the risk until we could hire more. I've heard Ishillians make great guards and fighters. We'll see if anyone's available when we pull in for supplies.'

Gora and Daiki paused and watched the Ishillian merchant ship slide past, its crew running to the side to call out and wave at the *Sea Guardian*. Their traditional headscarves twisted around their heads proved they'd been correctly identified as an Ishillian vessel, just leaving their home port, fresh with expensive cargo to trade elsewhere. With such cargo, Gora expected them to have a strong team of guards to help defend the ship should they run into trouble. His eyes searched the ship and found the black uniform and black headscarves of the Ishillian hired guards, fully armed with traditional curved swords and single-hand pistols.

Ishillian guards it is, he decided. He'd see if he could hire any once he'd dealt with the sea scum ahead.

As the crew of the *Sea Guardian* rounded off the Ishillian merchant vessel and cut off the pirate ship, Frewin tried to get his ship to go around them. Gora called to Moori to raise the signal flag. As she hoisted it up the mast, crew from the Ishillian trader ran to the stern side and stared back Gora and his crew, mouths agape.

A ship wanting to communicate with pirates? Gora reckoned he'd think the same if he'd seen it from their side, too.

9

Communicating With Sea Scum

Gora strode to the starboard bow and jumped up onto the wooden gunwale, holding on to the shrouds for support. He watched Frewin's ship drift in closer, no longer bothering to try to go around. So, he was going to talk, was he? From this distance, Gora could see pirates grouping at the bow of the vessel, arms drawn and faces pulled into fierce and intimidating grimaces to ward off those who dared to raise the communication signal at them.

What an ugly bunch.

Gora searched the ugly faces for Kipp. The pale-haired pirate wasn't there. Gora wondered if he'd died in the battle back in Hié but could barely believe that possible. That man was too aggressive and could wriggle out of anything. But then Yoshiko hadn't told him much of when she returned from Frewin's ship with the Hizen children, and Gora hadn't probed. He had always wondered what had happened but never wanted to ask.

A figure strode through the group of pirates, and Gora's breath caught.

The figure was burned beyond anything Gora had ever seen: all red, brown, and ghastly sores and boils, as if his face had bubbled and cracked. Gora swallowed back bile. Even from here, he could see the curling of the old pirate's lips. When the 'keep at Shon Wa had said Frewin was all red with burns, he hadn't been exaggerating. This would make anyone want to know what happened. When he thought back to Yoshiko's face when she came back, he finally understood her hesitance to say anything.

'Frewin!' he bellowed across the watery gap between the two ships.

If the old pirate's eyes could narrow any further, they would have.

'Lad?' Frewin's voice came out croaky, as if he was struggling to yell. Gora was amazed the man could even move his face.

'We need to talk.'

'Oh, aye?' The pirate sounded suspicious. But then, the last time the two of them had spoken, Frewin's crew had spotted and kidnapped Gora in Acrein. After Gora had escaped, Frewin and his crew had followed Gora's ship to Hizen, where they'd got mixed up in a war that had ended with Frewin and half of his crew being burned by a creature that was supposed to be myth.

In fairness, Gora justified to himself, *he had tried to steal from the country, including children.*

Gora looked about at Frewin's men, who were eyeing up his ship, and Frewin continued. 'Pull 'er in, lads!' His men ran to it the minute he ordered them to do his bidding. Gora saw his own crew freeze, imagining the pirates swinging on ropes to board the ship if they got any closer.

'You stay right there!' Gora yelled.

The pirates stopped and turned, eyes like daggers.

'And how'd yer propose we chat, lad?' Frewin guffawed as if he was speaking with an imbecile. Some of his men joined in but earned a glare for hanging about, acting idle.

'You come to me. Leave your men there.'

'Ne'er goin' t' happen,' the old pirate growled. 'Ye come t' me if yer the one t' call the talk.'

Dread shot through Gora's blood at the thought of being on that ship again. He knew the idea he'd get the old pirate on his own to talk was too good to be true. Easier to kill and then gun his ship and crew down with cannons later.

And the same the other way if he boarded Frewin's ship.

He swallowed and frowned.

Things were never that easy.

'Fine,' Gora growled back. He jumped down from the gunwale and addressed Moori, who'd moved closer after hoisting the communication flag. 'Arrange me to take a boat.'

The crew looked at him in horror, Miyoshi's face white.

'Captain, you can't be thinking of going over there alone?' Moori said, her voice high and hoarse. She glanced around Gora at the pirates nudging each other and grinning at the beautiful Hizen ship. 'You know what they'll do.'

'Just do it.'

She scowled but ran off to comply, and Gora instantly felt guilty for snapping. He called over to Shingo, who was standing down the deck and watching the pirates warily. 'While I'm over there, you're in charge. Keep an eye out for them distracting you and trying to board. Don't let it happen. Any problems, you sail her away—with or without me. The crew's safety comes first.'

'And leave you there alone, captain? With *them*?' He spat as he addressed them. Gora had never seen the man acting that way. It was almost like Yonemura swearing.

'If that be the need, yes.'

Shingo's eyes darkened, but he agreed and bowed. Gora gulped and rubbed his stubbled cheek nervously. He should have shaved last night, he realised. Not that it mattered now.

Moori called that the boat was ready, and he climbed the rope ladder below, watching it snake back up over the railing the minute he let go. He knew it was to reduce the risk of pirates getting on board, but sitting in this tiny, bobbing rowboat between two giants with naught to pull him back up to the safety of his own ship, he suddenly felt isolated. The foul, looming giant towered over him as he pulled the rowboat closer to the pirate ship, heart thumping what felt like tar throughout his body.

The pirates had lowered their rope ladder for his arrival but held it just out of reach so that he had to jump and struggle against the waves in the rowboat. When he nearly missed, they guffawed to see him hanging on to the edge, struggling to pull himself up. Below him, the rowboat was drifting back towards the *Sea Guardian*, pulled by Moori on a line, who had agreed to pull the boat back when he arrived so the pirates couldn't use it to get to his ship. She'd protested at the thought of leaving him there stranded, forced to jump into the ocean to escape, but agreed to cast a line and pull him back to their ship instead. As he hung from the Jacob's ladder, he turned to meet her anxious gaze. He knew she'd stand guard. As the deck's main gunner, she operated at the ship's edge.

'Make way for our guest, lads,' Frewin cackled as Gora pulled himself over the gunwale of the *Cutter*. From this close, his voice sounded more guttural, with wet noises thick in his laugh. 'It's been a long time since this young thing's been on my ship! Let's make him welcome.'

Gora snarled. *Long time? How about just a few months, now? This isn't some nanna's tea.*

Welcome was the last thing Gora felt. On the deck, the pirates had gathered just too out of range to stick him, but close enough to lunge in if they needed to. Despite the large, open deck and vast sky around them, the world closed in around him. The thick stench of too many men stuck on the same ship for many months on end clogged his senses. Frewin commanded a large crew and always had. Gora wondered if it had seemed overcrowded back then too. Perhaps it had.

'Come down to my quarters and let's speak in private, lad.'

'I'd rather stay here above deck, if that's all the same to you.' There was no way Gora would let them drag him below deck. He knew he'd never come back whole or alive.

'Don't trust me, lad?'

Gora remembered what happened to people in Frewin's quarters. 'Not even if you were on the other side of the ocean, Frewin.'

'After all I've done for ye?'

Gora chose to ignore that. What had this piece of sea scum ever done for him? He tried to keep his face blank and unreadable, like he had in the time he'd lived on this damned ship. 'All the same, I'd rather stay here.'

Frewin shrugged. 'Your choice. Ain't private, though.'

Gora glanced around and saw the others obviously listening in. He still couldn't see Kipp. That was strange.

Where is that piece of shit? Gora felt nervous. That man never failed to be around to gloat and taunt Gora. If he wasn't here, he'd probably be trying to find a way to sneak aboard his ship to cause havoc. He turned to look at Shingo to see if he'd spotted anyone doing anything strange.

'If yer lookin' for Kipp, yer'll not find 'im.' Frewin's face and voice clouded like a summoned storm as he watched Gora search the ship. The pirates tensed, their faces livid.

'Where is he?' *Had he jumped ship?*

'Dead. Killed by tha' damned demon woman we saw ye standin' with on the shore.'

'That's our leader. Don't you dare speak of her like that.'

'That's no broad. It's a monster!' Frewin stalked around him, body awkward and heavy to move, and Gora thought it ironic that this man was calling someone else a monster. 'You didn't see what that creature did to my ship. What it did to my crew.' The old pirate paused, looking at Gora warily. Then true horror crossed his foul face as his eyes widened with remembrance. 'Came at us from below, clawing its way up from the ocean, piercing holes in the hull. Then it landed right on top of me, and look at what it did!' He leaned forward and pointed to his face, burned and boiled, looking like a creature from the land of the dead. Almost like the *noppera-bō*, a faceless *yōkai* from Hizen folktales. Ill-set features buried in the wretched burned flesh, and rags of whiskers and hair hung tousled about him. Frewin spat on the deck, a piece of spittle still hanging from the curled-up corner of his burned lips. 'Then it turned into that demon woman and ran below, killing everyone it met. Shoulda seen how we found 'im, Kipp …'

Gora shuddered. Anger flooded through him. As if these people had any right to judge actions by others. The things he'd seen them do … that they'd made *him* do.

'You have no right to call her a monster after everything you've done. *I've seen it!* Stealing children from their homes, killing them, ravishing them, forcing them to work as slaves until they die. Then you throw them overboard into the depths like a rag.' He tried not to let himself look back there, the times when he'd heard the screams and seen the limp body of a child tossed over …

'The daimyō did what she had to do to bring those children back. I'm glad she did what she did! I asked her to. Nay, I begged her. I've seen what happens to those who don't get saved. I *lived* it.'

His throat felt hoarse, emotions bubbling up hot inside him as if he could also unleash Yoshiko's dragon power. He wished he could. How he wished he could add to the bubbling burns on Frewin's ugly face.

But the old pirate wasn't fazed. He let loose a burbling laugh, all guttural and gross. 'You know nothing about what happens to the children. Yer had it easy, devil's child.'

Gora flinched. He'd heard something about that before. Devil's child. It's what they'd called him for years. Since the moment they removed the sack from his head, the pirates had panicked and called him that. Why? The memory tugged at him from that day he was taken on the first pirate ship, captained by Foy. Two pirates had come to inspect the three captured children from Gora's coastal region. They'd moaned and cursed when they saw Gora in the firelight.

'Shit, we screwed up,' one had said.

'Wot you done now?' the other had asked.

'This kid's a devil's child. We can't use his soul. She'll kill us if we mess it up with a devil's soul.' The first peered at Gora with a fearful expression.

He could remember feeling angry at this, through his fear. Devil's child? He was the son of a carpenter! And who was this 'she' they were afraid of?

The other peered at him too and screwed his face up. 'Shiiit, how'd you get that wrong?'

'I couldn't see his red hair in the dark! Just looked like an ord'nary little flounder. Di'n't notice 'til now, in the light.' Looking uneasily at each other, they'd argued about who would tell the captain. Then they'd pushed him hard into the wooden wall and disappeared, leaving Gora alone with the other two children, who stared at him in fear.

Devil's child.

Ever since, he'd wondered what they'd meant about labelling him the child of the devil. What they'd meant about him having a devil's soul and who this 'she' they'd talked about was. When he'd finally been able to go up on deck, there'd been no sign of a woman. Women didn't last on that kind of ship. After a while, he noticed the pirates saying, *'A soul for the great sea witch'* when they threw the dead children overboard. Maybe that's who they meant by 'she'.

He was brought back to the now with questions burning on his tongue. This wasn't the time or the man to ask. That would be Foy—the man who had started it all.

He glanced at the pirates around him, making sure they were still there and not sneaking about. They were. They were leaning in, hanging off every word. Entertained.

Gora almost got it. The boredom on the open sea. How often did you really get this sort of entertainment?

Then he glared back at his old captain.

'Easy?' Gora continued from where Frewin had left off. 'That's not how I remember it. Working like a mule, forced to do things I didn't want to do. Kill people. Seeing other kids like me kidnapped and killed … helping you take them …' He trailed off. He didn't want to remember the times they'd forced him to take other children from their own beds.

'Yer still alive, ain't ye?' Frewin snarled. 'Be lucky the devil saved yer. You'd have been the same as them, otherwise.'

Gora had asked many times why they'd kept him alive when they killed all the others. It was always the same answer: that he'd been saved by the devil. Then they'd beaten him for asking questions and forced him to continue working to pay back the effort and resources they used for taking him and keeping him alive. As for the other children, sometimes they killed them quickly, with a blade or by dragging them into their quarters or onto the galley table and having their way with them while the child screamed. Other times, they fed the child strange potions and worked them hard until they became grey and lifeless and died of a slow illness. To Gora's fearful, childish eyes, it looked like they'd lost their souls. But he told himself that was something from the scary folk tales people told. Not for real life. But it kept Gora working hard. He was terrified of being the next one they'd turn into a grey one, whether it was like something from the old folk tales or not.

'Tell me why you did what you did to those children, Frewin. Why you made me do it, too. You didn't need to take and kill them, now. You could have just gone after treasure. Why the children?'

Frewin almost looked surprised Gora had asked. For a moment, he looked taken aback. Then his face turned fierce, and with the bubbled skin and burns, he looked like the true devil, regardless of what they called Gora.

'I thought we'd beaten those questions out of ye, lad. Or have you forgotten? Need we remind ye what happens to lads who ask questions?' He reached for the lash he hung at his belt, and Gora heard a round of low chuckles and excited murmurs from the surrounding crew, eager to see a deserter lashed.

Gora's skin felt the hot, white burning of the lashes even at the memory of it. He leapt back and put his hand to his sword, seeing the surrounding crew do the same. His heart lurched. He wasn't sure he could get out of this. From behind him, he heard a yell from Shingo on the *Sea Guardian*.

What was that? He strained his ears, hoping to hear. Nothing else followed.

'I want the answer, Frewin! I came all this way.'

'Yes, you did well to bring me such a pretty boat. When I kill you, we'll kill your crew too and take it for our own. I quite fancy another ship. Good job, boy.'

'The answer, Frewin. Why are you and your men hunting children, and why did you buy me from Foy? What are you and he involved in?'

Gora had never expected Frewin to spill all, but he'd thought he could at least trick the man into bragging about his successes and spill a few hints that Gora could use. May as well try to get information before he sank their whole ship and sent the lot of them to Davy Jones.

'It goes deeper than you know, boy. It's not just me and Foy, though that old son of the sea witch is one of the best. I'm just his pawn in this game. You wanna know why we do it, you'll have to ask him.'

Gora froze. A man like Frewin, a pawn? But he barged around the seas like he owned the place and burned any pirate ships that got in his way. He was just a pawn?

'He di'n't know it?' a pirate to the side guffawed.

Gora glared in his direction and then blinked. The deck looked emptier and felt less claustrophobic. He looked around, really seeing this time. There were definitely fewer people about. Another cry came from behind him on his ship, and he wheeled about to see pirates swarming up the side of his ship like insects. He let out a strangled cry. How had they got there? They couldn't swing that far with the ropes. Then he cursed. They'd just been stalling him and keeping him distracted. All this stuff about the past. Frewin had never really wanted to talk.

Of course.

Frewin stepped forward and drew Gora's attention back to him. He'd swiftly drawn his sword and was striding forward. 'But then, yer ne'er gunna leave this ship alive t' ask him, anyway. Our secret's safe.'

Gora rushed to unsheathe his blade—a Hizen katana given to him by Yoshiko. The pirates wouldn't have experienced fighting blades like this very often, and he knew it would at least afford him some advantage. Then Gora took several steps back. Everyone in front of him had drawn their arms and were watching their captain advance. Frewin would have first dibs. As always. But he could see them barely holding back, wanting to punish him for deserting. For challenging them. Gora took a deep breath, almost choking on the foul stench that wafted around this crew. Frewin was old now and severely injured by Yoshiko. He was sure he could handle the old pirate. But his crew of gargoyles would swarm him the second Gora showed signs of defeating their captain. He wasn't so sure he'd be able to handle that.

Blades clinked from the *Sea Guardian* behind him, and Gora prayed to the spirits that their training would help them at least a little. They knew that ship. They should know by now how to use it to their advantage. As for him, it had been years since he'd set foot on this one. This bunch of sea scum knew it better and would be able to outmanoeuvre him.

Steeling himself, Gora lunged at Frewin and darted past him, crashing the back of his blade into his to parry the attack and then swinging his sword around his head to slice at him as he pivoted past, inspired by a Hizen fighting technique he'd seen Daiki and Yoshiko use. The old pirate barely blocked it in time and was rewarded with a shallow cut to the back of his neck.

Hizen blades worked different to most of the swords these pirates would know. They sliced instead of hacked and worked best with circular movements and pivoting actions. It was a completely different style. That would be Gora's advantage, and he used it well. Before Frewin could react and raise his sword again, Gora had dug in his stance and used the force to flick the blade around to cut back up diagonally. Then he stepped back and leaned into his front foot as he cut upwards, slicing with the tip through the pirate's chest. This was something Frewin wouldn't have seen before. With Frewin being able to move quick enough to block, his chest received a shallow gash. Gora swore. It wasn't deep enough to kill him. The old pirate roared in pain and yelled at the others to 'stick the accursed lad'. That was their cue.

The gargoyles leapt to action, and Gora ran.

As he darted around the edge of the ship and wove between attacking pirates, defending and slicing, Gora could hear the commotion coming from the *Sea Guardian*. The crew were putting up a good fight, he could hear, and on many occasions, he heard the foul cursing of pirates as they were caught off guard or attacked. Gora grinned before slashing the face of a Shon Wa native who'd joined the crew since the last time he'd seen them. Must have been hired to replace those who'd died.

Reader, I don't want to tell you what it was like for Gora to see the man's face spill open. I don't think he'll ever forget it. Despite his desperation to defend himself and get back to the ship, he'll always regret killing that pirate in such a way.

Gora swung on the shrouds and kicked at the head of another gargoyle-like man. The man fell back, and Gora jumped onto the deck and stabbed him through. The man's face changed from pain to thunderous outrage, and he tried to be clever and stick Gora too.

Too obvious, Gora thought. *I've even seen that kid Miyoshi do that in training. Child's play.*

Gora pulled his blade from the man's stomach, and as he did, the pirate's legs collapsed beneath him and he crashed into the deck, landing on the deck and spilling blood into the wood.

That's going to be a pain to clean, Gora thought, realising that would have been his job a couple of decades ago. Somehow, a smirk managed to crack through his stony expression.

He looked back up, lungs screaming, and cursed repeatedly as he saw how many insects were still crawling about on both ships. Frewin was hobbling towards him, blood covering his shirt and coat until Gora was sure he wore red, not blue and brown. He truly looked like something from the old horror tales from Hizen or Gora's home country. He looked past the gargoyle crew over towards the *Sea Guardian.* Things were looking rough there, too. He cursed again.

We're going to die, Yoshiko.

Frewin lumbered closer, laughing with that guttural laugh that bubbled as if something was as destroyed inside him as much as the outside. 'Ye can't beat us, lad. Ye don't have it in ye. Ye ne'er did. At least ye can be happy ye lived thirty years longa than ye should've. Ye can thank me and old Foy fer that.'

10

Hunting Yōkai at Night

It was some days since the occurrence with the *kodama* in the forest, and Yoshiko was sat cross-legged on the tatami of her parents' favourite tearoom, her dark navy *hakama* making it easier to sit comfortably like this in comparison to having to kneel constantly on days she wore her mother's nicer kimonos. Now, as daimyō rather than noble daughter, she was able to wear the *hakama* and *haori* more often—the expected clothing of a warlord. This was agreeable for Yoshiko, as she always preferred the practicality of this dress, particularly in the comfort it afforded her. For now, alone in the tearoom, she leant back with her hands on the tatami and stared out of the open sliding doors into the private garden beyond.

A small water feature left a happy, bubbling water sound at the edge of her consciousness and a stone lantern sat in her immediate vision, but her eyes stared past it, and she was instead lost in her thoughts.

Footsteps padded in the hallway, but Yoshiko didn't stir, not even as the paper doors slid open. Chisaka. She recognised her footsteps.

'Lady Yoshiko,' Chisaka muttered.

Yoshiko heard fabric as the guard bowed, and she merely hummed back in response. With this as her signal, Chisaka stepped forward into the room and knelt at a side of the small tea table too, on the side to her left, just like she'd asked her to when she'd first joined her and made her feel uncomfortable with simply kneeling beside her. She'd requested she sit in her field of vision, joining her at the table, ever since. It was too lonely otherwise.

Yoshiko returned from her thoughts and leant forward, picking up her leftover tea. Cold. She frowned and drank it anyway, eyes sliding to her left to stare back at Chisaka with a challenging question in her eyes.

'I want to talk about the *kodama*,' the guard admitted, resting her hands on her knees as she shifted position and sat cross-legged also. 'I bring reports about more people going missing from outlying villages and wondered if it could be related.'

'*Kodama* don't take people,' Yoshiko said, knitting her brows. At least, not in the stories she'd read of them. 'Do they?'

'I looked into it before I came here. There are different types of tree spirit, it would seem. Perhaps those we met the other day were harmless, and perhaps others not so.'

Yoshiko watched as her guard and adviser also turned to the garden. It was a peaceful place and it was easy to organise your thoughts while watching it. Then, feeling a pang of hunger and wishing for tea that was actually hot, she turned and called a maid she heard passing in the corridor behind the room. She and Chisaka sat in a comfortable silence as the maid returned with a large iron pot of green leaf tea and a tray of toasted rice mochi on sticks—*dango*—and two dipping sauces: sweet soy sauce and sweet red bean paste. Yoshiko's stomach gave a satisfied growl. Then, as the maid dismissed herself and her soft shuffling footsteps faded away, Yoshiko nodded to Chisaka to continue. Best not to worry the people yet.

Yōkai stories had been a thing of the past. People lived in relative peace nowadays, at least where the spirits were concerned.

But since the events of last year, when the sky had torn open at the death of her mother and then again when she was in Acrein and had transformed and burned the city, Yoshiko had noticed stranger things happening more regularly.

'Sometimes *kodama* appear much like an ordinary tree,' Chisaka said, her voice still low. She leant forward and reached for a *dango* stick, and Yoshiko was already devouring her second. 'If one was to attempt to cut that tree down, they say blood will spill forth from the tree, and it would awaken and curse the axe wielder.'

Yoshiko's eyes widened as she listened in silence, licking some sweet soy sauce from her lips before continuing to chew near endlessly on the hot toasted *dango*. Impatient for more, she swallowed too soon, the chewy rice getting caught in her throat, so she grabbed her tea to help wash the mochi down. Chisaka looked back at her as if she was babysitting a child rather than her warlord.

Cheeks flushing, Yoshiko coughed a little and scowled at the guard. 'Continue.'

'People in different villages claim to see different things. Some a sort of atmospheric ghost light, others a moving tree, and yet others say they can turn into humans to trick people.' Chisaka paused to chew another mochi, her brown eyes staring again out into the garden. 'Some say they have started to hear echoes at night—what sounds like a tree falling, its crashing to the ground echoing in the dead of night. When they search for the fallen tree, it's unnaturally withered, as if the life force is completely vanished in days as opposed to years.'

Yoshiko felt ice crawling up her back. And while she knew these were ghost stories—tales her people had been telling for generations—something within her *knew* what Chisaka was talking about. She thought back to the little leaf creatures they'd seen in the forest. They had seemed perfectly harmless—nothing like the creatures of these stories Chisaka was referring to, for she knew of the old tales she spoke about—and yet there had been an energy that day that made them feel as if they should leave the forest immediately. An uneasiness that had stirred at their beings.

'I never saw them when I stayed there last year,' Yoshiko said airily, trying to remember back to the time she hid in the forest after her mother's murder. 'Indeed, it feels as if things have changed since—' She paused, not sure she wanted to say it. Chisaka looked at her and nodded as if she understood anyway, and Yoshiko thought some more. 'We should visit the shrine,' she said certainly, as if drawn to a new power dwelling there, and yet while her spirit had said those words, her head wondered why.

'Now?' Chisaka asked, looking just as surprised.

Yoshiko saw the hesitance in her guard's eyes. Chisaka, endlessly brave as if nothing ever stirred her, now looked reluctant to go back to that forest. A practical woman, the spirits left her on edge. But now, with her head catching up to what her spirit had suggested, Yoshiko thought that if they were to learn anything anywhere, the shrine in the forest where it had all begun might be a good place to start.

'*When hunting for spirits, go where the spirits go,*' she quoted, smiling as she cupped her hands around her pot of hot green leaf tea and thought back to her father's poetry. It had been a while since she'd last quoted his work. 'And we'll go tonight, when the castle compound goes to sleep.'

She looked up from her tea to see Chisaka's eyes boggling, looking at her in pure horror.

'At night?' She put her own tea down with a wobbling tinkle of china on the wooden surface—the only clue of her nerves—and leant forward. 'You want to go hunting for spirits at *night*? When the *yōkai* are at their peak?'

Yoshiko nodded. Instantly, Chisaka's face paled. And for the first time since she'd met her, she leant back onto her elbows, all decorum vanished, and stared up at the ceiling.

'You'll have a dragon with you, of course.' Yoshiko grinned. 'What could go wrong?'

* * *

The last time Yoshiko had snuck out of the keep at night was that fate-changing night over a year ago when her mother had come to smuggle her from the castle compound. Asumi, adept at castle escapes seemingly due to some reckless youthful side of her, had astounded Yoshiko with her agility. Now, it was Yoshiko's turn to look so comfortable at it that Chisaka was the one left reeling.

'Seems my mother's training paid off.' Yoshiko shrugged as the guard commented on her scrambling across rooftops and walls and tried her best to keep up.

'Why are we sneaking out, anyway?' Chisaka hissed at her when she caught up, crouching low behind a wall before they stepped lightly into the passageway and ran down the stone steps to the next compound layer. 'Can't we go through those caverns you said were under the town?'

'The entryway in the compound is blocked, and the one in the moat wall is tiresome. As for sneaking, it's a pain if we're seen and they decide they want to come with us.' Yoshiko pouted as she imagined it. While she knew her guards were looking out for her and meant the best, being followed by a great number of them would make this trip a challenge. The spirits wouldn't reveal themselves to such a group, and it would be a slower journey. Any time she wanted to do anything on her own terms, she now got used to sneaking off on her own, with Chisaka close by. It was hard to shake her off.

Now she knew why her mother was so good at stealing away from the compound.

'Besides,' she said as they turned into the courtyard towards the stables, 'we're not sneaking out. Not fully. Just until here.'

A whinnying broke the silence of night. Yoshiko smiled and ran the rest of the way towards her horse. Yukako must have smelled her across the courtyard. Yoshiko dug her hand into a satchel hanging from her shoulder and brought out a wrapped cloth parcel. From it, she produced a handful of grain and let the horse nuzzle her hand to feed. Yoshiko grinned and stroked the mare's forehead.

'Can't really get to the forest easily on foot, can we?' Yoshiko smirked at Chisaka, who rose her hands to admit defeat. 'Not easily, anyway. We have to be back here early on the morrow.'

The women mounted their horses and navigated the wide road towards the *oté-mon* gate.

'So we're just riding through?' Chisaka turned to Yoshiko, frowning.

'Of course,' Yoshiko replied. 'What did you expect?'

'Something grander and more chaotic, with you.' Chisaka pursed her lips and looked directly ahead, and Yoshiko couldn't help but smile in return.

'I'm sure you're starting to enjoy the chaos, Reina,' Yoshiko said, playfully adding an emphasis on the woman's given name. 'You seem to seek it out. Here.'

Yoshiko nudged Yukako into a run, leaving the guard crying out behind. Chuckling at Chisaka's surprise, Yoshiko knew if she were to look back again now, there'd be a small smile on the woman's face. But when Chisaka caught up, she'd be chastising her—or at least pretending to—all over again.

With the crashing of hooves echoing in her sensitive ears and the wind rising and whipping her hair about her face, Yoshiko lost all her cares. She called out as she reached the *oté-mon* gate and hailed the guards happily, tossing a casual 'see you later' over her shoulder as they dived out of her way.

Yoshiko craned around to look back as Chisaka followed, sending out polite apologies to those on duty at the gates, pausing for a moment to explain before egging her gelding on to catch up. *Now she'll* definitely *tell me off!* But the guards grinned as they watched the two women ride off, and Yoshiko found herself comparing it once more to that time a year ago when the guards had been against her.

Not against me, she reminded herself. *Not all of them.* Yoshiko recalled the moment she and her mother had been hanging on to the stone under the main bridge and a messenger from the castle had brought the news to block off the castle and find them. A couple of the guards on duty had seemed worried, asking about her and her mother's wellbeing. *Just like Daiki.* Her mood dropped as she remembered some of the loyal samurai had been blackmailed with the safety of their families, or just had their families outright killed. By the time Chisaka caught up and flashed a disgruntled frown her way, Yoshiko's mood was sombre. The woman didn't even pester her.

They rode in silence to the forest, letting the stillness of the night soak in. Yoshiko looked up at the stars, as she always did in the dark of night, and let their stillness clear her mind. The constant chattering inside her head slowly faded out. Even her questions about what they would find today and where Gora and his crew were slowly edged out, until her only focus was this moment.

The glittering of silver on black above.

Yukako's swift footsteps pounding the ground.

Her own body as she rode.

Chisaka's stern expression beside her.

Yoshiko took a deep breath and refocused her gaze ahead, the forest in the distance.

The two women left their horses roped to the trees at the mouth of the mountain forest, and Yoshiko saw Chisaka shiver a little, huddling her thick *haori* closer.

'Let's get moving,' Yoshiko said. 'You'll warm up quicker then.'

Chisaka nodded and met Yoshiko's stride as they clambered over ancient roots and scrambled up the hillside, the darkness thick about them. And while Chisaka held out a firelit lantern, it offered little light beyond the small orb ahead of her. Eventually, she sighed and put it out, placing it hanging on a branch and leaving it for the way back. Instead, Yoshiko held out a small rope for her and led the way, her cursed vision allowing her to see, leading Chisaka on. Eventually, Chisaka's eyes adjusted a little to the dark forest, and she was able to vaguely see the way, though she still clutched the rope.

Yoshiko pretended not to see the whites of Chisaka's knuckles or the woman's jittery glances about them, squinting deep into the forest.

Besides, who was she to comment? Her own breath felt shallow as she stared ahead, wondering what they'd meet.

Please don't be a bleeding kodama *tree!*

The cute, tiny ones were strange enough.

Finally, the two women found the stairway to the ancient shrine, and the moss-covered stone steps led high above them. Here, Chisaka's breath came in short, sharp bursts as she tried to steady her breathing after their quick climb, and the two paused for a rest and to drink from their gourd *hyotan* flasks.

'What do you think we'll find?' Chisaka asked, wiping her mouth and looking into the trees above. 'I see nothing.'

Yoshiko followed her gaze. 'There's nothing unusual up there at the moment,' she said.

'Not even with your special vision?'

Yoshiko shook her head. Whether Chisaka saw, she wasn't sure. Either way, the woman seemed to understand. Chisaka had a knack for understanding her these days. The samurai shrugged and straightened up, tossing her thick braid over her shoulder before gesturing they continue. Yoshiko saw the whites of the warrior woman's knuckles were still visible as she now gripped the handle of her katana. She couldn't help but smile.

'Alright,' she agreed and took light, careful steps up the old stone stairway.

When they finally reached the top, Yoshiko's eyes ran over the wooden *torii* and the stone kitsuné guards, but she gave a double-take when she realised there was only one.

'One's missing,' she muttered.

She looked about. *Thieves?* But no-one would steal a guard from a shrine. It would be terrible fortune. No-one tested the gods that way.

'What is?' Chisaka huffed as she met Yoshiko at the top, eyes squinting, still barely able to see. At least up here, a slither of moonlight entered through a gap in the trees.

'A kitsuné shrine guard—the *komainu*,' Yoshiko said, crouching and inspecting the ground where she was sure it was supposed to be. 'The female one. You know, the one that stood on the right—here.'

'*Komainu?* This is an *Inari Jinja?*' Chisaka asked, following Yoshiko and crouching beside her. 'It doesn't look like it's been forcefully moved. Maybe she just wandered off. Wanted a change of view.'

Yoshiko turned to glare at Chisaka but found the woman wasn't looking sullen. Instead, she looked almost peaceful, and the joke had been in good grace. Yoshiko let out a small huff of a laugh at her guard's remarks and replied that perhaps that was so. She'd want to move, too.

But a crack of a footstep on a twig in the forest ahead of them, behind the shrine, drew both women's heads snapping up, and Yoshiko peered into the dark abyss ahead.

'A tail?'

Chisaka rose and crept forward, her hand back on the handle of her katana. Yoshiko rose to follow, watching ahead of the woman.

'You saw a tail? A wolf?' Chisaka's voice was low, wary.

Yoshiko shook her head, not expecting Chisaka to see. 'I've never seen wolves here before.'

'Perhaps they came down from the mountains to the north.'

Sometimes, wolves were spotted in the mountains between Hié and Shogo.

Perhaps.

'It will be bad news for the local farmers if there are wolves,' Yoshiko hissed. 'We must be certain.'

It was Chisaka's turn to nod, and with Yoshiko's cursed vision, she was able to see. And so, the two women stalked the pathway from the shrine, heading deeper into the forest, following the light footsteps of the creature ahead.

'I'll go first,' Yoshiko said, overtaking Chisaka and passing the rope end back to the guard. 'Hold this and stay close.'

The buzz of thrill she got every time she hunted returned, and her blood boiled with anticipation. Legs itching to run, Yoshiko knew this time she'd have to continue quietly stalking the creature ahead. She sighed, trying to push down the frustration.

'There!' she whispered back to Chisaka.

The woman appeared at her shoulder instantly, squinting ahead, following Yoshiko's pointed finger.

The creature came into view after a giant tree trunk, its golden skin softly glowing with an unknown light. Kitsuné. A fox spirit. *The missing one from the shrine?* She almost chastised herself. Stone didn't come to life and walk off. The fox turned and looked back at the two women, and Yoshiko felt its gaze stare straight into her own. She froze. Yellow eyes pierced her own with an energy she'd only felt from those tiny leaf creatures, but instead of feeling anxious and as if she had to leave like she had back then, Yoshiko found herself thinking the fox was welcoming her.

'What is it saying?' Chisaka's voice felt like a moment shattered, and by the time Yoshiko had blinked, the fox had turned away and vanished.

'Did you see that?' Yoshiko asked, barely believing it. The space it had stood seemed to empty and undisturbed.

'Yes, and it seemed like it was speaking with you.'

Yoshiko shook her head. She'd not heard anything, though she'd had a vague feeling it had wanted them to follow. Now, she felt as if she'd missed the chance.

'I see.' Chisaka frowned and turned around, looking around the forest once more as if the moment really had passed. 'And did you see its tails? There were nine!'

'Nine?' Yoshiko hadn't noticed. She'd been too in awe of its eyes.

'How could you not see? They were huge!'

Yoshiko looked back to where the fox spirit had disappeared, wondering if she could still follow. Instead, the leaves rustled, and the feeling she'd missed it returned. *Maybe another time.*

'We should head back,' Yoshiko said, disappointment heavy on her heart. 'I have a feeling we've seen all the forest will show us tonight.'

They returned to the horses and followed the track back to the main town. Out here away from the zen of the forest, Yoshiko's head was filled once more with questions, wondering what was happening with the tree spirits and the fox spirits. Clearly, something was happening. She'd seen neither when she was here before, and the old stories were just that—old. So why were the creatures in them back?

'Do you think it's because you revealed your powers? Perhaps they feel more comfortable?' Chisaka seemed energised by the sighting and, for the first time since Yoshiko had met the woman, genuinely interested in something beyond her daily habits.

Yoshiko shook her head. 'My family's been here the whole time. Why would it change?'

'But none of them really revealed themselves. No-one transformed into a dragon. Not since the old days. But you did.'

Yoshiko frowned and focused on watching Yukako's head bobbing ahead of her as they slowly rode back to the town. 'But I'm not a dragon spirit. Just a curse.'

'Who says it's a curse or a blessing that matters? It's a creature of magic, nonetheless.' Chisaka expressed her interest to investigate further, to find out just how many more sightings there had been.

Yoshiko stared at the scenery, watching rice paddies and little lanes and farm folk walking about with their torsos bare and trouser legs hitched up. It was such a simple and honest scene. Were creatures of magic really coming back? And had anyone else seen them? She wished to speak with Gora. He'd mentioned travelling the world and seeing creatures, hadn't he? He'd not been surprised when she'd told him she had the powers of a dragon—what did he know of the creatures of the world? Was it just happening in Hié—close to her because of her increasing powers, as Chisaka suspected? Or was this happening everywhere?

11

A Boy's Chance

Miyoshi's mouth felt dry. He peered over the gunwale, squinting at the old pirate's ship. Frewin. He tried saying that name to remember it, but he was so nervous, barely a whisper came out. He tried to swallow and kept squinting, trying to look for his captain.

He'd asked Shingo for a spyglass, Yonemura too, but neither had given him theirs. Didn't want him to see what could happen over there, they said. The boy knew they were trying to protect him, but not knowing made it even worse.

He scrunched up his eyebrows.

Miyoshi had looked up to Gora ever since he first saw him when they took the ship back to freedom and Hizen last year, leaving Acrein behind them. The man had been his perfect vision of a role model, and the boy had wanted to do anything to help him. Now too. He wanted to be on that other ship now. He didn't care if it was dangerous. Miyoshi just wanted to help.

But what use could a little boy be on a ship full of fully grown pirates? He wasn't good at fighting yet.

Miyoshi rested his chin on the gunwale, brooding, imagining how skilled he could be if he could fight like Ikeda or Jelani, when a crash below caught his attention. He was glancing over the edge, scanning the waves for the source of the crash, when he saw small boats trying to creep around the edge of the ships, coming in with a curve to avoid being seen.

The boy looked behind him at Yonemura, who was at the helm, eyes piercing something ahead. Had she noticed?

She made no attempt to sound an alarm, and Miyoshi realised she'd not seen. She was too busy watching Frewin's ship.

Then Miyoshi looked around at the others. Too busy with their own tasks, getting weapons ready for a fight or glaring at what was happening on the other ship, not noticing some of the crew had slipped away to mount an attack on their own.

Their crew's much larger than ours, Miyoshi thought, *if they can spare extra to attack us and still have what looks like a full set on deck.*

He looked back over the gunwale, trying not to be seen by those below. They were reaching the hull.

Knowing they'd have lines to pull them up, Miyoshi launched himself back onto the deck, sprinting at Shingo. He interrupted him talking to Moori about gun firing ranges.

Not wanting to cause too much alarm and give away the secret that he knew to the pirates trying to sneak aboard, he whispered what he knew, watching Shingo and Moori's eyes open wide.

'Spread the word,' Shingo said in a low voice, nodding his head in Yonemura's direction.

Shingo watched Moori slip to the edge, gun in hand, beckoning Ikeda and Daiki silently.

The boy felt his heart shuddering in his chest. Any minute now, they'd open attack on the pirates, and the secret would be out. The pirates would jump up here and attack, and Miyoshi would have to be left with the realisation he was still useless. After relaying his message, Yonemura told him to go below deck where he'd be safe from the fighting for a while. Her face was solemn, and he knew what she didn't have to say.

If we can hold them back.

He paused as he plodded across the deck and squinted back in the distance towards Gora. He could just make out the glint of red-gold amongst a mass of yellow, grey, and brown.

The alarm sounded below—a yell in Traders' after the sharp firing of Moori's gun—and thuds on the wooden hull below. Miyoshi crept to the gunwale and, holding his breath, dared to peer over again. There was an empty boat below.

His heart didn't shudder anymore—it crashed about in his chest like a crow caught in a metal cage trying to get free. Where were they?

Expecting a shadow to loom over him and a blade to cut him in half any moment, Miyoshi launched himself away for the gunwale and ran for the stairs, a cry caught in his throat.

Then he stopped and remembered, looking back behind him at the pirate ship beside them.

There was an empty boat below.

12

Small Blades

Gora gritted his teeth and lightened his stance, planning to dart back around them and slice through anybody that came close, to wear them down bit by bit. If he could only get past some of them and back to his own ship … Just as he readied himself and angled his sword to run, there was a thump to his right as a man collapsed with a roar, blood spilling onto the deck from a gaping neck wound.

Gora's head snapped to stare bewildered at a figure on the gunwale beside him, a bloody blade in their hands from their desperate slash to the pirate's neck.

'Miyoshi?' Gora's breath caught in his throat. What was the boy thinking?

Miyoshi jumped down from the wooden gunwale and looked up at his captain innocently. The fear in his dark eyes made Gora shudder. How could he have let the boy come on such a trip and risk him seeing such things? To see such death. To kill …

'Captain?'

'What are you doing? How did you even get here?' Gora didn't even know which point was more important. He glanced urgently behind him at the foul gathering closing in. They had little time.

'There was a rowing boat. Then I ran along the gunwale.'

The boy said it so simply.

'As if that's such a thing to do!' he roared, pulling at the boy's hand to get as far away from their pursuers as possible.

Gora eyed the tiny blades in Miyoshi's hands and compared them with the cutlasses the pirates wielded. He wasn't hoping to fight with those, was he? But when Gora eyed the blades more carefully, he frowned; he recognised those daggers, but it wasn't the time to ask the boy about them when they were both close to dying.

Blood shone on one of the dagger's blades, and Gora wondered whether that had been the boy's first kill. Gora felt guilty. He'd hoped to protect the boy from instances such as this, keeping him free of the weight of taking another person's life. When the boy had begged to join him on the mission, Gora had intended to keep him to a cabin boy's duties, not getting involved in the dirty work. Perhaps he had been too naïve.

He looked about them again, hoping to find a safer alternative to get the boy back to their ship. Pirates were snickering to one another, planning to 'cut the little girl in half and send her soul to the sea witch'. Another wanted his comrade to save splitting 'her' in half until he'd been able to have his fun with 'her'. Gora instinctively stopped in front of Miyoshi to hide him from their view.

'Miyoshi, we must get back to the ship. The crew will be ready to fire *that* soon. It's been long enough. We need to be away from here, tell Yonemura to turn her bowside.'

The young boy nodded and raised his daggers to fight. The pirates had closed in around the pair and Frewin inched in, baring his teeth in his melted *noppera-bō* face.

'Good try, lad. But you and your little girl aren't getting anywhere. We'll keep you alive long enough to watch us show this little flower what happens to little girls on pirate ships. You remember, right?'

Gora did, but he didn't want to.

'I'm a boy!' Miyoshi cried out in Traders', poking his head around Gora's arm.

'You understood that?' Gora roared back at him in Hizen. 'What difference does it make right now? You know what they'll do to you, right?' *Boy or girl …* Gora hoped the lad didn't know. He hoped the lad never needed to know. Right now, it was his job to make sure it never happened. Before Miyoshi had come, he'd planned to run and cut down anything he could, even should it risk him getting hurt. But now Miyoshi was here and the pirates had crowded around, ready on their own terms, even if some streamed with blood and were covered in injuries.

Gora wondered if they could jump into the ocean to make their escape. He'd heard in so many sailors' tales of men jumping from ships to save their lives and being able to swim to another ship. In reality, he knew it wasn't as simple as it sounded. The ocean was wild, and secret currents were ready to sweep you away at a moment's notice. Up here on the ship, sometimes the waves didn't seem so big. But, when you were down there, with the tiny body of a mortal, they were treacherous. But sometimes it could be done. It's what he'd been preparing Moori for when he left. If he stood close enough to the *Sea Guardian* on this ship, there'd be less ocean to navigate. Less chance of being swept away. But now Miyoshi was here, and they were far from the *Sea Guardian*. He wasn't sure he wanted to take the chance. It was just too far, and the boy looked so small compared to the amount of ocean they'd have to swim until Moori could cast the line.

That won't work.

He observed the arch of pirates closely and looked for an opening. Miyoshi jumped as a pirate crashed his cutlasses, taunting the boy.

There!

A pirate to their right limped slightly as he moved onto his left leg to adjust his position, watching his captain with uncertainty. If Gora and Miyoshi could just rush him, push him and cut at his side, they could run past down the side of the ship, back to the bow.

'Follow me closely. Be quick.' Gora rested his hand on the lad's shoulder. The boy jumped and looked up at him before grimacing and wiping his mouth with the back of his sleeve. Miyoshi nodded.

Gora nudged him forward and darted towards the right-most pirate with the limp. The pirate's eyes widened, and he lifted his short blade to attack, the others leaping into action as soon as they realised Gora's plan. Gora knew a pale-skinned pirate beside their target would be the problem. He closed in quickly, so Gora slashed out with his blade in his left hand before pulling the sword back around and grasping it with both hands. Miyoshi ducked underneath his captain and dug both of his daggers into the man's stomach as he tried to attack again. The pale-skinned pirate dropped his sword as he fell to the floor, elbowing Miyoshi in the head as he did.

Miyoshi cried out and tumbled to the deck, scrambling on hands and knees, grabbing again for his daggers, which almost skidded out of reach. Gora reached out and pulled him up, half-dragging him towards the limping pirate, and kicked the man in the ribs. As expected, his left leg failed to catch him properly. He flew backwards more than Gora had anticipated, and his arms separated as they flew backwards to balance himself. His blade remained in his right arm.

'Miyoshi!' Gora yelled, panic flooding his face, realising this made the blade closer to Miyoshi.

The boy cried out and dived to the floor, rolling in front of Gora's booted feet and scrambling up to the pirate's left, near the railing of the ship. The boy twisted onto his knees and thrust a dagger into the man's thigh, giving Gora the time to change his grip on his sword to avoid catching Miyoshi and cut down the pirate at a sharper angle. The blade slipped through the man's left shoulder, giving him a deep gash, and he dropped his sword from his right hand to hold his bleeding shoulder. Gora grabbed at Miyoshi again and ran him across the deck with the rest of the crew on their tails. Frewin growled and limped towards them, cowering behind the defence of his crew in his injured state.

Maybe we'll have a better chance, now, Gora wondered, looking into the ocean as he and Miyoshi reached the bow of Frewin's ship and saw they were closer to the *Sea Guardian*. He looked down at the undulating waves against the hull of the ships and held his breath.

'They're turning!' A cry came up from the *Sea Guardian*, and Gora looked to see what they meant.

The Ishillian trader had turned and the sound of cannon fire cracked the air. Wood splintered, and the pirates' deck shook with a force that knocked Gora onto his back. Miyoshi crashed down into his stomach, knocking the wind out of Gora with the force. Gasping, with eyes glittering with white lights for a moment, Gora hoisted them both up to their feet. The ship swayed and the other pirates stumbled on their feet, too. Another crack broke the air and water sprayed their faces. This time, the Ishillian vessel had missed the ship, and the cannon had plunged into the ocean close by.

'They're firing at us, captain!' Miyoshi screamed, the white of his eyes showing as he started out at the Ishillian merchant vessel behind the *Sea Guardian*.

A third crack came, this one closer and more deafening, from the *Sea Guardian*. Gora's ears rang and the ship lurched with the force of a closer and more accurate hit. It had barrelled straight through the hull. Gora wondered what had taken them so long to fire. Perhaps the pirates had overwhelmed the gun level, too.

'Then it's *definitely* time to go. How did you get here?'

The boy pointed to a boat below, one from Frewin's ship. It bobbed on the waves, tethered roughly to the ship. Gora rubbed the lad's head with pride and swung over the side of the ship. Frewin, who had pulled himself up from the deck after the second cannon strike, roared and lunged after the two trying to escape. He pulled a pistol from his jacket. His arm shook terribly as he aimed it, but Gora could tell it was meant to be aimed at their faces. With a cry, he pulled Miyoshi over the side and kicked off with his feet, plunging into the ocean by the little boat waiting below. The round cracked overheard, firing to the side. It would have missed anyway. The old sea scum never missed, Gora realised, wondering what had made the old captain's arms so shaky. Was that why he'd not bothered to pull it out before, relying on his sword? At least in close quarters with a blade some damage could have been done, shaking limbs or not.

Maybe he's closer to death than he's tryin' to let on.

* * *

Underwater, the fourth crack of cannons was softened by the ocean above their heads, but the damage from its hit rained broken parts of the ship around them. Gora held Miyoshi close to him below the waves until he was sure it was safer to go up. They broke the surface the second wood stopped raining down. He signalled at Shingo to stop the cannon fire. The two in the water were too close. He wouldn't live with himself if Miyoshi got hit by shards of broken ship. Shingo ran, and even from here he could hear him roaring at the team in the gun deck. Gora pushed Miyoshi into the boat and climbed in after him, slicing through the rope with his sword instead of bothering to untie it. He pushed the boat away as the giant brown hull of Frewin's ship came closer.

He swore.

Frewin's ship was turning to get into a better position to fire back. They'd left themselves open far too long, overconfident they could overwhelm their enemy with manpower alone. Before, they'd wanted to take the Hizen ship for their own. But now, with Gora's crew putting up too much of a fight, Frewin would just want to end it all. To down them and be done with it. He was risking too much of his crew.

Above, Gora and Miyoshi saw pirates jumping ship and returning to their captain. Even they knew it was a lost cause. Gora grinned. Daiki and his crew must have been putting up one hell of a fight.

Miyoshi yelled as he rowed, eyes squinting shut, straining with the effort to row faster than the pirate ship could turn. 'Captain, it'll crush us!'

'No, it won't.' Gora grimaced, ignoring the pain in his back as he pulled faster through the water. He looked back to see Shingo leaning over the side again. 'Shingo, get Yonemura to turn starboard for the bow to face them! Get Moori to give them the figurehead's fire!'

'What about you, captain? You'll get it, too!'

'No, we won't! We'll make it.'

It was a race for who could turn and attack first. And, somehow, Gora and Miyoshi had to make it out of the way before either party could.

'Come on, lad! Show me how much you've grown! I've seen the crew toughening you up.'

Their little boat crashed through the waves as the two ships turned to meet them somewhere in the middle, giant black and brown hulls looming either side. From behind them, the black hull of the *Sea Guardian* sped closer as she turned the bow towards them. Gora cringed. Perhaps they wouldn't need to worry about rowing faster. It looked like she was going to meet them in her turn and crush them.

'Turn, Miyoshi. Quickly.' They turned and rowed to the side, trying to go around the ever-closing-in *Sea Guardian*. The bow narrowly missed them, and they rowed down the port side. From this close, they could hear a loud whirring noise from within the belly of the ship. The figurehead's flame was getting ready.

A couple of ropes dropped from above, and Tomioka and Sakai leant over the railings.

'Quick, captain! Yūki!' they yelled.

Gora lifted the boy to grab a rope and he held fast as Sakai heaved him up the side of the ship. Gora grabbed the other and started to pull himself up, Tomioka straining to hold the weight. When he finally climbed over the gunwale and jumped down onto his own deck, Gora felt relief flood through him so heavily he was sure his knees would buckle. He grinned and patted Tomioka and Sakai on their shoulders and thanked them as Kimura was sent for with hot drinks and blankets to warm their soaked and shivering bodies.

'The figurehead is ready to fire, sir!' Moori yelled from a platform on the bow, just diagonally behind the dragon lady figurehead. In preparation of giving the figurehead's fire, she'd cranked up a large mental contraption from below the bow deck. Now, she stood with her feet on two metal plates, eyes squinting into the metal crosshairs of an aiming support. She was the best at long-range fighting, of course.

'Alright, Moori. Let's give it to them!'

13

The Figurehead's Flame

The figurehead's flame: something special.

Gora ran to the bowside gunwale, closest to Frewin's ship, and bellowed across at him. The man's boiled and burned face couldn't look more livid.

'Frewin, you'll recognise this. The daimyō sends her regards.'

Even from here, Gora could see the whites of the old pirate's eyes as he aimed his pistol once again at Gora's face. He could even see the old man's arms shaking. The sounds of the flame powder's crack echoed in the air and were the only thing to reach him. This far away, the shot never would have. Snarling, the pirate captain yelled at his crew to ready the cannons faster and 'fire already'.

The pirates were distracted when the *Sea Guardian* reverberated, and the loud whirring Gora had heard from within the belly of the ship got louder until it was all they could hear. The pirates stared in concern, some edging closing to peer mouths wide at the *Sea Guardian*. They'd never heard anything like it. Their ship hadn't made it, and they knew they'd lost. Frewin never gave up, yelling at his men to fire at all cannons. He was desperate. A cannon cracked and missed, to Gora's surprise, skidding over the ocean towards the horizon before sinking below the depths. He cried out in rage and roared at them to hurry and try again or be thrown to the sea witch for her dinner.

The whirring grew louder, coming now from the figurehead, too. Standing at the bow, Gora watched as the dragon lady's mouth creaked open, and large wooden hands withdrew from her carved kimono sleeves. Hinges stretched, and the figurehead's arms raised, reaching forwards towards her enemy. More hinges unfurled her closed fists, revealing what was hiding in her great palms.

Her mouth and palms glowed white, and Gora squinted his eyes.

Frewin's men stopped running to do his bidding and stared in horror. Gora was sure a man collapsed with shock.

The roaring and whirring froze the air, and everyone threw up their hands to cover their ears from the head-splitting noise. Before he could blink, a flash of light harked three streams of white fire: one from the dragon lady's open mouth and one from each of her palms. The three beams of white flame merged to create a large river of light spitting out and shooting for Frewin's ship. Gora searched through the blinding light for Frewin's face. He'd never forget the look he saw before the blinding white flames took Frewin and swallowed his ship.

Terror mixed with hatred.

And the dying memory of the last time that fire had burned him.

* * *

The fire burned hungrily, slowly fading from white, to yellow, to orange. The pirates' cries died out quickly; they burned too quickly to suffer and scream for long. But the ship creaked and screamed and crashed into the ocean for much longer, and the water surrounding it bubbled and fizzled with the heat. Gora's crew took the *Sea Guardian* away towards the port of Ishil before the flame powder on Frewin's ship erupted and burst into a ball of flame. But they never stopped looking back, watching as the pirate ship burned like a beacon of hell.

The sea witch will feed well tonight. Or, rather, he wondered whether he should say 'a soul for the great sea witch' again, like old times.

Many souls, more like.

The dragon lady figurehead closed her mouth and clasped her hands inside her kimono sleeves again. She would sleep until the next time she was needed. Moori cranked the metal aiming platform back beneath the deck and, with Quinni's aid, heaved the trapdoor that covered it shut. Gora and Daiki each clapped her on the back jovially.

'Didn't I tell you she was the best for aim?' Daiki beamed as if looking at his star pupil. The young woman blushed and bowed, pushing her shoulder-length hair behind her ears.

As Yonemura steered them closer to the port of Ishil, the crew saw the Ishillian trade vessel had turned away once more, raising a signal flag for gratitude and respect. Though Gora's crew had saved them, who could tell what they really thought of them: the mysterious black ship that spat white fire. His main concern was the story of their ship spreading and pirates discovering a black-and-red ship was willing to face them and destroy them. With the pirates expecting them, perhaps their mission would get all the harder.

He leant against the bow railing and looked up at the figurehead. She stared ahead towards the port as if nothing had happened. When he looked back at his crew, on the other hand, their eyes filled with the looks of folk who'd never forget a horror.

The figurehead's flame was a weapon Yoshiko had worked on with craftsmen and weapon-makers especially to make up for not being able to go and fight with them. He knew how it was wired and what it did. But he'd never expected that. How they'd been able to make such a thing, he'd never understand. It was beyond him. A weapon that spat dragon fire? In the wrong hands, such a weapon would be world-ending.

The *Sea Guardian*. The ship was aptly named with such a weapon on board. Deep in the ship's belly, a slither of Yoshiko's fire wriggled brightly in a special cylinder, ready to split and be used when an enemy needed sinking. But the weapon used a large number of resources and took a long time to recharge. It was a one-hit attack. If they hit, it guaranteed victory. If they missed, they'd be stuck and unable to re-arm it for a long time afterwards, leaving them vulnerable to the greater powers of the enemies they faced.

Gora looked about his crew, nursing wounds and rushing to help one another patch up. Kimura had come onto the deck away from his place in the galley. Though he had a thin gash to his arm, he ran about tending his comrades first. A bucket of steaming water he must have heated on his stove splashed by his side, and he used a bundle of different cloths to clean wounds and bind them with strips. Gora was immediately grateful for such a man. Kimura often looked and sounded like a lighthearted young man who loved to play with people. He'd grown up in the higher classes of the Hizen empire, born to wealthy restaurant owners. His ability to cook up anything from any mix of resources made him valuable to the mission, and his love of adventure meant he'd agreed to join the mission. But now, this playful young chef offered Gora more than he ever knew Kimura had been able to offer: the care for his comrades, feeding and healing them.

As he caught up with his crew afterwards, he discovered that only Daiki and Quinni had been able to bring down pirates. The others had struggled to go toe to toe, neither seriously maiming the other. Yonemura and Ikeda had good reviews, but Gora knew this still wasn't enough. They wouldn't be able to hold up against pirates the whole time, and Kimura wouldn't be able to mend all injuries. It wasn't enough. Without the figurehead's fire, they would have been screwed. They really needed fighters.

Gora ran a hand over his chin, feeling his growing beard catching in his fingers. Thoughtful, he turned to the young boy still hiding in his shadow.

'Miyoshi,' he called out, turning, catching the boy's attention. 'Where did you get those daggers? They look familiar.'

The boy flinched a little, almost as if Gora had accused him of stealing them.

'Lady Yoshiko gave them to me,' he cried out, voice higher than usual and body tilting as if to guard them where they sat in a pouch at his waist.

Gora raised an eyebrow, sensing the boy's nerves, and crouched down, trying to look less threatening. He probably looked a right mess, covered in blood, and would scare anyone to look at. 'Did she now?' He smiled. 'Can I see them again?'

Hesitantly, the boy pulled one of the daggers out, holding it out in both of his palms. He looked into Gora's eyes warily, as if he was worried Gora would take them away.

Instead, a smile split out on Gora's face as memory gave him a moment of peace he'd not felt in a while. He'd seen Yoshiko using these and knew where they'd come from.

He ruffled the boy's hair and stood up, resting his hands on his hips.

'You look after them well. They're very special.'

The boy looked curious as he put the dagger back.

'Yoshiko's mother, the previous daimyō, Asumi, gave them to her. One of her last gifts for her birthday—her coming-of-age day—the year they escaped the palace after her father was killed. They're precious to her, which must show her good faith in you.' Gora smiled sadly as the boy realised how precious his gift was, Miyoshi's expression becoming reverent. 'Use them well. It looks like you have a good future ahead of you.'

14

Mercenaries of Ishil

The port guard narrowed his eyes. He'd demanded to be let aboard for proof of seal.

'We don't recognise your flag.' His red headscarf wrapped tightly at the crown of his head then hung down the side, a metal pin keeping it in place. Beneath the headscarf, the man's eyes were a dark brown, and these eyes were glaring at him and his crew with suspicion. 'You'll have to show me your seal before we can let you any further.'

A seal was needed for trade and navy vessels to prove they were legitimate, not pirate or mercenary ships. Usually, they were given by local leaders for the smaller vessels, and diplomats for larger vessels. Very rarely would a noble decree be given, as was their case. Gora handed the port guard the scroll of rice paper with Yoshiko's decree. He'd transcribed it for her into Traders' so anybody could read it. She'd then stamped it with her noble seal, and again with the shogun Kazuhito's, who'd given his personal decree for many of Hié's new ships. The guard ogled the stamps, mouth dropping open slightly. It wasn't often the port guards saw such decrees.

'So.' The man pulled himself together. 'That's the empire flag you've hoisted? Never seen it before.' He looked back up at the flag. 'I'll spread news to the other guards. What's your purpose in Ishil?'

Gora rubbed his stubbled cheek, exhausted and feeling as if he looked like he'd clambered from the land of the dead. How he looked probably only helped support his case. 'Putting in to stock up on resources and rest up a bit. Been at sea a while.'

The port guard nodded and looked around at the crew, all haggard and slumping. 'News has spread about a battle just beyond the cliffs. Would that have been you lot?'

Gora sighed. 'An Ishillian trade vessel couldn't shake their pirate tail. We were nearby, so thought we'd give them a hand.' He wasn't about to tell the guard they'd hunted the pirates up here. It might give the guard a reason to turn them away.

'Pretty tough to face off the pirates. There was a great ball of fire. What happened?'

'Flame powder must've caught,' Gora lied.

The port guard shook his head and pulled a disgusted face. 'We thought so. Sounds terrible. Well, the amount they've been pestering our trade routes lately, that's karma for them. We've had to seriously raise our guard. Glad one's finally dropped. If you fancy doing that to the rest of them, we'd be very grateful. You can go in, just let me off.'

The man marched off and started gesturing to the ship at the other port guards, clearly telling them the story of the pirate vessel. The others looked on in amazement as the crew pulled the *Sea Guardian* past their guardhouse at the edge of the cliffs, into the port and the assigned dock ahead. It wasn't until the crew had dropped anchor and tied the ship to the dock that Gora felt like he could finally breathe again.

'For a moment, I thought they weren't going to let us in.' Shingo let out a sigh of relief. Gora agreed.

'Yonemura, you're in charge of restocking. Shingo and I will head into the port town to see about hiring some extra crew. Get the resources stowed away in the cargo hold. I'll send Jelani to help Kimura order the food supplies. Think you can handle it 'til we return?'

'Yessir, leave it to me.' She nodded.

'Good. Now, Miyoshi,' The boy turned from where he was tying off a sail and looked down as Gora addressed him. 'You're with us.'

After what had happened, Gora wanted to keep an eye on him. A first kill wasn't easy. The boy bound down the shrouds and stumbled up to the two older men, trailing after them like a lost puppy into the port town.

* * *

It was a far cry from the last port they'd pulled up in. Compared to Shon Wa, Ishil was a place of luxury. Known for its high-quality silks and spices, Ishil residents flashed its rich colours and smells about them as they pushed through the bustling streets. People with dark hair and skin dressed in colourful fabrics that hung loosely about them, headscarves and wrapped jackets floating behind them as they moved. Gora kept the boy close so he didn't get lost in the life of it all, resting his hand on the boy's shoulder to steer him through the colourful crowds.

Unlike Shon Wa, Ishil was a government port and generally safe. But you could never be too careful. Pickpockets operated anywhere money changed hands and, in such places as this where rich trades took place every second, money was always changing hands. While Miyoshi was gawking at everything in sight, turning his head everywhere but ahead of him where he was walking, Gora knew that the boy simply bumping into someone could cause a problem. They'd think it was a thieving lad pretending to bump into them to cause trouble.

Gora pulled the lad out of the way just in time for a woman with long, deep-orange silks wrapped about her, with a headscarf of the same colour hiding most of her long, thick black hair, to drift past them. Shingo and Miyoshi both stared at her, jaws dropped. Then their heads turned in the opposite direction as a warm, spiced smell followed the sounds of frying pea crackers. They sniffed. Gora laughed.

'It's quite different here, right? So many tempting things,' he teased them. They agreed.

Ishil was high up in the world with rich trade and sought-after goods. A new centre of trade, it offered goods that were difficult to find in other countries.

'Are we going to bring some of that food onto the ship, captain?' Miyoshi asked, voice thick with hope.

Gora wondered. 'That's up to Kimura,' he said. But, knowing Kimura's love of food and trying new things, he was sure the young man would take this opportunity to get as much as he could.

Miyoshi looked excited. 'I hope Kimura gets some! I'd love to try it.'

Shingo agreed, looking once more at the carts of vegetables in spiced sauces.

'Well, we're resting here tonight. You'll be getting your pay when we return to the ship. You can come back on land in your rest shift and spend it on whatever food you want, then.'

Miyoshi cheered and started babbling to Shingo about all the things he wanted to try. For once, the older first mate didn't seem bothered by the high-speed waffle. He was looking about at places Miyoshi was pointing to and joining in just as much, both with big, excited smiles on their faces and black eyes lit up like burning onyx.

* * *

After asking a local food vendor where they'd find the local government hiring office, they finally stopped in front of the small, wooden building. Inside, a woman standing at the desk took their request. She told them to return tomorrow to review the selection. Feeling a little put out that there wasn't an immediate list to review, Gora pulled the other two back into the bustling streets and headed back for the ship. Miyoshi was in the middle of asking why the woman had three black painted dots above her eyebrow when two figures stopped them in their tracks.

'You're looking for guards?' one said, their Traders' speak thick with the Ishillian accent, glaring at Miyoshi's hands as he instinctively reached for the daggers he kept at his belt. The fight with the pirates had made him more wary.

'Where'd ya hear that?' Gora asked, revealing nothing in a calm, blank voice. He tried to take in as much of the two Ishillians as he could.

Both wore the traditional Ishillian headscarves, one dark red and the other blue, not black like the official Ishillian guards'. But both were clearly well armed with all manner of Ishillian arms. *Mercenaries, then*, he thought. They wore Ishillian clothes, deeply coloured tunics in light fabrics and baggier slacks that billowed around the place their boots fitted to their ankles. Ishillian silk sashes tied their tunics to their waists and belted their weapons. When he looked at their faces, seeing dark brown eyes and thick-set brows, their dark expressions confirmed his theory that they were mercenaries. This might cause a problem.

'Overheard you in the office,' one said. Gora didn't remember seeing anyone like them in there.

'News all around the harbour. They say you destroyed the pirate ship,' the other said. Their voices gave nothing away.

Shingo and Miyoshi looked at their captain, concerned. He wondered how much they could understand. So far, the crew had mostly stuck to orders and basics in Traders' speak, though Miyoshi was picking it up quicker than anyone else.

'You don't look like guards. Look more like mercenaries to me.'

One of the Ishillian mercenaries frowned.

'We're private hires. Usually any ships that need help, particularly with defence, hire us.'

The other continued, 'The official guards can't help you there. They're tied up in official rules. They're not allowed to be hired privately. You'll be waiting a long time to get approval from the officials to have Ishillian guards on board. Could be months. That's why you need us.'

Gora couldn't wait months. The two Ishillian mercenaries looked at one another gravely and then back to the three Hizens standing before them.

'You'd get more money hired by one of the rich Ishillian merchant ships, surely? We won't be able to offer you as much as them.' He watched them think about it. One scrunched their hands into fists and took a deep breath.

'We want to fight the pirates.'

'Why?'

'Why are you asking? Didn't you want to hire guards? What does it matter why?'

'I need to hire fighters, yes. But not to hire mercenaries who are just looking to pick fights with pirates.'

'What's the difference?'

'The difference is motive. We have a motive. We don't want bloodthirsty glory-hunters getting in the way of our mission.'

They thought for a moment, one nodding to the other.

'Our friend was stolen by pirates when we were children. We made a vow to do what we could to fight back.'

Gora blinked. They were like him. He opened his mouth but closed it again when Miyoshi chipped in.

'Captain, why are they pretending to be me?'

Shingo clapped his hand over the boy's mouth so he couldn't say anything more, not wanting to risk him saying anything in Traders' and giving the two mercenaries the wrong idea. He and Gora looked at the pair more closely. The mercenaries' guards went up and one reflexively reached a hand towards their blade. Shingo glared. Gora, on the other hand, remained relaxed. He clipped the boy lightly around the head.

'Don't be rude, Miyoshi. You're not one to talk about looking feminine.'

'But they're clearly ladies!' the lad protested, pulling at Shingo's hand on his mouth so he could speak.

'What're they saying?' one of the mercenaries asked, looking at the boy with suspicion.

Now that Miyoshi had pointed it out, Gora could also pick out the voice of a woman trying to be a man. And the faces … he wondered why he'd not noticed it before.

'That lad here is wondering why two ladies are trying to pretend to be men just to go off fighting with pirates. I didn't think that was the sort of thing Ishillian women did.' He tested it. Their faces flared as if they'd been caught.

'*He's* clearly wrong,' one of the mercenaries said, eyes inspecting the lad.

'I'm not!' Miyoshi cried, chipping up once more in Traders' and making Gora wonder how much he knew.

The two mercenaries leaned close to one another and talked quickly in Ishillian. Gora couldn't understand a word. They looked back at the Hizen trio.

'Does it matter if we are women or men? You need fighters. We're looking for hire? You won't find many others hanging around willing to fight pirates.'

Gora shrugged. 'How you dress or what gender you are doesn't bother me. But how much you'll lie about who you are does. I like to know my crew are honest with me. If you can be honest and prove you're skilled enough for the job, it doesn't matter who you are.'

One of the mercenaries fished about in a bag she kept at her hip, pulling out a scroll. 'Here. This is our letter of recommendation. Our training master and the harbour guard have signed it to prove we can work as fighters for hire.'

It was written in Traders', so obviously they'd prepared themselves for international work. Shingo peered over Gora's shoulder as he read it.

'Are they good, captain?' he asked in Hizen.

Gora nodded. He returned the woman her scroll, memorising their names: Eshnaa and Simrita. Then he told them to be at their dock the next morning, before noon, ready to sail with the afternoon tide. If they couldn't fulfil his expectations of them, he said, he'd drop them off at the next nearest port.

The two mercenary women nodded.

'Good. In the morning, then,' Gora said cheerfully. 'Come early and you'll get a tour of the ship before the work's to be done.'

Then they parted ways. The two mercenaries marched through the crowds and Miyoshi trotted after Shingo and Gora, asking a hundred questions about the two women they'd just hired as if the grown-ups somehow had all the answers about two people they'd just met.

* * *

'Captain, there's two women standing on our dock.' Kimura was carrying a crate of food up the gangplank as Gora was preparing to set off once more into town to meet the recruitment office. Gora looked past the trail of crew and port members helping Kimura load up the food and drink. He pointed a slim arm lazily down the gangway, Tomioka leading the way for the port hands.

'Two women?' Gora said. He took a moment to realise it could be the two he'd met yesterday and ran down to the dock to meet them.

'Captain,' one greeted Gora as he stepped onto the deck in front of two women in the traditional colourful garb of Ishil, long dark-brown hair loose down their backs in soft waves. He recognised that voice, though it was a higher pitch than yesterday.

Hearing a noise from above, Gora turned to see some of his crew peering over the side of the ship, including Miyoshi, who loudly announced he knew them.

'You're early,' he said, boggled at the transformation.

Gora scratched his arm, wondering how polite it would be to ask why they'd suddenly changed their appearances. It was a complete change. They'd swapped the tunic and billowing loose trousers of the Ishillian men for a loose, tucked-in undershirt with a long, loose silk tunic and overshirt that the women traditionally wore. The trousers still billowed and tightened where the boots met their ankles, but the colours were lighter and brighter. They'd kept the coloured sashes around their waists for their weapons, but they'd tightened them to more highlight their waists. The dark-coloured male headscarf had been swapped for a looser, bright silk that Ishillian women wore, wrapped more softly around their heads. Even their faces had changed. He could barely believe it. Their brows were thinner and more shaped, cheeks were more filled out, and the shading he'd thought was stubble had disappeared. He wanted to know what magic they'd used. Disguise abilities like that would be unthinkably useful.

'So is the way to assure the captain of his right choice to hire us,' the other woman said, drawing Gora's attention from their transformation to their words. Her voice was soft and light, as if it belonged to a woman who was calm and assured. He wondered if her personality would fit her voice, or if she'd be an uncontrollable showboat like so many mercenaries were.

'Is that so? Well, good to hear.' He suddenly felt awkward and rubbed the back of his neck, still not quite sure what to say.

This was his first time officially hiring. The crew from Hizen had either stayed on with him after the escape and war with Acrein, joined to help the cause, or been recommended by Yoshiko. Gora wondered if this was the sort of skill someone was born with, being a captain, or whether he'd have the chance to learn it. If someone was born a captain, he was screwed. He felt as if he was fumbling through each day.

'Well, come aboard. I'll have one of the crew show you about, as promised.' He beckoned them up the gangplank. 'Miyoshi.' He called the lad over to stop him from acting idle. 'Show them where the women's quarters are. They can stow their packs there for the time being. Then see if you can find Yonemura or Moori to help shift the room about a bit for two extra bunks.' Then he spoke to the two women in Traders'. 'I'll admit you caught me a bit off guard. You look completely different to yesterday. I barely recognised you.'

Simrita and Eshnaa looked at each other, confused.

'We thought it would be fine to dress like this, thinking your crew were used to having females aboard, what with dealing with *her*.' The woman gestured at Miyoshi. Gora realised he still needed to ask which name belonged to who.

'Did she call me "her"?' Miyoshi asked in Hizen. Gora nodded. Miyoshi then spoke to the women in clumsy Traders': 'I'm a boy!'

The same Ishillian woman, with near-black hair and a yellow silk headscarf, frowned. 'Whatever you say. But you can't fool us. We've hidden our genders long enough to spot others like us.'

Miyoshi looked at Gora imploringly, not understanding that much Traders'.

'They say you can't fool them.'

'But I am!'

'Be that as it may,' the calmer of the two, with mid-brown, wavy hair and a green headscarf outlining her curls, interrupted. 'Captain, are you still happy to hire us as we are? Are your crew content with us being here like this? You must understand, we dressed as men as many crews think it unlucky for women to be on board. In fact, in Ishil, women aren't allowed to fight or work on the ships. It was the only way we could fight the pirates.

'When we met you yesterday and you still hired us after the boy revealed us for who we were, we assumed you were fine with us as we were. Did we get the wrong impression?'

Gora suddenly felt overwhelmed, but he saw the serious expressions on the women's faces and relaxed. They were in the same position as him—wanting to fight for their past.

'Doesn't bother me,' he said. 'We have women on board. Just not him.' He gestured to Miyoshi. 'No-one here will care how you dress or what gender you are as long as you work well with the crew.'

The two women looked uncertain, so he continued, 'I'll get the other two women to greet you once you've taken your packs to the women's quarters. They're off preparing to set sail now.'

Simrita and Eshnaa relaxed, but the former had another question. 'And the crew won't bother us? Many men cause … problems for women. Particularly in such close quarters as a ship. They find ways to get around the rules. We only revealed who we were because we thought *he* was a girl when we met you in town and thought the ship might be safe to work on as women.'

She worded it carefully, but she didn't need to tell Gora. He'd experienced what she was on about. He'd sailed with the worst sea scum on the earth.

'I understand your concern. Truly. But buggery ain't allowed on this ship against anyone. No-one bothers anyone. That includes them and it includes you and anyone else we hire.' Their faces brightened a bit. 'Besides, most of the crew are Hizen, and from a matriarchal region run by a daimyō who has no sympathy for people taking others by force. I report directly to her. If I give a bad report, they know how much they'll be punished.'

'We have your word, captain?'

'You have it.'

Yoshiko had told Gora about what happened to her friend in the barn, why she'd burned the barn down. He knew what she'd do if anyone disrespected someone's honour, Hizen citizen or not. Jelani and Quinni had vowed their loyalty to her as honorary citizens, too. No-one had been allowed on this ship without clearly set rules, rules Gora would also share with any new crew.

'Right, Miyoshi, show them the women's quarters to drop their packs. Bring them back afterwards. How handy are you two on a ship?'

The calm one in green answered. 'Ten years' experience each, sir. At sea and on river charters.'

Gora's eyes widened. That was a long time and lots of experience. In that moment, he saw Yonemura returning to the deck. He pointed to her.

'Ahh, there she is. Right, see that woman over there? That's Yonemura. Once Miyoshi's shown you where to take your packs, go report to her. You'll be in her group for now. And ... see that fellow, there? That's Jelani. He can help you with translation. The rest of the crew are still learning Traders'. I'll spread the news you're both here and will get Moori, the other lass, to come and greet you, too.'

He watched Miyoshi bound off, excitedly leading the two Ishillian women to the women's cabin below. Then Gora turned on his heels and stomped back down the gangplank, ready to see if the Ishillian hiring office had any other fighters for him.

* * *

'Just one, sir?' Shingo muttered into Gora's ear when he returned from the Ishillian government hiring office later than morning. Gora huffed.

The lady at the hiring office had gathered all of three men to question. None of them had looked particularly the part. And, when he'd questioned if any female fighters were available to pick from, she'd repeated what Simrita and Eshnaa had told him previously. In this country, women weren't allowed to fight and be hired on ships. He sighed and reviewed the option in front of him.

One wore a black headscarf and navy tunic, likely trying to give the image of being an Ishillian guard. His slightly relaxed attitude dismissed the image he was trying to portray, and the man's face had a strange glint to it that made Gora nervous. He seemed the sort to chase glory—the sort Gora was trying to avoid.

The other, a man with a dark orange headscarf hanging low by his chest, was scared off when Gora mentioned to the three men their mission. The man looked uncertainly at the hiring office woman and snapped at her. She'd said nothing of pirates! He stepped back and bowed several times, apologising over and over, but dismissed himself from the office and quickly disappeared in the crowd outside.

That left the third man. Gora looked him up and down. He seemed smart enough. He stood straight, with good posture, as if trained well. His purple headscarf and tunic were kept clean and neat, and his dark blue trousers, too. The man was neat, spoke politely, and showed an official seal similar to the ones Simrita and Eshnaa had, showing him as a recommended fighter for hire. Seeing this man's face, with thick eyebrows, a strong jawline, and well-tended facial hair, Gora thought of how good a job the two women had done disguising themselves.

'What's your name?' Gora asked the man in purple.

'Rijul,' he replied, still standing as if to attention. His large brown eyes looked very serious, Gora thought.

'Rijul, I'd be happy to hire you. If you're willing to go after pirates.'

Rijul's eyes darted to the office woman for a moment but returned to meet Gora's blue ones with determination. 'I will protect your ship and your crew from pirates and mercenaries, sir. It is what I was trained to do.'

A good enough answer, Gora supposed.

The lady in the government office told them the terms of hiring, and how Gora would have to guarantee payment for Rijul or be penalised by the Ishillian government. If he wasn't happy with Rijul's performance, he'd have to return him here and file a report.

So much paperwork, Gora moaned. He suddenly realised what Simrita and Eshnaa had been on about before. If the Ishillian official guards came with more waiting times and paperwork, he was glad to miss out on that.

Even so, returning to the ship with just one man, three new fighters in total. Somehow, thinking of his foes, it still wasn't enough.

'Well, we'll have to see how they do, and try another port later on, too,' he told Shingo as the two of them strode the deck, checking they were satisfied with how the crew had got her ready. 'Rijul will be here shortly. It seems Ishillian women aren't meant to fight or sail. Let's hope he's open minded, or we could have a problem when he meets Simrita and Eshnaa. Even Yonemura and Moori, if he's strong-willed.'

'Let's hope it doesn't come to being like that,' Shingo agreed. 'We need every fighter we can get our hands on at this point. We're still a small crew, compared with the crews we're up against. If it came down to letting one go, who would it be?'

Gora couldn't decide. He felt he'd need to see them fight for that. But then, Simrita and Eshnaa had more reason to be here. He didn't feel comfortable with the idea of letting them go just because an Ishillian man had a problem with women fighting.

'More women on the ship will be cheerful,' Gora said as an answer. 'Yoshiko would be happy to know Yonemura and Moori have company.'

Shingo nodded and tested a rope Miyoshi had finished tying. The boy looked at him expectantly. Shingo nodded his approval and ruffled the boy's hair, telling him to go do the same for the others. 'Moori's helping them shift the bunks about now to make room. Yonemura offered to help too, but I said we needed her up here to handle the deck. Seems like a good start.'

'That's good.' Gora watched Quinni and Jelani climbing up the shrouds, ready to check the sails and loosen them when the ship pushed out of the dock. They gestured and teased one another even at such a great height, sitting confidently up on the beams of the main mast as if they'd been born that high in the world. They pointed to one another down the gangplank, and Gora followed their gaze to see Rijul standing on the dock. Gora ran over to meet him.

'Rijul, come on up. We're ready to sail.'

The man nodded and stepped onto the gangplank, eyes roaming the ship in surprise. It was like none of the other ships in port, and Gora had grown used to the constant stares of the others docked nearby.

'You have quite the ship, sir,' Rijul said, bowing politely as he met Gora at the top.

'The craftsfolk will be happy to hear.' Gora wasn't sure about mentioning a large part of the ship had been Acrein. It was too long a story for now.

He took Rijul to meet Shingo and Yonemura at the helm, both reporting to Gora they were ready to go. They all greeted one another, and Rijul eyed Yonemura carefully. Shingo narrowed his eyes a little in defence of his comrade, though Yonemura made a point of acting normally and pretending nothing was going amiss. Gora would speak with Rijul and the other two Ishillians about the expectations on the ship. She knew that.

'For now, I'll place you in this man's care.' Gora gestured as he ushered the man over and clapped Daiki on the shoulder. 'His name's Daiki. His Traders' is minimal, but that man, Jelani, can help you if you need anything. His Traders' is pretty good. My crew's still learning, so please help them where you can.'

Daiki greeted Rijul, and Gora translated for them while they introduced themselves and Daiki ran Rijul through the basic expectations. It was then that Simrita and Eshnaa came back onto the deck, following Moori. The two Ishillian women caught sight of Rijul and froze, making Moori turn in her tracks to see why they'd stopped. Rijul looked with uncertainty between Gora, Daiki, and the two Ishillian women. His brow furrowed.

'I didn't realise you gave passage to people,' Rijul asked Gora. 'You have a few women on board. Are they paying for travel? Where will they get off? Will it not be dangerous for them if you are hunting pirates?'

'We're not a ferry. We don't offer passage to people.' Gora raked his fingers through his hair as he always did when thinking of how best to solve something. 'Those are members of our crew.'

Rijul looked at Gora in surprise. 'Those two, they are from Ishil, too, are they not? They look like my countrymen.'

'They are. We hired them yesterday.'

The man looked taken aback. Gora frowned. Moori had guided the two Ishillian women towards the helm for instructions from Yonemura, who now directed the three other women for their take-off duties.

'If there is a problem with your working with my crew, I'd hear it now. While we are at port, we can arrange your return. If there isn't a problem, then we can set sail. It's time. I need your decision quickly.' Gora's voice was low and firm. He'd not be having any nonsense on his ship.

Rijul looked over towards the Ishillian women once again. Then, after thinking a moment, he turned back to Gora. 'No, sir. There won't be a problem. How you run your ship is not my business. My business is helping you protect it.'

'Good choice. Daiki, show him the armoury. I want it reorganised after the latest attack. We need to be quicker at getting what we need when we need it, cannons included.'

Daiki bowed and gestured for Rijul to follow. When the man's head disappeared below deck, Gora sighed. He always hated politics.

'Right, crew. Time to leave. Sakai, release the ropes. Ikeda, raise anchor. Yonemura, get us into the open sea.' He looked up at the crew perched in the masts and gestured for them to loose the sails. The thick canvas billowed down and caught the wind, causing the ship to lurch from its place in the docks and edge further away, pushed out by Tomioka and Sakai on the ship and several port hands below. Gora turned to see Miyoshi resting on the railings, trying to get a final glimpse of the colourful port before they hit the open sea, his face glowing as he soaked up the bustling energy.

15

Journey to the Other Side of the World

'Where next, captain?' Shingo and Yonemura watched Gora expectantly, standing beside him.

They'd just pulled past the cliffs that gave a natural gateway to the port of Ishil and been waved through by the ogling port guards. Now, Gora stood absentmindedly by the bow railing, looking out into the great expanse ahead. Yonemura nudged him with her elbow and repeated the question.

'Next, we try to find the *Devil's Corsair*. Frewin said old Foy's the one in the know. Said there's something bigger than we knew and that Foy's connected to it. So, he's next.'

'He's the one who kidnapped you?' Yonemura asked.

'That's the devil.'

'But where would we find them? Weren't you born on the other side of the world?' She couldn't imagine how far away that was.

Gora laughed. 'Halfway there. Foy controls the Sinfell Circle: a group of trade routes in the Western Ocean. Every sea and gulf attached to that route is in his domain, and he terrorises everything that gets in his way. Traders pay a lot of tax money to have strong guards and escorts to take that route. It's the only way to go, so there's no other option. He knows that. It ain't gunna be pretty.'

'We can't search an entire ocean for one man!' Shingo looked at Yonemura in disbelief.

'We don't need to. He usually operates in the same few places. If he's hunting for kids, there're only a few countries he tends to visit. Then, once in a while, he takes his quarry to a pirate town where they hold slave auctions and trade the things they stole. I was thinking we could try going undercover there.' Simrita and Eshnaa's disguises had given him an idea. He'd wait for Foy to come to them.

The other two still looked unsure, but they nodded. 'Where am I taking her, then, captain?' Yonemura looked ahead, towards the horizon.

'Towards the Western Ocean. From there, I'll update you. Yonemura, take us south-west for now. Let's catch the devil and figure out what their game is.'

She bowed and returned to where she'd left Taro at the helm, releasing him and taking it herself. She turned the ship towards their new destination, towards the devil Gora hoped he'd never have to see again.

* * *

'Father, you're old. Let me do that bit.'

It was only a few days sailing from Ishil when Gora watched Kyo as the young man insisted he take over from his father, Taro, in shifting some of the cargo. Kyo was usually silent and kept to himself. When he did speak, it was only when necessary or when trying to help out his father.

'I'm not so old that I can't move cargo, yet,' the older man insisted.

'You can move that bit.' The younger man pointed to a stack of smaller crates. 'I'll do the barrels. We've got a long journey. Don't overdo it.'

Taro sighed and looked at his son's still-gaunt face. Kyo had been one of the first to be taken by Acrein to work in their plantations. Over the many months forced to work with little food, the young man had become gaunt and his long, black hair had lost its shine. Since returning with Gora and Yoshiko and reuniting with his father, Kyo had been trying doubly hard to work to make things easier for Taro, insisting on taking the heavy work. The extra stress on the lad's body, still trying to regain the nourishment it had lost, meant he was taking longer to regain a healthy weight and body. Taro's usually sharp eyes were now looking at Gora for help.

'Captain …'

Taro needn't say anything more. Gora understood. Taro had been away trading with a nearby kingdom up the coast from Hizen when his only son, Kyosuke, had been taken by Acreins. A fit, young man had been a great catch for them. Taro's wife had been forced to work their shop alone, the grief of her son's disappearance piling on top of the stress of having to handle the family business alone. She'd fallen ill. When Taro was able to come home, unaware of his son's disappearance, she was on her deathbed. She'd died, leaving Taro alone forever, not knowing if his son would ever return. Now his son had, Taro had a fierce determination to stay beside his son and had followed him when Kyo had joined Gora's crew, unable to stay in Hizen after his experiences as a slave.

Both now wanted to make it up to the other—if a bit too much.

But this pain hit home for Gora too much. He wondered how his father had felt, knew what he'd have done with his family if he'd have been able to go home, and knew the pain of seeing Yoshiko suffer on the ship to Qecla before she disappeared from his side when they were separated on the other side. He knew what he'd do for her now, what Taro would want for his son.

'Kyo, Taro, both take a break. Go to Kimura for your mid-rotation meals.' Kyo still needed greater rations than the others. He didn't have the stored energy the others did.

Both men heaved cargo to the side and glanced with uncertainty at their captain before bowing their way out. Taro lingered behind his son, a smile slightly visible beneath his untrimmed facial hair.

'Thank you, captain.'

Gora nodded briefly. 'Crew's gotta be a family, right? Look out for one another.' Then, as the two men disappeared above deck, he called over to Sakai, who'd been working with them, 'You too, Sakai. I'll get a couple of the others to finish this off. You've done enough.'

Sailing, he reflected, was a constant series of shifting resources to ensure the ship remained balanced. What a pain and a waste of the crew's time. Though, what else they'd be doing in the endless hours of vast ocean, he didn't know. Learning, perhaps? He'd never had much of an opportunity to learn, having spent so much time on the ocean. But the time he spent with Yoshiko and now Moori, Daiki, Ikeda, and Kimura—all from positions of privilege and learning—made him realise how little he knew. He'd quite have liked the opportunity to learn. Perhaps, after fighting and language, that was something he could look at for the crew.

'Rijul.' He met the Ishillian fighter when he returned to the deck. The man's dark hair had been combed back neatly and his clothes were well cared for. This man was every image of a government hire.

'Sir?'

'Daiki looking after you three?' He deliberately referred to all three Ishillian fighters. He wanted it to be known they'd work well together on his ship or find themselves off the ship altogether. He responded diplomatically, to Gora's approval.

'Mr Daiki and his associate, Ikeda, are instructing us well in your ways. And the two women have great knowledge of sailing. They seem fine. They rushed off to handle the ship quickly.'

'Do you have much experience sailing?'

'I am merely a fighter. I was hoping to train to become an Ishillian guard. It takes lots of experience. So, I never gave myself the time to learn to sail. I'm sorry.'

'I see.' Gora wondered why the man was sorry. He'd hired the man for his fighting skills, after all.

They paced together across the deck as Gora watched the crew. All was well.

'I heard the story of the fire strike. You destroyed a pirate ship like one of the gods smiting a demon. Where did you gain such power?'

Gora shifted his gaze uncomfortably, finding solace in staring at the endless horizon. Even then, he could feel Rijul's strong gaze on his face. He felt the familiar burning in his ears whenever anyone expected a determined answer.

He thought for a moment, until he spotted Moori nearby. 'Moori,' he called out to her. The young woman hurried to finish what she'd been doing and jogged over.

'Sir?'

'Rijul wants to know about the figurehead's fire. As you worked a little more closely with Yoshiko on it and are one of the few allowed to fire it, would you mind explaining it to him?'

'Everything, captain?'

'Just the main idea, I guess. Is your Traders' comfortable enough to give a rough idea?'

'I think I can handle it,' Moori said.

Gora shrugged his stocky shoulders and looked at Rijul, switching back to Traders' language so the man could understand. 'Moori knows it better than me. Happy for her to run you through it?'

Rijul said he was.

'Great. Give her a bit of space for her Traders'. The crew's still getting there. But I want them to use it to get the hang of it.' He clapped his hand on the Ishillian's shoulder and nodded to them both, striding off to find Shingo. As he glanced back behind him, he could see Moori excitedly padding over to the bow of the ship, pointing to the figurehead. He smiled to himself. *That woman and her projectile weapons.*

Shingo was monitoring Nishimura at the helm. As Yonemura was on the night rotation, the young Nishimura was taking longer stints as the navigator. He was less experienced than Yonemura, but she and Shingo had been monitoring his progress out at sea and testing him when there were no stars or landmarks to guide him. He'd been doing well.

A spiritual man, known for being just as religious in the care of his looks, Nishimura was a ruggedly beautiful man in his thirtieth years and liked to talk about how his body was his temple. His long, wavy hair was the envy of many women back in Hizen, and his well-kept yet wild appearance meant he'd been well admired. Nishimura, however, had paid more attention to the world about him. He took long trips out into the mountains when he wasn't working on the merchant ships, loved to watch the moon and stars, and spoke poetic stanzas that sprung to his mind. For him, the opportunity to sail the ocean and experience the greater world had been his driver to joining Gora's *Sea Guardian*. How people could rid others of their freedom and personal spiritual journeys had been detestable to him. So, now, this young man who Gora could only describe as other-worldly used his knowledge of the stars and of sailing as one of the few ship navigators. To top it off, when they shared shifts, Nishimura had taken it upon himself to teach Miyoshi how to appropriately look after and braid his traditional haircut. Nishimura's patience far out-spanned Gora's.

'Shingo, Nishimura, how goes it?' They bowed their heads towards him as he approached.

'Steadily westward. Though something is making the water stir more than it ought.' Nishimura's eyes returned far off into the distance. They gave Gora the impression of someone all-seeing. He shivered slightly at the thought.

'Moon cycle?' Gora and Shingo looked at one another with a similar thought.

Where the moon was in its cycle could affect the mood of the ocean. Any seasoned sailor knew that.

Nishimura shook his head. Gora noticed he'd tied back the top half of it to keep it out of his face as he steered. It brought to his attention how windy it had become lately. So, it wasn't just the ocean stirring more than it ought.

'If not the moon, then—' Shingo's eyes widened as he once more met Gora's gaze. Both men froze.

'The sea witch,' Gora finished for him.

Nishimura nodded.

'What could have riled her up?' Shingo said, more to himself than in need of being answered.

'Could be anything, knowing her kind. They're known to be just as wild and unpredictable as the oceans themselves. Strange, because the moon seems so steady.' Gora barely paid any attention to what he was saying, staring at the ocean surrounding them.

Soon, they'd be entering the Casnia Strait, and passing near Qecla, he realised, one of the north-western kingdoms of the continent the Casnia Strait ran above. He wondered how Nubia and the others were faring after retaking their home country from the control of the Acreins. Then, as Kyo, Taro, and Sakai bound back up to the deck from their lunch in the galley, Kyo's many slave brandings covering his pale, thin skin like crude patches covering holes in a tunic pulled him back to his current reality.

'If we can make it into the strait before the ocean gets too wild, we might be okay. If the waterway becomes a problem, we'll just have to find a port to hole up in.'

'The energy of the sky isn't going to be a problem. It's just the ocean we'll have to worry about,' Nishimura said, eyes turned peacefully to the sky.

'So the crew won't have to fight a storm, at least.' Shingo sounded relieved.

Gora's mouth twitched upwards as an evil thought flashed into his mind. Shingo saw the glint in his eyes and frowned, expecting something ridiculous to follow.

'If it's just the ocean, could be a sea monster.' Gora let the grin take over his face. His smile felt it would stretch off his face, past his ears, and his eyes crinkled until they were almost shut. He only laughed out loud when Shingo gave him his old fisherman's glare and threatened again to hang him over the bowsprit.

Making his quick escape before the threat could be actioned and his reputation and position ruined in front of his crew, Gora excused himself to go check en route ports they might pull up if in need.

'And Nishimura, you and the others are to take us as directly into the strait as possible—like a crow flies. Before the sea witch really flies off the handle.'

* * *

The sea witch.

A holder of an ancient, supernatural power that passed only through the veins of women in a northern tribe. When one sea witch died, her powers somehow passed to a young woman-child in her tribe. Gora didn't understand how it worked. What he did know was the sea witches had been watching the ocean for thousands of years, living in the cold regions on the top of the world. There, they could look down at all the oceans.

Like the ocean, the sea witches' moods were wild, unpredictable, and could switch from calm to tumultuous and back again without warning. A sea witch would always watch the oceans. She'd always put ocean life first, no matter the cost of human lives. For that, many pirates, who spent most of their lives on the sea, treated her almost like one of the gods. They feared her, gave offerings to her, tried to bribe her, and those who were brave enough asked for her aid.

Gora didn't know how long the pirates had been giving the sea witch the souls of children or what it gained them. Perhaps they'd made an agreement with her or thought it would act as an ultimate offering to give them safe passage. Either way, such a payment disturbed him.

The previous sea witch had been murdered by pirates a couple of decades ago, while he was still a cabin boy on Foy's ship. He'd heard the news, of course. The pirates had been trapped and eaten by ice sirens after dumping the sea witch's body in the Penrath Expanse, deep in the Southern Ocean (as far away from her northern tribe as possible). They'd hoped it would stop the cycle of the sea witch dynasty.

It hadn't.

If anything, the pirates now feared the new sea witch would be trickier to handle than before, her ancient memories showing her what had happened to her previous body. Pirates, Gora grunted, always thought other things and people were theirs to control and own. As if one could control or even influence an ancient power as strong as the oceans.

Which was exactly why being on the ocean at a time the sea witch was angry was a bad idea. It was normal for her to toss ships about or send storms their way. But primal anger was a thing to avoid. Whirlpools, sea monsters, and hidden currents to pull unsuspecting ships against unseen rocks. Every sailor knew the tales. Miyoshi and Shingo's fears of sea monsters were well founded. At the sea witch's behest, whole crews could be taken to the depths into the waiting jaws of monsters.

Then there's the big one. The one they never said out loud. Or even think about it unless they could help it.

He shook the thought from his mind before it called the creature to them and hoped Nishimura's sense of the natural world and hidden powers would guide them to the Casnia Strait in time. At least there, there was less water for them to run into trouble with. So long as the sea witch didn't try to drain the waterways. This was the quickest way to the Western Oceans without sailing for weeks, risking getting closer to the more treacherous Southern Ocean.

There, terrible things lurked.

16

Nerves and Burning and Talk of Yōkai

The burning was getting hotter. Each day, she escaped to train in her mother's old training courtyard, trying to find any way possible to release the energy that grew inside her. Sometimes she was joined by Chisaka, who sparred with her, both women collapsing on the floor by the end dripping with sweat and chuckling at one another about how they'd kill each other next. But each time, both kept up. Other times, Yoshiko trained alone, trying to keep her mind running over the things her mother had taught her the year before when they were alone in the caverns.

At least up here she had fresh air and constant light, though now and then, she dared to challenge herself in the dark, running in seemingly endless circles through the dark passageways and letting her senses take over. It was the perfect form of moving meditation, keeping her ever-chattering mind occupied.

She'd still not heard from Gora or the crew. Moori, at least, should have reminded him to check in, or Ikeda.

Yoshiko's fingers clutched the wooden training *bokken* with such a sudden and aggravated force that it snapped in her hands, and her attention was tugged back to reality to stare at the mess ahead of her. Smoke wafted from the remaining wood in her hands, and the rest of the *bokken* splintered at the floor by her feet.

There was an impatient clearing of someone's throat ahead of her. Yoshiko looked up to see an annoyed Chisaka. The woman was clenching her teeth and had her hand resting on her hip, her other holding her training *bokken* to her side.

Few would get away with treating the daimyō like this, but Chisaka had been getting bolder and less formal, and ever chastised Yoshiko for her form. Training the young daimyō, she claimed, to make her a true leader.

'That's the third you've broken this week,' Chisaka reminded her, closing her eyes and sighing. 'At least it didn't explode into a flaming ball like the last one. I needn't remind you how you nearly fried me.'

Yoshiko rose her eyebrows at Chisaka, failing to find the right words to say. The woman was right. With the shogun Kazuhito visiting in mere hours, Yoshiko couldn't afford to let her curse take over, but she was feeling more tense by the day, and her body was burning up.

Since it had exploded in Acrein, she'd not had the same fever symptoms she'd had at the plantation or on the death ship, but increasingly each day, her heat rose, and she wasn't sure how to escape it.

If only Mama was here, Yoshiko thought, knowing Asumi could share ideas. And while Asumi had never transformed, the evidence of the white fire at the old farmhouse she'd died by had proven Asumi could use some form of advanced curse powers. And she'd had scales all over her arms and other parts of her body. There must have been this uncomfortable heat for Asumi, too. How did she deal with it?

Cursed for the power to take over fully. And once you turn into a dragon, you're cursed to live in that form forever, unable to turn back into a human, doomed to live a long, slow life until you go crazy and try to take revenge on whatever looked closest to something in your past that might just be able to undo the curse.

'You're worried about the shogun's visit?' Chisaka was nudging the splintered wood on the ground with her boot.

'Not really,' Yoshiko admitted. 'I want to ask him about the sightings, so it's good timing that he's visiting to check on the ships.'

Chisaka nodded. More reports had come to the castle compound about sightings of creatures that had been dismissed as myth, legend, or folklore, and more people were getting hurt.

'Still no word from the *Sea Guardian?*' Chisaka guessed next.

Yoshiko shook her head and stared at the slowly burning piece of wood remaining in her hands. She let it tumble to the ground, watching embers spark into the air. Chisaka made a huffing noise. 'You'll cause the armoury to run out one day,' the woman sighed. 'Come on, I was told to bring you in after training. May as well go now. The messenger said the shogun was due this afternoon. You burning everything won't be a good way to greet him.'

Agreeing, Yoshiko clapped the guard on her shoulder and smiled. Strict as she was, this woman kept her grounded and her head above the water. Without her, Yoshiko wondered if she'd just spend her whole days these days worrying about all the responsibilities piling up on her.

I feel ill-prepared for it all, she finally admitted to herself, knowing her mother would have shown her what to do when she came of age. That had never happened, and now Yoshiko felt like she was floundering to pick up the pieces and fix the region after what had happened.

The people of Hié were incredible. They'd worked together smoothly, and the newly created local leaders had worked with Yoshiko to create a council that would take some of the decisions from Yoshiko. The tidy-up from the battle was nearly complete, and Hié was finally looking like it was before the Acrein's had invaded.

And while the mental scars would never fade, people were getting on with their life again and picking up the pieces. With a new shipbuilding industry kicking off with the Acrein ships' skeletons and plans, what was a simple fishing port was becoming livelier by the week, and the shogun's visit today and for the rest of the week would only bring more prestige to the area.

Hié, with its excellent position, farming, fishing, and trade opportunities, could only go up from here, and Yoshiko was proud to be a part of that and guiding them, with the advice of her diplomats to assist her. But this matter of piracy and human trafficking troubled her, and she regularly woke in the deep hours of the night in a cold sweat, shivering despite the burning curse inside her, remembering the death ship, the people lying dead or dying in their own mess around her, the moans of the ill, the pain from the branding, and the blackened figure of her friend, Haruki. Each night, she mourned the missing space of her parents and Haruki. Masa, Ishikawa. Those names would never leave her soul, etched there in grief forever. And with no-one to truly share her grief with, Yoshiko felt alone. While she had good people around her, those who had shared those horrific experiences with her were so far away—Nubia searching for her husband and rebuilding her own country, and Gora and Daiki and Ikeda on a ship who knew where. Who knew if the ship was even still sailing at all and wasn't sunk to the abyss with the weight of the ocean crushing them in eternal darkness where the light couldn't reach?

She clawed her fingers into the slave branding on her chest and let out a shaky breath, knowing she couldn't think like that.

'Gora's alive,' she whispered into the dark. 'Moori, Daiki, Ikeda, Yūki … they're all alive.'

Each night this happened, and then each day she tried to banish the thoughts with the burning flame by running, training, working, distracting herself constantly.

'Chisaka,' she said, breaking the silence as the pair of them strode through the keep towards Yoshiko's chambers to meet Suki and prepare for the shogun's arrival. 'I want to find a way to help those who suffered. With the town repaired, the people's wellbeing comes next. You've been in battles a few times before. How do you banish those dark thoughts that linger?'

Chisaka frowned and followed Yoshiko into her room, greeting a bowing Suki. 'Trauma is a serious thing. I won't pretend that it doesn't weigh on me and the other samurai I know. I had suspected it was troubling you.'

Suki fussed about them, letting the two women talk as she helped Yoshiko change into her mother's long-sleeved kimono, the dark navy one Yoshiko had loved, with the moon rabbits. Suki had suggested Yoshiko wear it when the shogun came, as he had been like an uncle to her mother and would recognise it. Yoshiko, however, felt ill-suited to wearing it. Her mother was far beyond her.

'It is, and I know it will be affecting our people too. How can we help them?'

Chisaka hummed. 'I will think and ask the others.'

Yoshiko nodded, appreciating. She sat still while Suki twisted her hair up with *kanzashi* pins. The silver mirror showed haunted black eyes, and she tried to liven up her face. This meeting would be important for her region. When the shogun arrived, she had to be prepared to welcome him.

* * *

The shogun arrived in a clattering of hooves and rickshaw wheels, and Yoshiko had little time to think of anything else for the few days following. With her keep full of guests, the castle workers were rushing, and the corridors were bustling. Meals were energetic, diplomats loud and jovial, talking over one another to vie for attention, and Kazuhito, ever calm and generous, engaged all. His *haori* billowed behind him as he walked as if there was a breeze only for him, and his firm, dark eyes seemed ancient and all-knowing. Lines were etched on his face, but still the years didn't betray him. He was a man of power and seemingly eternal energy and youth, and he strode everywhere as if unhindered by age.

Yoshiko took him to meet the shipyard workers and craftsfolk, and they walked through the town with their escorts trailing behind, and Kazuhito greeted the people of Hié kindly and cheerfully. And though he was a man of incredible power and renowned for his prowess in war, little did he strike fear into those he met. Instead, he was gracious, and Yoshiko found her mother's stories of the man were true. This was her first time meeting him, yet she felt she'd known him forever.

'Your rebuild is going very well. You should be proud of the work of your people,' he said as they returned to the castle grounds late that evening.

The sun was setting, and people were hurrying indoors. Kazuhito frowned.

'And yet, people still hide?'

Yoshiko bowed her head and agreed with both statements. She had told him of everything over the last few months since her father's death, and how the strange sightings were impacting people's lifestyles again. People had finally felt free after their curfews at the hands of the council the year before, and now they had to hide for their safety again.

The shogun let out a low growl as he thought. He walked closer to her. 'Here, take my arm, young one. Your mother and I used to walk together like this when she was small.'

Yoshiko did so, and they walked quietly up the hill through the town.

He spoke again, voice low. 'Your reports are not the only ones reaching my ears. Several domains have had odd sightings—ghost tales, they say, creatures that only existed in stories before. People going missing, found dead, attacked or with a strange stare in their eyes.'

His voice trailed off and they both looked behind them to their escort, who had conveniently dropped back a little. Chisaka bowed her head as Yoshiko caught her gaze. The woman stood tall, vigilant, and watched the shadows as Yoshiko returned her attention to the shogun and the castle compound rising ahead of them.

'I saw a kitsuné,' she whispered. 'In the forest by the mountains.'

They greeted the guards at the *oté-mon* gate before Kazuhito spoke again. 'A rare sight indeed. No news of those have reached me yet. Do tell, do they have nine tails as the stories suggest?'

'They do,' Yoshiko said, smiling at the memory. 'They seem peaceful, quiet, and the eyes suggested an eternity of understanding.'

'They are beyond us. The spirit world is something we cannot comprehend.' His gruff voice betrayed his awe. 'Have you seen anything else?'

'We think *kodama*, young ones. Thousands, looking like little leaves. Though fortunately nothing like the ones in the scarier stories that attack you or bleed if you chop them down.' Then she added, 'Not yet.'

'A good thing, too. Some of the stories we've had are horrific.' They paused at the steps as some of the escort filed away to the guards' quarters, and Yoshiko guided the old shogun up the stone steps towards the top platform where he was staying with her and the other higher-level guests in the *tenshu* keep. 'Some say the creatures are returning, that something that had stopped them before has now come undone. We are having a hard enough time with more foreign ships bringing guns and stirring trouble between regions. Your mother knew their weapons would bring back the feudal days and tried to stop the gun trade, and for that, I think her council betrayed her, seeing only the money that comes with the sale of armaments. But to control guns *and* the return of the old magic, I see this as causing quite the stir among the nation.'

Yoshiko sighed. Before her father died, Chinen had told her of the prospect of war returning. What he hadn't mentioned was he was going to be a part of the cause, trading the people of Hizen for access to new armaments and guns and trade connections. If that was continuing elsewhere … she asked the shogun if he knew of any other region with people going missing due to possible human trafficking, and he shook his head.

'We relayed the news. The searches have thankfully brought back nothing yet.' He looked at her sadly. 'Hié is one of the easiest places to access for trade. Likely, you were the first point they tried. I am sorry for the suffering your people have experienced.' He stopped and looked up at the evening sky. 'Unfortunately, I do not think this suffering has ended. If the predictions are true, both guns and creature sightings will get worse from here before they get better.'

He looked at Chisaka, who was following at a private distance further down the steps. He left Yoshiko with one final clue before they stepped into the castle compound and closer to prying ears.

'Your heritage is a rare one. Of all people able to research the old stories, your family is the closest to the source. For the sake of all of Hizen, I ask you to use your family's past as its strength. There are things your ancestors may know that give us the clues we need.'

Yoshiko bowed in response and watched as he strode away, through her keep and towards the castle workers who rushed to help him. His words had struck deeply. He'd known about the curse for years, he'd said—since her grandmother's days—and yet he'd kept it silent and private. Having known both her grandmother and her mother, Kazuhito would know more about her family than Yoshiko could, and if he said there was a secret to learn, Yoshiko had no doubt it would be there.

That night, when the night sweats and nightmares awoke her, she rose from her futon instead of cowering in the warm blankets. She lit a flame lantern with the heat of her fingers and padded silently through the sleeping keep.

Records of her family. Was there such a thing?

Her mother had left behind a wealth of scrolls and notes, and they had a room of records of the daimyōs' governance. Would something be in there?

And so, spurred on by the shogun's hints, Yoshiko used the terrible night hours to search through her family's recordings of all that happened in Hié. Long after the shogun departed, Yoshiko kept this up, trawling through meeting notes that made her eyes droop and her shoulders sag. Often, she fell asleep at the small desk, knees cramping as she woke up. Until one day, something her mother wrote made her stop. Asumi had explored something her grandmother had told her about, and though it was just a hint, Yoshiko took it.

A trip to Tatsushima—dragon island. It was a small, near-insignificant island that lay just off the southern shore of Hié. So small Yoshiko had barely paid it attention before. Now, with its name written in front of her, she chastised herself. It was too obvious. There were no notes beside it save Asumi writing she'd taken a boat there for the day.

But, Mother, what did you do there?

Yoshiko clicked her tongue, wishing her mother had written more. She sighed and slumped back onto the tatami flooring, frustrated at the only thing she'd found in her weeks of hunting being so tiny. Her search would have to continue. Yoshiko stared at the dark ceiling above. What if her mother hadn't written what she'd done there in case it was discovered by the wrong person? What if all along they made it seem like an insignificant place?

Tatsushima. Dragon curse. It had to be connected. And only a short distance away, she could easily take a day trip there to find out more for herself.

17

Serpents of the Straits

Miyoshi was leaning over the gunwale of the ship, eyes and mouth wide in awe and uncertainty of his view below. Eshnaa and Rijul ran to his side, their hands swiftly reaching for the weapons at their belts and pulling the lad from the edge. Their faces mirrored his when they peered into the ocean and then turned with dark eyes to implore Daiki's aid.

'What's the trouble?' Gora joined them to translate. Though his crew were getting better at Traders', it wasn't enough for deep conversations.

They gestured their heads past the gunwale, into the sea, and Miyoshi leaned over to look again.

'There's lots of eels and things down there,' he cried, pointing to a particularly large swarm.

Daiki peered into the ocean and made a strangled cry, pulling the young lad back, pinning the boy to his side with a grip that made Miyoshi's face scrunch up.

'I've never seen anything like it before,' Eshnaa said, carefully edging closer to the gunwale to peek down. Her curved blade was fully drawn, her muscles primed to swipe out if anything were to jump up at her. 'There are so many.'

Gora followed her lead and leant over the gunwale. Swarms of eel-like bodies pulsed and pushed below, some huge enough to be

140

seen with all their detail from up on the deck. And it seemed as if more were arriving each moment. He gulped and met the gaze of Shingo, who hurried over to join them, his face pale and staring like stone at his captain.

'Sea serpents?' Shingo dared to ask, knuckles white as he gripped the gunwale to see for himself.

Gora met Eshnaa's eyes, and both nodded.

'Sea serpents,' they both replied.

'Though, they are smaller than I expected,' Eshnaa added thoughtfully, expression nostalgic. 'They're always huge in stories.'

'Could be young ones.' Gora rubbed at the stubble on his chin as he tried to think back to ever seeing anything like this.

Rijul stepped forward again, returning his gaze to the undulating, snake-like bodies below. 'This is what they look like? I've seen nothing like it before. They are said to be a rare sight, keeping to the depths of the ocean where no ships bothered them.'

Eshnaa and Gora nodded. 'This is unusual,' Eshnaa agreed. 'Sim would want to see this.'

Simrita was taking the night rotation with Moori, both now resting in the ladies' quarters. Even so, Gora could see the decision in Eshnaa's eyes—should she go wake her friend to see this? The decision flickered from her gaze when something big nudged the hull and her curved blades raised once more, and she faced the edge of the ship full on and face set with determination.

'They are all swimming in the same direction. It's like they don't notice us at all. As if we are a mere object of inconvenience in their way.' Daiki had also returned to stand by the gunwale, taking Miyoshi with him, and was now also fingering the handle of his katana, but his gaze calmly swept over the creatures in the depths. 'Captain, it is as if they are fleeing something. I don't believe they are paying us much heed.'

Gora and Shingo both frowned at the seasoned samurai. His calm, analysing face in such a situation gave Shingo reassurance to edge once more towards the edge.

The six of them dared to rest their hands on the lacquered wood railing and peer over the side. Gora was surprised to see Daiki's impressions were true.

'It's like they can't see us at all.'

It was true, in a way, Gora noticed. More like a frenzy had overtaken them and their only focus was on getting away.

'Something's not right,' he thought out loud. He ran to the other side of the deck and peered into the ocean that stretched beyond, the opposite direction of the straits. The water was unsettled in all directions as thousands of serpentine bodies raced towards them. Some of the others on the ship were starting to look their way. Miyoshi's leg was twitching as he watched his captain, desperate to join him and see what was happening out in the ocean, but Shingo had ordered him to stay. The boy strained his neck to look instead.

'Over there.' Gora jumped as Quinni loomed beside him. He was quietly pointing into the distance and squinting. Gora followed his gaze.

A shadow lurked in the ocean. Gora looked back at Nishimura, who was gazing towards the straits. He couldn't see the man's face. But the man had warned something was stirring in the ocean. Was this something conjured by the sea witch? Were the serpents running from something her anger had stirred up?

Something else nudged the ship again, causing her to rock slightly as she was battered between large bodies below. At the helm, Nishimura rushed to half-tie his hair up again, pulling his long hair from his face to focus.

'Captain?' He turned back and bellowed across at Gora, his eyes serious now. 'I need Yonemura.'

Yonemura was below, resting from the night rotation with Moori and Simrita. But Nishimura's expression and how he quickly returned to hefting the helm around to keep it steady showed he needed the aid of his superior urgently. Another large body nudged the hull, making him stumble.

'Eshnaa, go wake the other women. We need Yonemura to help at the helm, and we could so with having Simrita and Moori ready if this gets ugly,' he said in Traders'. She nodded and ran off. 'Daiki, go get Ikeda from the sleeping quarters. Rijul, keep watch and let me know the minute they start noticing us and look like they're ready to attack. Observe all ends of the ship.'

Both ran off to do their bidding.

'What shall I do, captain?' Shingo's brow furrowed. 'And the boy? To keep him away from the edge.' He looked back towards the swarming bodies below.

'Miyoshi can warn the crew and pass the message to be ready for this to get ugly. Then he can go check the safety lines are tight. Shingo, go reassure the men sleeping below, but make sure they know to be ready to called upon. They can keep resting for now. Then we need to make sure we head to the straits at full speed. If the serpents are running from the shadow, we need to, too.'

They bowed their heads and ran off, leaving Gora watching the serpents alone. The sea was thick with them, and he could even see fish joining the fray and swimming blindly in the same direction as the serpents that battered and pushed them about.

'I'd almost believe I was sailing on serpents,' he sighed, and turned on his heels to direct his crew all speed to the straits.

The sea witch was testing him.

* * *

'It's there!' Nishimura cried out, pointing towards the opening where the paler water of the Casnia Strait met the Central Sea.

143

Yonemura had rushed up to join him, and they were taking half of the helm each to pin it in a carefully coordinated manoeuvre towards the straits.

'I'd almost believe it if there was a dragon down there.' Yonemura's voice was strained as she heaved the helm a couple degrees towards Nishimura. 'There's so much interference.'

The ship lurched as another serpent swam past the ship, barely noticing something was in its way.

'What could be so bad that so many serpents are escaping?'

'I don't want to find out. Just get us into the strait.'

'You think we'll be safe there?' She grunted, nodding to Nishimura as they both held the helm steady for a straight aim at the paler water ahead.

'Of course,' Nishimura said, giving them both a knowing look. 'You should always pay attention to what creatures are doing. If there's danger, follow the animals as they run away. It will take you somewhere safer. Their instincts are stronger than ours.'

Gora nodded. The ten years or so he'd spent living on the edge of the Hizen forest had showed him that exactly. Hizen was known to experience ground shakes. When the earth roiled and rumbled, animals seemed to know it before humans did. It had saved his life on many occasions, either by his hut or in the woods, where he could find a place to avoid falling trees.

'Keep following the serpents. By any fortune, if we travel the same way as them, they'll not see us as a threat. If we turn in any direction, we'll be battered as they try to push us out of their way.' He watched into the distance. 'We were headed for the waterways anyway. It's the best way to the other side of that continent.'

The two navigators nodded seriously, and he left them to it. They knew well enough to get the crew and ship there. They didn't need him breathing down their neck to do it, particularly at such a crucial time. Gora paced over, wobbling at further knocks to the ship, to Quinni, who was still watching the shadow in the ocean ahead.

'Will we make it, do you think?' Quinni asked, turning to face his captain. His deep brown eyes were wide, his usually dark face ashen with a fear only sailors knew.

'We'll just focus on doing our best to get there.'

'And will it be safe in there? We won't be followed?'

'Nishimura thinks not.'

'He is a wise man when it comes to the natural world, but I wonder how that could be the case.' Quinni frowned.

'Some creatures prefer different types of water. Or different depths. Perhaps that is it. If the serpents are escaping that way, it's a good place to start, at least.' Gora leaned casually against the railing and stretched out his arms, relaxing and looking at the sky. He hoped a show of confidence would relax the man. 'Deep breaths, kid.'

The man relaxed, if only a little. Gora stood straight again, clapped the man on the shoulder, and said, 'Keep up the good work. Let me know if you see anything else. I'm going to check on the others.'

And, with the quiet giant going back to staring at the shadow that followed them, Gora did his rounds checking on the crew. Moori and Simrita had come up to the deck and joined the defence team standing at points around the ship to observe the serpents that surrounded them, ready to shout if anything looked ready to attack. Sakai and Jelani were clinging to the shrouds, making their way to check the mainsail, and Miyoshi had been ordered to help Kimura in the galley to keep him out of harm's way.

'We're nearly there!'

Moori's voice from her place at the bow of the ship rang through the tense air on the ship, slicing above the low waves and the deep noise coming from within. Both Nishimura and

Yonemura stared unwavering at the Casnia Strait, and the rest of the crew turned to watch the same place until a bellow from above, high up in the crow's nest, drew their attention back to the waves.

'What's that?'

Everyone on deck stopped and looked up at Sakai, who was pointing and squinting into the distance. They followed his finger, and a shape appeared where the shadow in the distance had been. They edged to the gunwale and watched the shadow over the side. Below them, serpents squirmed and wriggled past the ship, knocking and nudging it.

The ocean exploded where the shadow rose, and water crashed upwards. Miyoshi gasped and searched the others for an answer, but none came. Everyone was as confused as he, even Gora and Yonemura, both staring open-mouthed into the distance. The crew turned in unison to Nishimura, who was still at the helm, his face calm as ever as he, too, observed the exploding sea.

'Nishimura, thoughts?' Gora asked in a gruff voice. He turned his blue eyes back to the exploding sea, furrowing his thick red brow and narrowing his eyes to peer into the shadow's depth.

Miyoshi did too, copying his captain and furrowing his brow, but he was unable to see what had made the ocean explode.

'None, just that we should continue following the serpents. I'm more confident than ever that we should head full speed towards the straits. We'll be safe there. Creatures have better instincts than us, so we should follow their lead.' As always, Nishimura's voice was calm and soft as if his thoughts were in a far-off place, and Miyoshi admired how he could be so tranquil in such a time. His own heart was pounding as much as a festival drum, and he wished the ship would speed up.

Gora, as always, thought well in silence before making his decision, and he nodded. 'Wake those who are sleeping. Full crew to get us to sail us to safety. Whatever's hiding in the ocean, we want to be as far away as possible.' Then he turned and strode to the doorway that led below deck, calling back over his shoulder. 'Follow the serpents!'

Miyoshi watched Gora until his red head had disappeared below, then wheeled on the spot and ran to be useful, tightening the lines and trying not to get underfoot. Simrita called him to help her in the shrouds to tighten the sails to catch the winds, and he pulled himself up as quickly as he can. He didn't want to get caught by whatever monster was out in the ocean.

'Do you think the sea serpents will know where to hide?' he asked her, trying his best in Traders', squeezing his legs tightly to stop himself falling off. The serpents below seemed to be nudging the ship more than ever, and he feared one knocking a bit too hard and toppling him to his death on the deck below. He eyed the frenzied sea below.

'Of course,' Simrita said, looking at the young boy through long, thick eyelashes with a soft gaze. She kept her sentences short so he could understand, something she'd been good at doing since she, Eshnaa, and Rijul had joined the *Sea Guardian* crew. 'They will not want to die.'

Miyoshi gulped and nodded, hoping that would prove to be right. Simrita was quiet and kind and seemed shy, and he doubted she would be the sort to lie just to comfort him.

The sea gushed with the craze of serpents below, and Miyoshi couldn't help but watch the shadow in the distance. The ocean hadn't exploded again since that first time, but the shadow still followed, and he knew it could erupt again any moment . He rushed about on the deck, running himself breathless and ragged, hoping that his extra effort would help them get to safety faster. Each moment he could, he stopped to check the straits getting closer and monitor the shadow, hoping it wasn't catching up. Before he knew it, he'd forgotten the serpents, the fear of death and the hope for safety driving him to ignore what he found most interesting, and he soon grew used to the rocking and butting of the ship to the point he no longer noticed it. Not until, that is, he heard another cry come from above.

'They've gone,' Sakai bellowed down at them once again. 'The serpents stopped.'

The crew turned to watch Gora, who had once again come up from below deck, Miyoshi wondering if it was because he noticed the ship had stopped being nudged about like a stick in rapids. The captain scowled and ran to the stern of the deck and peered into the ocean. Sure enough, there were no serpents. He looked behind, and they weren't there either. 'The shadow, Quinni?'

The tall man searched behind, face still ashen, and then he nodded. 'Still there.'

'Right. Either way, continue into the straits full haste. If the serpents are gone, that means they found safety. We must be close. Find somewhere round here that'll do.' Gora gulped and tried to steady the thumping of his heart. 'Maybe the serpents went down. Maybe they went ahead. But we still follow their lead. Let's just hope it doesn't follow us through.'

18

The Straits

Miyoshi ran once again to the edge of the ship and leaned over to peer into the depths. He frowned and squinted his eyes but, sure enough, he couldn't see any signs of the sea serpents anymore. The boy sighed and slumped his chin onto his hands as he slouched against the gunwale, staring disappointedly, wishing he'd been able to look at them again. They'd not looked anything like what he'd heard in the stories. They weren't big and scary and fearsome. Why had he got so anxious about something like this when he heard the captain and Shingo speaking? How embarrassing! Miyoshi thought back to what Eshnaa had said about them being young ones; did sea serpents just start off like these had and get bigger and scarier the longer they lived? Maybe he'd still have a chance to see one.

Now, unable to look for baby sea serpents, the young boy watched as the wide ocean view shrank, land coming closer, and the ship slipped into the first of the straits. It didn't look too different from a huge river, so what was the difference? He mused, pouting at the shoreline far ahead. The boy stood up straight and peered down the bowside of the ship, sure enough seeing the twisting strait path as a giant, winding river, with the water of the ocean guiding them through the gap between two countries.

'So that side's a different country to the other one?' he muttered. Well, that was different to a river. The boy jumped as someone called his name from behind him and he spun around to see who it was. 'Tomioka?'

The man smiled and clapped a hand on Miyoshi's shoulder. Then Tomioka looked into the distance at the shores of the strait, and Miyoshi watched the wind ruffle through the man's wavy hair. Tomioka looked peaceful.

'You're in the day shift now?' Miyoshi asked, still looking up at the man and trying to read his face.

'Yep. It's nice to be able to see ahead again.' Tomioka grinned, eyes still on the land ahead.

So, that's why he looks so peaceful? Miyoshi wondered. 'What's it like on the night shift?'

Tomioka looked down at the boy now, soft, dark eyes meeting Miyoshi's gaze. The man looked away as he answered, staring once more at the view. 'Dark—so dark you can't see much ahead of your lamp—and quiet on still nights. It's peaceful, but too much of it, you feel you might go mad. The night crew don't talk as much as the day crew, and it's harder to keep a watch out for other ships. The night changes how you think, and you worry there's something there you can't see.' Tomioka shrugged and smiled kindly at Miyoshi. 'That's why we do it in small bursts. Usually no more than five days at a time. Day's better. Get to see, spend time with the crew.'

'Who's leading the night shift next, if you're here?'

Tomioka was one of the experienced leaders on Gora's ship, along with Yonemura and Shingo. Tomioka was the least strict with Miyoshi, or so he thought.

'It's Shingo next.' Tomioka stretched and looked about them at the others on the deck. 'Ain't got anything to do, Yūki?'

Miyoshi blushed and frowned at the man. When he, too, looked about them, he saw much more of a rush than even a few moments ago. Simrita dashed past and clambered up a shroud with greater agility than even some of the most capable of the Hizen crew, and Miyoshi couldn't help but watch as she fumbled with tightening one of the sails. Tomioka cleared his throat.

'Want something to do, Yūki?'

Looking at those around him busily helping the ship along, Miyoshi felt a loneliness from being the one to stand aside. Didn't he come here because he wanted to help them? He searched the deck for Gora, to see the face of the man he'd decided to follow. Even from back then on the slave ship back from Acrein, Gora had been the one who kept them all going. Him and Yoshiko.

Miyoshi reached for the daggers at his belt, fingers gliding over the leather of the pouch Yoshiko had given them to him in. The boy set his jaw and nodded. He wanted to get better on the ship and help out more. He didn't want to get in the way all the time.

Tomioka smiled again as the boy met his eyes. 'Here, go and talk to Kimura and see if there's anything you can help out with in the galley.'

Miyoshi nodded and darted off, turning to look back at Tomioka as he ran across the deck. Tomioka was staring into the distance again, this time out into the ocean behind them, a frown on his face and eyes squinting to look for something far off. The boy couldn't imagine what might give Tomioka that kind of face. Was it the baby sea serpents? Or the shadow?

* * *

Yells came from above by the time Miyoshi had finished helping Kimura in the galley. He liked Kimura; the man was always bright and cheerful, his young, good-looking face often smiling, though often because he liked to playfully tease his fellow crew, even the captain. The others said Kimura was easy, often playing with beautiful women, but Miyoshi had never seen that side of Kimura, only the friendly young man who took his passion for cooking seriously. Even with the limited rations they had to plan on the ship, Kimura always managed to make the best meals Miyoshi had ever had.

'I guess that's what you get when you're raised in an upper-class restaurant family,' Miyoshi muttered to himself as he thought, skipping up the steps to the main deck and looking at the commotion about him.

Here, people were calling across the deck, leaning over the gunwale to yell back at Yonemura at the helm. Nishimura was beside her, his long hair pulled back completely into a single ponytail. Miyoshi gawped. If Nishimura's hair was completely tied back, there must be a lot to focus on.

The boy darted across the deck to join the closest crew member, Eshnaa, at the gunwale. He caught her eye as both looked sidelong at one another, and she smiled. Eshnaa hollered to Yonemura, holding up her arm tall to catch the second mate's attention. Miyoshi kept watching the Ishillian woman, eyes pausing on the colourful layers of silks of her clothes and then on her curved blade, wondering whether he'd be able to pull enough Traders' together to talk with her. The three new people all spoke Ishillian and Traders', not Hizen, and if he wanted to speak with them, he'd have to learn the common trading language better.

His confidence left him as the woman looked once more over the edge at the rocks below, and the boy slumped against the gunwale again and resigned himself to just standing beside her, hoping Eshnaa would at least understand that he wanted to try. Instead, he watched as the crew worked together to warn Yonemura and Nishimura of the rocks below and looked around at the straits. It looked different to before. When he was last up here, the river was wide and clear with low land beside it that could almost be beaches as the continents ran either side of them, winding and meandering gently. Now, the cliffs were tall, rugged, treacherous, with the two most skilled of the steering team working together and taking quick shifts to recover from the effort of weaving through the maze of rocks. The boy heard a voice from the other side and realised even Rijul, the other Ishillian guard specialising just in fighting and not sailing, was calling out warnings of rocks.

Miyoshi looked next at the rocks, wondering if it was this place that stopped the sea serpents from swimming through. Would they just cut themselves on the rocks? But, if a ship could get through, he was certain creatures could get through too. The boy frowned and looked into the water again, almost wishing to see the sea serpents, and didn't notice the relief fall over the deck as the straits eventually opened out to wide ocean.

He turned when Eshnaa left his side and watched her stride across the deck towards Rijul, meeting Simrita on the way. The two women spoke to the young Ishillian guard and laughed, and Eshnaa ruffled the young man's hair playfully. Miyoshi couldn't understand what they were saying, but he could imagine it was praising the guard for helping and for starting to pick up sailing needs. The first time Miyoshi had seen Rijul interact with the women, Rijul had had a problem with women being on the ship, particularly Ishillian women. Miyoshi couldn't understand why, but after a stern talking from Gora, Rijul had slowly been coming around and talking more with Simrita and Eshnaa, even smiling more as he spoke with them. Miyoshi grinned and searched the deck for Gora—that man could win anyone over, surely?

But Gora wasn't anywhere to be found on the deck. The boy frowned. He hadn't seen the captain since they'd entered the straits, which was unusual; the captain preferred to spend more time up here with the crew than down below in the study.

Miyoshi searched the deck for someone he could speak with, eyes falling on Satou, the young man who had just come from night shift. Satou was a craftsman from Hié, specialising in carpentry, and was here to help with the running and the repairs of the ship. Because of this, he had a great knowledge of things going on aboard the ship and how it ran. Miyoshi ran up to him.

'Satou, did the captain move onto night shift when your team moved to day?'

The young man turned and thought for a moment, tucking a tool Miyoshi didn't recognise into his belt. 'I don't think so, Yūki. Why?'

'Ain't seen him for a while.'

Satou smiled. 'He's probably worried about that shadow and all those serpents. Might be downstairs reviewing routes or something. A ship's gotta be careful with unknown things in the water.'

Miyoshi thought about the little sea serpents again and wondered whether that could be true. But if they were heading into the straits, wasn't that enough to take care of the shadow? They were heading into a new ocean.

'It's okay, Yūki. There's lots to learn about sailing. You'll get there. The captain's rightfully worried, but he's being cautious. It'll work out.'

At that moment, Shingo called out for Satou across the deck, and the young man clasped Miyoshi's shoulder before padding away to help. Miyoshi looked once more towards the door that lead down below the deck, wondering about visiting the captain, but was called away by Shingo instead.

It wasn't until much later, when Miyoshi was mopping the deck and daydreaming of getting better at fighting and being able to stand alongside those he admired, like the captain, Ikeda, and Daiki, that Gora came up onto the deck and started to rotate to speak with the crew. Miyoshi watched Gora from the corner of his eyes, turning now and then to mop in a place where he could easily see the captain and whoever he was speaking with.

'His face looks tired,' Miyoshi grumbled to himself, sloshing the water a bit too much and casting his eyes around to see whether anyone had noticed. They hadn't, so he quickly pushed it about and continued. As he did, the boy wondered whether it was a bad sign that his captain looked tired. Had he been up for a long time worrying about something? Maybe if Gora was tired, it was because he had things covered. 'I shouldn't worry.'

'Worry about what?'

Miyoshi's skin crawled and he jumped about to face behind him, coming face-to-chest with the giant Quinni. When Miyoshi looked up at the man's face, he saw Quinni was quieter, more serious.

'Nothing,' Miyoshi quickly fumbled. Then, 'Quinni, are you here for the night rotation? I've not seen you for a couple of days.'

The man nodded, laying his eyes on the distance where the sun was setting and then behind, where it cast shadows behind them. 'Was the day normal?'

The boy thought for a moment, wondering what to report. Nothing strange had happened. 'All clear. No new sea serpents or anything.'

'No shadows?'

The boy shook his head and peered up at the giant man, whose shoulder seemed to relax at Miyoshi's response.

'But huge, ragged cliffs. This part of the strait was very tricky. Will Yonemura be okay on her own at night?'

Quinni smiled. 'We won't be sailing tonight. We'll keep her anchored and steady and continue in the light. No point tearing the ship apart. Just gotta make sure she's safe.'

As Quinni spoke, Jelani padded over to them, moving fluidly from his years of experience aboard ships. The two men nodded to one another, and Jelani clapped the young giant on his shoulder with a Qeclan greeting and an ear-splitting grin. Miyoshi wondered what they were saying. Then Jelani turned to him and grasped his shoulder too, greeting him with the same grin.

'Yūki, boy. How's it going? Floor spotless?' Jelani nodded down to the mop. The boy's ears felt like they'd burn, and Jelani grinned. 'All good, boy. As long as you get it done. Don't want you getting punished for just chatting to us.'

The boy nodded, and the two men left to check out the position. They leaned on the gunwale, and Quinni pointed far into the distance, Jelani nodding and clapping the younger man on the back. Sighing, the boy hurried to finish mopping before his evening meal. When he next looked up, Gora was standing beside the two Qeclan men, speaking in hushed tones with them.

'We'll be entering the main ocean soon. Do you think it's safe?' Miyoshi just picked up what Quinni asked.

There was a mumble from Gora, and an affirmative noise. 'It'll be fine. That's long behind us. This is a new ocean.'

The three men continued, and Miyoshi picked up the bucket and ran to throw the water overboard. Then he rushed to put it all away to go to eat in the galley. He felt better for hearing the captain say it would be fine.

If Gora think's it's fine, then it's fine.

∗ ∗ ∗

The next day, when the light came up and the day crew relieved the night crew, *Sea Guardian* slipped past the remaining high cliffs and crags of rock teeth. Miyoshi, eager to see what the ocean looked like where the strait merged, rushed to finish his chores and dashed to lean over the wooden gunwale as the ship bobbed out of the rocky mouth and past the two countries. He peered into the water, squinting to see the difference in water colour—there wasn't any.

'What's up, lad?'

Miyoshi jumped at the sound of the familiar voice already so close and turned his face to see Gora leaning beside him. He hadn't heard his captain walk up to him.

'Looking for sea serpents again?' Gora continued, ruffling the lad's hair gently with his rough, giant hand.

Miyoshi stared up at Gora's face, hoping to see some sign of what was bothering the captain, or to see the captain was happier. But the red-haired man still looked closed off and serious. The boy turned back to the sea. 'I wondered if the water looked different where the strait met the ocean. Sometimes when a river meets the ocean, the colour is different.'

Gora hummed and leaned over too. 'That's because it's different types of water meeting, usually pure, mountain fresh water with salty. The water runs from the mountains clear and cool. But the straits, it's just a pathway of ocean water, so it's the same.' The man tilted his head to the side and thought again a moment. 'I guess sometimes oceans could have different waters, but I think that would have merged further into the straits.'

Miyoshi nodded and then looked towards the place the ocean opened back out into forever. Boots thudded, and Shingo's voice came from behind.

'We've cleared the straits, captain. They're just weaving through the last of the crags, and then we'll be out into open ocean again.'

Miyoshi heard Gora confirm this; then the three stood in silence. The boy cast his eyes over all the ocean he could see from here and knew more would open out as they travelled. They'd be hunting for someone here, wouldn't they? That was why they'd come. But how could they hunt for one ship in such a giant ocean? It would take forever.

As if voicing Miyoshi's thoughts, Shingo sighed. 'How're we going to find that ship in such a place, captain?'

Shingo stepped forward and joined the two in leaning against the railing, Miyoshi turning to see the older sailor's face creased with concern. Then the boy looked to his other side at the youthful face of his captain, whose brow was just as creased as he stared into the distance and thought, blue eyes darker than ever, as if a shadow had settled within them.

'We don't need to hunt the whole ocean,' Gora said, voice low and hesitant. 'Just part of it.' He looked to his right at the other two, and Miyoshi's eyes widened at just how serious Gora's face looked. 'In this ocean is an island where pirates gather to trade the things they've acquired. All manner of goods found and stolen, including people. There are slave auctions there'—Gora looked down at Miyoshi now—'just like the one we saw in Acrein when we arrived after the long ship journey. They sell and buy the people they use on their ships.' The captain paused, pain flashing through his ocean-blue eyes. He ran a hand through his hair and looked back over the ocean. 'I was sold there at one point, when I was in my teens. Foy, the man we're hunting for, sold me to Frewin there.'

Miyoshi's blood boiled and he clenched his fists, memories of the slave auctions in Acrein flooding his mind and ringing in his ears. Black spots pricked across his eyes, hurting his head, and he blinked to stop them, bringing his jaw together tightly to focus. He looked into the blue sea and tried to focus there—this was where he was now.

A warm hand settled on his head and his attention was brought back to this ship and this time. Gora smiled down at him sadly. 'It's okay now, lad.'

The warm hand didn't move for some time, but Miyoshi didn't mind. It felt comforting and grounding, and he focused on the warmth and not on the cold memories of the time he was separated from his mother. This was why he'd come here, after all. To try to fight back for what had happened. To get stronger. To protect his home.

Shingo rested his elbows against the railing and his face in his hands for a moment, a sign Miyoshi's recognised as thinking. When Shingo's face came back up, his dark eyes showed his concern. 'And we're heading for that island, captain?'

Gora nodded. 'Foy returns there fairly regularly, so we have a greater chance meeting him there. If we don't meet him there, we can ask around about his whereabouts.'

Shingo huffed. 'You know how dangerous it will be. And besides that, will you be okay? Will some of the crew? You know what we went through. There's barely anyone here who wasn't affected by that. Only a few, and even they'll be affected by the feelings and suffering of their comrades. Besides all that, it'll be dangerous. It's not just one pirate ship. There'll be hordes of them.'

'We survived Shon Wa,' Gora pointed out. 'We'll try to go about it a similar way.' Before Shingo could open his mouth to protest, Gora continued. 'What other option do we have?' He cast his hand further from Miyoshi around in a sweeping circle towards the ocean. 'Search the whole ocean for a man who's more slippery than an eel? I don't want to go there, either. Hell, I'd do anything to turn around now and be nowhere near that place or that man, but it'll help us unlock some of the mysteries and shit that's starting to reek around here. We promised the daimyō we'd make the seas safer—it means taking out the dirtiest of sea slugs in the dirtiest of places.'

At the mention of the daimyō, the three fell silent again, thinking of the moment she'd seen them off on their mission. They'd return home to a safe place with a strong leader who could protect them, so they had to do their bit to protect others out here, too.

Miyoshi thought of their new name, the *Sea Guardian*.

'Aye, sir,' Shingo sighed, rubbing his face in his hands. 'I know you're right. Just … this one will take a toll, I think.'

The warm hand left Miyoshi's head and he looked up as the captain rested both hands on the railing and looked out into the distance, eyes distant and face dark. The man nodded but said nothing more, and Shingo bowed his head and left, leaving Miyoshi standing beside his captain alone.

* * *

The next few days as they sailed towards the pirate trade isles, Gora grew quiet and sullen. Shingo led the crew a little more with his captain's direction, but even he was quieter than usual and felt stricter with the crew. When the lad bounded below to the galley for their evening meal, the captain never came to join them. The boy slumped into a space on the bench beside Tomioka, who greeted him with a playful nudge, and stared at the food Kimura dished up for him. Not even Kimura's easy grin got a response from the boy, and Miyoshi sighed and pushed the food around on his plate unconsciously. *Why isn't the captain coming? Shouldn't he eat? I thought he was fine again.* A noise around him made him jump and an arm rested over his shoulder—Tomioka's. When the boy looked up, the three others in the room, Kimura, Tomioka, and Shingo, were all watching him, concern in their dark eyes.

'What's up, lad?' Tomioka's arm was warm.

'You've been staring at that for a little while. Not hungry?' Kimura sat at the bench with them and rested his cheek in his hand, watching Miyoshi across the table. The almost permanent easy and carefree smile had left his face. 'You need to make sure you eat for your health. It's hard work on a ship.'

Shingo agreed, and the three of them waited for Miyoshi to answer. But Miyoshi felt as if he couldn't give them an answer. Was it wrong to worry about the captain?

Before Miyoshi could decide whether to tell them, footsteps came closer in the passageways, towards the galley. Yonemura and Moori entered, finding four serious faces around the table. Miyoshi wondered if he'd been here for so long already that it was almost time for the night rotation people to come for their first meal.

Kimura rose and gestured for the two women to sit, and he returned to the pots he had on the stove to serve them their meal. As the two sat at the table, Yonemura instantly hit on the mood.

'What's up with Miyoshi?' She turned to Shingo and Tomioka, her soft face and full lips pinched with concern. She met Miyoshi's gaze, and he immediately focused on his bowl, ignoring her eyes.

'Worried 'bout the captain,' Moori said between mouthfuls of food, voice raising slightly as if she were half guessing. Miyoshi looked up at her, wondering how she knew. The young girl stared back, her black eyes piercing his. He tried to hold her gaze defiantly, but the others all mumbled around them, drawing his attention back.

Shingo sighed and rubbed his cheek. 'Aye, aren't we all? But worrying and not eating our food ain't gunna help him.' He bowed his head slightly and reached a rough hand across the table to clasp Miyoshi's shoulder comfortingly. 'Lad, eat. The only way we can help the captain is if we have enough energy to keep the ship goin'. He'll want you to grow big and strong and look after yerself.'

Kimura, leaning back against one of the cabinets with his arms crossed across his chest, nodded in agreement. 'Besides, if you don't eat the food I give you ...' The young man rushed forward and ruffled Miyoshi's hair with both hands, laughing as Miyoshi cried out for him to stop. 'You should know by now a chef is protective over their food! It's a matter of honour.'

Miyoshi glared up at him and reached grumpily for his spoon. 'I'm just worried is all. He seems unhappy.'

'Aye, of course he will be. He's working through his demons. You know we're heading to the place he was sold as a child. Must be hard. That's why we gotta eat well and work hard to support him and keep the ship going. The quicker we can be in and out of that place, the quicker we'll have our happy captain back. He's handling it in his own way. Don't let it worry you.'

Miyoshi managed a mouthful, his stomach still not feeling up to eating. But he knew they were right. If he wanted to be helpful to his captain, he had to do his best.

'Okay,' he muttered, going for a second mouthful. He glanced up to see the others smiling—well, all but Moori, who was too involved in her own food, her small face closed and unreadable.

'Just in case, Yonemura, can you chat with the captain and just make sure he's alright? See if there's anything we can do t' make it easier for him? You're getting along well with him.'

Miyoshi caught a sly glance from the weathered face of the first mate and the sharp look shot back from the second mate. Beside them, Kimura snorted, holding back a laugh, and turned to hide his face when Yonemura glared at him too.

'Aye, I can do that,' she said, reaching for her own bowl, 'if that'll stop you getting more grey hairs.'

This time, Kimura did let out a light laugh, and even Moori smirked into her bowl. Miyoshi felt a small smile creep onto his face.

Maybe I was worrying too much, he thought, allowing himself to be taken up by the mood of the others. When he looked back up at Shingo, the older man smiled and nodded at him before finishing the conversation with one final piece of wisdom.

'He'll be fine. He just needs reflection time.'

Later that day, Miyoshi saw Yonemura talking to Gora, both leaning against the bow gunwale, Gora looking up at the figurehead and Yonemura looking firmly at the captain. The captain turned his head and nodded to Yonemura, and Miyoshi jumped when someone snuck up behind him. He whirled on the spot to see who it was. Quinni and Moori were standing beside him, both grinning.

'They're standing pretty close, don't you think?' Quinni said, voice low and melodic as always.

Moori chuckled. 'Could be in love,' she said in a sing-song voice, grinning up at Quinni, who raised a brow thoughtfully, wondering.

The quiet giant rested a large hand on Miyoshi's head. 'I'm sure the captain will be feeling better soon, don't you think?'

And he was right. Over the next few days, Miyoshi watched as Gora seemed to be chirpier, lighter, and more active again around the ship. While he wasn't sure what kind of telling off Yonemura had given the captain, Miyoshi was glad to know his captain was doing better. He was even teasing the boy again, and Miyoshi felt more comfortable.

Across the endless sea, an island appeared in the distance, surrounded by a web of sharp rocks, wooden structures and piers, old harbours, creaking shipwrecks, and docked ships. Miyoshi tried to make himself useful, running around the deck to help as Gora hollered over the sound of the waves crashing against the sharp rocks, guiding them through the labyrinth of stone and wreckage. After the long and tiresome mission, Miyoshi slumped against one of the masts while they finally docked, and, with no control over his heavy eyelids, fell into a deep sleep where he heard not even the drone of voices about him as people discussed who would go to shore with the captain.

He woke with a start when he heard boots thudding nearby and cries as the crew prepared for a team to leave the ship and head for the island, and he saw that someone had draped a thick hemp blanket over him. He blinked, rubbed his weary eyes, and then leapt up to look for Gora, hoping to hear the captain would let him come too.

'Absolutely not,' was Gora's stern reply before the boy even opened his mouth, his blue eyes icing over and his stubbled face frowning.

Miyoshi pouted, craning his neck to look up. 'But I really want to go! I want to see the pirate island.' He watched enviously as Moori strapped gun after gun to herself, hiding more in pockets of a giant overcoat before shoving on a hat to hide her face.

Gora's mouth turned down even more, if that was even possible, and his thick eyebrows furrowed until creases dug deeper into Gora's lightly freckled face. 'No chance. Not there. I'll not risk losing you. You know what happens there.'

'I'll be fine! I'll follow you. I won't get lost. I'll stick to one of them!' He pointed now to Kimura, who was swinging a bag over his shoulder, telling Ikeda something the lad couldn't hear as the young samurai passed him a katana and helped the young chef strap it around his belt.

Gora huffed and rubbed the back of his head, staring at Miyoshi. Miyoshi stood as straight as he could, meeting Gora's gaze, hoping his face looked hopeful and pleading enough. Gora's eyes softened and he sighed.

'Look, lad. You don't know what they're like. I can't risk you getting hurt. I promised Yoshiko and your mother. You stay here and help look after the ship.'

'But—'

Gora's face darkened again. 'No buts. I'm the captain, and what I say on this ship goes. I like to give you all the freedom to feel comfortable and listened to aboard this ship, but the rules are that you listen in dangerous times, and these are dangerous times.' Gora grabbed Miyoshi's shoulder and guided him with a rough grip to Tomioka, who was standing nearby, helping Kimura carry something to the boat they'd row to shore. 'Tomioka,' Gora called, his voice gruff. Miyoshi's heart dropped. 'Look after the lad. Make sure he's not outta your sight.' Then Gora turned to Miyoshi again, this time kneeling down onto one knee, grabbing both the boy's shoulders and looking up at him square on with a stern face. 'Lad, you go nowhere, not even on this ship, without someone else. Not while we're here. If they see a kid, they'll take 'em. I can't have that happen to you. You don't know what they do. Stay with Tomioka, and if he can't look after you, go straight to someone else. Make sure you do.' Then he stood and regarded the boy again, sighing. 'I mean it. Don't go anywhere alone. I can't have them get you.'

Gora nodded to Tomioka, who bowed his head in acknowledgement and looked at the young boy too. Miyoshi watched as Gora turned and strode away towards the port side of the ship, climbing over the gunwale and taking one last stern look at the boy before climbing down, out of sight.

Miyoshi sighed. He didn't need to be told who *they* were. He knew, but he'd hoped the captain would have been able to protect him. Gora was a strong fighter; he just knew it. To him, there was no-one better than Gora. And with him, Ikeda, Daiki, Jelani, Quinni, Eshnaa, and Simrita were all highly skilled fighters, with Rijul coming close. If they couldn't look after him, just one boy, then what kind of people were these pirates?

He shuffled across the deck and leaned on the gunwale to watch as the first round of crew landed ashore, dragged the boat up onto the sand, and hid it in some nearby bushes. He heard Tomioka stop beside him, and the man leant his arms on the railing too, smiling, eyes scanning the pirate island. Miyoshi followed his gaze, away from his disappearing companions, and finally took the time to look at the island and see what kind of place he would be missing out on. Trees with large, arching frond leaves dotted between huge boulders, with steep cliffs and a thick forest on either side of the small beach they pulled up in. To the left, where the boulders and tall fronded trees hid a rocky path, Miyoshi thought he could see something in the distance.

He cried out. 'Look, there's smoke! That must be the town!'

Tomioka chuckled beside him and ruffled the lad's hair, tugging the braid playfully. 'Aye, lad. That's the pirate slave markets. Let's hope the captain and the others are safe.'

19

Slavery Island Markets

'This fuckin' place again, huh?' Gora scowled as he stomped into the square. 'Even shittier than I remember.'

Beside him, Jelani sniffed and scrunched up his nose, swearing about the stench. Daiki looked just as nauseated.

'It's worse than Shon Wa,' the old samurai grunted. 'Didn't think that was possible.'

'Can't imagine there being any fun or exotic delicacies here,' Kimura said, brushing his wavy black hair from his face as he looked around at shoddy wooden buildings and gatherings of flies on both people and food.

'Meals or women?' Moori said from under a large hat, digging an elbow into Kimura's waist. Gora couldn't tell whether she was playing or chastising. Both, he decided.

Kimura cried out and pinched Moori's cheek. 'What's wrong with both?' He grinned and then caught Gora's eye.

'You'll not want any of either, here, lad.' Gora shrugged, turning to face blankly ahead, not wanting to think about it. 'Unless yer don't mind walking bow-buckled with numb lower parts the rest o' yer life.'

'From which?' Kimura smirked.

'Both,' Jelani and Gora said in unison, frowning at one another, before Jelani gave a wicked grin that lit his whole face, and Gora couldn't help but laugh too.

'Might as well head straight back to the ship now, eh, pretty boy?' Moori chuckled and pulled her hat lower again, shrugging her large overcoat on further to hide herself more. 'Nothin' for you here.'

'Eh, and if ye both keep flirting like tha' in a place like this, it's where yer'll both end up. Don't wanna give these sea slugs the idea yer both available for shit like that.' Gora glanced at the two shocked young ones. There was a reason he wanted to keep the young and pretty ones hidden on the ship. He'd had a hard enough time persuading Ikeda to stay again. But these two noble kids … At least Moori was keeping her face hidden.

Gora sighed and strode forward, leading the group in. 'We gotta book board if we're gunna try to fit in,' he said, squinting about him at the options. A door hung loose in its frame in one, and the other lacked any kind of window coverings. How did they expect people to sleep with the threat of peekers or people being able to sneak in? He glanced out of the corner of his eye at Moori strutting along the track with her hands shoved in her pockets, peering out under her hat. He frowned again. 'Hands out, lass. Yer never know when yer need to be ready.'

'Gun's in here,' she muttered, gesturing to the deep pockets.

Gotta hand it to her. Gora nodded his approval.

'Well, the crew will take a rotation in the inns, make us seem legit. But we gotta be careful. No goin' anywhere solo. Not even to shit. Not here. Yer'll end up raped, dead, sold, or on a ship somewhere close to being any of the previous three.' Gora eyed up an inn on the edge of the square, looking at least a little bit less shady than the others. 'We'll head there, first.'

'Is it true you were here as a kid, cap?' Kimura asked, taking the sights in surprisingly good stride.

Gora's body twigged with a spike of adrenaline, and he looked hesitantly at the other four, Daiki hanging back silently to scan the area and keep an eye out from behind. In situations like this, the old samurai wouldn't join in conversation. He was too into his job: protecting.

An instant cold sweat coated Gora's skin, a feeling akin to one he'd not felt for many a time, now. Was it this place?

'Aye,' he replied, voice gruff. He didn't want to say any more, but he felt the pounding of his heart would be loud enough that all four of them would know. Here, he was scared. He swallowed and tried to find extra words for the pairs of eyes waiting for his response. 'I was sold here.' He'd only told Shingo and Yonemura this so far. As far as everyone else knew, it was just a place they knew pirates came.

'That's why we're here?' Jelani said, voice low and eyes preceptive as always.

Gora nodded. 'The old devil we're after comes here for the markets. If anyone knows where he is, it's visiting sea slime, here. Never know, devil himself may show up if there's a big meet.' He gulped.

Kimura and Moori looked at one another, lips tight.

So, it just hit the young'uns what we're dealin' with? Gora sighed. 'A'ight. Let's head in.'

The door creaked like a strangled banshee as Gora pushed it open, and the dark inside swallowed them up until their eyes adjusted to the weak light of a measly fireplace in the lifeless tavern.

'Um,' Kimura began, clearing his throat to call out and peering around the empty room. Gora met his gaze. 'No-one's here? This isn't what I expected of a pirate tavern.'

Gora grinned ear-to-ear. ''Tis time for sleepin' off the drink. Some will be down for breakfast soon.'

'But it's already mid-morning,' Moori muttered, strolling further into the room.

'Aye, it is.' Gora smirked. 'But what time d'ya think they went to bed?'

The two youngsters shrugged, and Gora clomped across the scuffed wooden floor to a bar that could be the exact replica of the one he visited in Shon Wa: old and sticky with years of grime and drink. Mouth curling up at the edges, he crossed his arms over his chest and peered around the corner to identify a noise coming from a room out back—the kitchen. Daiki stopped next to him, mirroring Gora's stance with his arms crossed and glaring a moment at the bar before Gora could feel Daiki's eyes boring into the side of his face.

'This really a place you want to stay?' Daiki started uneasily, turning to look behind them.

Gora followed his gaze and saw Kimura and Moori strolling about parts of the room and nosing about, and Jelani standing in the middle and watching over the four of them silently.

'Gotta stay somewhere. Be weird if we all stayed on the ship and people realised where our ship was and questioned why none of us were on land. At least this way, we can say we're takin' shifts and tryin' to seem *natural*. Safer.'

Daiki's face showed justifiable worry, and Gora knew the whole crew felt the same. Heck, he did too. But when you've got pirates to chase, you gotta go where the pirates go.

Finally, a scuffling in the back room came closer, and a small, ashen-faced girl with loose, greying clothes appeared behind the bar. Gora nodded at the young girl, who was only in her teens, and asked about available rooms. She looked between him and the four others nervously and stammered a response that there were only two available.

'S'fine, we'll take 'em,' Gora replied in Traders'. 'For until the markets are over.'

Gora paid for the two rooms in advance, and the girl passed them two keys, muttering to them about where the rooms were. Moori had padded over to join Gora and was leaning in carefully to listen to the quiet voice speaking in Traders'.

'I barely understood her,' Moori moaned as they strolled through the inn to find the two rooms, fortunately next to each other but on the top floor of the inn where it would be harder to escape if there were problems.

'You'll get there.' Gora pushed open the doors to reveal small rooms with single beds. He sighed. 'We'll have to ask for extra blankets and get the crew to share rooms. Put up a sleep rotation to be sure someone's always on watch. We'll have five or six on land at a time. No-one's goin' anywhere alone in this place.'

'So, we'll have to sleep with boys?' Moori's nose wrinkled as she peered into the rooms.

'If you think I'd let you ladies sleep in your own room in such a place, you have another thing comin'. Yer'll be raided in no time. Even havin' yer here is a risk. Nah, you sleep with our lads. At least yer know they're the safe ones.'

Kimura smirked. 'You can rely on us to look after you!'

Moori turned and glared at him. 'In your case, isn't it that you rely on *us*? A kitten would beat you in a fight. Go back to your kitchen.'

Kimura's smirk held, and he threw out his arms in an exaggerated shrug. 'Only because the kitten would be so cute I'd let it win.'

'Alrigh', you two. You get the gist,' Gora sighed, knowing this could go on forever. He looked over at Daiki, who was standing in the corridor beside them, looking at the two young ones with amusement. He met Gora's eyes and bowed his head.

'I'll stay with the women,' Daiki said, his low, calm voice a reassurance to Gora's anxiety.

His dark eyes were steady, and Gora nodded.

'Thank you, my friend.' Gora clapped his hand on Daiki's shoulder. 'You have no idea what kind of place this is. I'd feel reassured they had someone with them while we were here, skilled as they are or not.'

* * *

The crew rotated regularly, holding the same rooms for the duration of their stay, Miyoshi being the only one not allowed to set a foot on the island. Regularly, Gora heard how the young lad was getting frustrated, flopping and grumbling around the *Sea Guardian*, but with the pirate slave isles being as they were, he refused to have it any other way. In mere days, Quinni had been viciously attacked by a fellow in a bar with small man syndrome who angered at Quinni for standing beside him as he ordered a drink, and Eshnaa had slashed another into a snivelling, submissive pile at her feet for trying to push her up against a rickety old wall. Kimura had moaned constantly about the food, suffering food poisoning along with several of the crew, and they'd narrowly escaped several mass brawls.

Exhausted, the crew trudged the island's paths defeated, their battered bodies and soiled clothes helping them fit in without even trying.

With the ship hidden on one of the furthest beaches on the island, Gora had little worry about it being found. But the distance to get there tired him and his crew, and little news was heard of Foy and the *Devil's Corsair*, no matter how often they eavesdropped or bribed drunkards for information.

Gora spent most of his days in a brooding silence, his mood fouled.

'What do we do now, captain?' Kimura asked as he slumped on the sticky wooden floorboards of one of their shared rooms, looking as foul as Gora had no doubt he felt. The young chef, once a thing of beauty, was pale, his shoulder-length hair limp and his mouth a perpetual frown. Once, it had smirked near-constantly and had frustrated Gora, but the man's warmth and energy had been a saviour for the crew in tough times. Now, his energy was fading. Gora wondered how he could reignite it—Kimura was one of the few who brought light to the crew—but knew on this island, at least, it was near impossible.

Moori spat out the window before slamming the shutters, and she curled her lips in disgust and smacked them. 'I want food and water that doesn't leave my mouth tasting like I've eaten something that died on the street seven years ago.'

'Seven? That's specific.' Jelani had joined them on this rotation, and he, too, lay on his back on the floor, feet up on Kimura's knees, arms covering his face. 'Make it eight.'

Gora rubbed his face and stared at them from where he slumped on the old bed, arms resting on his knees. He sighed.

'No news. How can there be no news on *that* man?'

The man was famous. The leader. He did what he wanted and acted like the king of the place. Someone *had* to know.

The other three looked up at him, eyes mournful.

'Fuck this,' he swore, and they all repeated it like a closing prayer.

He squinted at the light that stole through the gaps in the shutters. The ocean was beyond, and somewhere on that ocean was the devil himself. The man who knew everything about the reason Gora and countless other children had been kidnapped. Gora had to find him. For the sake of the dead children, their families, his promise to Yoshiko, for Eshnaa and Simrita's friend, and for himself.

'We stay one week more. In eight days, the next big slave markets are on. That's what we came here for in the first place. If we can't find anything else out before then, that'll be the day that something happens.'

They stared at him as if he'd shot them.

'It *has* to.'

20

Reminiscing With Foy

The day of the main slave markets was nearly upon them, and Gora felt like he'd tear his hair out from the stress. He and his crew had been stuck on this spirits-forsaken pirate island for far too long, and that old sea slug still hadn't shown up. Foy turned up for almost every slave market, from what he last recalled, but as it had been quite some years since Gora had sailed with the man and known him, he was beginning to worry that things might have changed.

'How old will that old demon be now?' Gora muttered to himself as he sat on the side of his bed in one of the shared rooms at the inn, pulling on his boot. *Probably fairly old.* But back when Gora knew him, it seemed the man would go on forever. If anyone found the secret to eternal life, Gora had decided long ago that it would probably be that piece of shit. *It's always the bad ones.*

Gora looked about at the other two crew members sharing the room with him and sighed. Sakai and Nishimura slept soundly, and Gora was amazed they slept here at all. It was their second rotation here, and he'd been trying to make sure to give people short rotations so they didn't feel worried about leaving the ship. The first time Nishimura had come here, he'd struggled to sleep and had just tried to meditate the whole night, and Gora had been worried about bringing him here again. Next door, Rijul was watching over Simrita and Eshnaa. Not that they needed watching over, he knew. But he didn't trust women in a room alone in a pirate inn, and Rijul had started to build a strong relationship with those two, almost like a younger brother, and he'd defend their honour and the two women from any harm well enough that Gora trusted him to be the one to ensure their room was safe.

Gora glared ahead of him in the room. He really hated being here.

In an ideal world, Foy would have shown by now. But of course, Gora knew it wasn't an ideal world, and things like that never worked out how you wanted them to. He turned once more to check on the two other sleeping men, and knowing he couldn't leave the room if they were both fully out of it, feeling a little guilty, Gora shuffled over and prodded Nishimura.

'Nishimura, I'm headin' out. Keep an eye out and an ear open.'

The man rolled over and pulled his long hair from his face. Even with the remnants of sleep in his eyes, his gaze had a strange, mysterious, knowing look to it. Nishimura nodded, and that was all Gora needed to turn and walk from the room. In the corridor, he took a moment to look at the door to the room the other three were in and then listened to the sounds of the inn. It seemed quiet. In the early mornings in places like this, it often was. It was the late nights you mostly needed to watch out for. But, in the early mornings, many sailors and pirates were making full use of their opportunity to come away from the ships and their duties, taking the time to relax, drink, and sleep in.

That was why Gora liked the early morning hours. He always had. As he padded gently down the steps of the inn, hoping not to stir anyone and cause trouble, he reflected on how the morning hours had been bliss for him from the start—even when he was first taken on the ship. The time when the night crew was getting itchy to finish their shift, eat, and go to sleep, and the morning shift hadn't yet woken up. It was the time he'd been least bothered by others on the ships and could just spend his time as he wished on the deck until the noisy ones had come.

He pulled open the door to the inn, knowing there'd be no point in even trying to get breakfast at this hour, and strode out into the street. The sun was just lifting from the horizon, lighting a spirits-forsaken town, brick and wood buildings with broken doors and empty windows. Smashed glass littered the streets, and dug-out drainage ditches clogged at the sides of a worn mud-and-stone track. Gora wrinkled his nose, wishing he'd got used to the smell by now.

With his mind worrying as it was, Gora needed a walk, even if it was down such a dodgy track. He wished there was a forest nearby like the one in Hié, where he could stroll through and feel at peace, and he wished Yoshiko were there for him to speak with. Somehow, she'd likely know what to say, or at least be there to listen to his worries. There was no-one else he could share these thoughts with. No-one else to tell his fears about losing face in front of the crew if things weren't to go as he planned here. As close as he'd become to those on his ship, and as much as he cared about them, there were just things in his mind he couldn't share with his crew. It wouldn't be right. And this, he was finding, was the dichotomy of leadership. You had to be true to yourself and honest, but there were still things you couldn't tell those you lead.

With no forest to walk to, Gora strode towards the harbour, much like he did every day. He felt like a kid. He knew just going to the harbour to watch the ships come in wouldn't bring Foy in. Yet, every day, he went anyway, if but to quieten his head and convince himself he did something that day that made a difference.

What if he never comes? What if he doesn't come to them all anymore? What do I do then?

These same thoughts went through his head every day, too. And he'd stare out to sea, wishing to see the old sea demon's sails as the ship pulled in but wondering what he'd do if he never came.

There were only a few pirate markets a year. If Foy didn't come to this one, it would be a few months before the next one. What would Gora tell the crew then, and what would they do until then? It would be hopeless to leave here and search for Foy. They couldn't expect to run into him randomly on the open blue, and he didn't have any other news on him other than that he'd likely be here, unlike with Frewin. They'd got lucky with Frewin, he knew that. With Frewin's new injuries, he'd have been taking things easy for a while. But with Foy, knowing that man could almost go on forever, there'd be no way Gora could find him any other way than this. This was the only place Foy would come to trade with other pirates, and very rarely did he pull into other pirate ports. With the world opening up, there were fewer places for pirates to gather and to hide in. Gora knew this would be one of their last hopes.

He sighed and watched the tide. He usually loved to hear its reassuring, hushed whispering, but this morning it felt too quiet, too heavy. Gora's eyes slid over the other ships in the port, and he wondered how his crew were doing and whether they'd had any run-ins with pirates finding them. They weren't particularly hidden, and he didn't expect to not be found. What they'd tell whoever found them, he had no idea. Probably something about needing urgent stopping and not even being able to make it the last few corners to reach the harbour, so now they were fixing it. He'd leave that for Shingo and the other leaders to decide between themselves. His worry was here, and that old sea dog.

Giving up for the morning, and thinking himself foolish for once again coming to watch the sea as if he was a young boy waiting for his parent to return, Gora stomped back up towards the pirate town and to the inn, where finally the kitchen was preparing breakfast. A few other creepy sods were awake now and sitting in the eating area, glaring into their cups from the hangover or yawning. Gora ordered a simple meal, one he'd ordered here daily in the hopes it would be the least dodgy and least likely to make him sick, and sat himself at the edge of the room where he could see everything from, waiting for the other five of his crew to wake so they could get going with their days.

Later that day, once they were awake, fed, and wandering about the island, looking out for signs and listening in on talks to see what they could learn and spying on the market area for the few markets that had already opening and the stolen goods being traded there, they heard news that finally made Gora's ears prick up.

'Aye, hear old Foy's finally come in. Gets later every year. As if we'd wait for him.'

Gora caught Nishimura's gaze, the young man staring right through him as always, and Eshnaa's gaze wasn't much easier to bear; both of them always seemingly knew what might be on your mind.

'Aye, that's him,' Gora muttered to them, answering their gazes.

Finally. Gora never thought he'd feel happy to hear Foy was arriving, but he knew it was the thing that would help his mission come along. And now the man himself was here, he didn't plan on staying on the island much longer.

'No need to linger. We wanted Foy, and that's all we'll need to wait for. No need to risk stayin' any longer, and no need to see the markets. I'll speak with him and do what we need to, and then we'll go. You all hang about here and see if you can find out any last bits of information about the markets—anything that will tell us about stealing children or anything else dodgy you think might be good to know—and then we'll go. Questions?'

Simrita's face flushed with anxiety. She looked at Eshnaa, and then Simrita turned back to him and nodded, setting her face into a frown. Sakai was the only one to speak, but Gora knew the others would be wary now with Foy coming in and eager to leave.

'Captain, how much longer do you expect to be here? Can we anticipate when we can return to the ship?'

'Not sure, sorry. I have no idea when I'll be able to wrangle a chat with him. I'll do my best. Until then, continue as normal, but at least we know we'll be able to slip away soon.'

The man nodded, and Gora turned away.

Fuck, Gora thought, clenching and unclenching his hands as he stomped up the track towards the part of the pirate town where all the inns were. He could feel his heart squeezing tight as if it'd burst in his chest, and his body suddenly felt cold, even under the sun. Gora looked around him as he walked, seeing the colours fade away, feeling his head numb and his heart drop, knowing all this was just like last time. He hadn't changed. Foy would be coming up to the island on the first rotation from the ship, he knew that. And though he needed to see him for his mission, he wished he could run and hide. He wished he could be the one protected on the ship like Miyoshi, knowing he had his crew to keep him safe and away from places like this.

Back then, no-one had protected him. Now, no-one could.

Gora sighed. Foy would be striding up that track from the harbour any moment, and he'd have to be ready. For the sake of his crew and their mission. He squeezed his eyes shut, took a deep breath, and licked his lips, wishing he could grab a drink for a bit of liquid courage. But he knew he couldn't; he had to do this right.

He's coming.

The loud guffaws of the first group of pirates coming up from their ship into the town to take rooms in the inns echoed up the tracks, and Gora darted behind a corner to let them pass unseen. He spied around the edge, seeing Foy taking his time at the back, flanked by a pair of slouching, overgrown men trying to settle as guards. And just like Gora had thought, Foy looked like he'd go on forever. His sharp grey eyes shone bright in his ocean-tanned face, and his white hair and beard was more platinum and sophisticated than an aged grey. He had more youth and vigour than the two cronies surrounding him, and that same old, annoying smirk resting on his face. Gora narrowed his eyes and watched them pass, almost letting the dread that flushed through his blood like heavy mud stop him from going out there, letting him stay hidden. He took another deep breath.

'Oy.'

Gora stepped out in front of the old pirate, who turned back and eyed the younger man curiously. He spoke in Gaean. This man was from his own country, and it almost hurt to use the language that had become a nostalgic memory of home with this beast. 'Old man. We need t' talk.'

'I know that face, and those eyes—still filled with hate, I see. Ye got ol', boy.'

As if he can talk; hair's as white as sea scum.

'Don't call me "boy",' Gora growled. 'Now, get rid of yer monkeys. I said we need to talk.'

Foy nodded at the two pirates flanking him, telling them to bugger off and have a good meal and a woman 'while I catch up with our little pup'.

The older pirate let out a sly smile, and Gora knew he was expecting a reaction. He stood taller, pulling back his shoulders, and stared the old man down. He was no longer the scared and hate-filled wee nipper he had been back then. He was now a proud citizen of Hié, supported by the dragon daimyō, captain of her *Sea Guardian* to defeat old sea slimes like this. He stared into the man's sharp grey eyes until the older man gave in and stepped to the side, gesturing beside them with his head.

'Let's go in there, somewhere more private. I want to eat. And you look like you have questions. Go on, I'll give you time without killin' ye, fer ol' time's sake. Yer could say I raised yer, after all.'

He didn't even wait to see Gora's face erupt with rage. He swiftly turned and stomped over the wooden veranda and into the whorehouse and inn, one limited to the higher-ups of the crews, one with slightly higher quality and cleaner whores. Supposedly. As Gora followed and padded in after his old captain, he couldn't help but narrow his eyes, trying to avoid any further reaction of disgust. *As if this is any cleaner or better,* he questioned, trying to keep his face unreadable. Offend a whorehouse, you're in trouble. These people had a surprisingly huge amount of control, and it could be life-ending, in one way or another.

Just as Gora remembered, Foy turned on the charm, the old fox leaning casually against the bar and smiling seductively at the house ma'am, who batted her overly long, painted eyelashes and smiled back, reminding Gora of a cat. This lady must have known him, as she looked overly comfortable for a house ma'am, who was usually strict and sceptical with the running of her whores. She lounged across the bar and smirked at Foy, who played along and no doubt ran his silver tongue in a way that won her over because she soon led him personally, practically purring, away through the halls and up some steps into a larger, more private room with a table and a huge bed, Foy making sure Gora followed. When Gora stepped uncertainly into the room behind Foy and noticed the bed with no girls waiting, his breath caught and his ears rang, and the same dread flushed through his body, not allowing him to take another step. Sparks washed over Gora's eyes, and he paused in the doorway, eyes taking it all in. Foy, already in the middle of the room, pulling off his black cap and dropping it on a stool, stopped and looked around, his face reading Gora's too easily for Gora's comfort and his face washing over with a cruel smirk.

'Aye, no worries, boy. There'll be girls servicing me soon. Ye've been let off, unless you want, o' course?'

That sly ...

Memories Gora never wanted to cross his mind ever again flooded back, and he was reminded of why he took to the spirits in the first place. Since working with Yoshiko, he'd come off them, but now his eyes instinctively looked for the nearest glass bottle of golden liquid as he tried to calm his breath.

'That's not what I'm here for,' he managed to say, mouth dry and voice croaky, wincing at how pathetic he sounded when all along he imagined facing off this old sea demon with a fire in his belly and vengeance burning like dragon fire. Instead, the young, lost boy in him came to the fore, and he hesitated to step further into the room.

The old pirate shrugged off his black overcoat and tossed it over the back of a chair, relaxing back into an old but comfortable-looking red velvet chaise lounge, kicking up his legs and staring at Gora, daring him to come in. Gora did. His foot managed to step into the room and out of the doorway, just enough for two girls to swan in and place a variety of foods and drinks onto the side tables, including, to Gora's relief, spirits. He tried to avoid it. He had a crew to go back to now. He couldn't come back plastered. He wasn't going to be that captain.

'This place bring back memories, boy?' Foy asked, keeping up the Gaean, eyeing up the ass of one of the girls as she bent over seductively to place a plate of assorted cured meats on to the table right in front of Foy. It looked much more edible than the slops they were given at the inn they were staying in, and one of the main reasons he gave such short rotations to his crew here was so they could go back and be fed by Kimura. At least here, in this inn for the higher-ups, the food didn't look quite so gut-destroying.

'You could say that,' Gora muttered, stepping to the side once again as the girls pushed back out of the room, and Foy leant forward on the chaise to reach for a plate. Gora still didn't want to get any closer.

'So, what brings yer here, if you don't wanna remember?'

'Hunting fer you.'

'Why? Goin' t' kill me, boy?'

'Not yet. I want answers.'

Foy's piercing grey eyes bore like blades into Gora's, and he chewed a piece of cured meat slowly, deliberately making Gora wait. It was an old habit of Foy's, one he'd done forever, making people wait for a response.

'Oh?' was all the old pirate offered.

'Why didn't you kill me, like all the other kids? And why are the pirates hunting kids?'

The steely eyes kept their gaze, and Gora tried to hold them, just like always. He felt his breath come quicker and shorter, but he tried to hide it. The older man on the chaise huffed a short, sharp breath of amusement and then leant forward for some more meat.

'And what made you think it wasn't because we saw somethin' special in you, lad?' The older man's voice was melodic and like liquid treasure, but Gora knew this was his way to win people over and catch them off guard—to bring them to his side.

'Don't lie to me now.'

The man smirked again, and he leant back on the chaise, bringing his booted feet up onto the fabric, an arm casually behind his head, eyes back on the *boy*. He looked as if he was calculating something for a moment, eyes narrowing as he stared into Gora's before he sighed and decided to tell him something.

'The queen wants us hunting kids. We collect and sacrifice them for her, she compensates us. Quite well, actually. Simple as that.'

'The queen? You mean the pirate queen?'

Gora had heard mention of her before, on the ships, and though he'd never seen her before, he remembered a time their ship had sailed to a meeting where Foy would supposedly speak with her and the circle of pirate leaders. At the time, he'd grumped and hidden, thinking it a farce. Fake queens. No-one could rule pirates, surely? They were too selfish, too focused on their own gains.

'Aye, that's the one. And we'd have done good to keep yer away from 'er. She'd of kept ye or killed ye. Neither way did we benefit.' The older man shrugged, his steely grey eyes looking up for a moment as if he was recalling something.

Gora shivered. Did that mean they had wanted to keep him? *Why?* He tried to find somewhere to sit. A simple wooden stool was close enough to the edge of the room and out of the old pirate's way. He took that, but hated how his leg twitched and hoped Foy wouldn't see.

'I'd have thought you'd have wanted to be rid of me. The number of times you all moaned at me or beat me. I never knew why you didn't just kill me like ye did the others. So tell me now, why?'

Foy calculated him again, settling back in his chaise, then cast his eyes to the door where two girls had appeared, blouses loose, hands pulling up their skirts, and eyeing the older man knowingly. He nodded, and they rushed in, flaunting themselves to him. Foy's expression was unreadable as he let them playfully undress him, and Gora had to look away.

'Your hair,' Foy said, eyes meeting Gora's through the movement of the house whores. Now Foy was speaking again, his steely eyes locked onto Gora's, and Gora couldn't look away. 'Red hair—it's a sign of the devils. Killing yer like we did the other kids would have ruined the queen's plans. She needs untainted kids, innocent kids. Giving her the devil's child would have ruined it all.' Foy gave a breathy laugh, and his attention switched back to the girls for a moment as one grabbed at his crotch, unlacing his breeches, and the old man helped himself to ripping one of their blouses off. Then his gaze returned to Gora. 'That's all. And rather than waste our work, we made you work. It's as simple as that. And why I never let the queen take you—I'd trained you up by then. Not losing a well-behaved lad who knows what I need on my deck just for that royal pain.'

A moan came from one of the girls, and Foy seemed to return it appreciatively. Gora flinched and felt his face burn. He cleared his throat.

'So then why here? You brought me here to sell me. Why?'

'You got too old and too reluctant. I needed a cabin boy, and while age doesn't determine that, your attitude did. You know I like my nippers eager.' The older man grinned knowingly at him, eyes bright and stabbing into Gora's worst memories, and then he looked away at the women, letting them pull off his shirt and breeches, running his hands up the from her waist up her bare torso. The old man's hands then slipped down to the woman's buttocks, pulling her closer to straddle him, lifting her skirts, lips teasing her breasts. She giggled and wriggled, grinding on him, and the other woman, not wanting to be left out, knelt naked on the chaise beside them, kissing and licking the old pirate's bare skin, letting desperate moans slip of her lips to bring his attention to her. The old man turned his face to bury it in the woman's breasts.

Gora looked away again, his ears rushing with the sounds of waves and his eyes darkening over for a moment before sight and sound returned to him.

'Can ye all not wait now?' Gora muttered in Traders', knowing the lasses wouldn't understand Gaean.

A scoff came in answer from Foy. 'Yer chose to follow me in here, lad. You know what we do in here. I'll be nice and offer fer you to join in, this once. You know I'm not usually as nice as that. One-time offer, fer old times' sake.'

Gora didn't need to see Foy's face to know he was likely smirking, eyes able to force their way into your brain and see your deepest thoughts and fears. He chose the wisest option and didn't respond. The giggles and growing moans of the girls would have drowned it out anyway.

'Our old times together turned you off that much, eh? Can't get with a lass now, eh?'

Gora still didn't respond.

'Well, I ain't letting a sexless monk get in my way. Stay and chat if you want and put up with it, or bugger off.'

This time, a low soft moan that he knew could only be Foy crashed through Gora's hearing, and his eyes faded over to blank again. His head pounded, and he stared at the floor, blinking the darkness away.

Gora's voice was hoarse when he spoke again. 'Keep goin', old man. Keep talkin'. Why'd you sell me to Frewin if you were so anxious not to let the queen have me?' Gora's stomach felt like it would churn itself out at this rate, and he was so tempted to turn tail and leave. Not like he was going to get much out of Foy anyway, especially now. The old pirate was just playing with him. But Gora felt like there was some important missing piece that connected everything that his mission needed, and he was certain Foy would be one of those pieces.

Amongst the moans and the sounds of flesh against flesh, Foy finally piped up again. 'I needed a cabin boy; he needed a crew thug. I had no place on my ship for a boy who wouldn't do what he was told. That was all.' The sounds stopped for a moment. 'Not still bitter? Did you want to stay with me, lad? Miss me? How cute. Yer should've said.'

Gora glared over at him, wishing he hadn't. The trio had moved over to the bed, the woman who'd been kneeling beside them on the chaise now sprawled below, legs outstretched, and Foy's ass right where Gora was looking, having a disgustingly easy view of the old man's balls as Foy pushed into the woman. The other woman previously atop Foy's thighs now lay beside them, servicing both with her lips and hands.

Gora's vision sparked over, and the ocean roared again in his ears, and before he knew it, his breath and caught and his blood thickened to lead once more, and he stormed out of the room gasping for air.

'I'll get nothin' more out of him. The old dog's playin' me,' he gasped, crashing down the stairs and throwing himself out into the open street and taking great lungfuls of air.

It wasn't until his vision fully returned to him and the ocean stopped roaring in his ears that he looked up to realise he was surrounded—the men he'd seen from Foy's crew earlier had come, the slouching, gruff goons that had been following Foy now looking pleased with themselves.

'Ahh, you brought friends,' Gora let out with a huff of breath as he tried to regain his breathing. 'How nice.'

21
Explorations

Miyoshi sulked against the black wooden railing of the ship, staring out once more at the rocks and frond-leafed trees dotting the nearest shore of the pirate slave isles. Several rotations of crew had already been ashore to dig for information about Foy and the kidnapping and trade of children, but still, Gora had refused to let him go ashore too. Even Tomioka had got cross at him last time for asking to go ashore.

'Again, you ask? Do you not remember why we're here? Do you not remember what they do to children? Do you not trust your captain and your crew to know what's best for you?' Tomioka had put him to good work as a lesson, making the lad refold the flags and scrub all the floors.

'I just want to explore,' Miyoshi muttered to himself as he wrung the water from the cloth and finished the storeroom floors. He wiped his brow with his sleeve and frowned.

Less than a year ago, he'd been able to escape from Acrein and come back to Hié after being taken as a slave. It had been scary to be kidnapped and taken on that giant slave ship, with people crammed in and death gods waiting to take them, then to work until he collapsed every day, only to be given tiny rations and no joy. When the now-daimyō Yoshiko and Gora and their friend, Nubia, had given people the chance to escape and come back, he

"

had, and he'd looked up to them like they were gods in their own right—without a shrine, without the powers, but good enough to be looked up to. When Miyoshi had said he wanted to join Gora on his mission, wanting to be helpful to Gora and learn as much as he could from him and help make the world safer so other people didn't get taken as slaves, Yoshiko had even given him her special daggers! He patted them in his pocket where he knew they were safe and sighed, lying on his back and stretching out his arms and legs like a starfish, looking up at the storeroom roof beams and wondering how long he'd have to wait before he was seen as a strong and valuable member of the crew. Would he have to wait until he got older?

'But that's ages away.'

He turned his head to the side and looked at the bucket of water and the cloth, knowing he'd have to go and do the next rooms.

Of course I know why we're here and what they do to children, he thought, recalling Tomioka's cross lecture earlier that morning. Miyoshi pouted. *That's why I'm here!* He knew exactly what it was like to be taken as a child and how scary it was and didn't want it to happen to anyone else. And the captain was just like him. Both he and the captain had been stolen as children and made to work as slaves, and while the captain had been taken by pirates and Miyoshi hadn't, he wanted to prove that he knew and that was why he was here. If only the captain would give him a chance!

He sighed and looked at the ceiling again. *I know they're just looking out for me, but I just—*

What did he just? Miyoshi wasn't sure. He knew what Gora, Tomioka, Yonemura, and everyone was trying to do to protect him. He knew as much as Moori and Kimura joked about with him, and as much as the crew called him Yūki as if he were a girl, that they'd do anything to keep him safe. But he wanted to help them, too! And he was in a new place, away from Hizen and his family in Hié—he wanted to explore and see and learn new things and go back with lots of stories.

The new rotation only just went to shore yesterday, and it's still morning, he thought, feeling a plan come to mind. *If I'm quick, I can just pop down to the beach and look over those rocks, then come back again. No-one will notice.*

Excited by his plan and wondering whether it would work, he leapt up and grabbed the bucket and cloth and hurried out into the corridor. He looked left and right, peered down a corridor, and felt his heart leap when Taro padded around the corner. The man's thin face flooded with surprise at seeing the boy then fell into a soft smile.

'Yūki! What are you doing? You look lost.'

Miyoshi liked Taro and his son, Kyo. Both were soft and quiet and mostly kept to themselves, particularly after what had happened in their family. But, whenever Taro saw Miyoshi, he often treated him like an extra son. He stepped forward and placed a hand softly on Miyoshi's shoulder, warm eyes lit up.

'Tomioka wanted me to scrub all the floors. I was wondering which room to do next,' Miyoshi lied, guilt twisting knots in his stomach for not telling the truth to someone as nice as Taro.

The man let out a soft chuckle. 'All in one day? Sounds like he's punishing you!'

Miyoshi bowed his head and looked at the floor, mumbling that Tomioka was indeed punishing him. Taro let out a soft breath.

'Ahh, and why's that, lad? Got in an argument with Moori and Kimura again? You know what to do if they push you too far.'

'It's not that,' the lad mumbled again, looking to the side, not sure whether he should say. It might spoil the plan. But when he looked up at Taro, he saw a gentle face and knew he wouldn't be the sort to judge or tell. 'I just wanted to go to shore, but they wouldn't let me. Tomioka got fed up with me asking. I know they're just trying to protect me, but I didn't think it would hurt to ask.'

Taro nodded silently, his face still gentle and smiling. 'Aye, lad. But let me tell you this. It ain't such a good place. I'm happy to stay here and never go back there again if I have the chance. But I know what it's like to just want to know. Kyo was the same too, when he was your age. It's alright to be curious; just know when to look after yourself.'

Miyoshi was surprised, expecting to be chastised again, not expecting to hear Taro hadn't liked it. Didn't all the crew always like exploring new places? Back when they went to Ishil, everyone had been excited to go to port.

'You really didn't like it?'

The man shook his head, and his face fell. Miyoshi realised how old and weary he looked, still not having recovered from the anxiety for his son and wife, now aged permanently. Taro ran a hand over his short, dark-grey facial hair in thought, eyes looking at Miyoshi carefully. 'That's right. It's not a good place. It felt greasy and unclean, and eyes watched you wherever you went. I felt like someone would jump out and rob me or kill me if I even blinked.' Taro nodded, mostly to himself. 'Yes, I'd be quite happy if we turned and sailed away this moment.' Then he looked fondly once more at Miyoshi, a soft smile lighting up his face again. 'I hope you never have to feel such a way.'

The man said something about needing to report to Yonemura on the deck and padded away again, leaving Miyoshi standing in the corridor alone, looking straight at a wall and not seeing it, doubting himself. On one hand, he still wanted to go and explore. And on the other, hearing Taro put it that way had made his heart drop a little, and he didn't want to worry the others if that's how they really felt about this place. He turned and watched Taro's feet disappear up the steps towards the deck, wondering what to do. But that little voice in the back of his head still piped up louder, and he couldn't help himself.

If I just go to the shore, surely that's okay? I won't go into the town, if that's what Taro thinks it's like. I can just peer at it over the rocks.

Decision made, and trying to push the guilt down, Miyoshi stashed the bucket and cloth in one of the next rooms, thinking he could come back quickly and still finish his chores as if he'd never left, and snuck up onto the deck, ready for his adventure ashore.

Up on the deck, he peered about to see who was there and who would spot him if he left. Taro was talking to Yonemura at the bow, and Quinni was up in the crow's nest, staring out to sea. Ikeda and Rijul were sharpening their blades, and Eshnaa was helping Kyo carry something below. Tomioka was nowhere to be seen, likely below somewhere, and no-one else was around. Miyoshi hoped none of them would look around to see him. He crept over to the port railing and pulled himself over into one of the rowboats hanging off the side for one of the next teams to go ashore. Once in there, he waited, lying in the boat, wondering if someone would come running, having seen him, dragging him back to the ship. No-one came, and he felt his body spike with excitement and energy. Next, he pulled himself up into a crouch and reached up to lower the boat into the water. With both sides tied, he'd have to lower them both one by one, and found himself feeling stressed at the time it took to lower one a little, shuffle over to the other and lower that one too, slowly edging the little boat down to the bobbing ocean below. With each tug of the ropes, Miyoshi worried that someone would discover his escape, and he kept his ears alert for any signs of a cry up above about the boy going missing.

None came.

His heart soared once more as the small boat hit the water, and he fumbled to find the oars and pushed off, trying to silently row himself to shore to the stern of the boat, where he hoped fewer people would be keeping an eye out.

His slow journey found himself navigating around some rocks where he could land on the small stretch of sandy beach unseen, and he strained to pull the boat up onto the land alone, where he hoped it would be safe if the tide came in.

He looked at the boat and then out at the rippling ocean. He wasn't expecting to stay here too long. Just a peek. He'd be back again before the tide came in.

Nodding to himself, the boy grinned and turned to run up the sandy beach, ducking below the rocks, eyeing the ship carefully to see if anyone had spotted him. The small figures up on the huge deck seemed unaware, and he ducked below a final rock before darting into the tree line on the edge of the beach.

Once in the tree line, Miyoshi paused to figure out where he wanted to explore first. He knew he wouldn't have long. Just a short explore, see a pirate island town, go back. He wanted to see if things were really as worn-down and unkempt as the crew made it sound, particularly when Kimura came back from the inn from his sleeping shifts on the shore. For an upper-class Hién like Kimura, Miyoshi thought of course anything would seem unkempt. But did that mean it really was?

The boy picked through the undergrowth at the edge of the tree line, trying not to come too out of the shadows of the trees and be spotted by a member of his crew on the beach. Here, he didn't know if he'd run into trouble with snakes hiding in the grass, but in his young mind, it was better than being spotted by a crew member and being made to go back to the ship before he saw anything interesting.

Once he'd spanned the width of the small beach, Miyoshi edged out of the tree line and scrambled over the first of many large rocks creating a blockade from the beach to whatever came past it. Whenever any of his crew went into the pirate town on their shift to shore, they could weave through these rocks by a little pathway. But, with the fear that the crew might be monitoring that little walkway to see if any of their crew were returning, Miyoshi stuck to clambering over the blockage at the far edge of the beach, hoping he was out of sight. It was much more effort, and the boy's breath soon came out in short, sharp huffs, but Miyoshi was never one to give up. As the son of a long line of fishing families, he took pride in his family's hardiness.

I'll have to figure out how to tell Kimura or Satou about these scrapes, though, he thought as he grazed himself again sliding down another of the rocks, knowing he'd have to get them checked and cleaned. He looked down at the scraped skin and decided that, if he had the choice, he'd go to Satou. The ship's carpenter was much more forgiving about looking after random scrapes and would dig less for an explanation than Kimura would. Kimura, too much like a teasing older brother, would give him grief about it until Miyoshi wound up telling him what idiotic adventure he'd been up to this time.

Finally over the last of the rocks, Miyoshi slipped down onto a winding pathway through more rocks; sandy dunes; sparse trees with those tall, straight trunks and huge, feathered leaves right at the top; and smaller cliffs. From up on the ship, Miyoshi hadn't realised how towering these dunes and cliffs were and how far it actually was to get around the corner to the pirate town. But then he wondered whether, if it were smaller and shorter, the pirates might have seen them by now and come to pester them about why they'd not pulled into the main docks. He panted as he rounded a corner, skidding to a stop and hiding behind a boulder as it opened up onto another beach, this one leading at the farther end to wooden structures, walkways, and eventually to the main docks and the pirate town. He turned to look behind him. It was much farther than he thought but, spurred on with a leaping heart, Miyoshi ran and stumbled across the loose, powdery sand towards what he hoped would be the exciting part of his adventure.

On the other side of the beach, a natural, rocky harbour curved into the island. Here, Miyoshi felt like he'd finally found something exciting. Wonky wooden planks and structures stretched from the harbour, providing separate walkways and bays for ships to pull into and their crew to walk on. Several vessels were already settled, and Miyoshi's eyes widened at the number and variety. He wondered what kind of pirates lived on those ships and how many had crew aboard now. Did they all leave the ship and go to port together, or did they take shifts like Gora's crew did? He didn't know enough to be sure, and while a part of him wanted to get closer to have a look at each ship, he settled for hiding behind a tree and peering at them for a while. If he went down there, he was sure he might be spotted by a pirate, and that's what he was afraid of. It wasn't that he didn't listen to Gora, Tomioka, and the others. He knew pirates should be something he was afraid of, and he was, so he wanted to stay hidden and not get caught by them. But that didn't mean he didn't want to see other things.

Miyoshi hid behind the tree for a while, peeking at the ships and anxiously looking around him to make sure he was still safe and no-one was creeping up on him. He had the knives Lady Yoshiko had given him, but he doubted that would be much good against someone with a full blade. So he watched the ships between hesitant looks around him and was in awe over the different sizes, shapes, styles. Some had ornate woodwork and high backs, others had painted hulls, some had two masts and others had three, and others black sails rather than the usual white. A man stomped across the wooden walkways towards one of the ships, one with a navy painted strip on the hull and two main sails. He had a slight waddle to his walk, and Miyoshi wondered whether he'd come from drinking or just wasn't used to walking on land anymore. He felt strange coming off ships once he'd got used to his sea legs, and it took a while to get the land legs back. The man, he was amazed to see, looked just like a normal man, other than this waddle. Not as scary as the others had painted them all out to be, though his experience with Frewin and his crew certainly had met the expectations. This man looked normal, with tanned, leathery skin, brown hair pulled into a braid, and a normal-looking face. There were no warts or scars or overly funky teeth, and he looked more tired than squinty-eyed, and he wasn't missing a limb, like some of the stories said.

Miyoshi suddenly pulled himself back to hide behind the tree again and look about him warily, realising he'd been staring too long. He felt his breath quicken, and it felt like hundreds of pairs of eyes were hiding behind him, watching him. Miyoshi shook his head and tried to gather himself together, thinking it was time to move on and explore something else, to make sure he got to see everything he wanted to before he had to go back to Gora's ship. So he looked around before diving from his hiding place and moving along the harbour, looking for a pathway that would take him into the pirate town that he could see the smoke coming from when he was on the deck of the ship. If that brown-haired man had just come from somewhere, then there must have been a few walkways nearby to let the pirates into the town. Still worried about walking straight down one in case a pirate came through it at the same time and caught him, Miyoshi tried to edge down the track from the side, dashing between trees or rocks and carefully looking and listening out before he moved, heart thudding in his chest and making his breath short and stilted. He barely wanted to breathe for fear it may make him miss the sound of any pirates' footsteps, and he tried to make his own footsteps as light on the wood as possible. When he finally managed to get somewhere high enough to see parts of the town, he ducked behind a rock and hid.

From here, there wasn't much he could see. It seemed the town had been built away from the harbour, with walkways stomping past trees and large rocks to act as a protection against wild weather. Unlike when they'd pulled into Shon Wa, where you could see much of the pirate town and bars close to the harbour, here it was embedded a little more inland. Miyoshi couldn't see much unless he came in further, and he wondered if that was because they'd been unable to move the rocks here or whether it was as protection against storms.

What he could see, though, through a gap in the walkway, was an area that led to a few tall buildings, a few floors high, built of stone and wood and looking quite rickety. Were they one of the inn buildings that the others had been telling him about, where they slept a few to a room with one always on watch, and where Moori was certain the floor had seas of woodmites living in them, and where the building creaked while people walked? He tried to peer closer, to see if he could see any more of those buildings or hear the creaking. It was impossible from his hiding space, unless he walked out from the walkways and past the rocks and into that open space.

In his head, pirates were either killing, stealing, fighting, or drinking. And certainly in Shon Wa, many had been drinking. But here, he didn't know where the drink houses were. Where were the lines of drink houses filled with rowdy, fighting drunkards? Was that down a different area? Did the path bend off to the side and lead to a strip with other sections? Miyoshi wanted to know, and his curiosity almost pushed him to look further, but he knew he'd been missing from the ship for too long. They'd have likely found out he'd gone by now, and he needed to get back. The boy bit back his curiosity, trying to convince himself that he'd got to explore, at least, and turned to dash back down the walkways to the harbour and then back across the beach, diving behind the first tree or rock he saw. And as he did, he heard stomping up the walkway again, this time from the harbour. Miyoshi froze and crouched low to hide by a tree, hoping to make himself as invisible as possible as this person came past. He held his breath, eyes wide, listening. Miyoshi hoped they'd stomp right on past, but the stomping stopped. Miyoshi froze.

'Oy, what's this?' A rough voice spoke out in Traders', and a hand suddenly grabbed at his shoulder and pulled him up.

Miyoshi cried out, finding himself staring at a tall man who had sun-pinked skin and a shaven head. As the boy stared at the man's face in shock, he noticed a scar leading down the edge of his cheek, right by his ear. This one, he thought, looked just like the pirates he'd been told about, with an aggressive attitude to boot. The man was staring at him, waiting.

'You waitin' t' kill me, boy?'

The man was speaking in Traders' again, and Miyoshi could understand enough to figure out what the man was saying. He gulped and shook his head quickly, trying to look as innocent as possible. The man didn't look convinced. And while the man was frowning at him, Miyoshi tried to figure out how he could escape. He darted his eyes to each side, trying to look for an opening to run away, but the man still had hold of his shoulder. Should he swipe out with his daggers and then run?

The pirate said something else, but Miyoshi was in such a panic that he didn't understand. With a narrowing of his eyes, the bald pirate grabbed Miyoshi's collar and pulled him in close, bringing the young boy to his toes as he was pulled upwards towards the man's face. Miyoshi held his breath. The man's breath was terrible, and the grasp on his collar hurt. The boy knew he had to do something quickly or he'd wind up dead and hidden in the bush.

He quickly grabbed at one of Yoshiko's daggers and swiped at the man's hand. The man roared in pain and let go of the boy, who used this moment of shock to quickly dash past the man and run down the tracks, back towards the ship.

It wasn't long before the man turned and followed him, and Miyoshi knew the man would easily catch up, so Miyoshi pushed himself to run as fast as he could on the laid wooden planks, looking behind him regularly to see how close the pirate was. His breath coming in short, sharp, terrified gasps, Miyoshi tried to ignore the yelling, cursing pirate closing in behind him. He skidded around the corner at the end of the walkway, making the sharp left turn that would take him past the harbour. From there, the beach next to it led around the coast and towards the hidden beach the *Sea Guardian* had pulled up in.

'Come here, you little—'

Miyoshi squeezed his eyes shut just a moment to push himself faster and leapt onto the sandy beach, taking it in awkward strides. Running on the beach was so much harder, and the boy knew if the pirate was to catch up, it would be here.

Anxious, Miyoshi turned to see the pirate too close for comfort, almost within an easy distance to reach out and grab him, but the sand was just too difficult for Miyoshi to run on and gain any distance. And though the pirate seemed to be struggling too, his longer, more loping strides were giving him an advantage over Miyoshi.

Miyoshi saw blood on the man's hand and wondered if there was anything else he could do to give himself another advantage. He didn't want to throw a knife at him and lose one of the precious daggers he'd been gifted from Yoshiko. But if it was that or his life …

The boy dodged to the side to avoid the man's grabbing hands and cried out as he tried to push himself faster over the fluffy sand. He reached the area at the end of the beach where the rocks separated this beach from the next, smaller one over, and this time, he didn't bother clambering over the rocks. He'd run right through the path he knew the others took when they headed into the pirate town, even if it meant running right into someone else who would find out he'd escaped—especially then; they might be able to help him with his angry pirate trouble.

Almost catching him, the pirate kept growling out and cursing at him, and Miyoshi could catch the odd words here and there enough to know the man was threatening him with what he would do if he were to catch him. Miyoshi would do anything to not be caught, and he had the benefit of young age and being used to running around. The man's breath was straining, and Miyoshi knew then he might just make it.

He dashed between the rocks, a little unsure of the way through from here but feeling confident there was a way out and that he'd then be able to see his ship on the other side. The pirate, not knowing there was a way out, became more hesitant. The boy used his hand to help him divert off a rock on a tight turn, not caring if it grazed, and darted out onto the beach, looking up at his ship in relief. Now he just needed to get up there and away safely, and no doubt the pirate would be scared off by the others. Miyoshi was desperate to get on board now.

Sure enough, a cry came out on deck, and Quinni's face appeared, shortly followed by his whole body as he clambered down the side and onto the sand, his huge figure loping across the sand towards Miyoshi, hands gesturing and voice calling for him to quickly come. The pirate behind Miyoshi seemed to hesitate, but he carried on towards them, yelling out again.

'… your lad? Little—tried to kill me!'

Quinni looked past Miyoshi, who crashed into his towering saviour as he finally ran to safety.

He has to leave now, right? He can't hurt us.

The boy hid behind Quinni, peeking out from behind him at his pursuer, who was red-faced, angrier looking than ever, and whose chest was heaving to catch his breath. The scar down the side of his face pulled as the man snarled.

'… ignoring me? I'll kill ya! Give me the boy.'

Miyoshi looked up at Quinni to see the calm giant's eyes hooded as he stared at the man, and his body was wary, as if he'd strike out if he needed to. But Miyoshi knew Quinni would rather find another way to deal with it. The boy peered around to see Quinni without a weapon and realised the man had jumped down here to help him, not even giving himself time to grab something to defend himself with. If the pirate drew his sword, they'd be in trouble. And, sure enough, the pirate, grinding his teeth at not being given an answer, though Miyoshi knew Quinni would be able to understand enough of what he was saying, drew his sword and stepped forward to take things into his own hands.

Another disturbance on deck, and the trio on the sand looked up, pirate surprised, to see Ikeda jumping over the gunwale, grabbing the rope with one hand and swinging down it towards them, sliding down with ease. He had his katana drawn, and the rope lurched as it arched the young samurai to the ground. He used the momentum from the swing to let go of the rope and launch towards them, taking the last few steps at a run to stop his momentum and land between the two from his ship and the pirate.

The pirate's face looked as boggled as Miyoshi, and with Ikeda's katana blade pointing right up at his nose but his own blade by his side as he watched the young Hién's acrobatics, the pirate realised his situation. He quickly drew up his blade and tried to meet Ikeda's, but the young man parried him away, kicked at the man's stomach until the man toppled over in the sand, and then once again stood waiting with his katana blade pointed to the bald pirate, warning him off.

Quinni picked up Miyoshi and put the young lad over his shoulder, turning to walk away, starting his climb back up the rope. Miyoshi called out at him to wait and help Ikeda, but the giant ignored him, and Miyoshi was left with no option but to hang over Quinni's back, watching Ikeda warning off the pirate, each time easily parrying the pirate's attacks and kicking him to the ground.

'Why won't Ikeda kill him?' Miyoshi asked Quinni when Ikeda kicked the pirate down for the third time.

'It's not a light thing to take a life. If the pirate shows no real threat and Ikeda can beat him without killing him, why should he?' Quinni's voice came low and soft, as always, and his words were always well thought out.

Miyoshi hummed in thought. 'Then why won't the pirate give up? He won't win.'

'Pride. He does not want to admit the younger man is better than him.'

They were near the top now, and Miyoshi was trying not to focus on how high up they were and what could happen if Quinni should drop him or he should slide from Quinni's shoulder. Instead, Miyoshi watched as Ikeda raised his katana again and leapt at the man, trying to scare him off. This time, the man gave up and stormed off, cursing at Ikeda, spitting in the sand, but leaving all the same. Just as Quinni pulled himself and Miyoshi over the railing, Ikeda was turning to make his way back to the ship.

Quinni landed on the deck with a soft thud and pulled the boy down from his shoulder. Miyoshi, too relieved to be back and safe, had forgotten about the fact he'd slipped away unnoticed and only realised too late when he turned around to face the deck to see Tomioka standing in front of him, hands on his hips, face unreadable. Suddenly, it all flooded back, and he gulped.

'Um …' he started, wondering what to say and looking awkwardly to the side, seeing some of the other crew watching him. He looked back at Tomioka when the man didn't respond.

But instead of punishment, the man stepped forward and scooped Miyoshi into his arms.

'You're alive; thank goodness. Don't do that to us again.'

22

Escaping the Isles

Negotiating with these sea slugs wasn't going to get him anywhere, Gora knew that. Here he was, stuck between Foy's crew, who'd do anything gruesome to people just for fun, and a whorehouse where the devil captain who'd stolen him as a child was pounding away at his own self-gratifying oblivion. He remembered the days on their ship. It was even worse than Frewin's. Foy, though he looked more of a decent human and had a way that the ladies and lads couldn't resist and a sickly charm to win anyone over, had a heart rotten as a ship sunken in the greatest depths for hundreds of years. The sorts of things that went on on that ship … Gora didn't want to return there. Not even in his thoughts.

He took a great breath, eyes finally blinking away the black spots that had swum in them as he ran from the brothel, and stood straight, eyes glancing around him at the gathering of Foy's goons. They'd formed an arc around him, hoping to block him in. He knew they'd attack then—when they were closer and guaranteed not to miss. They'd jump on him all at once, kicking, bashing, skewering … Gora had until then to figure something out. He reached for the handles of his twin blades at his left hip, hands pausing, knowing if he drew them it would be an instant attack. They all slowly closed in, eyes gleaming, glancing at once another and grinning. Then one of them slid their eyes to the door, and Gora realised they were stalling. They should have jumped him by now, but they were still waiting.

Not like these slimes to have self-control, Gora thought, wanting to follow that slime's gaze towards the whorehouse door behind him but wondering if it was a trick to get him to look behind him, where they could then easily rush him without him being ready to defend.

Until the door shut with a thud and boots stomped the ground behind him.

Gora whirled on the spot and took a step back from the door, digging his feet into a ready stance so he could move in any direction he needed at the smallest hint of attack from around him. Foy stood in the doorway, tucking his undershirt into his slacks and looking rather pleased with himself. His face held a deeper smirk than usual, white hair and beard bright against his suntanned face, eyes glinting like liquid metal.

'The lads caught you, eh, boy?'

Gora glared at the old captain, but the sound of footsteps scuffing on the ground behind him made him jump and look around, instantly drawing his blades to defend. The arc of Foy's men had closed into a circle around him, their captain stepping through into it.

Shit.

Holding both his cutlasses out, Gora turned slowly to watch the horde. He didn't recognise many of these men. Likely, in the years since he'd been sold to Frewin and left Foy's crew, most would have rotated out or left or been killed. No-one friendly to play to, then, he knew. Not that any of them had ever been friendly. And even if they had, they'd not lose face in front of the rest of their crew by being weak on him.

Gora sighed.

'Where'd you get those nice blades, lad? Frewin give them to you? Steal them off some unfortunate naval officer?' Foy smirked, eying up both his blades.

Gora gripped them tighter and ignored him. He had to get back to his crew. The others would still be looking around the markets, wouldn't they? Or had they finished up and returned to the inn by now? He'd have no way of knowing. Even if he could escape from here and run to find them, he'd be runnin' all over the damned island with this ugly lot on his tail, likely getting others involved, too. *Intruders on the island,* they'd say. *Kill 'em. Burn their ship. Sink 'em. Stuff holes in 'em.*

He grimaced.

'Aye,' he said, eyes sliding to meet Foy's. 'When you suckers taught me how to kill innocent people and steal their effects. Looks like I wasn't as useless a disappointment as you thought, now, eh? Got summat out of it.' He twirled a cutlass lazily in his hands, using the hand balance to swing it about his finger. 'When I kill the lot of you, can I take yours, too? I'll make a set.' He met Foy's sharp eyes and held the gaze, keeping his hearing out for anything from behind.

The ugly motley crew behind him sniggered. 'This one's forgotten what you do to insolent boys, eh, cap'n.'

'Aye, I should teach him again.' Foy's eyes went dark, and he snarled.

Gora shivered, and his heart thudded too fast again, and his arms felt weak. He swallowed and looked away, disguising it as looking around at the sod who'd called out, so Foy didn't see his weakness.

'What can I say? I'm a rogue, I'm pretty, and I can't blame yer for thinking such things,' Gora said, trying to keep his voice light and joking. He winced as he heard it shake a little. He knew Foy would spot that. *Time to leave before it happens.*

The pirate who'd spoken, a man older than him by perhaps half a generation and with slicked-back long braided hair and a nose red from the sun, gnashed his teeth. Looking closer at him, Gora thought he saw hints of a naval sailor in him. He had that bearing, clothes remnants of official sailing gear, patched up and mixed with stolen clothing. *So, he fell and joined the free side*, Gora thought. He looked like he was harbouring a grudge and could be the weak link Gora needed to barge and leave through.

Running his mouth as bravado to hide his weakness.

Gora grinned lazily at him and pointed one cutlass ahead. 'Upset I called you out, now? Think I'm pretty? Or are yer upset the captain never chose you?'

As expected, the man fell for it and broke his ranks, storming forward, unsheathing his sword and raising it to attack Gora. Foy called out for the man to stop, but he didn't. Gora smirked. As the man's blade came down, Gora raised his own, parried with one and brought the other slicing down in the same movement and sliced across the man's side. Not deep enough to kill, but enough to maim and run through the gap this man had now created in the circle. Gora immediately pivoted on his foot and darted towards that gap before it closed up. He brought up his right blade to block an attack from his side as the next nearest pirate rushed for him. Gora didn't bother attacking back. It would slow him down. He just ran, Foy yelling behind him for the others to bring him back, mostly alive, so he could kill the lad himself.

Ain't gunna happen. Gora's breath heaved as he skidded around a corner and jumped to the side to dodge a clueless pirate walking past. He had to get to the markets and find the others and get back to the ship.

He dared to look behind him to see the whole bunch of them pursuing him. They were mostly slow, lumbering, and Gora thanked the fact that he'd been living on land where he'd been able to run long distances recently. This bunch wasn't used to that anymore, confined to the space of a ship.

The markets came into view ahead as he rounded the hill and navigated the decline to reach them. Movement from the corners of his eyes made his heart leap.

A flash of black hair and yellow silk crossed his gaze. His eyes widened as the figure rushed past and he realised he recognised it.

'Sim?' Gora cried out, skidding to a stop and turning to see the Ishillian woman jump between him and the closing-in pirate rabble, circular *chakram* blades adorning her arms and *talwar* outstretched to ready. As he turned, he saw Eshnaa run in from the other side, her *talwar* blade cutting at the legs of one of the heavy-set goons who had been tailing Foy that first time Gora saw him before the whorehouse. The goon stumbled and hit the ground with a thud, crying out and cursing as he looked up at the woman who walked past him as if he'd barely been there, standing beside her friend. The two women looked quickly at one another before diving forward, cutting into the front line of Foy's crew.

Gora jumped as Rijul ran up from behind him, gasping from running up the hill and stepping past to join the other two, crying out their names. 'Eshnaa, Sim, don't just run off like that without telling us!' He looked back at Gora in surprise as he ran past. 'Captain! We found you.' Then he dodged as one of Foy's goons tried to jump on him.

'Are the other two with you?' Gora called out, looking behind, down the hill to the markets. Just as Rijul replied, he saw Nishimura and Sakai running up the hill towards them. He called out, beckoning them with his arm.

Though the three Ishillian fighters were good, he knew they couldn't hold off enough of Foy's men, and around them, a crowd was gathering to the noise. Gora rushed in to join the three, barging his shoulder into one to move him away from Eshnaa and then kicking at someone to move them enough away from Rijul that he could pierce the man's stomach with his *talwar* sword.

Gora watched Nishimura and Sakai reach the top of the hill. Those two weren't strong fighters. Not enough to deal with this many people, and someone from Foy's crew was yelling out at the gathering crew to help them.

'They're intruders! Get them!'

The crowd looked confused, but it didn't take much persuading for some to step forward, simply wanting to join a brawl.

'Oy, we need to go,' Gora growled out to the others, seeing this only get worse. They couldn't fight off multiple crews, and some idiot was spouting nonsense about them being navy.

'Look at his swords! He's no pirate.'

True, he had stolen naval swords, but no-one here was going to listen to that anymore. Even the mention of someone being navy, not pirate, or even anything other than pirate, could get a whole ship sunk. If you weren't one of them, you didn't belong, and that meant you got killed.

'Now!' Gora yelled, grabbing Sakai's jacket and pushing him away before they were surrounded, pushing him into a run towards the northern side of the island where their ship was docked in that hidden beach.

Simrita turned to run, but Eshnaa was surrounded by goons muttering obscene things about fighting women. Rijul leapt in to help her free, firing a well-aimed punch to someone's temple and grabbing Eshnaa's wrist and pulling her away. Simrita, knowing her friend was safe, turned and ran after Sakai, followed shortly by Nishimura, leaving Gora and Rijul bringing up the rear with Eshnaa just ahead of them.

'What did you do to rile them up, captain? Kill theirs?'

'I wish!' Gora gasped as they sprinted down the track towards the main harbour, feeling blocked in with the trees and rocks either side. There'd be no way to dodge or escape the chasing horde now. 'It was a trick all along. He sent his goons to get the rest of his men while I tried to get information out of him. Slimy fucker.'

'Of course he would!' Eshnaa yelled back at him from ahead. 'What did you expect?'

Gora frowned, having no answer to give. Instead, he grumbled at them to keep running and skidded around the left, turning to the side of the harbour to leap over the rocks onto the middle beach.

On the beach, some idiot behind them thought of firing their guns, knowing they were unlikely to catch up. Iron rounds whizzed past and hit the sand ahead, and the sounds of gunfire behind made Gora's heart seize up, as he never knew what would happen next and whether they'd be hit.

'Don't run in a straight line! Move out a bit! Run in different directions!' Gora barely managed to cry out, his breath coming in harsh gasps with the fatigue of running over powdery sand.

A cry came up from Simrita as a bullet skimmed her arm, leaving a bleeding line dripping down her arm and onto her *chakram*s. Gora winced. They were nearly at the end of the beach, the rocks that separated loomed ahead, and he could see the masts now stretching up ahead. If he could just get them past those rocks, they'd be safe a moment from the firing bullets and could call out for the crew to get the ship ready to leave.

He leapt over the rocks and bellowed Shingo's name.

There was a flash of the sun catching a spyglass at the gunwale. A yell came up on the ship.

Simrita and Eshnaa weaved and dived out from the rocks first, sprinting ahead on the hidden beach towards the ship, waving and crying out. Rijul and Nishimura followed, silent and looking behind at Gora and Sakai and those who pursued them. Behind Gora, the bullets ricocheted off the rocks, and he pushed a struggling Sakai, whose age was causing him suffering from this running. Gora glanced up at the ship to see rope ladders lowered into the water below, and the ship swung on the anchor.

Gora crashed into the waves, feeling the cold chill race through his burning legs, pushing Sakai ahead of him. Bullets whizzed past once again as pirates passed the rocks, but this time, his heart leapt to hear attacks of their own.

High above, a higher-pitched yell went out, and Gora strained his neck to see Moori standing at the railing, gun in her hands, and then the thunderous roar of gunfire as she fired into the oncoming crowd. Gora grinned. Moori's aim with the guns was uncanny, and somehow, even with the inaccurate guns, she hit a mark. Ikeda stepped up beside her, and while the young samurai looked a little more out of place with the gun, his serious composure was reassuring to Gora. With those two protecting the ship, they might just have a chance.

Gora waited in the water as his other five crew members clambered up the hull, and when he finally clasped the ladder, muscles burning from the run and the swim, he held on for dear life and tried to pull himself up. Above, Daiki was pulling Simrita over, mindful of not cutting himself on her *chakrams*, and then rushed to pull Nishimura over too and met Gora's eyes with a nod before turning to nod to someone behind him. 'All here!'

Still climbing, Gora heard Shingo's response. A cry from high in the masts went out, and the wind caught the sails, pulling on the ship as the anchor was torn free from its holding. Gora cried out and hung on like a spider swinging from its web, heart leaping as a bullet hit the hull beside his leg.

23

Dragon Island

The boat knocked against an old wooden dock on Tatsushima Island, and Yoshiko rushed to hook the rope over the post.

Their skipper sat and looked warily at the island, his weatherworn face scrunching up. 'Not sure what you want here, my lady. Ain't nothing here but a few stray cats.'

Yoshiko smiled. She was quite fond of cats. Then, as she gestured her head at Chisaka to stand, the two women thanked the skipper and reached up to pull themselves onto the deck.

'The warrior stays here,' a voice said on the breeze.

Yoshiko paused and looked back at Chisaka cautiously. 'Did you hear that?'

Chisaka scowled. 'I did. And it's not happening.' She continued to follow her daimyō, but the voice repeated the words and a strong wind rose like a growl.

Yoshiko swore she felt a heat to it.

'It's fine,' Yoshiko said, searching about for a sign of the speaker. 'You stay with the skipper and watch the boat.'

'But what if you're attacked?' Chisaka was looking around too, glaring and grasping her katana.

The skipper tugged at Chisaka's sleeve, edging her back into the boat to sit down before she caused it to tip. She glared at him too, until she noticed a fear in his eyes. 'That's not a voice you want to anger,' he said, tilting his head to the island. 'Her ladyship's strong. She'll be fine. The island's inviting her, not us.'

'But—'

The older man raised his finger, begging her to stop. 'There's an ancient shrine on that island, along with the cats. Let's not anger the gods.' He looked up at Yoshiko, who now stood with her own hands at her katana warily. His face looked steady, and he didn't seem the superstitious or drunk sort.

He nodded, and she turned her back, staring into the island. A cat crossed a worn path and stopped, turning to look at her. The green stare seemed disinterested, and it turned and walked away from her, padding soundlessly over the stone pathway. Then it stopped and looked at her, and Yoshiko swore it narrowed its eyes before continuing.

She felt like she should follow it.

Yoshiko left Chisaka grumbling with the skipper as she dashed to follow the cat, looking around at the abandoned island. Cicadas sang in the overgrown vegetation all around her, and she knew she'd see snakes winding through the grasses if she tried to look out for them. Sticking to the path for safety, Yoshiko followed the cat deeper into the flora until they got to an old folkmade stone mound with an inari shrine at the top. Even from here, she could see it was centuries old—an ancient style.

Yoshiko padded carefully up the stone steps, feeling anxious for some reason. Two old stone kitsuné guard statues sat proudly guarding the entrance to the shrine, one with mouth open, the other mouth shut, and ahead an old shrine. It was oddly well kept considering its age and that nobody lived here to look after it. Yoshiko bowed at the entrance before she passed the kitsuné statues, and then again as she stepped up in front of the shrine. A scraping of stone on stone set her heart leaping, and she turned in a flash, staring behind her, eyes wide, scanning for the source of the noise. There was no sign of life behind her. As she turned back towards the shrine, her eyes caught the kitsuné guards again. There was only one. The female was missing, but Yoshiko could have sworn she'd seen two as she passed. She stared for a moment at the back of the male kitsuné guard's head, expecting it to suddenly turn and look at her, setting her own heart blazing with a thumping fear at the thought.

'Idiot,' she muttered to herself, speaking aloud as if to break a heavy spell that lay over her, causing her to feel skittish. 'That's not going to happen.'

Then the noise of a straw brush sweeping on the stone right behind her and a soft voice welcoming her to the shrine really set her blood pumping through her body and her heart leaping from her chest, and Yoshiko spun around, mouth and eyes wide, to see a shrine maiden—dressed in traditional red *hakama* and white kimono, long, black hair trailing down her back—standing not a couple of feet ahead of her. Yoshiko hadn't even heard her move.

'How—' she started, then realised it must have been an odd thing to say. No-one expected her to be able to hear them walk close to her. Instead, she paused and asked the maiden to repeat herself as if she'd not heard what she'd said.

'Welcome to Tatsushima Shrine.'

Yoshiko paused to think. She'd not heard of this shrine, and there had been no mention of it in her mother's diary either. She looked more closely at the shrine maiden. She was very beautiful. Yoshiko couldn't place an age on her, but she must have been about Gora's age, and she had a small face and elegant posture. There was something unending about the depths of her dark eyes, almost magical, and her mouth turned up either end, much like a kitsuné fox. Yoshiko let out a small huff. Here she was again, imagining things.

The woman spoke again, voice soft and mellow, much like the echo of a shrine bell. 'Daughter of Kiyohimé, it has been many years since your kind visited us.'

Yoshiko thought back to her mother's report. It must have been years old.

'What is this place?' Yoshiko asked, not daring to bring her voice more than a whisper.

'An ancient place, marking the burial of a god.'

'A god?' Yoshiko couldn't believe it. She looked around. From every angle, this place looked like an overgrown wild island, left to nature. Whatever purpose her mother had had in visiting here, Yoshiko had no idea, and she was starting to doubt it had any use for her in discovering more about her heritage at all. She sighed and turned to do one final check of the place before she left, wondering what the politest way to dismiss herself from this mysterious shrine maiden's company was.

'I see you.' The shrine maiden's eyes, black as ink, bore into Yoshiko's, who paused midstep in confusion, the toes of her foot resting lightly on the stone ground. 'I have seen a great many of you, since the very first.'

The shrine maiden acknowledged Yoshiko's confusion.

'Your scales are progressed for your age.' There was no accusation or fear in the shrine maiden's voice. In fact, if anything, it was toneless.

'You know my history?' Yoshiko breathed, barely daring to move. *Who is this woman?*

The woman merely nodded, her black hair slipping lightly past her shoulders. Her red lips pursed into a small, tight-lipped smile, like the one the geisha mimicked. Yoshiko had a feeling this woman's was ancient, authentic, as if anyone else's painted-lip smile was merely a copy.

'Shrines host their god's spirits. The spirit of this shrine rests below.' The shrine maiden turned. 'Come.'

Yoshiko's heart shuddered. See the resting god? Blasphemy!

The shrine maiden turned and locked eyes on Yoshiko, and Yoshiko felt her cheeks heat up as if she'd been caught out with a thought. So, taking a breath and hoping retribution didn't follow, she followed the maiden round the back of the main shrine, discovering a small door rested in the earth. The shrine maiden lifted it deftly, and old stone steps led into the ground.

More underground passages? Yoshiko grumbled to herself, wondering how prevalent these were beneath her domain.

But this time, an ancient energy emanated from within, almost alighting Yoshiko's flight senses. It was a power beyond anything she'd felt before, more powerful than her mother had been. More powerful, she imagined, than how Gora had even described her to have been that time she transformed in Acrein.

The shrine maiden entered peacefully, as if she had no fear, and looked up at Yoshiko. 'If you want to know the truth, you must enter.'

It was always Yoshiko's curiosity that got the best of her. Gritting her teeth, she untied her katana and rested it at the entrance. It wouldn't fit down there anyway, and entering the resting place of a god with a weapon would be a sin. She climbed into the darkness, blinking rapidly and willing her enhanced vision take over.

But how is she seeing? Yoshiko wondered as she followed the shrine maiden through tunnels of black, wondering if the woman had just been here so many times she knew the route by heart. And impressive that would have been as, though the tunnel was short, it was winding and treacherous with steep stone steps, and Yoshiko was sure she'd have stumbled and cut her leg multiple times if she hadn't been able to see in the darkness. Finally, though, the steps ended and the tunnel bulged out into a giant cavern, simply circular and carved into plain stone. Nothing as great as Yoshiko had imagined for the so-called resting place of a god.

She didn't know what she was expecting. But when she saw a huge, hulking mass coiled in the centre of the cave, towering over her, her blood froze in place. She took a step back, and the shrine maiden turned and looked deeply into Yoshiko's eyes.

Too deeply. She can see in this blackness. Even better than me, I think. How?

'No need to worry. Your ancestor sleeps. Eternally.'

Ancestor?

Yoshiko looked more carefully. Then she saw the hulking mass was merely bone, and the following silence made her realise they were the only living things here, making her ears crave the sounds from above. It was too silent.

'Bones?' she whispered, wary that even her smallest voice sounded like an intrusion in this heavy silence.

The shrine maiden nodded, knowing Yoshiko could see.

'When a *kiyohimé's* spirit ages, it becomes dragon permanently. Unable to return to its human form. The more you use your powers, the quicker the curse locks you into it. Be careful.'

Yoshiko fidgeted, hearing her foot scrape on the stone floor. She'd heard that before.

'Worse is the power you will hold. There is a reason there are so few of your line to transform.'

Yoshiko's head snapped in the direction the shrine maiden was now speaking in. The woman had moved. 'What do you know?'

'I know it all.' The woman's mysterious voice was on the move, as if she was circling the dragon's bones. 'The heat, the energy, the power that is too great for a human's tiny body to hold. One day, whether you use the powers or not, you will transform, and it will be permanent. Many choose to die young, before the change. And while the fantasies show the power and impressive nature of a dragon's spirit and form to be glorious, the truth is far darker than that.' The shrine maiden stopped while Yoshiko took it in. 'A dragon ages slower than a human. Your life will be long, dragging out into the future's history, your loved ones and everyone you know dying long before you. Some go crazy, and in that craziness they seek out that which is closest to a memory of hatred they have, and rampage.'

Yoshiko's blood boiled at the memory of a rampage, and the heat of shame struck every inch of her body. But the maiden continued, unknowing or uncaring of Yoshiko's discomfort.

'When you do eventually die, promise me—right now in the presence of your ancestor—that you will remember this one thing: bury yourself as deep into the stone of a mountain as you can.'

'Why?' Yoshiko was shocked. She loved the sun, the sky, the fresh air and freedom. Burying herself in stone like this was the idea of a horror to her. She started to march towards the shrine maiden, ready to argue.

'Because the bones of a dragon holds the residue of their power. People will seek to use it.' The shrine maiden's voice was calm, untinted with emotion, and Yoshiko couldn't help but believe her. 'Long ago, magic existed. People blessed and cursed one another and used artefacts of power. They would grind the bones of creatures of magic to use in these artefacts, and in the use of potions and medicines, too. I have seen it before, and that is why your ancestor sleeps here, unknown. Lost.'

The woman's voice stopped, and a heavy silence fell once again. The looming dragon's corpse seemed to grow in the dark and the nothingness. Yoshiko felt trapped, as if the air was being pulled from her chest.

'The power to transform a human into a dragon spirit is massive. Think what others could do with that power.'

'I could not even imagine it,' Yoshiko whispered. And she couldn't. What would people even use bone for? What spells, enchantments? She couldn't think.

'Do not let them.'

The shrine maiden started walking again, and Yoshiko followed, head numb, heart heavy. Lost in her thoughts, she scrambled up the steps back to the daylight, eager to get back to the air and see the sky and get away from the suffocating earth.

Could she really bury herself in such a place? So deep down, so dark? She thought of where she had buried her mother, unable to give her a proper burning burial, and wondered if her mother's spirit felt the same at being buried.

At least she's not that far down, and has flowers and trees around her, she tried to reason with herself as she took the final steps, following the shrine maiden's quiet footsteps. *Maybe I should do what they all did too, and die early, while I'm still human. Maybe that's why no-one transformed: because they knew.* She frowned. *But why didn't Mother tell me?*

She shook her head, banishing the thoughts. Yoshiko imagined there were many things her mother was meant to tell her or had intended too, unable to for various reasons. Instead, she cried out gratefully as the shrine maiden hefted open the great, heavy trapdoor that led back out into the sun, and Yoshiko near danced out, taking great gulps of air and grinning at the sky. When she looked back at the shrine maiden, the small, tight-lipped smile was back, and she looked peaceful.

The woman walked about the small shrine, beckoning Yoshiko to follow still. 'I don't wish to scare you. It is my duty to look after your family. That is why I stand guard here, over your ancestor.' The shrine maiden bowed her head, and she moved to the bell, giving it a light nudge. It tolled lightly. 'I know you are here because of the change. It's true. Magic is returning, and the sky tore open. You saw correctly.'

'How did you know?'

'I can feel it.'

Yoshiko knit her eyebrows, but who was she to say something of such power couldn't exist? She thought back to the sky the day her mother died, and what Gora and Nubia told her the night she'd lost control in Acrein.

'Yes,' she said, thinking back, staring vaguely out to sea and the immense view from the top of the hill. 'The sky tore, and there were strange creatures lurking behind it. Now, creatures from stories of our past are being sighted once again, some causing harm to the people.' She turned to look back at the shrine maiden, who was standing unnaturally still, no expression crossing her face. Somehow, she seemed to expect Yoshiko to say this. After a silence, Yoshiko pushed again. 'How, and why, is magic coming back? What will it do? If harm will come to people again—'

The shrine maiden finally spoke, cutting in. 'Something, or someone, is bringing magic back. The two worlds had been separated for so long that creatures no longer passed between them, but with someone attempting to rejoin them and bring magic back to this world, the boundary is thinning.' The woman's face remained passive. 'That is what you saw.'

'Isn't it a good thing, for it to come back?' Yoshiko asked, thinking romantically of all the wonderful folk stories she'd heard in her lifetime and the wonder she'd felt at the creatures in them. 'Why are people being hurt? There can be good in magic coming back, but if it's bringing things that can harm us, too …'

'You mean, can humans live alongside them again?' the shrine maiden asked, as if she was separate from it all. 'Years ago, humans feared the *yōkai*. And you have just seen for yourself your future if you keep using your powers, and how you must hide from your fellow humans when you die. Can humanity really survive what will return?'

The wind stirred in the trees.

'*Yōkai.*' Yoshiko let her mind mull over the word and the creature sightings as she looked beyond the shrine at the bending branches.

She thought back to the bad spirits that also had been before. The world had been more dangerous, wild. Stories of people being killed or taken, and she thought of how people were disappearing again now, and it wasn't from being taken by other countries this time—she was making sure of that with the increased trade agreements and peace talks. Instead, people whispered of shadows, strange sounds, and ghostly figures. If this was because of the tearing sky, of magic returning, there would be more creature sightings, more disappearances.

Her people were in danger again, this time from creatures they couldn't fight. People of other countries, she felt she could handle. Hizen was joining together better. She was even building a better relationship with the domain to the west. But *yōkai* …

She thought back to the stories she heard when she was growing up. Good magic came with the stories of the *yōkai*. And her own powers, too, came from magic, though she'd grown up believing magic was dying. Now to hear it was returning … Yoshiko shook her head and knew she'd need to think on this a while. If it was happening here, it would be happening all over the world.

'Is there anything we can do?' *To survive, to live alongside the* yōkai. Yoshiko wasn't sure which she wanted to ask most.

The shrine maiden blinked, and a smile crossed her face. 'Humans thrived without *yōkai.* They were too weak to survive them and had no way of protecting themselves from the forces of the spirits. The years of dwindling magic helped humanity to spread out. How would humans fare if the *yōkai* returned?' A light wind caught the woman's long, straight black hair, but she didn't flinch.

Yoshiko nodded. That's what she'd meant. 'Then what will happen to humans if magic comes back?' she asked.

A harsh, warm wind rose, blowing in from nearby, and Yoshiko turned to see where it had come from, why it was so warm. When she turned back, the woman had gone, but when the wind died down, a voice called out softly, just like the bell she'd struck.

'That depends on which side you're on.'

24

Sea Battle

Yonemura stood at the helm, her hair pulled back with a *kanzashi* pin to keep it out of her way as she guided the ship from the shore and weaved it through the towering rocks surrounding the pirate isles. One of the reasons the islands were so well protected and a place the pirates sought as their own was this network of rocks. The pirates lived a life on the sea and learnt the dangerous labyrinth, but others, like slave-catchers or naval sailors, weren't so experienced. Tricky places like this were the ideal hiding place for pirate towns, but not ideal for Gora and his crew to make an urgent escape. Only Yonemura would be able to get them out of here. Her family had been fishing and trading folk on the coasts of Hié for generations and had been notoriously skilled at navigation. Yet even she grimaced as she heaved the helm suddenly to miss a rock, and Quinni yelled down from the crow's nest with warning from the starboard side.

'Nishimura, go help her.' Gora patted the young man on the shoulder. Yonemura's skill with his uncanny intuition created the best navigation team he knew, even amongst some of the pirate crews.

Nishimura nodded and padded off, tying his long hair back into a bun at the back of his head with a piece of twisted cord he kept around his wrist, and he and Yonemura took a side of the helm each to fight against the tide and the surging water upon rocks.

Quinni yelled down from the crow's nest again, and the crew grounded itself for a sudden turning.

'Pirates!'

A high-pitched voice cut through the calling of the crew, and Miyoshi ran up to Gora, pointing back towards the island. Gora followed where he pointed over the rocks towards the harbour. The pirates had left the beach and returned to their ships.

'They're actually following us?' Gora ran his hand through the back of his hair as he thought. He'd never expected the pirates to follow them by ship once they'd left the island. Surely their leaving the island would have been enough?

He stomped across the deck to the starboard quarter and peered back towards the island. They'd not got far, so it was easy to see the ships pulling out with a scurry of activity. One he easily recognised.

'Foy,' he growled. 'He's comin'.'

A small figure appeared beside him to look at the incoming ships too, and Gora looked down at Miyoshi, his dark hair neatly twisted into a single braid behind him, recently done, Gora thought, knowing how easily Miyoshi's hair got messy again. The boy looked up at Gora with wide, dark eyes, and then he looked away, Gora recognising the look of guilt crossing the young lad's face. Gora frowned and followed the young boy's gaze to Tomioka, and both grown-ups' eyes met. Tomioka nodded gravely, and Gora sighed.

'Miyoshi, go below and relay the powder to the team below. Take care.' Gora turned on his heels, not even waiting to see the boy run down the steps. He'd have to grow up and listen to orders without being watched, and Gora would have to make certain that happened more. He'd have to get stricter with the lad. He caught up with Tomioka. 'I need you helpin' guide the crew. You get your group manning the cannons and the balance. Yūki's down there too. Look after him, as always.' Gora looked into the distance back towards the island for a moment before meeting the man's dark eyes again. 'Ready the stern chasers.' He clasped his hand on the man's shoulder and the two nodded at one another before Tomioka padded across the deck, calling in his group. Then he, Kyo, Taro, and Sakai disappeared below to man the cannons.

From here, it was a race to see who could arm and fire their chaser cannons first: Tomioka and his crew, or the pirates.

Gora looked about to find the fighters. He'd need Daiki, Ikeda, Simrita, Eshnaa, and Rijul defending the crew and the ship, leading the attack if needed. Shingo and Moori would prepare to fire the figurehead's fire at Foy, the only way to bring down the devil. The man had survived the worst battles at sea, but dragon fire would be his downfall.

'Get the figurehead set up and get Moori using guns in the meantime. Look after her,' Gora said gruffly, keeping an eye on the ships behind.

They were already catching up. He called up to Jelani and Quinni up in the shrouds to tighten the main sail and focus on helping sail. Gora wished he could have had them help fighting. If it came down to a battle, they'd be invaluable, but they were also some of the most skilled at keeping the ship sailing, and he'd need them up there, out of harm's way, keeping the ship ahead, helping the other crew.

Lastly, Gora searched the ship for Satou and Kimura. The young chef wouldn't be much good in a fight, and Satou had too kind a heart. But they were both better than anyone on this ship at taking care of the others, and were the crew's main healers. Gora would need them somewhere they could be safe but also be ready to aid anyone with injuries. He stomped down to the galley to find Kimura rushing about and grumbling to himself.

'Oy, stop moaning about the supplies and listen for a moment,' Gora sighed as he swung the door shut behind him. 'We got bigger things to worry about. I need you and Satou ready on aid. Know where he'll be?'

Kimura leaned against the table and brushed his wavy fringe from his face, looking at Gora almost absentmindedly for a moment. 'Satou? If he's not up on deck, he'll be fixing something in the men's cabin. He mentioned something about it earlier.'

'Can you get him and make plans to be ready when needed?'

Before Kimura could respond, Rijul crashed into the room, swinging the door open widely and nearly hitting Gora with it. His eyes wide and face panicked, he took a breath before crying out, 'Captain! Come to the deck.'

Gora met Kimura's gaze one more time, nodding as the young man bowed his head in acknowledgement to him, and then followed Rijul back onto the deck. A chaotic scene of people running about met him, and Rijul pointed aftward, where Gora didn't need a spyglass to see the pirate ships catching up.

'Five? That's a bit much,' Gora groaned in Traders', rubbing his hair.

'They really want us dead for stepping on their island.' Rijul crashed his fist down onto the gunwale.

Gora looked at the young Ishillian beside him, arms folded across his chest and thick, dark brows furrowed. 'Aye, you're right.' Gora strode aftward to look closer. His crew watched. He'd changed his clothing since Gora had gone downstairs and was now wearing his full fighting gear. Gora pointed ahead. 'Well, *that's* the one we want. It's the one that, no matter what, we need to destroy. Just like Frewin's. The others, let's do our best. But Foy's high up in that circle or whatever. I'll explain more later. If he's allowed to leave here free, he'll go tell the queen, and we'll have bigger problems to worry about.'

There was a muffled acknowledgement, and Gora turned to face a deck full of pale, closed faces, some staring at him, others staring at the following ships.

'Aye, just do what you can to leave this place. We'll do the rest from there.'

Gora didn't blame the crew for looking worried. After their last scrape with pirates, many were injured, and that had been after fighting only one ship. But, last time, the team were still not prepared to fight. This time, they'd been training longer, and even the three Ishillian fighters had given the crew extra training. Gora had ensured those who were slightly weaker at fighting had gone below to fire the cannons instead, and those above were stronger. That should help. And even then, the goal was to do this without having pirates on deck. Not that they'd have much choice in that. Gora knew if the pirates had a chance to board, they would, and he wouldn't be able to do much to stop them. Until then, his crew's goal was to keep the pirates away, try to gun down Foy, and get away.

Yonemura called out as they passed the last giant rock from the island and hit open sea. Gora's heart both soared and lurched. They'd managed to get free of the rocks and would be able to sail more smoothly, but so would the pirates, and he knew they'd catch up.

'Full sails!' he called, looking above at Quinni and Jelani. 'We can't let them close in.'

They nodded and clambered off to adjust the sails, calling out to one another in Qeclan. Immediately, Gora strode again over the deck, this time towards Yonemura and Nishimura at the helm.

'We can't let them board. Can I leave you both to handle that?'

Yonemura looked warily behind at the ships closing in. Then she frowned and looked at Nishimura.

'We'll do our best. Have the defence team backing us up there.'

Gora nodded, and as if he knew he was soon to be summoned, Daiki soon ran up to them.

'Ready and armed, but what to do of projectiles for now? Will Moori come and take gun while she's not firing from the figurehead?'

The four watched Moori and Shingo readying their greatest weapon. They'd have one chance to fire it today. It took too long to ready otherwise, and it would need to be used on Foy. Gora couldn't chance it being used on anyone else. Foy knew too much about whatever was going on, and now he knew Gora was after him. If he got away alive today, he'd warn the pirate queen and the whole lot of them under her lead. Then they'd stand no chance in their mission. For his plans to work from here even vaguely, Gora needed them to not be aware—to sneak about unknown.

No, if Foy was life alive, their mission would fail.

Even if they managed to kill him, there was so much ahead and at stake that Gora wasn't even sure if they could achieve their mission now with just one ship. This had become so much bigger than he imagined. It wasn't just a few ships run by a few captains going about and stealing the children. It was a larger, planned organisation led by someone else who was controlling the pirates.

Clearly, they had a reason for doing it, and Gora knew he'd never be ready to find out why.

'Shingo can finish setting up from here. We need Moori now. Daiki, ready what Moori needs. Are Ikeda and the Ishillians on the guns, too?'

Daiki nodded. 'They're all set. They're watching now for which way they'll be needed. Cannons would do a better job for now. I want the guns to be the last resort. How are the team downstairs? Is Tomioka ready?'

Gora met Daiki's eyes for a moment and paused, thinking. The time since he'd sent them down should have been enough to ready. He'd have to send a runner with a message to fire the stern chasers. He knew to expect a bow chase attack at any moment, and they couldn't have it hit.

A rumble below interrupted his thoughts, and then the ship lurched as a deafening boom of exploding gunfire rang in his ears. Gora winced at the noise and instantly turned to see what had happened.

'One of ours?' Yonemura murmured, as if knowing but needing to be reassured, her face showing a hint of concern.

'Aye.' Gora grinned. 'Looks like Tomioka read our minds!' He clapped his hands together. 'See, Daiki? We've got a chance. We fired first.'

Tomioka won the race.

'Are you saying that for your benefit or for mine?' Daiki grinned back.

Gora laughed. 'Perhaps more for my own.' He clapped a hand on Daiki's shoulder.

Gora's smile faded as Daiki ran off to continue preparing his fighting team, and Gora bowed to Yonemura and Nishimura to go and call on Moori. As he walked on the deck, he knew that shot had signalled truly the start of the battle.

First shot's fired. It begins now. They won't wait long to fire back.

He didn't even think about whether that first one had hit.

'Shingo!' Gora hailed the older man who was growing the flame in the opening on the figurehead's fire control. Moori was standing carefully behind him, holding open the little metal door for the white flame to feed safely.

From there, the flames would spread throughout the contraption, through hard metalworks and up towards the figurehead. Once it was ready to fire, the flames would shoot up and out. Both looked uncertainly back at Gora, and it was obvious from their faces that he'd interrupted them in the zone.

'Shingo, can you do the rest alone from here?'

The older man nodded, his face still serious. 'You need Moori elsewhere?'

'Aye, on the guns. If those ships get closer, she's our best shot. We won't need her firing the figurehead for a while, until we can at least clear enough of this mess up that we can swing around to clearly burn Foy.'

Shingo took a deep breath and stood up, drawing the flaming stick away from the hatch. Moori closed it up, and both looked at one another and bowed their heads lightly before meeting Gora's eyes again.

'Aye, captain,' Moori said, her usually playful and certain demeanour wavering.

Gora couldn't blame her. They were against five ships.

'We trust ya, lass.' Gora instinctively reached out and rested a hand on her head, just like he always did with Yoshiko, and the girl's face flooded with confusion. 'Ahh, sorry, old habit.' He grinned, but she seemed like she'd relaxed a bit. 'Come now, let's go see Daiki.'

The ship lurched again with another shot as the stern chasers from below fired again. Gora's heart lurched, too, each time these damned cannons fired. And this time, his heart nearly lurched out of his body as he realised their shot had a response as a second shot answered from behind, and an iron ball whistled into the ocean just beside them, sending up towering sprays of water.

They took longer to fire than I thought. Tomioka's first shot freak them out?

But he had one thing to be happy about. At least Tomioka's second cannonball had hit, if the distant crunching sound was anything to judge by.

* * *

The bastards caught up. Gora knew they would. It had only ever been a matter of time. His only consolation was that one ship was down and another was practically limping, so they'd only have three to fully deal with. He prayed to the spirits that the fourth would finally piss off back to the island for repairs and realise it wasn't worth losing his entire ship just to catch one ship already chased by three others.

But he knew that wasn't the problem here. It was the pride and the glory: the chance that it could be them who caught a ship that had sneaked into their turf, and if they got shot down during, then they'd at least be able to have the glory of going down in a fight.

He didn't understand that side of pirates. For Gora, getting the ship to safety to be fixed and able to try another day was what mattered.

He shrugged and ducked down into the belly of *Sea Guardian*, running to the cannon deck.

'Tomioka,' he bellowed, skidding around the corner and locking eyes with Taro, who looked weary and wary.

The crew down here were light. Too light to man all cannons. Gora gulped as he stopped to watch them for a moment. Setting one up on the stern chasers before running to fire another, before running back to fire the stern chaser and then back to set up another cannon again on the port side. It looked exhausting just to watch, and by the looks of it, they'd now set up a break rotation.

Good job, Tomioka. As always. Lookin' after the crew.

Taro, on first break rotation, watched Gora, and when Gora was about to feel uneasy with too much watching, the older man padded forward and called Tomioka.

'Want to swap rotation and take a break for a moment? Looks like Captain wants to speak with you.'

Tomioka wiped his forehead on his sleeve and looked across at Gora before wiping his hands on his slacks. He padded over to

Gora, patting Miyoshi briefly on the shoulder as the boy entered the cannon deck with a new lot of powder, looking just as exhausted but determined like the rest. Both men nodded at Miyoshi as he disappeared again to run for the next round.

'Makes a good little powder monkey, doesn't he?' Gora noted.

Tomioka frowned. 'Aye, but it's a dangerous job.'

Gora sighed and ran a hand through his hair. 'Ain't it all …' Then he paused, watching a darkness slide over the ship, feeling his heart darken with it. 'The sea scum's gettin' pretty close.' Gora frowned, crossing his arms and watching the shadow of a hull beside the gun hatches.

Beside him, Tomioka nodded and re-rolled up his sleeves. 'Easier to aim at, though.'

He called out for his team to fire, and with such close aim, they couldn't miss. The thundering roar of flame powder exploding a heavy iron ball right through the hull was second only to the sound of the cracking, splintering ship. The ship beside them lurched, and even from here, looking through the cannon hatches, it was easy for Gora to see the ship fall behind as Yonemura, Nishimura, Jelani, and Quinni kept the ship sailing straight.

'Finally, the limping ship's down. Bastards better go back, now.'

Tomioka looked at him, an eyebrow raised. Gora gestured with his head to the disappearing hull.

'They made things worse for themselves by sending so many ships. Two or three would've been more effective. They're tripping over each other. They can't fire freely for shooting at each other, and now that one's down, he's in the way for another to get in position. They'll have to go around him.' Gora sighed and rubbed his stubbled cheek. 'Not that it's a problem for us.'

'But wouldn't they just shoot each other? I've never thought of pirates as being conscientious of one another. Aren't they all separate from one another?' Tomioka asked as he watched his crew run and fire the stern chasers again. Both men flinched at the noise.

'Depends who else you're sailing with. No-one will want to hit Foy. And if there's another high-level captain up there, too, they'll also not want to hit them.' Gora paused as everyone below looked back at him, confused, and even those preparing the cannons paused. 'Pirating is very hierarchical. If you're a notorious, high-level pirate, everyone's scared of you. If anyone here other than us even so much as fires an iron ball within the water near Foy, they know he'd destroy them. Even us, he's trying to destroy anyway. He's that kind of man.'

He thought for a moment.

'Like I said, they're tripping over each other.'

A shout went out above deck, and a chill ran down Gora's spine. He knew what that meant. He looked to Tomioka, who nodded and padded away, calling out, to help the others in the cannon deck fire on the starboard side hastily. This time, a pirate ship had succeeded and was close enough to board.

Gora sprinted up the steps towards the chaos of guns firing and shouting from both sides, watching open-mouthed as pirates stood on the side of their ship, ropes at the ready to swing over and board. Gora's ship lurched as Yonemura tried to pull their ship away—to widen the gap so pirates couldn't catch up. Rijul and Moori fired, both hitting their marks. Ikeda was ducked behind the gunwale, reloading, and Simrita ran down the deck, grimacing as she ducked against gunfire, to shoot at any pirate ready to take the stern side.

'What shit is this?' Gora groaned to himself, eyes wide.

Nishimura helped Yonemura pull the helm, and the *Sea Guardian* lurched away just as a pirate swung over, leaving them helpless and dropping into the ocean below.

'Pull away!' Gora yelled, waving a hand at the others, knowing they were too close to avoid cannon fire here. They had to get where it would be difficult to aim.

'It looks like they're focusing on boarding.' Shingo padded up beside Gora, frowning, arms crossed at his chest.

'Get Daiki and the team firing grapeshot,' Gora said, gesturing to the cannons on deck. 'Save the shotguns for next.'

Shingo nodded and hailed Daiki, both men meeting. Gora crossed the deck, looking for openings to pull away.

There has to be a way, he thought, looking out over the open sea. They'd been freed of the labyrinth of rocks, so they had a whole sea to sail in. Surely there was a way to get away.

'Yonemura!' he called. 'Take us sharp starboard before another ship closes in.'

If they could sail away at an angle, they would be less of a target to the pirates but have the full target for Tomioka and his team below to fire the stern chase again.

Gora looked behind as the ship turned, watching the three ships following them, Foy's right in the centre.

'What's the old sea devil doing?' Gora frowned, realising Foy hadn't been fighting or putting up too much of a chase compared with the previous two. Was he letting others do the hard work and then fall, ready to swoop in and get the win? Gora shrugged. It sounded like something Foy would do.

A ship closed in on the port side, no matter how much Yonemura and Nishimura tried to wrangle free. Rijul and Simrita fired grapeshot from the cannon on deck, and Gora could hear crew crying out on the pirate deck as they got hit with shrapnel. Ikeda, Moori, and Eshnaa prepared to fire shots at whoever tried to swing over, once again standing on the edge of the ship to board Gora's ship. But this time, even with the young ones shooting at them, the number of pirates was too many, and Gora's ship was boarded.

He grimaced, pulling out his handgun and one of his swords. 'Don't mind!' he yelled. 'Get ready, now!'

His disheartened crew looked at Gora for a moment before they, too, set their faces again in determination. And before Gora could even lay his eyes back on the first boarded pirate and step forward, Ikeda had sprinted across the deck, drawn his katana, and sliced upwards across the man's front.

The pirate fell.

Ikeda, sword held low by his side, turned to face Gora, face and eyes serious as always and fringe slightly covering his face. He was in his element now. Gora let out a breath as a chuckle.

The young man looked once more to the other pirates swinging over, raising his sword to the ready out in front of him. Beside him, Daiki prepared his blade, too.

Gora's ears rang near constantly now with the sound of Moori firing shot after shot, aided by the grape rounds from the on-deck cannon being fired by Rijul and Simrita. But still, pirates boarded, and the two Hién samurai guards rushed to deal with those themselves, their sharp steel meeting anyone who dared step on deck.

Gora huffed, stepping forward, gun pointing ahead and blade out, ready to join his crew. He took one final look behind, at Foy still hanging back.

What is he doin'? Gora wondered, not surprised if Foy was waiting for Gora to be overwhelmed and pinned in place by the other two ships before firing on all three.

In fact, looking again, he was almost sure that's what Foy really would do.

Gora grimaced and pulled his sword free from a pirate's stomach, cutting again through the man's arms before he could think about committing the final, dying action of killing Gora too.

Gora lunged back towards the helm, kicking another pirate off their path and firing his handgun. It hit, but the pirate was tough and didn't fall. Instead, they continued hobbling ahead, aiming for Yonemura at the helm.

Gore went ahead once again, this time bringing his sword down and across the man's chest. He had to keep his crew safe at all costs, especially those sailing the ship right now who couldn't join the fight to defend themselves. Yonemura and Nishimura needed the space and the protection to steer, and Gora yelled out at the nearest crew member to come help him. Rijul answered, and the two defended the two steering the ship, still trying to free them from the grasps of the pirates.

'If we can get away, we at least don't have to worry about more boarders and can focus on those we have,' Yonemura growled when Gora next got close.

Gora agreed and left her to it, more focused on ensuring no pirate managed to get past he and Rijul to attack her or Nishimura. 'I'll leave it to you,' he answered. Then he looked up at Jelani and Quinni in the rafters, making sure they were safe. The two men were looking at something, and Gora followed their gazes. A couple of pirates were climbing in the shrouds, eyes eagerly pinned on the crew above.

'Eshnaa! Ahead!' Gora roared, unable to move and leave those at the helm, but needing Jelani and Quinni looked after too.

The Ishillian woman immediately caught his eye and then followed where he was pointing, and she ran across the deck.

A blade flew past and hit a pirate across his body, lodging itself in his chest. A circular throwing blade: a *chakram*. Both Gora and Eshnaa looked back at Simrita, who grinned at them.

Eshnaa laughed and pulled the *chakram* from the man's chest, putting the circular blade on her own wrist for later.

As the battle wore on, Gora tired. Satou and Kimura had come up from below, rushing across to bind the wound of an injured Rijul, and joined the fray to help defend their team.

Satou's fighting had improved greatly, more and more skilled as they go, using his sharp tools well, but he was more of a doctor and carpenter, so he and Kimura found more creative ways to fight. Satou's axe and saw found themselves buried in unfortunate pirates, and Kimura looked like he was having fun with kitchen knives.

'You'd better clean those well when you're done,' Gora overheard Satou grumble to the chef, who was highly focused for once. The chef flashed a charming grin at the craftsman.

'Nothing wrong with a bit of extra iron! Hard to keep the crew high enough on iron, though you'd be the one to know all about that, with all your nails.'

Satou frowned and looked pale, but Gora wondered whether that had more to do with the fact he'd just smashed an old-looking, toothless pirate in the face with a huge carpentry hammer. He heard Kimura chuckle and tease the young craftsman.

'Glad I'm not a nail! Though, I wouldn't mind being hammered by you.' The young flirt grinned at the carpenter, who glanced back with uncertainty, flushing slightly.

'Is this really the time? We're surrounded by people who want to kill us.'

'Want me to say it again when we're in private?'

Gora shook his head and stormed off, diving into the thick of the fight again, keeping an eye on Foy's ship still hovering in the distance. He didn't like whatever was going on there. It didn't bode well.

Daiki, standing near the top of the stairs that led down to the lower decks and stopping anyone who tried to go down, looked like he was reaching exhaustion. Gora barged over to join him, thrusting his blade through the back of a pink-skinned man with a smaller build who was trying to creep up on Daiki from the side. As the man fell, Daiki looked over at Gora, and the two men met each other's eyes.

'Bit much, this, isn't it?' Gora stretched out his arms and sighed, looking around again. Then he nodded to the area Daiki where was standing. 'Good job protecting the steps. Wouldn't want any pirate down there. Especially to get the others on the cannon deck.'

Daiki nodded back. 'I haven't heard a cannon in a while. Are they well?'

Gora shrugged. 'I'd have to go see. We're a bit close, though. If we fired at any ship now, it'd blow back on us, too. And if it sank, it could tangle and take us down too or tumble over and fall on top. Tomioka is probably being cautious and waiting until we're at a safer distance.' Then Gora looked over at Yonemura and Nishimura, and then up and Jelani and Quinni in the masts. The ship wasn't going anywhere very fast. Their attempt to pull away wasn't working—the other ships were just keeping up, too.

Then Gora had an idea. 'If we shake those two ships, we'll just be left to fight whoever is already boarded. Then we can shoot at the other ships again and then turn to fire the gift.'

Daiki looked at him uncertainly after slashing his blade across the front of a pirate running up to sneak past him and down the steps, stabbing through him to be certain he fell. 'Can we get away, though? Yonemura looks like she's struggling.'

'We could do the opposite. Drop anchor and stop moving, swing her around. If we can't outrun them, we can get behind them. Not ideal. But they might not expect it.'

Gora grinned to himself. It was always worth trying. He patted Daiki on the shoulder and then ran off towards Yonemura to tell her and Nishimura his plan. Rijul was still ensuring the two were protected, and Gora was pleased to see him fighting well. The Ishillian, donned in his red tunic and darker brown, wide-legged slacks, and brown boots with Ishillian leather protection pulled over, had a frown on his face, and his thick, dark eyebrows pinched low on his face. He lunged past Nishimura, cutting with his *talwar* in one hand and then leaping ahead again to finish off a pirate with his *katar* knife in his other hand, kicking the pirate out of the way as he fell so his body didn't get in the way of Rijul defending from whoever came next.

'Nice one, Rijul.' Gora managed a grin then turned to Yonemura as Rijul darted off again to block another enemy. Through the chaos and noise of the fight, Gora tried to quietly pass on his idea to the two at the helm, both leaning in to listen to him.

Yonemura and Nishimura looked to one another for a moment and then looked around, trying to see if it was doable with the two ships either side of them and Foy's behind. But, like Gora, they noticed Foy's was hanging quite far back, and though they frowned at the realisation, both agreed it could work.

'Just pass on the news to Jelani and the other crew. We will need them to handle the speed. We can turn the ship,' Yonemura answered, returning to the helm and nudging it to avoid crashing into the ship to their port side.

Gora nodded and left immediately, barging into a pirate to shove him out of the way and then rushing to the shrouds, cutting his blade through the back of someone racing at Moori, who was changing guns. She'd be needed at the figurehead soon, and Gora would tell her as he passed back this way. For now, he clambered up the shrouds, realising it had been a while since he had done so, and he felt exposed to gunshots in this situation. He'd have to note that for when he sent his crew up here in battle.

'Jelani!' he called over the noise towards the two men, Quinni up in the crow's nest looking towards Foy, and Jelani standing below, looking at Gora. Jelani navigated his way across the beam towards Gora, crouching to listen to Gora's idea.

He nodded, and then he added his own information. 'Quinni's been watching that third ship, the one with the captain you're aiming for,' he said, gesturing up at Quinni, who still watched Foy's ship. 'Says they're sailing away.'

'What?' Gora squinted over to where he'd last seen Foy and realised he wasn't there. Just in the time Gora had been fighting off the sea slimes that had stolen onto his deck, the old devil had up and sailed off. He scanned the waves and looked to where both Jelani and Quinni were now pointing, and Gora frowned. 'We need to get after him. He's the one they want. These others can go to the depths in their own time as far as I care. I need you and Quinni to help Yonemura drop anchor, slide behind these two, and then we can sail around them to Foy.'

Jelani agreed, and Gora returned to the deck, stopping for a moment to shoot at a pirate climbing the shrouds. He was pleased with his crew. They were competent, knowledgeable, and worked well together. And no sooner were his feet touching back down on the deck than he felt the ship slow, and Jelani and Quinni were hastily tying down the sails then rushing back down the shrouds to the main deck to push the crank and drop the anchor.

The ship lurched, and a murmur went out on the deck, everyone, including Gora's crew, looking around. The two ships beside them paced on, pushing slowly ahead. A cry went out on either side to stop the ships, but Gora knew in the time it would take them to prepare to stop, his crew would have just enough time for a sharp turn to get out of their way and fire.

Gora stared in awe at the speed of Jelani and Quinni as they raced back across the deck and up the shrouds to pull the ropes for the sails, allowing Yonemura and Nishimura to turn the ship sharply enough as soon as the ships either side of them had sailed ahead. Gora held his breath and then cut at an anxious pirate on a frenzy, realising he couldn't get back to his ship. Gora kicked him over the gunwale, trying to ignore the scream.

'Hold fast!' Gora bellowed, bracing himself, digging into his stance, and holding on to the railing. 'Brace yourself.'

The stern side of the portside ship sailed past them, and Yonemura and Nishimura turned the helm wide and swung the ship around. The ship lurched, and for a moment Gora worried it might capsize. It didn't, and he swallowed back down his heart as he continued to hold on.

No sooner had they turned did a thundering boom sound from below, and Gora let out a victorious cry as Tomioka read the situation and readied the cannons to fire. The first iron ball skimmed the ship, slicing just a little through the wood before crashing into the sea beside it. The second hit its mark and crashed through the hull, the splintering echoing in the air.

Eshnaa and Simrita ran down the ship, disposing of any remaining pirates in their path. In the time Gora watched, Simrita slid a *chakram* blade from her arm and launched it across at a pirate standing near the railing wondering how to get back to his ship. Her aim was true, and his head slid from his shoulders and into the sea, his body slumping onto the deck and oozing blood. Simrita rushed over and immediately heaved the body over the edge, too. Eshnaa, in the meantime, her red-and-green embroidered silks flapping in the ocean wind as she ran, leapt up and grabbed the shrouds with one hand and sliced down onto a pirate with the *talwar* in her other, launching her body over his futile attack and cutting through his shoulder. She dropped herself back onto the deck behind him and pivoted back to turn and slice across his back before immediately dashing after another.

Ikeda wasn't far behind them, picking off those left on the stern side, slashing his katana upwards through a pirate's stomach and then turning and stepping to bring his katana back down through the head and face of another, shouldering him out of the way and leaping to parry and cut through a third. His eyes regularly darted back towards the steps to below deck to make sure Daiki was well, and then he returned to his own situation, helping rid the entire ship from their boarded enemies.

Gora stomped across the deck as Yonemura turned to go around the ship they'd just blown a hole into, shielding themselves from the second ship. Now, their concern was Foy, who was sailing away. Gora felt a burning rage flush through him, wishing he had powers like Yoshiko and could turn into a dragon to fly after the old sea devil and burn him and his ship till they were dust floating on the waves.

'After that ship,' he growled.

25

Distant Focus

Gora ground his teeth as he watched Foy and the *Devil's Corsair* sail towards the horizon. The old sea slug had used the distraction of Gora's ship fighting the others to make his escape, and now Foy'd be going back to the pirate queen and reporting all he knew about Gora's mission to her and the other pirate sea slugs. He took a deep breath of the smoke-filled air to try to calm himself. It was no use.

Yonemura was already guiding his ship around the others, but Gora could already see that second, unhit ship following suit and turning to sail after Foy. With their smaller, lighter ship, the pirate crew pulled ahead. Gora grimaced more. Now he was chasing two pirate ships, and if this one kept ahead, it would get in the way of their plan and block the firing range of the figurehead.

'Moori, ready to fire the figurehead,' Gora yelled, preparing himself to think of a way to ensure it hit Foy. If he had to fire at both Foy and that other ship in one go, so be it.

The young girl laid down the guns and ran over the deck towards the bow platform, up towards the figurehead where Shingo waited. The mechanism was ready, and they both worked together to prepare it to fire whenever Yonemura was able to bring their ship closer. But there was quite a gap to cover, with Foy taking plenty of time in the distraction to sail onwards.

Gora ran his hand across his stubbled jawline, trying to think. It was so much easier when he was crew and not in charge—it wasn't his decisions impacting things then. Gora nodded to Shingo, who was standing with Moori, both looking at him. Moori's hands were hovering over the safety catches, ready to take them off to be able to fire when needed. Gora gestured that she pause for now, and he strode over to Yonemura and Nishimura at the helm, looking up at the sails.

We're only going to have a small opening. Gora grit his teeth and frowned as Foy's ship drew closer. *If we don't catch up now, we'll have no chance.*

All the while, the rest of the crew hurriedly tossed the dead or injured pirate enemies from the deck and over into the sea, their ship finally free of their boarders. Grime spatted their deck, and Gora knew he'd have to order an intense clean-up before that stained. Ahead, he saw Satou pacing, already noting the people he'd need to tend to and the ship he'd need to fix. The young man ran a strong, tanned hand through his black hair and ruffled it slightly as he thought, eyes staring, focused, as he figured out what exactly he'd need to do to fix the ship.

Yonemura called over that she'd locked onto the angle to chase Foy and was gaining on him, and that the second ship ahead, too, was in range. Gora sent Daiki down to the cannon deck to get Tomioka ready to fire the bow chasers at the second ship. That one had to be out of the way for their plan to work, but it didn't look like they were going to be.

Now he strode back to the bow of the ship, looking over the waves towards Foy's ship as the distance decreased. He thanked the spirits back in the forest shrine that Quinni had spotted them when he had. If they'd waited much longer, there'd have been no way they could try to catch up with Foy. As it happened, over this short distance, Gora's powerful ship had the advantage in a chase, and they were soon catching up and within range, *Sea Guardian* cutting through the sea that slid past them with a roar.

Gora grinned as Yonemura took them in at such an angle that even that second ship catching up to Foy didn't matter. It didn't matter that that second captain was trying to take his ship next to Foy's for them to sail away into the sunset together. It wouldn't happen. Gora would burn Foy down and have Tomioka strike down the other.

Gora strode towards the bow to guide Moori. She was set up and had her arms in place on the metal mechanism to pull the levers and fire, and Shingo was standing beside her. They both greeted him as Gora reached them, Shingo bowing his head and Moori humming a response. She was focusing, and as she peered her eye through the sight, Gora knew not to speak or disturb her. Instead, he watched, and he watched Foy's ship get closer, and as if he could even see Foy on the ship, his heart rate spiked, and he worried something would go wrong. That the devil would somehow survive even this.

Moori frowned, squinting her eyes in the sight and waiting, muttering to herself.

Gora met Shingo's gaze, and both men waited with bated breath for the young girl to fire.

From the corner of his eye, he saw Moori's fingers drum lightly on the lever, waiting for her moment to come. Foy would soon be in range.

Yonemura held fast the helm. It was her steering that helped aim the weapon, and she knew it was a combination of her and Moori's coordination and aim that would solve this for them all, so Gora knew she'd be fully focused now, eyes locked onto Foy's ship as they closed in on them. Nishimura was standing beside her, ready if called upon, twisting his long hair up into a half bun in his own way of focusing as he, too, watched the old pirate's ship come within range.

Gora tilted his head, knowing the attack would work better if they could get even closer, right up and personal so the figurehead could spit fire over the whole ship, but even this distance would do. If the back of the ship caught, the heat of the dragon fire would spread quickly, and the crew wouldn't be able to put it out. They just had to be close enough for it to reach.

Moori's short hair lifted in the breeze, distracting Gora for a moment. It was only at times like this that she focused for long, but now, she was so still she was unmoving, save for her hair in the wind and her fingers measuring out her patience.

'Looks like they're both trying to sail away. Wondered why that other ship wasn't firing anymore. Didn't want to risk us firing back if they missed,' Gora muttered to himself, thinking out loud as he watched the second ship catch up to Foy's, dropping in beside it. He shrugged. Not that it mattered now. As long as it didn't get in the way of Moori firing at Foy.

Yonemura pulled their ship ever closer, and Gora saw Moori press her face against the sights once more, assessing the distance. Her fingers clenched around the levers, and she pulled her lips tight to focus. They were in range. She squeezed her fingers in towards her palms, and a loud whirring reverberated from the belly of the ship all up the bow towards the figurehead. Here, so close, it was all Gora could hear, and the sound of loud pulsing and buzzing, just like that night in Acrein when Yoshiko had first transformed in a heat of anger and despair and burned half of the upper town and the palace, filled Gora's ears once more. This sound, he was starting to recognise. The sound of fire so hot it pulsed and throbbed in the air, sending out loud waves that blocked all else.

It was as if the ship was growling.

Gora watched the figurehead's hands pull free from her kimono sleeves, and they latched together in a ball, the pipe of the metal passageway that guided the dragon fire resting between them. The pulsing buzz of sound waves grew louder, and a ball of light appeared in the figurehead's hands. And as if the ship roared while launching a fire breath attack, a beam of pale yellow-white flames spat forth and leapt through the air like light trailing a shooting star in the darkness above over a calm night sea. Gora felt his heart roar with it.

The beam of flame arched towards the back of Foy's ship, and Gora could almost imagine that old pirate racing to the stern side of his ship, hands on the gunwale as he looked in surprise and anger at the incoming attack. Not much surprised Foy, but Gora knew this would. A ship—the figurehead, no less—attacking with a beam of fire. Even the old devil wouldn't expect that from him.

Gora let out a roar of laughter, and he let his heart soar just for a moment as he wondered what the old man would be thinking.

''S what you get for stealing kids, you sick shit,' he dared say out loud, the reverberating air still swallowing his words the minute they left his lips, but his heart felt better for saying them.

Unable to take his eyes off the beam of light launching at Foy's ship, he watched the flames latch onto the *Devil's Corsair*, and the hull lit up.

A smile dared tug at Gora's lips. Just at the corners. He couldn't celebrate yet, not until he was sure they'd succeeded. Gora tore his eyes away from Foy's ship just for a moment to look around at his crew and saw them all staring with him, some leaning over the railings on the sides of the ship, others standing where they were a moment ago, paused in the half-finished task, all mouths wide open and all eyes staring. Gora looked back too, and he saw the flames grow, eating up the lines and the back sails and seeping across the *Devil's Corsair*'s hull.

The reverberating of his own ship stopped, and the comet of dragon fire stopped with it. The figurehead had done her role.

Beside Gora, Moori and Shingo moved slightly as they both woke from their stupor from staring too at the attack, and now quickly returned the safety latches and shut the gift down before they drained the ship of the last of the dragon fire. Once that was done, they returned their gaze to staring at Foy's ship.

Gora didn't mind his crew's lack of action right now. It was a momentous event to watch. If they could do this, once Foy's ship was down, they could keep going with their goal, getting ever closer.

Amongst the increasing brightness of the flaming ship in the distance, Gora squinted at small figures moving. Rowing boats dropped from Foy's ship, distant figures of people in them. In a hurry, people were diving from the ship or dropping in the row boats, all aiming for one thing: the second ship.

Gora's heart paused. He watched teams of Foy's crew jumping ship, all making their way to the other ship. One rowboat caught aflame before it could escape, its line cutting and dropping like a flaming rock to the ocean below. In his wildest dreams, Gora hoped it had been the one with Foy on it, but he knew Foy would have been on the first. He wouldn't have stayed back with his ship. He was too vain for that. The flames took Foy's ship quickly, but not quickly enough to take the crew with it.

Gora's heart dropped. He tore his eyes from the escaping crew to look at Yonemura. She must have seen him turn, as she, too, tore her eyes away and met his gaze. Not knowing what else to do, he shook his head. She nodded in response and gripped the helm, showing she was ready.

And just like that, the spell of focus and anticipation that held his crew in a stupor cut, and they all looked at him, wondering what came next.

'Bastard got away,' Gora growled, his voice loud in the silence of his ship, slamming his fist onto the railing as he pulled out a spyglass and looked at the ships in the distance.

Foy's crew had jumped ship, their boats and lines already crossed the distance to the second pirate ship, the lines being cut to avoid the spread of fire that was now eating away at the second half of Foy's ship.

'We got him, but he escaped,' Moori mourned, leaning back against the metal railing of her weapon firing zone. Shingo nodded sympathetically and crossed his arms, squinting past her into the distance.

'What will they do now, do you think?' Daiki and Ikeda had padded up behind them, both looking ragged from the battle, blood streaking across Ikeda's clear skin from where he'd wiped and smudged his cheek. His eyes were dark and unforgiving, and both men watched the ship sailing into the distance. 'Will the other captain drop Foy and his men back at the pirate isles?' He gestured with his head behind them.

Gora shook his head and closed the spyglass, sighing. 'He won't. Foy's the stronger power. He'll overrule and take the ship as his own. The others will have to join him or get off where they are.'

'Ruthless,' Shingo muttered.

Gora hummed in agreement. He rubbed his cheek, feeling the fatigue of it all wash over him now. The evening would be washing in soon. That escape had taken all day, and his crew looked dog-tired from it all. How they'd manage the rotations, he wasn't sure. He tried to think.

'They'll be headin' to the queen. Foy knows what we're up to now, and he'll tell her. The whole pirate circle will be in the know and out to get us. We have to stop him before he gets there. Round everyone up. Clean up the ship. Tip the rest of those dead sea slugs overboard.' He gestured back towards the remaining corpses of the pirates they'd defeated. 'We gotta keep goin' now. There's no turning back. We're too into it, and there's just too much goin' on to go back home and ignore it. Come on. Where's Satou and Kimura? We need them checkin' everyone out and takin' care of them before illness sets in. Go bring them to me.'

Ikeda nodded seriously and dived off before anyone could respond, and Gora and Daiki raised their eyebrows at one another.

'Daiki, tell Yonemura to lead the chase. The crew listens to her. We must catch up.'

Then Daiki too ran off, and Gora returned to looking through the spyglass at his distant enemy. Foy's old ship burned, and with it, those old memories. The flame powder and cannonballs caught, and the flames finally exploded in an air-rippling boom. He felt the ship lurch with the pressure of the heat waves pushing out from the burning ship, and then his ship slid into action as Yonemura called up for the sails to take them ahead, and Gora watched as *Sea Guardian* passed the burning wreck, now falling slowly into the sea like a burning tower, crumbling into something even his nightmares wouldn't forget. He shuddered as he watched it burn before slipping beneath the hungry waves, the black smoke still billowing. He covered his mouth and nose with his sleeve, and even though Yonemura took the ship wide to avoid the smoke and further explosion, it still made his eyes sting, and he heard his crew around him coughing too, covering their own noses.

'The old man's goin' to kill me,' Gora sighed, tearing his eyes away from the wreck.

No-one messed with Foy's ship. You even so much as scrape it as you clean, you get a beating. Gora remembered that all too well. And now Gora had burned and sunk it. The only way he'd ever have been able to do this was if he managed to take Foy down with his ship, but he hadn't, and Foy would be back for revenge. He'd stolen it from one of the most infamous pirates of the north seas off the coast of Eire, and Foy had been very selective about the one he'd chosen to steal.

The death he'd bring to Gora for destroying his ship and leaving him alive would be brutal, slow.

Gora shuddered again and turned instead to watch the fleeing ship disappearing ahead. He looked behind and saw Taro, Kyo, and Sakai jogging up from below deck to join Jelani and Quinni above. Yonemura gestured her arms to them, and they all nodded. Gora let a small smile tweak at the corners of his mouth.

At least he had a good crew to keep up.

'Captain?'

Gora jolted from his thoughts at the sound of a low, serious voice behind him. He turned to see Satou and Kimura, and Ikeda walking away behind them to meet again with Daiki and the other fighters to help tip the pirate bodies overboard. Gora looked at Satou, the one who had spoken, and cleared his throat.

'Good job earlier. I saw the two of you helping defend the ship. You've improved greatly.'

Satou bowed his head quietly, face still serious, but Kimura let a smile spread across his face and he cheerfully took the compliment.

'I heard you wanted us to check on the crew. We've started with those who came to us with injuries or were reported, but did you want us to do a full inspection in case they're trying to be tough or hide injuries?'

'Aye, within limits though, of course. No forcing people to strip or anything, just quiz them. Especially the women,' Gora said, raising a brow at Kimura. 'And I want a report of the injuries we gained. It might help us see how we're faring against the pirates.'

Satou agreed and walked off, leaving Kimura behind to bow to Gora and catch up, moaning to the carpenter for leaving him behind.

Gora leant on the railing again and looked up at the figurehead, her hands still lightly smoking from firing the figurehead's fire.

Across the bow from him, Moori and Shingo were tidying up from firing her and running below to prepare her for next time and ensure they kept the mini dragon flame burning. If that went out, they'd not be able to fire her again until they could next see Yoshiko, and Gora had no idea how long it would be until then.

As much as he wanted to visit Hié, see Yoshiko and tell her about what they'd learned so far, and rest up, Gora wanted to make the seas safer, and he wanted to stop the pirates from stealing and killing children. Now he knew it was an organised thing, he felt even more uncomfortable. Someone, the pirate queen, by the sounds of it, was planning something by making the pirates in her reign go around kidnapping and killing children. Gora had been one of those children, but he'd survived, just because of a mistake a pirate had made and the colour of Gora's hair. How being a redhead had made him the child of the devil, in the eyes of the overly superstitious pirates, and unsuitable to kill.

Thank fuck.

Now, he had his crew to think of, and the children who had been getting taken and killed for decades to think of. And he'd helped kidnap them back then, too.

Bile suddenly rose in Gora's throat, and he leaned down against the railing and put his head in his hands, trying to remove that thought from his mind.

That was why he had to save them now, when he had a choice in what he did. To atone.

26

Chasing the *Devil's Corsair*

Miyoshi returned to the upper deck and pouted, eyes heavy with fatigue from the day. He knew they'd failed to hit the pirates they wanted to take down; they'd heard about it from Daiki running down to the cannon deck to tell Tomioka, but Miyoshi had refused to believe it. Now, coming up to the deck and watching his friends running about to ensure they could catch up, it hit him that it was true.

The young boy padded across the deck to the bow gunwale to look where the pirate ship sailed towards the horizon. To him, it looked a long way away.

Boots plodded up behind him, and Miyoshi turned briefly to see his captain coming to stand with him, and the boy bowed his head respectfully before turning his gaze back to the fleeing ship.

'Will we catch up?'

He sounded miserable, and he knew it.

Gora rested a hand on the boy's head and ruffled his hair gently then leant on both hands on the railing.

'We'll do our best to. We need to,' was all Gora replied as he too stared out at the pirate ship, blue eyes bright with the now sinking ocean sun, but looking just as disappointed as Miyoshi felt.

'We hit him, didn't we? Moori got them. Why did he have to jump ship and sail away?'

'Everyone's goin' to do their best to survive, lad. That's only natural. But we can't let him get away. There's a lot at risk if he does.'

'Like what?' Miyoshi looked back up at his captain now, wanting to see his reaction.

'Like him telling those we're hunting that we're coming for them. We'd do better if no-one knew. They're too big a group for us to go against if they know.'

'You mean it's not just those couple of ships? How big are they?'

'That's the question, isn't it, now?'

They leant on the railing in silence for a while, listening to the wind in the sails and the hull cutting through the waves. Miyoshi yawned and stretched out, and Gora spoke again.

'You did well to help the crew below, earlier. Well done. Tomioka told me how reliable you were.'

Miyoshi felt his ears burn, and he mumbled an embarrassed thank you. He still felt worried about Tomioka telling Gora of his explorations that morning, and he couldn't help but wonder whether, if he'd been out there even a little too long, the captain would have run back as he had with the horde of pirates on his tail and left without him. Miyoshi would have been stuck on the island, then, with no-one knowing he was gone until too late.

His face burned more, and his eyes almost stung, but he blinked back the tears and settled for staying quiet, listening to Gora's faint chuckle as he patted Miyoshi's head again.

'Go rest, lad, you've done a lot today.'

* * *

When Miyoshi awoke, the ship was still chasing after Foy. His heart sank. Miyoshi shuffled into the galley and plonked himself onto the bench to receive a bowl of hot rice broth from

Kimura, who smiled kindly at the young boy for once instead of teasing him.

'Did we chase them all night?'

'Yup, and we'll keep going until we catch up,' Kimura replied lightly, turning back to the counter to keep preparing the food for whoever came in next.

Shingo and Sakai were already at the table, both looking tired, though Miyoshi knew they'd been in the sleeping quarters at the same time as him and had just woken for their rotation.

'We've got smaller, tighter rotations to make sure the crew can sleep and sail and that we don't slow down,' Shingo explained between mouthfuls of broth, looking over at the boy. 'Yūki, you'll be working hard today, too.'

The boy nodded and scoffed down his food, enjoying the clam broth and hot rice. He chewed in huge mouthfuls, cheeks bulging, and watched Kimura thoughtfully. The young chef, playful and teasing as he was, especially to Miyoshi, was very kind and reliable. He'd helped Miyoshi and many others with their injuries and was a bright personality on the ship when things got tough. Miyoshi admired his cooking and felt lucky they had someone as good at cooking on their ship, and he wondered what restaurant his family had owned in Hié town. He knew it was one of the upper-class ones, but Miyoshi had never been in that part of town. Not that he remembered, anyway. He was almost too nervous to ask. As kind as Kimura was, Miyoshi wondered if he was allowed to ask higher-ranking people such questions. Was it considered rude or private?

Miyoshi didn't ask. Instead, he thought back to what the other three had been speaking about, and he piped up. 'Do you think we'll be able to catch up? They won't get away, will they?'

The other three looked at him, Kimura turning back around, spoon in hand, and Shingo and Sakai glancing across the table.

'Well, we have to. It would bring worse things if we don't,' Kimura said, turning back around to look after the food for others coming in after them.

'Is it bad to be hunting and killing the pirates?'

'In a way, I guess. But it's the only way to stop them from kidnapping and killing children. If they're still at it from when the captain was a boy and they take three or four at a time, I wonder how many they've taken overall,' Kimura continued.

Shingo and Sakai were silent but watching Kimura, thoughtful. Shingo closed his eyes and nodded gravely. Miyoshi's body flushed with anxiety. He thought back to how it felt with the pirate chasing him back on the island and how they were going around stealing children. What would have happened to him if the pirate had caught him?

'Don't worry, Yūki. We'll find a way,' Sakai said, reaching over and patting Miyoshi's arm.

Miyoshi opened his mouth to ask more questions, but as he did, the galley door swung open and Ikeda and Rijul poured in, both looking exhausted. Ikeda's hair was wild, and he untied the cord to shake it free with his hand as his tired, dark eyes met Miyoshi's.

'Yūki, the captain is looking for you. You should go as soon as you finish that,' the young samurai said, plonking himself on the table and putting his cord in his mouth to pull his hair back again.

Kimura served two bowls of broth and rice for the two men joining them, and Miyoshi hurriedly nodded and raised his bowl to his mouth to push the remaining meal into his mouth with his chopsticks. He watched the young samurai over the top of the bowl, wondering if Gora had given him any other message.

'Want me to make that pretty for you?' Kimura smirked as he lay the bowl gently in front of Ikeda, gesturing with his eyes to the young warrior's hair.

Rijul dug in, grabbing his spoon and focusing his eyes on his meal to ignore the two young ones. He'd learned they bickered and wanted no part of it while he was tired and hungry. Ikeda, it seemed, was much the same, and his eyes hovered warily on Kimura's face as he took his cord from his mouth and wound it around his ponytail, saying nothing.

Kimura, wanting the man to take the bait, continued, 'Even young Yūki here knows how to braid now. Perhaps he should do it for you.'

Kimura grinned over at Yūki, who raised his brows in surprise as he finished his bowl, pushing the last, large mouthful into his mouth, cheeks bulging too much to reply. But by then, Ikeda had already finished tying his hair back, and he sighed, reached into his kimono, pulled out his chopsticks, and started to eat.

'Last night was tough, and the captain has barely slept in the last couple of days. You should try not to keep him waiting, Yūki. He needs to sleep'—then he added pointedly, glancing sidelong at Kimura—'and so do we.'

The young chef chuckled and turned his back while Ikeda thanked him for the food and dug in, and Miyoshi jumped up from the table, quickly washed his bowl and chopsticks in the bowl of water beside Kimura, and raced from the room, hearing low chatter start up again as Sakai began asking the two new incomers questions about the night's rotation.

Miyoshi was surprised. He didn't hear of the fighters doing night rotations often. Did that mean they expected a night attack? Would Foy's ship stop and turn to try to catch them unawares?

Stomping up the steps to the deck, Miyoshi realised he'd not asked Ikeda where Gora would be. He looked straight to the helm as he stepped onto the main deck, taking in a deep breath of fresh sea air. Gora wasn't there. The boy then looked down the ship to the bow—the place Gora was most likely to be found if he wasn't running duties or making checks or cooped up in his room, and the place the captain loved best, by the figurehead where he could look to the horizon and talk to the figurehead as if talking with Yoshiko. The whole crew knew he missed the daimyō, who was like a younger sister to their captain, and wished she could have joined. They knew she'd have wanted to, too, if not helping to rebuild their region of Hié back in Hizen.

Surprisingly, as Miyoshi ran down the deck to see, he wasn't there either. He spun about and searched the deck, running about. Kyo, on his way down to below deck since finishing the night rotation, caught him looking lost.

'What's wrong, Yūki?'

Miyoshi spun to face him, looking up at a very tired and gaunt Kyo, whose long hair was pulled back into a messy ponytail after a windy night. 'Do you know where the captain is?'

'He's in his stateroom,' Kyo said, yawning, and then he bowed and plodded off below to the galley.

Miyoshi padded after him, turning in the other direction to knock on Gora's door. Gora called out for him to enter, and Miyoshi entered to see Gora and Tomioka stop chatting to turn and watch him enter, Gora sitting back in his chair, Tomioka standing in front of the captain's desk.

'Close the door.'

Miyoshi did, suddenly holding his breath. He had a feeling it would be about his little adventure. He was right.

'Tomioka here tells me you had a little trip onto the pirate island, now,' Gora started, leaning forward with his elbows on the desk. His blue eyes pierced Miyoshi's, and the boy froze. After waiting a while for the boy to respond, Gora sighed and continued. 'Do ye know now why we tried to keep you here?'

Still frozen, the boy managed to make himself nod.

Gora, obviously seeing the boy's distress, scratched his head and closed his eyes a moment, thinking. 'Aaah, lad. You have no idea how much you worried us all.' His eyes opened again, and this time, the blue eyes were caring and worried. 'Tomioka told me about Quinni and Ikeda coming for you. If they hadn't …' He paused, and the two men met each other's gaze, a silent communication. 'We all just want you safe. You know now what we're up against. I believe what you experienced was shocking enough that you'll not do it again now, but understand we still need to give you a lesson for it.'

Miyoshi nodded again, anxiety swapping with misery. He didn't want to upset Gora; he wanted to show Gora what he could do and become someone like him. Instead, he just seemed to be showing him and Tomioka his careless side. The young boy stared at the stateroom's wooden floor, fidgeting with his hands.

'After the fight yesterday, the deck's still in pretty bad shape. Satou's still fixing things, but we'll need someone to help him and tidy up the place. Today, I want you going about making the place ship-shape. See what he needs, tidy up after him, and when he doesn't need you, tidy up the rest. That means blood scrubbed off the decks before it sets in and anything the crew wants you to do. Double work.'

The boy looked up at Gora hesitantly, and he bowed, bending at his waist and waiting to be told to stand before he stood again. Then, to Miyoshi's surprise, Gora stood up, padded around the desk, and rested his hand on Miyoshi's head, looking down at him with care.

'Really, thank goodness you're safe. When Tomioka told me, I near lost my heart. I promised your mother we'd take care of you, and that's what we're going to do. Me, Tomioka, everyone. This crew's a family, and we all look out for one another. We can't do that if you run off on your own, and we'd worry sick about you.

You did a good job yesterday helping Tomioka and his team on the cannon deck. I know we'll be able to rely on you again. So, keep up the good work, and believe us when we say we're thankful you're alive and made it back. We'll be thanking Quinni and Ikeda, too. Without them, I hesitate to think what would have happened.'

Gora looked now over Miyoshi's head at Tomioka, who nodded. 'We're here for you, Yūki, remember.'

The boy's ears burned, and he nodded, embarrassed. The two men chuckled and dismissed him, and the boy thankfully ran off, grateful that worse punishment hadn't come. And, true to his word, he worked as hard as he could to repay them their kindness and cleaned the deck with all his might, spending the day brushing and scrubbing to tidy up from the day before's fight. Satou was working silently, as usual, to fix scuffed or broken parts of the ship, having to completely rebuild the part of the upper stern deck that had the cannon ball crash through it. Miyoshi helped him by running to grab tools and materials from the lower storage holds and sweeping up or washing after him. Kimura popped up to deliver the young carpenter his meals, much to Miyoshi's surprise, and other than that, the two worked in silence together or apart until they were happy the deck was put back into good shape. By the afternoon, the boy was done and exhausted, wiping sweat from his forehead with his sleeve and looking over at the ocean stretching beyond, wondering where they were and how close they were to catching up to Foy. In his hard work, he'd almost forgotten.

Miyoshi dodged crew as they whizzed about keeping the ship sailing, scooting past Yonemura as she swapped duties with Nishimura to sleep through the afternoon, ready for night rotation. To the side, Daiki and Eshnaa were sharpening and polishing all the weapons and blades, keeping them ready and usable. They seemed to sit in a comfortable silence, turning to one another now and then to say a few words in Traders'—what little Daiki knew, and Eshnaa teaching him new words—but generally content in their company of mutual warrior respect.

Miyoshi ogled the weapons and how skilfully they handled them, even to clean, and wondered when his next lesson would be. It had been a while since he'd learned, the lessons stopping while they'd been on the pirate isles. He couldn't get better if he didn't practise or learn more. Now that he'd finished his chores, would Gora let him practise on his own if he didn't disturb anyone?

He reached the bow of the ship and leant on the railing, staring out over the sea for Foy's ship, scanning the waves. He couldn't see it straight ahead and panicked, looking left to right.

'There,' a quiet voice said, and the boy turned to see Gora standing behind him, pointing. His heart leapt, and he wondered how long Gora had been there and whether he'd missed him earlier. He'd not heard him walk up behind him.

Miyoshi turned to look where Gora was pointing, off to the port side at an angle. The boy frowned.

'Are we okay here? Will we catch up? What if we miss them?'

Gora rubbed his cheek. He looked tired still, and Miyoshi wondered whether he'd slept at all while he'd been cleaning up the deck and helping Satou. If he had, it hadn't been long, by the looks of it. Gora's face was pale, though usually lightly tanned by the ocean sun, and shadows covered his lower eyes.

'We'll find a way. As long as we can see them, we're fine.'

'I've finished cleaning. If I help them sail, would we be able to go faster?'

Gora looked down at the boy, hand hovering on his head from where he ran it through his hair. He looked slightly surprised, and by then his face settled into a gentle smile.

'Nah, it's alright, lad. One extra person will not make much difference. That's on the wind and the currents as much as those who sail the ship. The only way we'll get faster now is to have a bunch of strong arms rowing us.'

Miyoshi looked down at his arms, suddenly feeling very flimsy. He didn't think he'd make much impact if he rowed a ship this big.

'Aye, it's alright. We need your help elsewhere. That's enough for now.'

Gora leant on the railing too and looked out over the sea, his eyes settling on the pirate ship ahead. He had a sad gaze, and Miyoshi knew why. This pirate had stolen Gora's life and home from him. His captain had been his age when it happened, and Miyoshi thought back to the Acrein slave catchers that had taken him and his mum away from their homes, too. It had been terrifying and lonely, especially when they'd been bought by different people in Acrein. Fortunately, they'd been sold to work in the same town and had found each other by chance. If it hadn't been for Yoshiko, Gora, and Nubia helping people escape, he'd still have his life stolen, too. Unlike him, Gora hadn't been able to escape until he was much older, and he'd had to live with pirates. Miyoshi shuddered. He couldn't imagine it. The boy, too, looked at the fleeing pirate ship and glowered at it. Those ships took kids like him and killed or made slaves of them. He wouldn't let them get away with it. He wanted to do as much as he could for his crew to help them save all the future children from being taken, which is why he had to work hard now.

'They need to die,' he muttered, feeling upset again that the old pirate had escaped the day before, jumping ship and taking over this other one.

Gora chuckled, though it sounded much more lifeless than usual. 'Don't get so caught up in dealing death and justice, or you'll blur the lines for yerself. Then you'll never know which is which.' He paused for a moment. 'Don't end up like me, lad.'

Then Gora ruffled the boy's hair and turned away, padding over the deck, hands shoved in his pockets.

Miyoshi wanted to run after him, to ask him more questions and to ask him to help him get stronger, but the captain's shoulders were low, and he was plodding over to Shingo. Miyoshi knew they'd be talking business and didn't want to get in the way, so he returned to staring over the ocean, looking now into the endless waves. Boredom overcame him, and he wished he was bigger and stronger to help with the sailing and make an impact, to help them gain on the ship ahead.

'Why aren't we catching up?' He pouted as someone passed by him a little later, and the person stopped beside him. Miyoshi looked up at who he'd talked to; it was Taro. Miyoshi was surprised. Usually, Taro and his son Kyo had their rotations together.

Taro thought for a moment, eyes squinting to watch the pirate ship ahead.

'It's to do with the differences in the ships. Their ship is smaller and more streamlined; it's made for sailing, and sailing fast. It can manoeuvre well, too. I believe pirates favour ships like that because it helps them chase ships to rob them and then run away. Our ship is bigger. While it's a very good ship, it's a warship, made for strength, not speed. We're only keeping up by grace of the winds and by Yonemura and Nishimura's great navigation skills keeping us in the right place.'

The boy pouted again, thinking it not fair. He stared at the waves again.

'Do you think we'll see a sea serpent again?'

The waves had been quiet of creatures since that first time they'd seen the serpents, and he wanted something entertaining to happen again.

'I hope not,' Taro chuckled. 'Just dealing with pirates is enough. Besides, remember that shadow that followed them?'

'But they could eat the pirates,' Miyoshi piped up, feeling hopeful.

Taro laughed. 'Yes, but us, too.'

'Oh,' was all the boy responded, before he focused back on the waves, hearing Taro walk away behind him.

27

Something Hidden in the Waves

On the fourth morning of chasing Foy, Gora awoke from another disturbed sleep. With memories of his pirate days haunting every moment, Gora wanted nothing more than to catch up to Foy and put an end to that nightmare once and for all.

Gora heaved himself out of his bunk and slipped on his boots, tying his slacks and pulling on a *haori* jacket. Looking about the captain's stateroom, Gora rubbed his cheek sleepily and wondered why they were still having such trouble with Foy. The man Gora had known would have got frustrated about having a ship constantly on his tail and turned and fired on them or tried harder to lose them. Foy didn't seem to be doing that. He paced about the room as he thought, still unable to get these nagging thoughts out of his mind. He'd lost sleep over it the last few sleep rotations now and knew there had to be something up.

Either he's deliberately leading us somewhere, or that other captain's killing his stride. Gora wondered at that. Foy *had* gone onto that other ship. It was very likely that Foy would have taken over, being one of the higher up and most dangerous pirates he knew—not wild, but his intelligence and cunning was what was scariest. *Or perhaps he's just lost his grit in old age.*

Gora snorted. As if. He'd seen Foy back on the pirate isles, and it was as if he'd not aged a day, *Except maybe a few more wrinkles and his hair turning white, though you'd not believe his age if he told ya.*

True enough, Foy's white hair looked good on him, and many women and men alike fell for his charms, but underneath that silver look was an age not many knew, and it had to be getting to him sometime soon, right?

Gora could only hope.

Bet he's leading us somewhere, the sly old sea devil, Gora reasoned. As he stretched and cracked his back slightly, a spark suddenly tweaked in Gora's mind, and he darted to the desk and pulled out a scroll showing the map of the world's oceans, running his fingers along it to the point he'd estimated they'd sailed to that night.

He frowned at the scroll and looked closer, squinting his eyes at a smudged marking.

'Well, I'll be damned,' he whispered to himself, knowing full well he already likely was, as would the rest of his crew be if they kept up this path.

Gora rolled up the scroll and, keeping it in his hands, stormed out of his quarters and up to the main deck, looking for any one of his leaders, whoever was on rotation at the moment. He locked eyes with Tomioka and Yonemura, Tomioka directing young Miyoshi to something at the main sail ropes and Yonemura standing at the bow looking through a spyglass ahead. He noticed her angle. She wasn't looking at the pirate ship, but at something else ahead.

Bet she's realised.

Gora bellowed to Tomioka and then strode over to the bow deck, joining Yonemura. She turned, her face calm and unreadable, as often it was.

'Captain,' she greeted him, closing her spyglass with her brows furrowed. 'There's something ahead.'

'Aye, and I'm not liking our chances.'

They both turned as Tomioka jogged up to them, seeing the boy peering in their direction after him as he continued with the rigging. Gora was satisfied that they were keeping the boy busy and giving him new things to learn. He nodded appreciatively at Tomioka before hitting them with the news.

'I think he's leading us somewhere. That's why he's not tried attacking or shaking us off.'

The other two glanced at one another and then back at Gora, their faces confused.

'I did wonder why he wasn't attacking. I thought it might have been because he worried the dragon fire would overpower him again,' Tomioka said, crossing his arms and resting his hands in his opposite kimono sleeves.

'So, that thing ahead,' Yonemura started, turning back to face the bow side.

The three looked into the distance.

'Tell me, what direction is it?' Gora asked, reaching for his pocket, clicking his tongue as he realised he'd left the compass in his stateroom for his haste to get up here.

Yonemura reached into her bag to pull out her own compass, often having one on her person for navigation at the helm, and held it out for the three of them to see. Tomioka and Gora stood either side of her, all watching the needle. While she held her hand out in the direction of the strange region ahead, the compass swung back and forth, not settling.

Yonemura and Tomioka both turned to Gora, seeking his answer. He continued to stare at the needle, praying to the spirits for it to settle.

It didn't.

He rubbed the back of his head and then looked to the distance, taking his time before answering.

It was around about these parts, wasn't it?

He sighed.

'Have you ever heard of the Wandering Abyss?' Gora said, speaking low, directed only at the two of them. He looked around him to see if anyone else had heard.

'Only in stories,' Yonemura said, her voice hushed, eyes darting between the two men conspiratorially.

Gora was comforted that at least she knew enough that it wasn't the sort of thing to say out loud on a ship. Not carelessly.

Tomioka, on the other hand, hadn't. But then, Gora wasn't surprised. It was far from Hizen and not a place the Hizen sailors knew about, keeping their sea trade close to their waters, at furthest to Chuuko and Kannko, perhaps some of the smaller countries and archipelago in the eastern areas. But the Wandering Abyss was far west from there in the central seas. It was likely only Quinni and Jelani would have heard of it. Yonemura's family were famously wide traders with contacts in other regions. No wonder she'd heard stories of it.

Gora wondered how he'd explain such a place to Tomioka in a way to get him to understand the situation they'd be heading into if they continued chase.

'Imagine a place the compasses stop working and fog settles low over the seas. The stars abandon you, and monsters hunt the lost. The seas spin and churn and swallow ships whole, and they say there's a curse in those waters: those who go in never come out.'

Tomioka paused, his face blank as he processed it. Yonemura had returned to watching ahead, spyglass out, clearly trying to see if it was the place of the stories she'd heard.

'Why would he go to such a place if no-one can leave? Would he risk himself and his crew just to lose us?' Tomioka said in a harsh whisper.

Gora thought for a moment, back to the days of old, the place he hated to return to. He was just a lad then his voice hadn't settled for long, and he still hadn't had fluff appearing on his face. When he did, that had been when they'd sold him. He thought of the stories he'd heard at that age and wondered.

'The crew told of rumours that Foy knew a way through. That he was one of the few pirates alive today who had survived it. They say he's a hoard there and no need to worry about others taking it. If that's true, he needs no fear of it.'

Yonemura looked back at him then, her face sceptical, eyebrow raised and eyes dull from disbelief. 'That's ridiculous. No-one can sail through the Wandering Abyss and leave. The monsters there don't let people through.'

'Be that as it may, he's heading there now, and he must have something up his sleeve,' Tomioka replied, pointing to the ship ahead. 'Is he trying to call our bluff? To make us turn and give up, thinking it impossible and mad, and then he'd turn at the last minute and shake us off?'

'Perhaps.' Gora hummed thoughtfully to himself, hand on his chin, looking unseeing at the water churning below, leaning his hip against the railing. *Sea serpents before, shadows in the ocean, and now monsters in cursed places.* Gora thought about the stories he'd heard of this place. He didn't know whether it was just his imagination stirring up, but he swore he saw a pale shape slide past below. Gora looked again, his breath stalling a moment.

Nothing there.

He looked back up again. The place was far into the distance. Gora asked to borrow Yonemura's spyglass. Towers of rock rose crooked from the sea, and a pale spray of mist already blanketed the landscape ahead. In there, you'd not be able to see the spiralling, swallowing water holes; the ship would have no hope without being able to see where it was steering, and he couldn't risk taking his crew in there.

But they had to end Foy.

The pirate queen lived in the warmer parts of these central western waters. If Foy cut through the Wandering Abyss, he'd be there in no time.

'We have to try to end him before he gets there. Is there nothing we can do for one last spurt of speed?'

'I don't think so,' Tomioka started slowly, looking now to Yonemura, who had a little more of an idea of where they were with the ship. She shook her head and mentioned Shingo being the best one to know about the ship's capabilities.

Gora rubbed his cheek. Shingo was on rest rotation, so he couldn't wake him. They'd just have to do what they could.

'Is Moori awake?' he wondered, half speaking to himself as he looked about the deck.

'I believe she should be,' Yonemura said. 'She was asleep earlier but should be on morning rotation with me today.'

Gora looked to the right at the figurehead's weapon, waiting be reloaded. 'Can anyone help her set that up, or is it just Shingo and me?'

'Daiki might be able to,' Tomioka said. 'Or Ikeda. I believe they may have been with the daimyō Yoshiko when it was being built, when they were her guards.'

'Good. So, we can make one last chase before Foy heads in there. After that, who knows when or where we'll find the old sea devil again?'

With that, Gora turned, returning the spyglass to Yonemura and nodding to both of them. 'Let's speed this ship up. One last sprint.'

The ship was a scurry of activity as every person awake rushed to get the ship ahead. Daiki and Eshnaa stored the weapons away, and then Daiki sorrowfully rushed below to awake a sleeping Ikeda. Ikeda, he'd told Gora, had been the one paying the most attention when they worked on it with Yoshiko. Both men knowingly smiled to one another, knowing why the young lad had been paying such fast attention to it.

With the young samurai awake, they both returned to the bow to help Moori ready the figurehead's flame. In the meantime, Yonemura was calling out instructions to the team to catch the wind in the sails. She heaved on the helm and took them in at an angle, catching a cross current that would speed them towards the place the compasses spun worst.

Towards the Wandering Abyss.

As the ship pulled closer, Gora finally saw the moment he'd been waiting for: the ship that had been in the distance grew a little larger as they gained, their last sprint and effort coming to fruition. He called excitedly across to Moori, Daiki, and Ikeda to see how they were doing with the preparations of the flame and was satisfied to hear that soon they'd be able to fire on his old captain and kidnapper.

'For all those children, I'll end this,' he muttered to himself, feeling joy as the wind rushed through his hair and caught his *haori* sleeves, and he took a deep breath as he watched his crew take their last stand at the sea devil before he hit the Wandering Abyss.

He meandered to the port railing, keeping an eye on Foy and what the old pirate and that other captain aboard—if he was still alive, that is—would do to discover Gora's ship gaining on them just as they thought they'd shaken them.

'You really goin' in there?' Gora growled, looking from the ship to the towers of rock now visible with the naked eye. Ahead, a white blanket covered the waves, and the bases of the towers disappeared into faded clouds before being swallowed by an ocean darker than any he'd ever seen before, darker even than the black sea in the north Enssan ocean where the waters were saltier and a deep gulley below it could swallow colour and light. But here, a dark power lingered, and the water darkened with it.

Gora felt a chill reach his bones, and he wasn't sure whether it was superstition or real, spreading across the breeze from the mists.

He pulled his *haori* over this chest and glared once more at the fleeing ship. Was the old sea slug really going there? To the Wandering Abyss? Perhaps the old pirate had done it before. Either way, Gora doubted the odds, and he knew that if his crew was to fire on Foy, they'd have to do it sooner rather than later and then turn tail and get out of there. Who knew where the Wandering Abyss began, and who knew where the monsters would reach?

'It looks like they're slowing,' Tomioka said from beside him, making Gora's heart pound from a jolt of surprise.

Gora coughed to hide his blunder. 'Aye, but I can't figure out why.'

'Think we called his bluff after all?'

Gora thought for a moment before responding. 'Not likely. Look, they're not turning. They could fire at us from the stern chaser, but they're not. That shows me they're not sure of either our reach or how many iron balls they have left from the fight a few days ago. They're also not turning to go another direction.' He observed some more, and Tomioka stepped forward to look closer too, both men's eyes squinting into the distance. 'It looks more like he's slowing to take deliberate action. They must not be able to enter the Abyss without a certain understanding.'

'You mean knowing if there's a monster, a swallowing pool, or rocks?'

'Aye, perhaps. But he's not that close yet. Look, there's a little ways off yet.'

Tomioka looked again and nodded. 'The Wandering Abyss …' Tomioka thought out loud, watching. 'Does it truly move?'

'Aye, who knows where it starts? Could be something else beneath those seas.'

Then, once more, something white below caught Gora's eyes, and he saw in the depths something that made his heart freeze over.

White, ghoul-like shapes were flickering about below the waves—small creatures, half fish, half spirit.

'Merfolk?' Tomioka breathed, following Gora's gaze. He stepped back. Gora admired the man's knowing.

'Aye, you know about them?'

The man nodded, face paling. 'We can't let the crew see them,' he started, before realising that would be a near impossible mission. He clamped his mouth shut, wondering what to do. He looked about, brow furrowed, thinking.

Both men startled as a light thud came from below, and they both turned slowly, pale, to look once more at the white figures below. One of the merfolk had launched from the waves, digging its claws from its long, pale arms into the hull to hang on. The near-flat face looked upwards, small, colourless eyes staring up, mouth open to bear tiny rows of needle-like teeth.

'Fighters!' Gora bellowed, stepping back from the edge. 'Daiki, get your team up here, all of them, awake, now. Leave Ikeda to help Moori. Get the gunwale. Let no-one over, and nothing comes on this ship.'

Daiki looked rightfully confused, but he leapt into action and ran below, ushering Eshnaa to wake Simrita as he awoke Rijul. Gora ran both hands through his hair, feeling fear flooding through his body. Would that even be enough? Just four fighters? Without Ikeda and Moori, and with the ship needing everyone else to sail, their numbers were down, and he could only do so much while monitoring everything else too. And merfolk … he'd take serpents over that any day.

To add to his stress, while Tomioka was off relaying news to a confused Nishimura to continue their plan and guide the young man steering the ship, Miyoshi sprinted up from below deck and ran to the edge, seeking excitement.

He must have heard from the galley. Gora cringed, running up to the lad and pulling him away.

'Well, lad, you got your wish. Something interesting for ye to see. Though I wish it were something nice-interesting—not that you get much of that in the open seas. Perhaps a pod of whales, but otherwise …'

Gora paused, thinking about the superstitious tales of seafolk. No wonder pirates and sailors were so superstitious and dark-tale-minded. Out here away from humans, darker things reigned.

The boy pulled on Gora's arms as he tried to run back to the gunwale. 'What are they?'

'Merfolk,' Gora said, not wanting to offer anything further.

'Mermaids? Aren't they good?'

Gora raised an eyebrow and turned the boy around, looking him directly in the eyes. 'They're not like out of folk stories, boy. Nothing beautiful and magical. That's sirens. And they're bad as it is. No, these are more like *yōkai* spirits. You know the stories of evil creatures beneath the water, dragging people down to death?'

The lad looked up at him, falling still and no longer pulling on Gora. '*Yōkai*? There's *yōkai* this far from Hizen?'

'There's *yōkai* everywhere, lad. They just have different names.'

'But I thought magic was dead? Why are we seeing so many weird creatures if magic is dead?'

Gora thought back to the story he'd heard about Miyoshi and Sakai coming face to face with the *funayūrei*.

'Dying. But it still lingers on. The dark stuff will last longer, drawn to the power of nightmares and the dark places to live, thriving off the good. As is always the way. Stay away from the edge.'

The boy looked at Gora with more understanding than Gora had ever seen from anything he'd explained to the boy before. Something in Gora's tone must have clicked with the lad if he wasn't trying to race to see, that or he'd finally understood the sorts of powers they were up against.

One of the merfolks' pale hands clawed over the edge and dug into the woodwork, dragging its bedraggled body behind it, grey-white face peering over the edge. Miyoshi cried out and clung onto Gora, angling himself away from the creature but unable to look away, glancing around Gora's body.

''S okay, lad. It'll be fine.' Gora muttered to the boy as he reached to his side then swore, realising in his haste to leave his chambers below, he'd left his blades behind.

'Fool,' he muttered to himself, looking about for Daiki.

The guard ran up the steps onto the deck and across to the edge, slashing at the creature's face with his blade. Jelani yelled out from above, pointing to the other side of the ship, where another creature clawed its way to the railing. Daiki looked behind, face judging whether he could make it in time. Before he had to make the decision, a flash of silver flickered across the space and the creature's head sliced in two, Gora following the reverse motion back to Simrita, who held her arm out, full of throwing *chakram* rings.

Gora let out a breath. *Just in time.*

'Lad, go to my quarters. Get my blades. Off you go, now. Go.'

Gora ushered the fearful boy along, watching the lad look about a few more times in case ghostly creatures emerged at the railing, but then he turned tail and sprinted down the steps, stumbling a little but catching himself as he went.

'This going to affect us firing on the pirates?' Tomioka said as Gora backed his way towards the helm until the boy arrived with his blades, both men watching the edges of the ships to guide the fighters. Nishimura stared straight on, aiming as before towards the Wandering Abyss and the pirate ship about to enter.

'Hope not,' Gora said, eyes quickly darting to the place he'd last seen Foy. The old pirate hadn't moved much in comparison, and he was certain they'd soon be close to aiming. Gora wished they could aim a cannon at them to slow them down and stop them from running away: at least then they could get up close and personal, unlike last time, but with the merfolk here, he couldn't spare the hands. Others who'd been on the sleep rotation had awoken from the fighters being called and come up to join them, but with the ship being sailed, the gift being prepared, and the merfolk being fought off, no-one was free to go below to the cannons. Not here, not so close to the Wandering Abyss, where Gora had no idea how far out the tides would reach and pull them in, or how far out monsters would come to feed.

No, he needed his crew here, where all could turn this ship to flee if needed.

'Ready to fire, sir,' Ikeda cried from across the deck, he and Moori turning to look back from the contraption they'd pulled up from below the deck and locked on. The metal body of the contraption was up, and Moori was standing in the firing zone, hands once more at the ready and a determined look clouding her face. Gora knew she'd not let them get away this time.

An audible clawing from either side froze Gora's soul, and he could hear the claws digging in with little thuds as multiple pairs of hands climbed their way up the hull. The ghostly faces of the merfolk peered over the railings surrounding them, their tiny eyes wide and their needle-like teeth bared. Ahead, Miyoshi cried out as he ran out with Gora's blades.

'Back down below, lad,' Gora said, trying to keep his voice steady and calm and kind to reassure him. 'We'll do alright up here. You go see if Kimura needs help. Let him know there might be a few injuries up here if things go to the worst. And if you can find Satou in his workshop, bring him up too—axe or saw with him, preferably.'

The young boy nodded and ran off again, and Gora's smile fell into a grimace. He clapped his hand on Tomioka's shoulder, asked him to stay here and monitor the surrounds and lead the firing of the figurehead's flame, and then ran off to help the fighters to keep the merfolk from climbing onto the deck. If they dragged anyone below, Gora knew he'd not be able to live with himself.

As they got closer to Foy's ship floating on the edge of the Wandering Abyss, Gora felt his ship slow, and he looked about to figure out why. The sails were still full with wind, and Nishimura was looking about blankly. Then the man's face washed over, and his mystic gaze came over him. Gora realised now why Foy had slowed too.

'The Abyss,' he breathed, kicking at a merfolk's tiny, bony hands before it could pull its head up. The fingers were prised from the wood, and the creature fell into the ocean below. He didn't dare look at how many might be clinging onto the hull now. 'It's come out this far?'

He heard an enraged cry and looked down the ship to see Moori kicking air, running from her firing spot to look beyond the railing.

'No!' he yelled, getting her and Ikeda's attention.

Moori looked back, hands on the bow railing, not seeing the pale face appearing behind her. But Ikeda did, and he rushed forward, unsheathing his ever-present katana and grabbing Moori's sleeve, pulling her back with his left arm as he thrust out his blade with his right. Moori stumbled to the deck behind him and twisted to see what he'd done, shuffling herself backwards on the floor when she saw he'd stabbed through the small body of the ocean creature. With Ikeda's blade raised, the creature hung by the wound in its torso, spindly arms reaching out to claw and swipe at Ikeda, who held his blade as far as he could. But the claws cut at his arms, and he quickly wiped his blade along the railing, pushing the creature off to fall back into the ocean. The young man raised his blade to scrutinise the dark, grey-red blood oozing on his katana, and he turned with a disgusted look on his face. Not sheathing his katana, he strode over to Moori, held out his hand to help her up, and then guided her back to the gift-firing zone. There, she stood, shaken, still, and now looking ahead at Foy's ship.

By then, Gora had shuffled over to them and asked what was wrong.

'We're out of range. Just. We can't get any closer. The ship slowed. Just like his did.' Moori sounded mellow, but she spat 'his' as if it was the same blood that Ikeda had found on his blade from the creature.

'The Wandering Abyss,' Gora said again, this time more certain. 'It's this far out.'

The two younger ones looked at him with tired, confused expressions. Gora explained.

'Where different seas and different currents meet, it changes how you sail. We're crossing from one to the other and moving to one notoriously dark and dangerous. Where we are now, both cross. But if we go any further'—he gestured ahead—'we'll get sucked in and find it difficult to leave.'

Sure enough, as they watched, they saw the pirate ship rock a little and then sail ahead with renewed vigour, as if favoured by a wind or some unseen current. The latter would be the case, and Gora watched with a heavy heart as Foy sailed ahead, soon to disappear into the mists.

'That's it, then?' Moori asked, sounding just as down and shocked as Gora felt. Disbelieving.

Gora nodded, miserable. He started ahead, watching as the boat disappeared into the white mists at the base of a tall stone tower, and then he sighed. 'Aye, that's it. We'll have to find him again, but it'll be harder now that he's looking. And when he gets through there—if he gets through there—he'll be heading straight for the pirate queen, and we'll have a bigger problem.'

'But we always had to have gone after them, right?' Ikeda said, eyes serious still, the only one standing tall still and not sounding filled with despair.

Gora nodded. 'We always had to, I guess. We just didn't know it all until we spoke with Foy.'

The young man nodded. 'Well, they might be showing us where we need to go. It'll be easier to find them all if they're in one place, though harder to fight them all.'

'I ain't sailing through there,' Gora growled. 'Not even following him. No inch of ocean's the same in there. We need to leave. Forget Foy. We lost him.'

But then Gora met the young man's eyes, and he realised he didn't have to.

'We'll go around. It'll take longer, be we know the pirate queen is this way, in a place it's quicker to reach by sailing through there. It will help us narrow down the ocean.'

Ikeda nodded, and he turned to help Moori take down the figurehead's weapon. The young woman sighed, looking dejected. Gora left them to it, not saying a thing. To have crew know what they need to do and get to it was a gift enough. He'd not lose that by telling them what they didn't need telling.

Instead, he strode off to relay the news to Tomioka and get Nishimura to turn them around and get them away before the grasp of the Abyss held them. As he did, the ship lurched, and a fast current caught them, pulling the ship back towards the place Foy had gone. Gora cried out and rushed over the deck, waving his arms widely for Nishimura to turn the ship around.

Nishimura did, but he strained against an unmoving helm. Tomioka quickly jumped on to join him, both men leaning their weight in the wheel.

'Don't sail against it,' Gora yelled. 'Sail aside! That way, that way!' he pointed to the side, telling them to sail north, perpendicular to the pull, where the current wasn't pushing so much against them.

The ship creaked as it lurched against the waves that tried to pull them closer to the Wandering Abyss, and Gora, knowing they'd be lost forever if they didn't make it out, ran across the breadth of the ship to the starboard side to squint inside the reaching mists. The mists stretched out and brushed the ship, and something large moved within—something so large that the merfolk yet hanging on to the hull turned their ghostly heads, glared into the white cloud, and dived back into the sea.

Gora heard words of gratitude from Eshnaa that may have included a curse word. At least, that's how he took it from the reaction Rijul gave her, not wanting to hear such language from one of his two new sisters. She looked over at him, face showing how tired she was and that at this moment, she didn't care about being caught swearing.

The world fell eerily quiet, and when the sound of a shout rang out from above, the white cloud easy swallowed it shortly after it was called. Kyo was yelling and gesturing ahead: a tall, looming shadow was getting closer.

'Stone tower,' he cried. 'Ahead!'

Nishimura and Tomioka struggled against the helm, trying to turn around the tower. They ended up letting the ship turn starboard, as the current was trying to take them, and them momentary letting go of the helm lurched the ship closer to the ghostly seas but helped them quickly dodge the tower. The ship skirted past it, and when it was behind them, the two men launched themselves at the helm again to continue sailing alongside the mists, not letting themselves go any closer.

Gora jumped slightly as a small hand grabbed at his sleeve, not having heard any sounds of someone coming up behind him, and he looked down to see Miyoshi clinging on to him and looking around—probably for the merfolk. His eyes were wide, and Gora let out a gentle huff of air.

'They've gone, lad. Something worse in there scared them off.'

Miyoshi turned towards the mists, eyes still wide, but the boy was too curious to return below and not look. He looked over the starboard railing, letting go of Gora's sleeve, and Gora could see the wind lifting the boy's stray hair, and the mists reached out, near brushing the boy.

'Get away, lad. I'm not sure we should be letting the mist touch us.'

'If it did?'

'Not sure, but there's something in there. Don't want to get too close.'

The boy nodded and stepped back. A rumbling came from within the mists, and then a yell from Tomioka as he shouted out in an effort to push the helm aside again.

His yell rang like a ghostly call against the swallowing silence of the mists, and as a shadow within lurched closer, Tomioka's final yell was joined by Nishimura, and the ship groaned as it lurched across a wave peak.

Then it slid down the other side, and the ship twisted away from the mists.

The crew held its breath and turned to Tomioka and Nishimura, watching them more easily pull the helm into control, turning their backs on the Wandering Abyss. They watched as Tomioka let go, letting Nishimura steer alone, seeing the relief on their faces as the ocean no longer fought to swallow the ship. The crew looked back at the Abyss and the shadow in the mists, just in time to see the shadow move—a long, unseen arm or tail of sorts thrashed out with a roar against a stone tower, which toppled noisily into the sea somewhere on the edge of the Abyss inside the mists.

'I think I'll repeat what Eshnaa said, sorry, Rijul. Thank fuck,' Simrita said, in Traders' this time so most could understand, slouching to sit on the deck, looking up at the sky.

Rijul's face widened in shock for a moment, but then he grinned and laughed. 'Okay, me too. Thank *fuck*.'

Gora grinned as the rest of his crew laughed with relief, and he turned to look back at the distance they were making away from the mists. He thought of Foy's ship lurching and disappearing within. Foy had let the ship be pulled in; that meant he must know a way through, even sailing through the mists near blind, dodging stone towers, avoiding or fighting the monsters within.

Gora rubbed the back of his head, now turning to watch Nishimura pull the ship back to sailing northwards, up the Wandering Abyss, but at a safer distance. They'd go around and find their way close to where Foy was aiming to go. How long it took to go around the Abyss, Gora didn't know, but he was pleased his crew had come together when it was needed once more, and though tired, they still came together to help them sail away.

Back to normal rotations now, though, Gora thought, now not needing to worry about Foy's ship suddenly turning to attack.

His final glance back to the mists was to look at Yonemura's compass once more, seeing the needles spin slower again as they got further away. Relieved there'd be no worry about being pulled into a swallowing pool from out here, Gora sent some of the crew to sleep to be there for the night rotation in a few hours. Then he too stomped below, thinking of merfolk, swallowing pools, and heavy mists, realising the strength yet in magic in the abandoned areas far from humanity. The boy had been right. Hadn't magic been dying? Yet it was still strong out here where humans didn't dwell, and if humans came close, magic was sure to swallow them up.

It was the scary part of the wild.

28

Escaping Through a Storm

Gora drummed his fingers on his stateroom desk, leaning back casually in his chair. How long had they been searching these waters after sailing around the Wandering Abyss? It had been endless enough trying to pass it, and now, after they'd finally found the open ocean on the other side of that monstrous mist, there was no clue to where Foy could be. The maps were empty, the ocean was empty, and he was bored.

'The sea slug can't still be inside,' he muttered, dropping his cheek into his hand resting by the elbow on the desk, 'can he?'

His eyes shifted once more across the map spread out upon his desk and saw once more that the map was clear.

This part of the ocean would be mostly uncharted. With the Wandering Abyss shifting as it wished here and there in this portion of the world, many people avoided it or couldn't charter it anyway. Any land here could potentially be swallowed back up if the Abyss returned, so there'd be no point.

'Where are you, ye bastard?' he growled, frowning.

His crew were getting restless. He knew that—how could he not? He felt it, he saw it, and no manner of learning activities now could help. They'd returned to their fighting lessons with the Ishillians helping Daiki and Ikeda teaching new skills, and the Hién crew's Traders' speak was coming along well. But now, idleness and unending waters were getting to them, and Gora knew they'd have to find port soon to break this mood and find purpose once again.

Give up on Foy? He wasn't ready for that yet, though.

Gora was about drifting off at his desk when he heard a yell and stomping down the passageway, and he jolted awake, sitting up straight and staring at his door. There was a quick knock before a young Miyoshi stormed inside with so much shock on his face that Gora didn't even bother to chastise the lad for not waiting for permission to enter.

The boy's chest heaved as he fought to catch his breath. 'Gora, sir! There's a ship. A different one. They're coming. We think pirates.'

Gora stood immediately and grabbed his *haori*, pulling it on and then grabbing his twin blades. 'Show me, lad.'

The boy nodded, spun on the spot, and bound out again, not even following the proper protocol of bowing, even a little. 'Gotta teach the lad manners again,' Gora sighed as he strode after him. 'We're far from Hizen, but the manners stay on the ship.' Grumbling to himself, Gora squinted into the bright midseason sun as he stepped onto the deck and looked about for the boy, who had paused halfway across the deck and was looking back at him.

'Over there!' the boy pointed portside, and Gora squinted into the distance.

Around him, Gora could see his crew turning to look at him, Ikeda and Satou standing by the portside railing to peer at the incoming ship. Gora joined them.

'Do you know who they are, captain?' Satou asked, greeting Gora as he arrived beside them.

Ikeda's face turned and his gaze bore into Gora's eyes as he too waited for a response. As ever, his gaze was heavy, and Gora rose an eyebrow as he turned back to look over the sea.

'Those sails: three masts with ribbed sails like a dragon's wing—middle Enssan style. Remember, we saw plenty of ships like that in Shon Wa? Local build to their mainland.' Gora looked closer, trying to look at the flag. He didn't recognise the symbol, but then, it had been a while since he'd known and studied them, and plenty of pirates could have popped up in the many years he'd been in Hié. 'Definitely pirates, but not sure who.'

'Could Foy have sent them after he left the wandering sea?' Ikeda asked, his hands leaning on the railing and face set more serious than ever.

'Perhaps. Who knows, other than them.'

'Is there a way to find out? It might help us find them.'

Shingo had appeared behind them, and he too now looked over the sea. The boy was beside him. Gora took a breath and held it as he thought, letting it out slowly.

'Not in a way we're going to like. But it looks like it'll happen anyway—pirate raid.'

The Shon Wa ship was sailing directly towards them, and Gora turned to see who was at the helm. Yonemura. *Perfect,* he thought. It was her skill he'd need to outrun that ship. He hailed her as he jogged over.

'Yonemura, take us away. We can't afford to get involved with another pirate ship. Outrun it, then find a place to moor up.'

'We're going to land?'

Gora's decision from earlier had been helped by the appearance of the Shon Wa ship. His crew were tired. Weeks of sailing on empty seas would do that to a crew, and another interaction with pirates in this state could be the end of them. He nodded to Yonemura, and her face showed understanding. She turned to monitor the Shon Wa ship, set her brow, and then turned the helm slightly starboard.

Gora sighed and then looked about the rest of the blue waters. Perhaps it was time to return to Hié for a while—to take stock, find a new plan, and figure out what to do from there. If Foy had got out of the Wandering Abyss and spread word about a black-and-red ship hunting the pirates, maybe it was best that they returned, found a new plan, and found out what Yoshiko advised. His eyes slid over to the figurehead, both his heart and head realising at the same time what it was that he needed right now and where his own hesitancy had been. He needed her advice. Gora had promised to return now and then and report, and it had been a while. And now, with the new information that he knew about the larger pirate circles and with Foy getting away to spread the word, he knew the situation had changed from what they originally set out for. They needed to return to Hié, and he needed to speak with his closest friend and leader.

Mind made, he nodded to himself and strode back towards Ikeda, who was assessing the Shon Wa ship from the stern deck, having moved to see it clearly with the turning ship. They both looked at it, seeing it having moved too, following them.

'They're definitely aiming for us,' the young man muttered to Gora, eyes sliding to look at him sidelong through his fringe. He tucked it behind his ear as he looked back at the following ship.

Gora hummed in thought. 'We're returning to Hié,' he told the young samurai, seeing the lad immediately turn his full head to face him, expression opening up and eyes alert. The dark eyes sought his for explanation, and Gora couldn't help but let out a little, amused huff with a small smile twitching across his lips. 'Aye, I need to speak with Yoshiko. And the crew could do with time at home.'

A spark that had left young Ikeda's eyes for a while now returned, and the lad's cheeks flushed slightly, and he turned away to watch the ship again in pretence to hide it. A small smile tugged also on the young warrior's lips, and Gora's heart settled. He knew it was the right thing to do, and the lad's reaction had settled it.

'Let's just survive this.' Gora gestured with his eyebrows at the incoming Shon Wa ship, and Ikeda nodded, standing taller and looking around the deck.

'I'll call the defence,' he said in a low voice, and then both men bowed their heads to one another.

'As you will,' Gora said, smiling and returning his gaze to the incoming ship. His heart soared. 'Let's go home.'

He turned to look at Ikeda guiding the fighters, now all awake, the young man's enthusiasm renewed. Gora knew Ikeda preferred Hié. He knew Ikeda would have stayed as the new guard for Yoshiko, a woman Gora knew the lad admired. If not for Ikeda's determination to help Daiki, who had been troubled at the time with the deaths of his family at what the old samurai felt was his own fault, the boy would never have come to sea. Gora looked now at Daiki, who seemed more bright-eyed and happier with a new purpose on the ocean. What would their decisions be when they returned to Hié? He felt Daiki would stay, fitting in well with this life of hunting pirates and helping to stop others from experiencing what he experienced with the loss of his family. But the lad … would he see his mentor's life renewed and then stay behind in Hié?

Gora went to speak with Yonemura at the helm and let her know the plans.

'What's a Shon Wa ship doing this far out to the middling seas?' she asked.

Gora too was worried about this, and he turned to look at the ship in the distance. 'Not sure. But I think it's best we do whatever we can to avoid it. Head east, and we'll figure out the rest later.'

Yonemura nodded and turned the helm, calling out instructions to the crew to help her sail east and escape the Shon Wa pirate ship. Gora quickly returned to his quarters, pulling out a map from his chest and flopping into his chair at the desk to review it. He joined it with the map of this region of the middling seas he had currently open and tried to figure out where they were compared with the full world map. They'd have a long way to sail east, and they'd need stops on the way. So, for now, which route was the best to head for to help them run from the pirates? He knew it had to be an official one. No more skulking on pirate islands for now. Not until they'd returned home, refreshed, and come back.

He sat for a while, staring blankly at the markings on the map. Shon Wa really was a trek from here, and he couldn't figure out what that ship would be doing this far from home seas. Mostly, pirates stuck to their regions and rarely spread out. Now and then, Foy and his circle would spread out and cause trouble and meet with others, but Foy was ruthless and a larger name in the pirate circles. Only known captains could spread beyond their borders. Others would get shot down by powers higher than them.

Either this Shon Wa ship was foolish and soon to die by other pirate hands, or they were a higher power. That or they were here for a gathering.

Gora thought of Foy's ship disappearing into the mists of the wandering sea and how they'd not been able to find him on the other side yet. Foy wasn't the sort to stay low for long, so it was unlikely he was still on the inside. That meant, if he'd not been killed by the Wandering Abyss, he'd have to have found his way out and headed somewhere else. Where was the pirate queen? Gora didn't know. He remembered being taken to a meeting place in his young pirate days, but back then, he didn't want anything to do with them and only thought about his escape. He never considered remembering or paying attention to where their leaders lived. He scolded his young self. He should have been more aware of everything, if only to save his own skin.

So if Foy's gone to the queen, and the Shon Wa ship is here too, could they also be going to the queen?

Gora furrowed his brow. Even more reason to get as far away as they could.

Over the course of the afternoon, Gora returned to the deck to see the sky darkening and the clouds billowing. Ahead, to the east, black clouds loomed, and the sea beneath it turned grey and choppy. Behind, the Shon Wa pirates still gave chase, and Gora knew their ship to be closer than last he was up here.

'What's with the storm?' Gora asked Shingo, who was monitoring Nishimura on the helm while Yonemura rested for swapping back in the night.

Both Shingo and Nishimura looked ahead to the storm, and it was the peaceful Nishimura who answered. 'It's no normal storm. Something stirs in the seas, and the sky stirs with it.'

Both Shingo and Gora looked at Nishimura uncertainly, but the young man simply looked ahead. He spoke again. 'It will get much worse. It will be a rough night. Should we turn back and go around?'

Gora looked back at the Shon Wa ship once more and realised that, should they go back, the ship would catch up with them. It would be certain danger if they did. If they were to go through the storm, they could lose the Shon Wa ship, and while it would still be dangerous, it would be less so than an enemy deliberately aiming cannon fire upon them.

'Go through,' Gora said, wondering if he'd regret his decision.

Shingo looked at Gora and studied his face for a while then nodded his agreement. The growing wind ruffled the older man's greying hair, but his alert eyes moved to study the storm. His jaw was set, and he spoke to Nishimura.

'You will need help on the helm, no doubt. Can you last a while to give Yonemura more rest? Though'—he looked again at the choppy seas ahead—'it may be a job for Tomioka to help you.'

Nishimura's face slid into a light frown. 'It may be a job for Tomioka, though with Yonemura's guidance and her skills at the ready. It will be a long one, and we will have need for rotating.'

'It'll be that long?'

The young man nodded, and he looked to Shingo for a moment and gestured to the helm. Shingo took it while the young man tied his hair out of his face, and Gora's stomach lurched to see the man tie all of his hair up into a knot at the back of his head. To have it all back meant full focus, and Gora only then realised how strong this storm might be that he was sending his crew into.

He observed Nishimura for a while as he took back the helm, but the man's face was closed and peaceful as ever. Nishimura was sturdy and had a strange affinity for the natural and spiritual, and if he said the storm was to be bad, Gora believed it. But the man showed no concern, despite tying his full hair back to focus, and Gora wondered if he could take that as a sign that Nishimura trusted their spirits to keep them safe. Gora thought now of the shrine in the forest back in Hié, and the old kitsuné shrine guard statues. He was a long way from home, but would they carry his message to the gods?

We're just trying to get home, and being made to choose between a storm or pirates is just taking the piss.

Gora watched Ikeda cheerfully darting across the deck to finish preparations for defence. He seemed lighthearted for the first time in a while—the journey taking its toll on the young man who wanted to be near home and not away too long—and the rising winds rushed through Ikeda's short ponytail and fringe and through his *haori* sleeves and *hakama* legs. The young man stopped, glared into the dark clouds in the east, and rolled up his sleeves, turning to meet Gora's eyes.

Both nodded to one another and then carried on.

I need to tell the crew we're heading for home, Gora thought. If anything could encourage them to get through this, it would be the thought of home.

As he told them of his plan, Miyoshi's eyes widened with the excitement of seeing his family, and the expressions of others mirrored his excitement. And just as Gora hoped, the mood of the crew rose, and their energy increased just in time to handle escaping pirates through a storm.

A gust of wind caught the sails and lurched the boat sideways, slackening the sails and causing them to flap noisily. Nishimura groaned with the effort of bringing the ship back, and Gora called Miyoshi.

'Fetch Tomioka. We need his help at the helm.'

The boy nodded and ran off—ever his only state of movement—and Nishimura bowed his head gratefully. Tomioka ran back up with the boy immediately, the wind lifting his soft, black, usually well-kept hair. His face immediately focused, eyes piercing the surroundings and stubbled face falling to a frown. He stood by, waiting for the time Nishimura needed his help.

'Reef the sails! Tie them down!' Gora yelled at his crew, watching Jelani, Sakai, Kyo, and Taro immediately clamber up the shrouds and edge along the masts to bring the mainsail down.

Gora turned to face the storm again and squinted through the sea spray.

He glared and rubbed his hand through the back of his hair as he thought. 'Shingo!' Gora hailed the man as he jogged up to him.

Shingo had been leading those in the masts in reefing the sails, and he stopped pointing upwards and turned to face his captain as Gora reached him. The two spoke with their voices raised against the rising winds, and Shingo too turned to face the storm.

'It comes from a right rotation,' Shingo said, looking carefully, 'so sailing portside will give us the best chance to sail away from the growing storm.'

At this, Gora nodded. He'd thought so too. The waves skimmed and pushed from the starboard side, so turning to sail portside would have a natural boost as well as helping them be free sooner. He clapped his hand on Shingo's upper back in thanks and left his first mate to continue guiding the crew.

Gora returned to the helm to relay the message to Tomioka and Nishimura, who agreed with Shingo's assessment and turned the helm easily portside. No resistance came from the waves from this move, and Nishimura's face looked just a little more peaceful at the move. With that, Gora felt encouragement enough.

'Aye, we'll make it through,' Gora told them, half to tell himself. And with the sails down and the crew harnessed with lines passed out by Miyoshi, they were ready to embrace the storm that had hit them.

29

Storms and Plain Sailing

The storms were always the scariest part of sailing, Miyoshi thought as he slipped over the deck, but nothing he'd experienced on his family's fishing boats was anything like the storms of the open sea. True, back in Hié, you got some incredible typhoons and storms, and fishingfolk at times never returned. But here, in the open blue, there was nothing to swallow the fury of the waves. Only the power of the spirits and gods could make it stop.

Miyoshi yelled out as the ship lurched again and then dropped down the other side of the wave. He heard a brief cry as Tomioka and Nishimura tried to keep control of the helm and stop the ship from capsizing. Their yells were soon drowned out in the noise of the storm, as was anyone's cry out here.

They'd tried to escape the pirates by sailing into the storm. And true, as Miyoshi looked around them, he could no longer see the strange sails of that Shon Wa ship. But the storm seemed bigger and more dangerous than they'd originally anticipated, and his captain's face was now in a permanent frown or grimace as he rushed about the deck to keep his crew alive.

'Either way,' Miyoshi muttered, pouting, realising that either way, they'd have struggled to get out alive.

He thought back to the pirate that had chased him on the island, yelling out curses and strange threats as he bore his sword. Miyoshi shivered, and he couldn't decide which was better or worse either. This storm was fearsome and tumultuous, and he felt like a giant creature had picked them up with its hands or tentacles and was tossing them about like a child plays with a toy. Nature was scary. But the people of Hié were used to fighting to survive against nature. In Hizen, earthshakes and typhoons and all kinds of other forces of nature reigned and made the humans fight to survive. His kinsfolk wouldn't let a storm like this stop them.

The boy grit his teeth. Neither would he. He'd prove his strength and worth for Gora.

He slipped the remaining way to the main sail post and grabbed at the lines. His job was to check they were tied properly and they were tight. If any one of these lines failed, it could be the life of a crew member. He gulped and checked again. Only when he was certain did he turn to meet the eyes of one of the leaders—Gora was somewhere on the deck with his back to him as he guided the crew, so Miyoshi hunted out Shingo. The man gave a smile of relief as the boy nodded.

Miyoshi felt relief too. Now, with this check done, he'd been told to head below for a moment of respite and to help Taro check the hold. Pleased to be free of the stinging winds and rains, Miyoshi rushed to the doorway and untied himself from his line with rain-numbed fingers, taking care on the steps for once with the lurching of the ship.

Miyoshi crashed through the galley doorway, making Kimura jump and turn from his place at the counter. Kyo and Sakai were here for the respite, too, with warm bowls of broth and blankets over their shoulders, and Yonemura was eating her first meal to begin her rotation, waiting here until called. There'd be no point in her heading up there to be soaked, not until she was needed,

Miyoshi thought. They'd want her down here as long as needed until they did need her.

The boy greeted them politely as he slid onto the bench at the table and watched Kimura preparing the broth, wondering how he could keep the supplies and cooking gear in control while they sailed in such conditions. Then Kimura drew his hand back quickly and swore, and Miyoshi looked awkwardly back at the table until Kimura passed his bowl over. The boy bowed his head and cupped the bowl gratefully in his cold hands, feeling the heat seep through until it was hot enough to the touch that he had to draw his hands away. The ship lurched again and some of his soup sloshed free, and the boy cried out, quickly slurping it from the table.

He looked up to see the other three obviously looking away, pretending not to have seen it. Kyo's gentle outbreath and awkward sidelong look at the wall gave it away, mirroring Yonemura's raised eyebrows as she looked over at Kimura and opened her mouth as if to speak, finding nothing to talk about.

The boy guiltily returned to his soup, trying to gulp the rest of it down as quickly as he could so it wouldn't spill again, crying out at the heat as it burned his tongue and the roof of his mouth.

'Take care, Yūki.' Kimura turned to face him again, and this time, the other three turned back with concerned looks on their faces. 'Take your time; it's still very hot.'

Sakai reached for the boy's water beaker and tipped some of his own drink in there for the boy to cool his tongue. 'Here. You drink yours too fast before the meal.'

Miyoshi bowed his head quietly at the man and took a sip, taking care to take it more slowly this time to show gratitude. He looked at Sakai. When Miyoshi had first seen Sakai joining the ship, he'd been a little afraid of him. The man was in his middling years and had a serious, closed face, made more serious by skin that was starting to sag and pucker with frown lines. This made him often look like he was frowning or unhappy, and the man's quiet personality made him seem all the more unapproachable. To make it scarier for the young boy, Miyoshi had seen tattoos on the man's chest, beneath his kimono, when the wind blew strong. In Hizen, tattoos meant the criminal underclass, and it wasn't often you saw them in Hié. Miyoshi had heard the stories of the gangs and the prisoners who decorated their bodies with permanent ink, and he imagined wild, loud, vicious people. He'd never seen anyone with a tattoo before, until Sakai. No-one really knew why Sakai was there, apart from the captain and maybe a couple of the other leaders. Miyoshi's wild imagination had him imagining Sakai stealing out of the prisons in the capital and running to a ship to take him away from prisoner life, or having a run-in with an enemy gang and having to run away. But, after months of sailing with the man, Miyoshi just couldn't imagine these anymore. Sakai was kind and thoughtful, and he took care of the crew well. He was a group man and worked hard in the background to keep people comfortable. Sharing his drink with Miyoshi after he had burned his mouth was just one moment of many where his kindness had broken through Miyoshi's anxiety around Sakai's tattoos and past, and the boy turned back to his meal, content.

He's really not so scary.

Miyoshi took care with the rest of his meal until it became easily drinkable, and then he leapt up from the table and charged down the hallway to meet Taro in the hold. Or rather, he imagined himself charging, when really the tossing boat made him tumble to and fro, crashing into the wall to the side of him and pushing himself back up to run the rest of the way, trying not to tip and trip over. At one point, the boy nearly swore that his whole body lifted off the ground with the drop after a surge, and his heart pounded.

His lips were dry when he reached Taro in the storage hold and hesitantly asked, 'Will we survive?'

Taro turned from where he crouched to tighten a tie and looked at the young boy standing hesitantly in the doorway, hands on the doorframe. Miyoshi's eyes were wide, and Taro smiled slightly. He raised from his crouch and padded carefully over to Miyoshi, stroking his wiry facial hair for a moment as he thought.

'Of course. We have the best crew to survive. Can you imagine we wouldn't?'

Miyoshi felt hesitant, and he looked up at the man for a moment, not knowing what to say. The ship lurched again, but this time, the boy's heart slowed, and he calmed. They'd sailed free of sea serpents, the shadow, pirates, and more. Surely they could survive a storm. Miyoshi nodded and then mumbled that the captain had told him to come and help Taro check on the supplies and help keep them tied down.

Taro's face washed with relief that the boy was settled, and he guided Miyoshi through his next tasks, keeping the boy so busy he had no time for worry. As he ran about the hold, Miyoshi wondered when the storm would end, or when they'd escape it. When he was up on the deck, he'd overheard Gora talking about sailing portside to leave through the side, avoiding the storm's direction of growth.

How do they know which way a storm grows? The boy wondered if anyone would tell him. If it could help him be a little more useful to the crew, he wanted to know.

He stayed below in the hold for hours, Taro keeping him busy. The ship still lurched, and the noise of the ocean and the growling of the sky still, even from the hold, drowned out his ears. Miyoshi was glad he was down here in the dry at least, rather than up on the deck where he'd be getting wet, cold, and miserable. But to not be able to see how things were going and feel reassured was a trouble to him.

'Sounds like the storm's ending,' Taro said casually, but not with a small amount of relief.

Miyoshi looked up at the older man, whose eyes narrowed in thought. The man looked up from his work and met Miyoshi's eyes—kind, dark eyes looked back. The man's face crinkled into a smile, and he repeated himself.

'How do you know?' Miyoshi asked, trying to listen.

'See, it's quieter, and the lurching has lessened. I imagine they're sailing out of the side now.'

Miyoshi longed to go and see, but he still had things Taro had given him to do. But as he pulled on the ties to make sure their hold was settled, he paid more attention to the rolling of the ship and the striking of the air and ocean. And, as Taro had said, the tossing was less and the world just a little quieter, and the boy took a moment now to realise they were sailing home.

He thought of his mother waiting. She'd been anxious when he asked to come on this journey, and he remembered her worried expression as he'd left. She'd tried to look happy and certain, wishing him safe travels as she'd hugged him farewell, but as he turned to watch from the deck of the ship as they pulled away from the Hié port, her face looked worried. He imagined her smile when he returned, and he worked just a little faster and harder to finish Taro's instructions, feeling happy they were returning home. She'd have been lonely while he was away—they were all each other had now. He'd make her proud of who he was becoming, and he hoped he'd grown even a little over these months at sea.

'Nothing's going to stop us now.' The boy grinned, rolling up his sleeves and standing tall, trying to make an impression as he and Taro finished with the hold and noticed the quieting of the storm even more.

Taro looked at the boy and laughed cheerfully. He reached over and rustled his hand through Miyoshi's hair. 'Aye, Yūki. We're going home. Nothing will stop us now.'

30

Foy Brings Friends

Gora's clothes stuck to his skin and clung like icy rags, freezing his body in the dying wind. He stood on the deck, watching the storm disappear behind them as his ship pulled free of the side, escaping the growing death trap inside.

Ahh, the spirits blessed us that that was only young. He ran a hand through his wet hair, stretching out his body as he turned away from the storm to look ahead.

About him, the crew looked just as relieved as he felt, their misery at the cold and wet temporarily forgotten as cheers of victory rose from about the deck.

We survived the storm, and the Shon Wa ship doesn't seem to be in sight. Gora plodded about the deck, examining their situation. He thought deeply and gave the crew instructions to take turns to run below, re-dress, and warm up. *Kimura would have water heating up by now for people to use buckets to wash.* Gora imagined a hot spring bath back in Hié, and his body stung from the cold at the comparison. He gave an involuntary shudder and tried to block out thoughts of the warmth just yet. His crew had to warm up first.

Gora nodded to Nishimura at the helm as he walked up to him and held out his hands to trade posts. Nishimura's face lit up with relief, and Gora held on to the spokes. 'Go and warm up, lad. You sailed well.'

Nishimura padded off quickly, releasing his long hair from the knot and letting it drop down his back as he ran below for warmth.

Gora watched as the young man disappeared below. He'd earned every moment of warmth—he'd sailed the entire duration of the storm and kept them on the path towards the end. It was even he who spotted the best route to safety, and Gora knew he was a key part of their being free right now.

Gora held the ship steady at the helm until the crew eventually drifted back. Warm and dry and fed, they filtered back to the deck and clambered about, releasing the sails again and releasing the safely lines. Gora watched as the canvas billowed and caught the wind, and he felt a smile creep onto his face. The ship sailed smoothly, and for the first time in hours, he truly believed they were going home. His heart soared, and not even the stinging cold of his clinging clothes could cool the burning of his heart and soul. And when Yonemura ran up to relieve him of the helm and give him time below, Gora took a moment to watch as his crew continued with a spring in their steps and light on their faces.

Home, he thought. This was the first time on a ship he'd felt this feeling—of sailing home. Last time, they'd been sailing back to Hié from Acrein to stop the war and release the people, and they'd had no idea what they'd be returning to. And all the times before that, he'd never considered anything home. But now, with a good crew, good friends, and the woman who felt like his sister waiting to hear his crazy stories and tell him her own, he finally felt like he had a home to return to.

The thought carried him through like he was walking on the softest of grass on the best of days back in Hié, and Gora rushed to warm up and eat, with Kimura hounding him to eat more and take a moment to rest. But with too much excitement and a fire still flooding his body from the survival of the storm, Gora couldn't rest. He couldn't sit still. He grew impatient at Kimura's constant forcing of more food, and though he knew it was for the best, Gora leapt up and returned to the deck before Kimura could hound him anymore, leaving the young chef calling out behind him.

But Gora didn't care. Any moment of stalling felt like it would delay their return, and he rushed to the forecastle to watch the route, the sea gliding past them peacefully finally, nothing in their way.

It seemed much that way for days—clear skies, smooth seas, and nothing to stop them. Gora planned their route with Shingo and Yonemura to take them safely below the middle continents, and then up and around the eastern ones until they reached the final climb to Hié on the edge of the world. Each day, he, Shingo, Yonemura, and Tomioka would meet and discuss the trip, the route, the crew's welfare, and their resources, wondering how long they could hold off before needing to port and restock. They discussed safe landing options and places to avoid if they wanted to stay clear of pirates. It seemed funny to them, now, that before they'd deliberately sought the pirates out, and now they were desperately trying to avoid them. Nothing could get in the way of their return home. They'd come back for the pirates.

The crew's mood had lightened, and people hollered cheerfully to one another and lessons for fighting and language restarted with the lightening of people's worries. On more than one occasion, Gora found himself glad of the decision he'd made. There were only so many pirates one could handle before needing to return home to something peaceful and beautiful, and Hié offered both.

This jovial feeling continued for four days after the storm, until the fifth. Gora ran up to the deck from his stateroom, and he found his crew silent and hesitant. He followed their gaze and fell to Shingo's side, taking out his spyglass.

'What is it?' Gora asked, positioning his glass to where Shingo pointed.

'Pirates, we think. Several ships appeared on the horizon earlier, and we've been watching them, hoping they were sailing in a different direction. It seems certain now they're coming this way.'

Gora's spyglass found its mark, and he peered through, finally silent and frowning.

'Fuck.'

Gora's skin tingled, and he felt like he'd been dunked in the ocean and dragged back out by the very demons he saw incoming now. He could feel the sting of Shingo and the crew awaiting his reply, all watching him, the weight of their expectations dunking him back into the ocean to be dragged out once more. Worse, he knew his answer would dishearten them all.

'What is it?' Shingo whispered, leaning closer.

Gora opened his mouth to reply, still staring into the distance, vision glazing over. No noise came out. His lips were as dry as salt, and his breath caught. Then Gora closed his eyes, forced himself to take a deep breath, and let it out slowly.

'Foy's back. And he brought friends.'

There was a murmuring behind them as the others speculated, and Shingo looked once more at the incoming armada, his ocean-weathered face sinking. He ran a hand through his salt-and-pepper hair and sighed then looked at Gora sidelong through his tired eyes. 'No chance they'll let us be? Just as we were happy to be heading home.'

'Aye, 'tis often the way. When you're happy, pirates smash you down. That's it,' Gora said, reflecting on his whole life and wondering how it came in circles like this.

'Can we outsail them?'

Gora shook his head. 'They're faster. Look—'

Both looked through their spyglasses once more, watching the streamlined ships sail for the Hizen-acquired Acrein warship.

'Can we out-gun them?'

'That's likely a no, too. Too many of them.'

'But we managed to break free of the others after leaving that pirate isle.'

'Aye, but that time there were underling pirate ships. They look like higher. See the quality of the ships, and the variety. I'd wager it's those that report to the queen. The old sea demon's gone to the pirate council.'

Gora turned on the spot and scratched the back of his head, feeling stressed and not wanting to show it to the crew. Once again, they were looking at him, and he met a few of their gazes. Eshnaa, Miyoshi, Sakai, Jelani, Simrita—their dark eyes seeking answers he didn't have yet, and likely would never have.

'We can only do our best,' Gora said slowly. 'Try to outsail them. We're near the middling continent. If we can find somewhere to lose them and hide for a while—to pull into port, restock, refresh, and lose them—then we should.' Gora looked about the ship and met Tomioka's eyes. 'Tomioka, lead the fast sailing of this ship. Shingo, come with me to plan a place to hide. Everyone else, if you want to go home, sail like your life depends on it'—he turned back to look at the incoming ships—'because it does.'

* * *

The pirate force was soon close enough to see without the spyglass, and they were making straight for *Sea Guardian*. The boat Foy had commandeered was at the centre, and several spanned out either side, with a giant ship behind them—a ship so large it would dwarf even the Acrein warship, and of a size like Gora had never seen.

How's that monster sailing so fast? he wondered, peering at the detailing through his spyglass. His eyes boggled even just looking at it, and he tore himself away. Watching the ships wasn't going to solve their problem.

If we survive, I'm sending out messengers all across Hizen for sailors …

Even with a greater sailing number, though, Gora knew there was no hope for his warship to sail fast enough to flee the pirate group. The dragon-winged ship returned once more from their starboard side, cutting *Sea Guardian* off. Gora grimaced. There was no hiding now.

'Why are they not firing at us?' Shingo slipped beside him again, having helped Moori ready the on-deck cannons.

Gora scratched his head. He had no answer and told Shingo such.

The man with peppered-grey hair tilted his head in thought. 'Do you think they want to talk?'

'Why would they want to?' In Gora's mind, pirates preferred killing and action—at least, all the ones he knew of did. 'Frewin only talked so he could try to steal our ship. Ain't gunna risk that again.'

'To find out what you really want. Foy knows you're out to get them. Maybe they don't know why.'

'I reckon it's more they want to rob and bleed us dry, then blow us up,' Gora sighed, rubbing his cheek. His good mood and his hope for returning home had left him, and he now felt that same heart-dropping defeat and hopelessness he remembered as a boy. Would he never be free of pirates? Could he not go back home for some happiness? He should never have come on this mission; then they'd have been fine.

Gora's heart stung. But the children the pirates took wouldn't be fine.

He looked about at the crew. Their faces showed determination, each one defiant.

'You know, they'll not be stopped. They want to go home, too.'

'Reading my mind?'

Shingo laughed a little and clapped Gora on the shoulder. 'We're all thinking the same. Like you always tell us: we'll figure something out.' Then Shingo nodded to the incoming ships. 'If they're not shooting us from out there, we have a chance. If they want to come and rob us and bleed us dry, then they're coming aboard, and we have a chance. I'll get the figurehead's fire ready— we have a chance.'

Gora met Shingo's gaze and saw the same determination as with the rest of the crew. The dark eyes burned like glowing embers, and Gora thought it was much like how Yoshiko's looked—that same look of refusing to let a bad situation get the better of them.

Gora let a smile cross his face, and he looked down at the deck a moment and rubbed the back of his neck bashfully, feeling slightly ashamed of himself for losing hope. He looked back up at Shingo and smiled again, this time broader. 'Aye, you're right. We still have a chance.'

But when the pirate ships drew closer and circled around them, blocking *Sea Guardian's* way, Gora wasn't sure he could convince himself of that much longer. The huge ship—the one greater than anything Gora had seen before—closed in from the left and towered over them, and the remaining ships gathered about, blocking all routes of escape. Not even a rowing boat could slip through. The dragon-wing ship hovered off to the side, and Gora could feel the sting of their watching.

Ropes lowered from the giant ship on the port side, and Daiki called out for the fighting team to spread out and watch all angles, his face closed and eyes narrowed his focus. Blades and guns ready, and Moori and Shingo waiting at the upper deck cannons, Gora's ship fell silent.

31
The Pirate Queen,
Sacrifices, and Magic

Waves licked against the hulls, and a shrill voice atop the giant ship cried out orders. More ropes dropped to Gora's deck with dull thuds as they smacked against the woodwork. Faces appeared over the edge of the large ship's gunwale, and then several women clambered over and down to Gora's deck. Gora licked his lips, tasting salt, watching, fists curling at his sides.

The first woman jumped the rest of the way when her journey was sure, and her boots thudded on the deck. She turned and scanned the deck, light brown eyes narrowing as she glared about them, pulling a gun from the belt at her hip. The woman was incredibly young, Gora realised, likely not too much older than Yoshiko. She had a narrow face, short, curly hair that ruffled in the wind, and a short, slightly upturned nose that made it look like she was constantly looking down on people, bored. She watched another pirate woman land beside her, both acknowledging one another quickly. Gora thought they were quite alike, the other one a few years older with longer wavy hair instead and curvier hips but a softer, warmer face. Four others followed shortly after.

Simrita, shifting on the spot where she stood and looking between Eshnaa, Daiki, and these women, gave up her patience and darted forwards, raising her *talwar* blade. As she did, the two women at the front gave Simrita a sharp bark to wait, and then looked up at their ship, watching whoever was coming down the ropes now. Gora looked up too, and his breath caught.

'Wait,' he said sharply, and Sim turned back and gave him a frustrated expression. Daiki and Ikeda beside him turned to look at him with the same expression mirroring their faces, and he gave them an apologetic shrug.

The six women on the deck hadn't rushed in to kill them all; instead, they stood about in a protective arch, waiting for the seventh member. A plank suspended between two ropes was lowered with a woman standing on it. Dark chestnut hair peppered with grey fell in soft waves, her face warm and homely. But in that face, shrewd copper eyes pierced those about the ship as the ropes lowered the woman onto *Sea Guardian's* deck. She wore a tailored, quality black jacket over a simple soft grey blouse and well-tailored trousers around full hips, and her high-quality boots looked nearly new. Two hand pistols and a blade hung at double belts that crossed over her wide hips, and a thick gold ring glinted in the sunlight as she held on to the ropes.

Before she even stepped aboard between the six women from her crew, Gora had already realised who this was.

'It's the queen,' he muttered in Hizen as way of explaining to those around him why he didn't want them rushing forward. If they rushed forward and attacked the queen, there'd be no hope of getting out of here and returning home. At least if they could play along and find out what she wanted, some of them might make it out alive.

The woman's boots clunked as the strode between her crew and stopped between the two that looked similar. Seeing the three together, Gora realised they resembled one another and wondered if they were related, she being their mother or aunt. All looked more normal and homely than he would have expected for pirates—soft-featured, fairly good-looking, and as if they were from one of the southern middling continent countries where fruits and olives grew rich and the people healthy and happy. From when he was a child, Gora had always imagined the pirate queen as someone frightening-looking—strange, with the eyes of a demon, a gaunt face, and a tall, spindly appearance. This woman looked like any other house matriarch, more suited to inviting people in for a warm meal and not letting them leave until they were full to the brim. What she was doing as the ruling figure of the pirates, he had no idea.

Her copper eyes finally landed on his after scanning everyone present, and Gora felt her gaze dig into his soul. A smile crossed her face, and her features became sly, knowing—too knowing.

'You're the devil's child I've heard about,' she said in Traders', not questioning.

'How much has the old sea dog told ya?'

'Enough.' Her smirk deepened, and her gaze refused to drop. It felt like she was trying to read everything about him. Then, without even breaking her gaze, she raised her arm and pointed. 'Give me that child.'

Gora blinked and tore his eyes away from hers and looked to where she pointed, seeing Miyoshi standing with gaping mouth.

There was a pause as the ship tried to process what she said, and Gora's brain clouded over for a moment before a laugh bubbled from his lips. He roared with a laugh that made him grab at his stomach to stop the pain that ached there, and deep within his soul, he wondered whether he'd finally lost his mind.

It's finally been too much.

Her face never dropped its look as he laughed, and when he finally finished, he grinned and caught her gaze. 'Never.' His voice was low and dangerous, he knew that, and he saw Miyoshi flinch.

'Did you really think you could get away with that?' Ikeda stormed forward, katana in his hand, face lit up in fury with a snarl more like Gora would expect to see on Yoshiko's face, and his eyes burned with rage just as hot.

'Ikeda.' Daiki's warning came low, but the young man ignored it as he stormed across the deck towards the queen.

The queen's guardians raised their weapons, and a chill ran down Gora's spine as he heard yells from the ships about them and the clicks of readying guns.

'Ikeda, really, stop.' Gora joined Daiki's warning, scanning about them. The crew had gone pale and were peering about at the guns from the surrounding ships pointing at them, and Ikeda stopped where he stood and whirled around, looking at Gora in disbelief.

'Do you want to go home, lad?' Gora said in Hizen with a low voice. 'Want to get out of here alive? We're not going to get back to those we love like this.'

Gora tried to hold a steady gaze with the lad, and the young man's face fell into a look of despair. His sword arm dropped and hung limply by his side. 'We're here to defend and look after the crew. How can we do that if we can't fight them off?'

Gora saw the other fighters do the same, putting away their weapons as they realised their roles were useless at this point. Simrita looked just as frustrated, and she huffed as she watched the pirates, fiddling with the bright yellow silk of her tunic and pouting. Eshnaa and Rijul looked to their friend and then to one another and shrugged, but then stood facing different directions and watching the other ships carefully. If they couldn't fight, they'd at least stand guard.

Gora stepped forwards and rested a hand on Ikeda's shoulder. The young man didn't move, so Gora let out a small huff and, bending close to the young samurai's ear, said, 'You know, she's waiting for us to come back alive.'

There was a pause, and in the pause, Gora could hear the seven pirate women muttering to one another in that middling continent language. He frowned. He had no idea what they were saying, but keeping his eye on them while he rested his hand on Ikeda's shoulder, he could see them sussing the crew out—pointing at Miyoshi, nodding towards Gora, eyes watching the others—figuring out how to get what they wanted. Then Ikeda nodded and put away his blade, and he glanced sidelong with sad eyes at Gora.

'Sometimes, lad, the best defence is not fighting.' Gora left him with those parting words before gesturing for the lad to step back, and he took his place in front of the pirate queen.

'Surely you didn't just come here for the boy. So, tell me. What do you want? What shit did Foy tell you about us?'

The pirate queen stopped muttering to the soft-faced one beside her, who looked like her family, and a smile crossed her face again, and she stepped forward to stand in front of him.

'I heard you were one of us, and now you're hunting us.' She looked about at the ships that surrounded them. 'Once you're part of the family, you don't hurt them.'

'I'm not your family.'

The woman let out a laugh. 'I'll tell you what you want to hear. You'll join us again or you'll die, anyway. Take me to your stateroom where we can talk more privately.'

Gora narrowed his eyes at her and heard a muttering behind him.

'Captain, I don't think that's a good idea,' Yonemura said hesitantly, getting agreement from the others.

'What if she kills you?'

'What if they kill all of us?' someone else hissed back.

Gora shrugged. 'Alright. But your girls stay here, and they don't hurt my crew. Nor do all your other goons there.' He gestured with a tilt of his head to the surrounding entourage, and the homely-looking pirate queen smiled again.

'That can be arranged.'

She called out something in her middling continent language to the women behind her, who nodded. The young one with the short, curly hair and the severe-looking face looked stunned, and stepped forward and protested, grabbing the queen's arm. But the queen just turned and reassured her, and Gora found himself wondering what their relations were. He'd expected the queen to be terrifying and strange, but she just acted like a mother. He sniffed. She may be friendly to those on her ship, but she led the pirates with an unrelenting rule, one that made such fierce and gruesome pirates as Foy and others not want to set a foot wrong. There was something dangerous about this woman, he knew, and the stories he'd heard of her must have come from somewhere.

His heart thudded in his chest as he took a step down towards the lower decks and to his stateroom at the stern of the ship, each step feeling like he was descending into the underrealms with no hope of stepping back into the light. Her heels echoed on the wood behind him like a Shinigami death god haunting his steps, and sweat pricked the back of his neck.

'Aye, in here,' he muttered, mouth dry. He noticed the bottle of liquor on the side. 'Drink? Liquor.'

The queen nodded, and she helped herself to his chair, leaning back casually and crossing one leg over the other, lounging with one elbow on the arm of the chair and her head in her hand. Down here, alone with her in his domain, Gora was sure he could easily dispose of her—though with terrible consequences from the surrounding ships if she didn't return to the deck alive. So she sat, smirking, as if death could never touch her, watching as he poured the glass, a hint of amusement on her face.

Gora scowled and tried to ignore her. *Bloody royals, thinking they own the place,* he groaned to himself, wishing he had some kind of poison to slip in her drink.

But he knew that wouldn't work, either. No matter the method, if for whatever reason the queen didn't go back up to the deck alive, he knew his ship and his crew would be sent down to the ocean's bed as a sacrifice for the sea witch.

'So, speak,' he said, thrusting one of the mugs of liquor at her.

She took a cautious sniff of the liquid and then looked at him, his eyes watching his own cup. Gora got the hint, and sighing, he raised his mug in a toasting motion, muttered in Hizen his thanks for the drink, and then took a grateful gulp. The sweet burning was a welcome distraction for him, and his mind stung with a moment of recognition at this feeling—all those times he'd drunk before to forget the memories of the pirates. He eyed the simple pottery cup. He couldn't let himself fall to those habits again, but damn, this was a good time to do so.

'The name's Mammie. Remember it.' The queen took a sip of the spirits and nodded with approval while Gora stared, boggled at such a normal-looking 'mother' with such a normal name ruling such a circle of pirates. 'And I'll say again, I want that boy.'

'What, so you can kill him? I know what you lot do to kids.'

'And you've helped us, too,' Mammie muttered, grinning slyly over the rim of her cup, her copper eyes glinting.

Dread flushed through Gora, and he felt his hand weaken. He gripped the cup and took another gulp, letting the welcoming burning slip down his throat.

'I hear Foy let you live, the old softie—who'd have thought?'

'Man's no softie. He's a monster.' Gora leant back against the stateroom wall and kept a steady gaze on her, trying to suss her out.

'Can't be that bad if he let you live.'

'You have no idea what he did,' Gora started, feeling the cold flush through him again and the room turn dark. He tugged at his collar and tried to take a steady breath, but it shook—audibly. He grimaced as he saw her face register his weakness.

Mammie took another sip. 'Oh, I'm under no delusions what my boys are like. There's a reason most of my crew are women.'

'Is that right, now?' Gora said, still trying to control his breath, barely listening.

'The boys tell me you're the devil's child. Is it true?'

'Ain't fuckin' true. My pa was a carpenter.'

The pirate queen chuckled. 'Oh, you really know nothing. Poor thing.' He glared at her, and she continued. 'They think your red hair makes you the child of the devil. Isn't that ridiculous? I can't believe that's what kept you alive.'

Gora watched her, mouth dropping open with bafflement. *All over my damn hair?* Then, slowly, he replied.

'Aye, seems they didn't want to ruin your pretty ritual. Can't have a devil's child ruin it. Superstitious fucks.'

'What do you care? It kept you alive.'

'What do you want with my boy?' Gora said, cutting back to the chase and controlling his world to prevent it from collapsing in.

'Your—?' Mammie eyed him up for a moment, narrowing her eyes, and then she thought for a moment. 'I guess there's no harm in telling you. You waited all these years to find out why your little friends were dying. And you'll be dead soon, anyway.' She put her cup down harshly onto the wood of his desk and leant forward, eyeing the maps with a raised brow.

Gora, a spike of panic spearing his heart, rushed over and ripped the map of Hizen off the table and slammed his hand down, making her jump slightly. Then Mammie laughed.

'I need the boy for my "pretty ritual",' she said. 'A final sacrifice, after years of sacrifices. So, don't worry; he won't die like the others.' The pirate queen looked up at him with cunning eyes. 'But he will die. Eventually.'

'Why are doing this?'

'You mean, they never told you?'

'As if they would!'

Mammie nodded as if satisfied with herself and leant back. 'True, I put the fear of fate into them to not tell their crew. As you say, they're a superstitious bunch of fools; it's not hard to control them if you know how.'

Gora didn't bother to ask. He knew she'd keep talking. Her eyes had glazed over, and she looked too settled in his chair.

'Did you know magic is dying?' She was looking into the distance now, out of the port hole.

Gora thought of Yoshiko's powers and how few people knew of magic anymore, and few believed in the magical creatures of old. 'Aye,' he said in slow response to fill the quiet.

She continued as if she didn't care for his answer. 'Few people can use it anymore, but my family can. Have you heard of seers?'

'People who can see the future?'

She nodded, still staring out of the window. This time, she leant forward to pick up the pottery cup again and took a sip before holding it absentmindedly in her hands. 'Years ago, when my girls were born, I saw the future.' She looked up to make sure he was listening. 'A future where terrible, deformed creatures ripped through my homeland and ravaged all in their wake. They tore the forests, devoured people and animals, and left the country bare and barren. Nothing could stop them.

'I sought out stories of magic, to see if there was a way to stop it, but few people believed in magic anymore. Even I'd had to grow up hiding my abilities.' She held out her cup for more liquor, and Gora obliged with a sigh. 'I thought the only way to save my homeland was to find a way to bring back magic. My husband didn't believe me; he didn't believe in magic. He wanted me to be a jolly housewife and raise our two girls. But after what I'd *seen*, as if I could!' Mammie gave an exaggerated shrug. 'Every day, I would look at the olive groves and the fruit orchards and imagine them being torn down. I'd imagine my beautiful town with its people dying, torn, bloody, eaten. So, I took the girls and ran away— imagine, a mother with two young children, one still a babe—and took a ship to sail and find the source of magic. I thought I could learn how to save my country.'

There was a heavy pause as she took a long drink and stared out of the port hole.

'Instead, I discovered magic was dying and there was no power left to face this incoming terror, so I sought out the only strong power left who might be able to help—the sea witch.'

The pirate queen stared at Gora defiantly, golden eyes daring him not to believe her. He kept his gaze cool and didn't say a word, so she continued.

'I travelled for months to the highest, most-northern regions of the world, where the world was locked in ice and snow and the very air froze all, even breath and skin. The sea witch was old, older than I thought people could live to, and told me there was a way to bring magic back, but to do so, you had to sacrifice young, pure souls—thousands—to even be able to replicate the magic source enough of pure energy to replenish itself. She looked at the two babes in blankets in my arms and doubted I would do it.' She sat up straight, jutting out her chin in what Gora could only guess was pride. 'But I thought of the future my girls would lead—a burning, scorched land torn to shreds by vicious creatures—and I knew it wasn't the future I wanted them to live in. If I knew it was coming, I had a duty to try to stop it. So I agreed.'

Mammie stopped, holding out her cup, requesting yet again more. Gora sighed, slouching as he poured more for her, even daring to pour more for himself. The spirits knew he needed it right now.

'I could never kill a child. You know, I had my girls. How could I? But then, how would I do it? But when needs must …' Mammie shrugged casually and twirled her drink cup in her hand as she looked at it and sighed. 'So I thought, why not have someone else do it for me? But who would take and sacrifice children out to sea for a young woman?'

'Who indeed?' Gora growled, fidgeting with his cup.

'So I went to the place with the most disgusting lowlifes imaginable—people who would. A place for the lawless. The pirate port. I got them to do it.'

'Why would pirates listen to you?'

Mammie smiled over her cup, almost like she was proudly watching a beloved child or grandchild and humouring their questions.

'Pirates are *very* superstitious. I set up a table in a drab old seedy bar as a seer and told them their fortunes.' She looked around at his stateroom. 'They like to know how they'll die. Or, rather, be reassured how they'll live. Doesn't take much. Just a few simple words and they'll do anything for you, for fear of finding out something ominous.'

Was that really it? Gora wondered. Had it really been as simple as being a fortune teller?

'I never intended to become pirate queen. But before I knew it, whole ships had pledged to me, saying I brought luck and fortune. They killed for me, and I gave them reassurance. I had women coming to me, mercenaries, runaways, bar wenches, begging me to have them around me—not many women in this trade—and they'd fight for me. That's where I met Franceska, my guard. You know, the one with all the curls. Then an old captain said he'd leave his ship to me when he died, as I gave him a good death reading. And, well, my girls were older then. I thought it would be interesting. An adventure. But his crew refused to sail under a female captain, so I fired the lot. Didn't need them. After all, I had the women around me. We started an all-woman crew, an irony, as pirates think women on ships are bad luck, but they did anything to follow ours as the fleet headship. The only men allowed on board are my girls' husbands, and they purely cook and look after my granddaughter.' She gave a soft chuckle, as if they were merely discussing the antics of children.

Gora didn't expect the whole life story, but it had been hard not to listen, like a grandma was speaking to you and would clip you around the ear if you tried to walk away.

'Of course, I have to end this—kill the last child … but I've had years to get over that. That's where your lad comes in. A lovely one he is too, at that. He's surrounded by magic. I know you know someone like me, born of the old magics, and the boy knows her, too. Residue of her power lingers around him. A gift, perhaps.' Gora's eyes widened as he realised what the pirate queen was saying, thinking about Yoshiko and the daggers she'd given Miyoshi. Mammie smirked. 'He's the last missing piece. A full circle—a child looked after by one of the first children we stole, the sole survivor of our sacrifices. A child pure and wholesome despite looking up to the devil's child. You've looked after him well, but now it's time to pass him over to us. Your fate was sealed the night you were stolen. You were destined to live, and he was destined to take your place.'

Miyoshi's face flickered in Gora's memories—his face when he was praised for doing something well on the ship, his face when he was given permission to sail with him, his face when he saved Gora and told him about the knives Yoshiko had given him. A happy, youthful face—too young to face the horrors Gora knew he had, yet still eager and wholesome.

'He was destined to take my place?' Gora muttered, toying with the words on his lips, twirling the pottery cup mindlessly in his hands.

'Fate is a wild thing—so cruel, so unknown, so unstoppable. There's nothing you can do to change it. You lived; he'll die. One of the first, and the last. I know your story, devil's child. Foy told me all about you. You can't stop this, and you can't run away. Give me the boy. The world can't lose magic. Surely even you have noticed the creatures disappearing to the hidden corners of the world. One day, they'll rear up, angry with being pushed into their small hiding places'—as she spoke, Gora pictured the writhing baby sea serpents swimming away from that giant shadow in the ocean—'and they'll come for us all. You were a pirate once, so you know what we're up against. The horrors that still exist in the world. Only those who dare sail in the quiet spaces of the sea know what's still out there. The folk on the land have no idea.'

His body prickled with a chilling sweat, and his heart rate rose again, more than he'd ever felt, even faced by Foy. 'I was never a pirate. I may have been on those ships, but I ain't one of you, and I ain't letting the boy die—especially not in my place.' The heat flushed back through him, and he launched his empty cup at where she sat.

To his amazement, the soft, matriarchal-looking woman dodged. Her motherly face turned sour, and her dark hair looked more matted than neat as her copper eyes glared with hatred. 'You can't stop fate, boy, and you can't run from it, no matter how much you try.'

She stormed from the room and up the wooden steps, yelling out in the middling continent's language. Gora, panic rising at his foolishness, ran after her, skidding around the corner and crashing up to the deck where his crew had gathered in a huddle with Miyoshi in the middle, each crew member armed and wary. They caught the look on Gora's face, reading his shock, which said it all.

Moori was the first to move, rushing to the control post of the figurehead's fire, stepping into the metal gate that helped her stand in place while the boat lunged through the waves. She readied and waited, turning to look back at her captain.

In that time, Simrita and Ikeda had finally reached the edges of their patience, and with the first word of permission, they both darted after the pirate queen, drawing their blades.

Mammie's guardians stepped out to meet them, and the two siblings closed in on either side of the pirate queen. Gora finally realised the resemblance. They were the two daughters Mammie had told him about. All grown up, not dead.

Of course she wouldn't sacrifice her own.

Mammie turned to look at him, and there was a final lull of silence as she scanned his crew once more.

'What yer lookin' for now?' Gora growled, hairs raising on the back of his neck.

She pointed at each of the four women in his crew. 'Which one is it?' When Gora looked confused, not answering, she continued. 'The one they told me about. The one who burned Frewin last year, and then his ship?'

Gora turned to regard them, his eyes meeting a wary glance from Yonemura, who pursed her lips.

'Ain't none of them,' he said as he turned back, brows knotting. Just a moment ago, she'd said the old powers had lingered on Miyoshi, as if she could see it. But now, she couldn't tell the powers weren't on this ship at all. Had she just *seen* that the boy was connected to it all previously, and was only connecting the dots now?

If anything, that was more concerning.

When the pirate queen looked at him, doubting, he rolled his eyes and continued. 'She's back in her country.'

Mammie's brows arched. 'Bring her here.'

'Wha—? As if.'

Mammie spoke again, more dangerously this time. 'I don't think you understand your situation.' She gestured to the ships surrounding his. 'Bring her, or this ship ends up in pieces—crew and boat.' All traces of the grandmotherly attitude had vanished, instead replaced by the woman who had led pirates for twenty years. Detached. All-seeing.

She turned, storming back to the ropes that brought them here, and her daughters followed.

'You've got one chance,' Mammie called back. 'Go home, fix your ship, bring the girl.'

'Fix my ship?' Gora spluttered, storming forward after her. 'Now, wait just a—'

'It'll be your only chance to save the boy.'

She stepped up onto the wooden step, and crew up on her deck raised it up the side, leaving Gora desperately searching about him for Miyoshi. He found him, on his deck, with Sakai standing protectively at the boy's side with body language that harked back to his gang days. Gora let out a relieved breath and turned back to face Mammie, confused. The pirate queen's daughters climbed after her, not even bothering to look back.

Blades crashed as one of Mammie's pirates clashed blades with Simrita, and the queen smirked down on them all as she neared the gunwale of her monster ship. Then, calling out in a loud voice, she cursed them in Traders' for all to hear. 'You'll regret this day, devil's child. The boy will be mine, and he will die in your place. It was told by fate, and fate always wins.' Then she signalled the surrounding ships. 'Destroy them, and get me that boy.'

32
Miyoshi

Miyoshi's heart froze.

The first clash of steel was soon followed by more as Ikeda launched his attack at one of the pirate queen's guards, dodging her defence and swiftly cutting through her waist. She cried out, lashing out with her blade as she fell, failing as Ikeda swept to the side and was soon upon another, eyes dashing to the ship on the other side pinning them into place, seeing other pirates swinging over on ropes.

Miyoshi watched, feet glued to the spot. Before he had even noticed, the ship was filling, and Tomioka was at his side, grabbing his shoulders and shaking him, looking into his eyes and crying out words that didn't register at this moment. Sakai shielded them, his bulky form wrestling with a pirate that had lunged at the boy.

Miyoshi flinched, and finally Tomioka's words got through.

'Yūki! Come on, we need to go.'

Tomioka dragged him off, lifting him over his shoulders to carry him down the steps below. The young boy caught Gora's gaze, and his eyes, which were usually blue like the freedom of the sky, looked dark and stormy. Gora's expression haunted him, and as the red-haired man drew his twin blades, Miyoshi realised he'd never wanted to see anyone suffer like that again. It was the look that had been in his mother's eyes on the days they were taken, and the reason he was here now—to stop others feeling like that again.

'No, stop! I have to help!' Miyoshi cried out, reaching up the steps towards the deck as Tomioka carried him away.

'If you want to help, all you can do now is stay with us and stay alive,' Tomioka said sharply, and then Kyo and Taro and Sakai appeared on the steps behind them, running down to help on the cannon deck.

'But—'

'Yūki.' This time it was Kyo, and Miyoshi was shocked to hear such sharp tones from the haunted young man who barely spoke. 'This is what you must do now. Next time, you can do differently, if you wish.'

The young boy fell silent, and he accepted his fate as Tomioka carried him to the cannon deck, finally letting him go with a promise from the boy that he'd not run off.

'Don't leave our sight,' Tomioka said, and then the four men looked at one another, nodding. 'This is all we can do to help you for now, until we can get free of this somehow.'

'What about the others?'

'They'll find a way. Think of yourself for now,' Taro said, patting the lad gently on the head before turning away to help Kyo and Tomioka with a cannon. Behind him, Sakai nodded gently, and the yakuza man's face softened briefly before he too rushed off to help with the cannons.

Miyoshi slumped against the wall, watching as the others rushed about firing cannons, listening to the crashing of iron balls and the clammer and roar of the fight above. He pulled his knees up to his chest and hugged his legs, clenching his teeth to try to calm himself down, wishing he could help.

He heard the clatter of people running in the corridors nearby and then the screams and crashes as those people were pursued and killed by others. The boy clenched his eyes shut and held his hands over his ears. He didn't know who was dying—he hoped it wasn't his friends, but he knew he couldn't be naïve enough to believe they'd all survive this. But he didn't want to hear it. He tried to block out the sounds of the fight and the cannons as Tomioka and his team fired them, and he tried to look brave as they checked in on him.

But it wouldn't stop his body from shaking, and it wouldn't stop his fear.

The pirate queen had said he would die soon, and in Gora's place. He gulped.

Does that mean the captain was meant to have died already?

It was as expected of his captain, the young boy thought, that he could do something as wonderful as escaping death. Could Miyoshi do the same? He recalled the despairing look on his crew's face as they found out the queen wanted him, and he didn't want to be the one to give them that expression.

There was a lull in the noise, and the boy removed his hands from his ears, listening quietly. He saw Tomioka and Sakai turning too, trying to listen. Sakai took a step forward from where he stood on the other side of the cannon deck, eyes locked on the door, clenching his giant fists. Miyoshi followed the man's gaze. Was someone coming down?

Afraid that it might be an enemy, the young boy slid away on his bum, pushing himself away as fast as he could. The door crashed open as a fearsome pirate kicked his way in, snarling, and the boy scrambled away faster as the pirate turned his way and grinned, licking his lips.

Across the room, Tomioka and Taro cried out in the middle of holding down a heavy cannonball while Kyo loaded it, neither able to drop it and run to the boy's aid. Sakai lurched towards him like a bear chasing travellers in the stories Miyoshi had heard about the mountain forests. He tried to get up and run towards Sakai too, but the pirate grabbed his leg, slid the young boy towards him, and picked him up, throwing him over his shoulders like a sack of grain.

Sakai bellowed as he gave chase, and Miyoshi heard Tomioka calling out, seeing him turn to follow as soon as his hands were free of the iron ball. The boy squirmed and wriggled and kicked to get away, and he tried to make the man's ascent of the stairs as difficult as possible, not even thinking about his own safety if they were both to fall. It didn't matter to him. The stricken looks on Sakai and Tomioka's faces as they raced to follow were all the boy could see, and the pirate yelled at him to stop wriggling and spun him to hit his head against the wall in anger. Miyoshi cried out and tried to protect his head, pain flushing through his fingers as they hit the wall instead. He saw a pistol and a dagger come from Sakai's kimono, and the stocky man aimed at the pirate's legs. The shot crashed true through the man's calf, and the pirate flailed up the last step and dropped Miyoshi onto the deck, swearing.

It was then that Miyoshi saw the chaos on the deck. *Sea Guardian* was still pinned between the pirate ships, and Daiki had blood oozing from his side and was resting against the main mast, defended by an exhausted Ikeda, who rolled to his side and pushed Kimura out of the way, forcing the young chef onto the deck as he stood up in his place and sliced his blade across the chest of a pirate about to kill the young chef. Kimura turned where he sprawled on the floor, kitchen knife in his hand, staring in horror as his would-be attacker fell to the floor, the young, dishevelled samurai standing ahead of him, chest heaving to catch his breath, hair loose about his shoulders.

Miyoshi turned. Rijul was limping as he rushed to defend against yet another pirate swinging over, and Simrita was wresting with one of the queen's guards. But Miyoshi didn't get much time to look, and he didn't get to see where Gora was. Not a moment later did the fallen pirate yell out to someone near him, who then rushed over and grabbed him instead, pulling him away before Sakai could clamber over the body of the pirate he'd shot down. Sakai roared out, shoulder-barging anyone who tried to stop him, digging his dagger into someone's throat. Blood bubbled from the wound as the man gargled and fell, pulling at Sakai's clothes and showing his chest and shoulder tattoos, smearing blood down him, making him look as frightening as Miyoshi had first found him to be. Sakai shrugged the man off and ran after Miyoshi, with Tomioka diving up onto the deck after him, pushing the downed pirate out of the way.

'Yūki!' Tomioka yelled from behind Sakai, sprinting over the deck towards him, eyes wild and desperate.

Miyoshi craned his head to see where the man was taking him—towards the pirate queen's ship—and wondered how they were going to get up there before Sakai caught up.

He's going to catch up, isn't he? the boy hoped, looking back at Sakai, reaching for him with a hand outstretched. 'Sakai!'

Then the boy peered about the deck for Gora, hoping he'd see him too. Gora could help him, couldn't he? Gora could do anything. He'd never let Miyoshi be taken onto that giant ship.

He found his captain on the forecastle.

But Gora's sleeve was red with blood, and his face was pale, and by the time Gora met Miyoshi's gaze as the boy yelled out his name, Gora's face whitened completely, and a pirate jumped on Gora's back with a grin and brought the autumn-haired captain crashing face-first onto the forecastle deck, the pirate catching Miyoshi's face and smiling with triumph as his captain roared and flailed beneath him.

No ...

Sakai fired another shot, narrowly missing this pirate's legs. The whizzing bullet drew the boy's attention to his friends again, and he saw Sakai was close. His heart lurched. There was a clatter on the hull above him, and the boy saw the plank the queen had used to get to her ship being lowered again, and voices called down at the man carrying him to step on.

A thunder-like clap drowned out even the sounds of fighting as a ship fired a cannon, and then the crashing, tearing noise drowned out the sounds once more as Gora's ship lurched with an iron ball tearing through the bow hull. Both Miyoshi's captor and Sakai wobbled to keep their balance, and Miyoshi feared they'd all drown.

Sakai roared, hand close to reaching as the pirate stepped onto the plank, but another pirate stepped in the way, jumping on the large ex-yakuza and crashing down with him to the deck, where, to Miyoshi's horror, the pirate plunged his blade into Sakai's stomach. But the pirate didn't stop there. He withdrew the blade and stabbed it over and over, laughing as he did, until Sakai's torso was pierced multiple times over and Sakai's tormented bellows rang in Miyoshi's ears. The boy stared in horror as Sakai's head crashed back onto the deck, energy lost. But with one final act of defiance, and a deafening roar, Sakai thrust his dagger into the man's forehead, his arm flopping down to the deck just before the man's body followed.

And with that, Miyoshi's captor stepped onto the plank, and it was raised. Miyoshi trembled, unable to tear his eyes away from the horror of his friend lying bloody on the deck, face frozen in death, contorted in pain and rage. Tomioka crashed into the gunwale, reaching up and crying out after him as a tear streaked the man's cheek.

On the pirate queen's deck, the boy was slapped and yelled at to be silent. They pinned him to the gunwale, hissing in his ear to watch his friends be destroyed, and another thunderous roar cracked through the air as an iron cannonball spun through the ship and skimmed the deck, tearing through the mizzenmast. His crew yelled as they dived out of the way, and Miyoshi saw Gora rolling away just before the mast and sails landed where he'd been pinned to the deck. Satisfied the boy had seen enough to despair, the pirates bound his wrists and dragged him to the holds below, where he was thrown in a small storeroom on his own, the door shut, and the boy was left in the dark with the memories of the death of his friend and of cannons tearing his ship apart.

33

Crushing Cannon Fire

Gora heard a sickening crunch as the mizzenmast crashed just beside him, landing atop of the pirate he'd wrestled off him. Heart thudding at the near miss, he searched desperately to see who of his crew was still alive, discovering with horror that Sakai was dead and Tomioka was crying out desperately at Mammie's ship. Gora hobbled down the steps of the stern deck and rushed to the man's side.

'Tomioka! Don't tell me they have Miyoshi,' he gasped, holding himself steady on the railing. To his dismay, the queen's ship pushed away.

Tomioka turned, ashen faced, and met Gora's eyes with all life disappeared from his own. Then the two turned to the giant ship again.

'No,' Gora breathed. He turned to scan the ship for Moori, who was yelling out as she fired gunshot after gunshot into fleeing pirates.

'They're all leaving?' Tomioka said, surprise filling his voice.

'Aye, I guess they were only here on the queen's whim and for the lad. They can destroy us from afar now. Prepare for more of *that*.' Gora gestured to the mizzenmast and then at the place the cannonball had crashed through the bow of the ship.

'Is there nothing we can do?'

'Aye,' Gora said. 'Fire back.'

He said nothing more as he hobbled over the deck to Moori, calling out her name multiple times before she heard him and turned, lowering her pistols.

'I need you to fire from the figurehead. Get them before they get away. Nishimura, turn the ship!'

Nishimura had been keeping the ship from crashing into those that had blocked them in, trying to find a space to slip their ship away, defended by Eshnaa, who was on the warpath like one of the warrior goddesses of her people. Now, with the other ships sailing away, they had room to turn, so he gratefully turned the helm, knowing where Moori needed him to be to fire.

'Not the queen's ship! They have the lad!'

Nishimura turned to look at Gora with shock on his face, and his eyes searched for another aim. The pirate ship ahead—the one now led by Foy.

Biting his lip in frustration at not being able to protect the boy, Gora did all else that he could. He called on Ikeda and Rijul to fire the on-deck cannons at a ship to the side while it pulled away, and he told the others to clean up the remaining sea slime on his deck.

In no time, Moori was ready to fire the dragon fire, and Nishimura was turning the ship aim at Foy.

Gora could almost feel the glare coming from Foy, and he knew the old pirate would have something up his sleeve, too. He was the only one not following the queen.

It's you or me, Gora thought, determined to be the one who came out of this alive.

The figurehead's hands pulled from her sleeves, and the now-familiar buzz as the figurehead's dragon fire powered up overcame the ship. The sound of all else drowned out, and Gora watched as a slight flare of light lit up across the way: Foy's crew lighting cannons.

A ball of light appeared in the figurehead's hands, and the buzzing noise grew louder, pulsing in Gora's ears. This time, he didn't put his hands over his ears to block out the deafening sound. He didn't want to forget the senses that this moment gave him.

The crash of Foy's cannonball came just as the figurehead's flames shot forth, but so too did a second, and an iron ball flew from the stern chasers of a ship following the pirate queen, tearing through the figurehead and shearing off her hands just as the flames began to stream out.

Moori dived from her standing point, ducking the splintering wood and the explosion of flames that billowed as the power subsided, and the iron ball shot from Foy's ship ripped through *Sea Guardian's* hull.

34
Desperate Choices

Moori pulled herself up from the floor of her gunning post and swung around the wooden gunwale to jump onto the deck. She ran over to her captain and strained to pull him up. Gora's face was pale, and his red brows furrowed in a mix of pain and frustration.

'It failed,' he gasped as he leant against Moori's small shoulder. His legs buckled a little, but she held him as hard as she could. 'The dragon fire failed. I don't understand how. We had one chance.' His voice wheezed as he tried to bring back the air in his lungs. His ribs barely complied.

'I'm sorry,' Moori whispered, eyes pinned to the deck. She didn't want to meet anyone's gaze. 'I failed you.'

'No. It wasn't you.'

Moori said nothing.

'Take me to the edge,' Gora growled, breath heaving.

'But, captain, your wound,' she began, her usually cool and confident voice shaken for the first time on their quest.

'Do it.'

Moori pulled his arm over her shoulder and half-dragged him to the edge of the ship. Even that small distance, with her tiny size, took an effort that left her panting. If not for him grabbing on to the wooden railing, Gora knew she'd have dropped him.

The pair squinted into the horizon at the disappearing armada.

'We'll never catch up,' Moori whispered.

Beside her, Gora nodded.

'Fuck this bright sunlight.' A voice from behind them made them both jump, the captain's face convulsing in pain as he twisted awkwardly to look behind. He crumpled in a heap, leaning over his wounded side and hissing in pain. Yonemura sat beside him, her back against the gunwale, muttering an apology for making him jump.

'You're getting too good at the swearing thing. You've all got to stop copying me.' Gora grimaced when Yonemura examined his bleeding side.

'What will we do about Yūki?' Yonemura hit home. 'And the crew. They are gravely wounded. Sakai is dead. He tried to bring the boy back. The crew suffer. How do we guide them? What do we do?'

Overwhelmed by the questions, Gora looked beyond the worried faces of Moori and Yonemura to the blurred figures of his crew beyond, either slouched and depressed or running about trying to solve problems. Satou tore between multiple places to heal the crew, grabbing a wet cloth from Kimura as they passed one another. Kimura's peaceful smile flashed through his view as he watched the young cook dash to the side of a wounded Daiki, tending to the older samurai while the young Ikeda watched anxiously, forgetting his own wounds over his mentor's. Kimura had been lucky. Ikeda had been there to save him. Now, the young chef was helping in his own way. Gora saw Ikeda bow his head to Kimura, furrowing his slim brows as he next chastised his teacher, who was equally chastised by Kimura too, by the looks of it.

'Those two get on surprisingly well when it comes down to it,' he chuckled.

The women turned in confusion.

'Captain, really, now?' Yonemura looked at him in frustration.

Gora sighed and looked at her with large, pained eyes. She paused.

'I can't lose that lad,' he whispered, finally. He pulled himself to lean against the ship railing and rested his head back, eyes closed. 'But I don't know what to do. I don't know where they're going.'

'They'll kill him, won't they?' Moori whispered, sliding herself to flop on the deck beside him. Yonemura followed suit, sitting on Gora's other side. The trio absentmindedly watched Quinni nursing a bleeding arm, puckering his face up and hissing in pain as he dabbed it clean with freshly boiled water.

'Aye,' Gora said, leaning his head back against the gunwale and clenching his eyes shut against the burning of tears. His voice cracked. 'Eventually.'

35

The Return of the *Sea Guardian*

Yoshiko climbed the last of the steps towards the top level of the castle grounds, heading into the *tenshu* keep and away from the muggy late summer heat. She pulled down her paper parasol and closed it, passing it to Suki, who walked beside her. It had been countless months since Gora and the crew left for their mission, and still there was no news. Each day her mind came up with some foreboding thought of what could have gone wrong, and nightmares woke her in a sweat more regularly than not. Yoshiko yawned, covering her mouth with her fan, and then looked at Suki, whose face looked just as closed and brooding.

Suki had opened up considerably with Yoshiko since they'd met again upon Yoshiko's return from Acrein. And since that night Suki had helped smuggle her into the castle grounds to take back control, the two had been close friends. Often, Suki would laugh and talk with her now, and Yoshiko welcomed having a friend to speak memories of Haruki to, telling Suki of all the things she'd learned about food and music from the town, asking if the young girl had seen any of them herself. Suki had, and now occasionally brought gifts from the town, and Yoshiko had even persuaded Chisaka to let her walk about in the town wherever she pleased and speak with those who lived there, learning more about it and seeing how it grew. Chisaka, strict as she was, left her to this whim and followed her graciously, seeing how much Yoshiko lit up to speak with her people and learn from them, hoping to become a better leader with their guidance.

It was one of such days on the hot summer afternoon that Yoshiko, Suki, and Chisaka had been returning from the town, when footsteps pounding up the stone steps brought a panting samurai from the main gate keeling over with his hands on his knees, looking up at her, wiping his sweaty brow on his sleeve.

'My lady,' he said between gasping breaths. 'They've returned. In the port. The *Sea Guardian*.'

Yoshiko snapped her fan shut and ran around him to the *tenshu* keep's main doorway, standing in the entrance and looking down the slopes towards the main town and the port. True enough, a ship sailed in through the last of the harbour, and Yoshiko turned to look at the guard.

'It's them?' She could hardly believe it.

The man nodded, and she turned back, pushing her vision to its limits to see the details of the ship. Her heart leapt to see the *Sea Guardian* flag flapping in the breeze and the black-and-red lacquered woodwork glinting in the sun. But her heart fell just as quickly when she saw the damage, and she blinked her sight back to normal, and she turned back to the guard, worried.

'They don't look in very good condition.'

The guard bowed, having caught his breath. 'Yes, the messenger said as much.'

'Well, we must go to them immediately,' she said. 'Suki, prepare the keep for guests and have healers ready to tend those who are injured.' The young maid bowed and shuffled off, catching the attention of other maids awaiting them by the entrance. Yoshiko turned to the guard, who was waiting to return to the gate. 'Can you call upon guards to meet the crew at the docks? They will need assistance.' The man too bounded off, and Yoshiko turned to the ever-there Chisaka, standing properly as usual. 'Chisaka, we're going to run.'

Yoshiko didn't even wait to see the woman's response. Instead, she turned and ran down the steps, calling out apologies and warnings to those she surprised as she ran past. It wasn't long before Chisaka followed, and she heard the steady footsteps behind. Yoshiko was fast, but she made sure to run at a pace the older woman could follow, mostly because she knew Chisaka would grumble for days if she didn't.

Yoshiko's mind replayed the dreams and worries she'd had over the months, and having now seen damage to the ship, she leapt to the worst.

Who's hurt? Did anyone die? The closer she ran to the dock, the more these thoughts refused to be shut out.

Unable to wait any longer, at the last hill, Yoshiko sped up, ignoring the cries of Chisaka behind her. She arrived as the gangway was lowered, and a crowd gathered at the port, flushing aside as the daimyō ran through like a wild child. She skidded to a stop as she saw the true damage to the ship up close—the disfigured and armless figurehead, the hole in the bow hull and the railing, and the missing mizzenmast and sails. Mouth agape, Yoshiko could barely believe they'd made it back.

'What happened?' Yoshiko whispered, not even turning as Chisaka ran up beside her.

'Looks like one hell of a fight,' the guard said through staggered breath, clasping her waist as she tried to stand up straight, flicking her long ponytail back over her shoulder.

They looked up at the ship, waiting for someone to come down the gangway. More than anything, Yoshiko wanted to run up there and see her friends for herself, but intuition kept her standing in place, and she bit her lip and clenched her fists to keep herself patient and waiting. She tapped her foot. Eventually,

Gora stepped onto the gangway and looked straight over them at Hié town.

'He looks exhausted,' Chisaka muttered, and Yoshiko nodded, noticing the deep shadows under his eyes and recalling the haggard look he'd had when they'd sailed back to Hié after escaping Acrein, and he'd barely slept then. This time must have been worse.

'He's grown a beard,' Yoshiko said, amused at the red-brown facial hair that covered the lower half of his face.

Eventually, he looked down at port and took a step, pausing when he met her eyes and saw her waiting at the bottom. A look of relief flushed over his face, lifting the look of exhaustion, and he stomped down quickly. Behind him, crew ran about, calling on deck as they finished docking the ship, and Daiki and Ikeda guided Moori and Kimura down next, much to Yoshiko's relief.

Gora stopped in front of her, and he bowed formally and stiffly rose, eyes shifting around him at the crowd. Yoshiko let out a light huff from her nose as he avoided her gaze.

'Captain—' she started, before Gora let out a sigh and reached out and pulled her into a heavy embrace. And with that, she relaxed. He'd not drowned. Nor had her other friends. Gora's smell of salt spray, ocean air, and sweat reassured her more than disgusted her, and she pushed her arms through his to hug him back around the waist.

'We're home, finally,' he mumbled into her hair before pulling away and running a hand through his curls bashfully, looking at the others around him once again.

Yoshiko grinned. 'Welcome back.'

But her grin failed when she looked back up at her friend's face and saw a haunted look return. Gora's eyes had slid back over the sprawling town that stretched up the hill from the port to the castle grounds, and his face darkened.

'What's wrong?' she asked, her voice barely coming out as a whisper. Her heart felt heavy, and she clenched her hands, turning too to look at the town.

He was silent for a moment, and the chatter of those coming off the ship and helping them off the ship merged into a background clang she tried to shut out.

'Miyoshi—' Gora started, and then his pained gaze met hers. 'He was taken. And Sakai is dead.' His lip trembled, and his words tumbled. 'What do I do now? How do I tell the boy's mother?'

Yoshiko faltered, and her heart dropped into her stomach. She tried speaking but nothing came out, and her mind fogged over. She took a step back and looked at him, seeing now the despair in his ocean eyes and why he looked so haggard.

'I promised her I'd protect him.' His voice cracked, and his gaze had fallen somewhere by her feet. 'We couldn't even follow them. The ship, it—'

'Do you have a plan?' Her voice was low, slow, but determined. Her heavy heart had lit with fire, and now Yoshiko knew she had to light his, too.

'What?' He looked up at her again, eyebrows furrowed. 'Yes, but—'

'Okay, that's all that matters now. And you're here as part of that plan?'

'Fix the ship. Get your help,' he said as if he'd been reciting it over and over, and he tilted his head to one side as he tried to read her thoughts, face furrowing with the effort.

Yoshiko bobbed her head. 'Alright. We can do that. That's what we tell her. Just tell me what you need.'

The guards sent by the palace filed into the port, and Yoshiko directed them into helping Gora's crew take what they needed off the ship and up towards the palace. It took some persuading to get the crew to agree to be taken care of at least for one night in the castle grounds, with an elected friend or family member joining them to reassure their families were safe. The two Qeclans and the three Ishillians would be treated as special guests, and Yoshiko had already spotted the three newcomers to Gora's crew and become excited at the questions she could ask them of their home country. Messengers were sent to family homes to collect the crew's guests and tell the families they were safe and would be returned to them after they'd been checked by the palace healers the next day.

Her body froze and a lump caught in her throat as she saw the horror in the eyes of her friends. Sakai, she decided, would have a proper send-off, though he'd had no family or friends in Hié. *It would do the crew good*, she decided, and she turned to walk back up the hill with Chisaka, anyone else following in their own time.

The sun had started to slip, and the shadows grew long as the group climbed the hill through the town towards the *tenshu*. Gora sometimes walked alongside her, both beginning to speak of what had happened in the time since Gora departed, and light conversation about the town and its recovery made the mood joyful as Gora observed the comings and goings of the town and how it could stay open again as dark drew in. Yoshiko felt comfortable, thrilled whenever Gora or any of the crew pointed to a place that had been hit in the battle and exclaimed at how it looked just like it did before, or even better.

Yoshiko and Gora laughed as they heard Kimura grumbling behind them about finding it difficult to walk on land again, and Moori teased him playfully, earning a laugh from Yonemura behind them. Gora dropped back and ruffled Kimura's hair and teased him, a grin crossing his face again and eyes lighting up.

'Need one of us to carry you, dear chef?' Yonemura called out. And when the young man pouted and threw back a less-than-polite reply, Yoshiko caught Chisaka's horrified expression and chuckled.

The chef didn't grumble for long, though, when he saw the white *tenshu* keep stretching up ahead. His eyes lit up, and when Yoshiko looked back, she saw the same gaze on all, even on Moori, who had been there many times as she grew up. And as Yoshiko turned back to look at it too, she remembered the time she'd been taken away from it and had returned after many months from Acrein, and how she'd had the same feeling of awe and relief at finally returning home.

Yoshiko and Chisaka were bowed through the main *karamété-mon* gate, and many greeted the young daimyō as she strolled across the bridge, followed by the large group from the ship. She smiled to herself, knowing what her castle workers were doing at this moment to make the crew welcome, and a light bubbled inside her at how her keep ran, everyone working together. There was a new life in the keep, with maids smiling easily at her and people talking to her, and she no longer felt lonely or restricted. She loved how the castle was now, and she looked forward to Moori, Ikeda, and Daiki seeing the difference and how much more joyful life was here, even among the guards.

They'll notice the difference, right? she worried.

As they entered the *tenshu* keep, the crew were whisked off by castle workers to use the baths and dress in fresh clothes. Suki met Yoshiko and Chisaka in the entranceway, and she showed Yoshiko the banquet hall and the guest rooms that had been prepared. Satisfied everyone would be treated well, the trio returned to wait for the crew, Yoshiko trying to keep her patience despite all her questions.

I'll be a pest again, she thought, recalling when she first met Gora and had hundreds of questions for him, and how he'd had to call for quiet the first few times, needing peace to think.

Suddenly, memories flashed back to less pleasant thoughts, and her breathing quickened and her face flushed hot. Her father's sword on the dais that day, escaping the castle, Haruki going missing, all the deaths of her friends, the death ship and the war …

A hand rested on her arm and a light voice interrupted her thoughts, someone calling her name. Yoshiko looked uncertainly at an anxious Suki standing before her. Without Suki and even Chisaka, Yoshiko wondered whether she'd have been able to manage as much as she had after the death of her parents and Haruki, with both Nubia and Gora leaving.

But he's back now, Yoshiko told herself, trying to pick herself back up again and reassuring Suki she was fine. *And it won't be long before we can talk like we did before.*

Gora was the first to join them. His autumn hair was still dark with being wet, and he pushed his kimono sleeves up to his elbows to keep cool after the hot baths as he padded down the halls towards where Yoshiko and her two guardians had been chatting.

'Fancy a stroll?' Yoshiko offered him, agreeing with the green kimono the castle workers had chosen for him.

'Gardens?' His blue eyes lit up, and Yoshiko couldn't help but smile back.

'You'll have to tell me all about your trip,' Yoshiko said in return as she led Gora away from Suki and Chisaka and down the stone steps towards the eastern palace gardens on the first level of the castle grounds. The sun was setting, and the castle was quieter, diplomats having headed home for the day, leaving the castle workers tending to the guests.

'So she always goes around with you, now?' Gora asked, looking back up the steps to where they'd left Chisaka in the entranceway.

Yoshiko let out an affirmative hum, not needing to turn to know the woman would still be watching her while she could see her. 'Most of the time.'

'Most?' Gora looked at her sidelong, eyebrow raised, his lips pulling into a cunning smile.

'When I don't outrun her!'

It was nearly dark when they arrived in the gardens, but that didn't seem to dull Gora's mood. Yoshiko smiled as he stretched and looked about happily, heading to the nearest stone lantern.

'You wouldn't believe how fuckin' long it's been since I've seen green things,' he said, crouching down to look at a clump of white flowers, their petals shining in the lantern light against the twilight.

Yoshiko lightly pushed him about the lifestyle they'd led on the ship, questioning how everyone had been. 'Did Kimura feed you well? How was the boy—Miyoshi? And Moori?'

Gora answered her questions one by one, as he always did, this time with greater patience than usual. Yoshiko felt anxious that her questions would seem endless, but Gora seemed almost relieved to be talking, and they strolled for what felt like hours, the moon rising and Yoshiko's keen senses guiding them through the darker tree-covered areas. When a pair of guards from the *tenshu* came to collect them for dinner, the two discovered they'd not been chatting for hours at all, and the evening meal had yet to be served.

'Aye, here's one for yer,' Gora started with a low voice, piquing her interest immediately with the conspiratorial way he said it as they made their way back up the stone steps. 'Did yer know yer have a giant living off yer coast?'

'A what?' Yoshiko whipped her neck to face him, trying to gauge his expression.

'Ever heard of an *umibōzu*?'

Yoshiko nodded. She'd read about them in old folk tales.

'Well, there's one of them lurking like a damned mini mountain in the waters to the south of here. Had a right job to get past it, 'specially with the ship as it was.'

Gora sounded like he was remembering it, and Yoshiko wanted to pester him to tell her more. She'd been wondering how much more they'd hear of magical creatures and spirits and had wanted to ask Gora what he'd seen on his travels but had held off for worry he was too tired and that she'd be too much of a pest. Now, here he was, telling her about giant sea ghosts, and her curiosity spiked.

Instead, she watched him as they followed the guards towards the feast, noticing how gingerly he used his arm and how he kept stopping to look about him, almost as if reassuring himself he was back. No, she thought. He was exhausted and recovering. Her questions could wait.

The meal was jovial, and Yoshiko was pleased the castle workers had put on good, hearty food full of colour and meats and vegetables—all the things she knew would have been rationed on the ship. The crew and their chosen guests' eyes almost boggled out of their heads, and Yoshiko happily listened to the banter and stories as her guests chatted about their experience, eager to share with their family or Yoshiko. She felt a pang of envy that she hadn't been able to join them but relished this opportunity to hear their stories, particularly to see how the young noble daughter Moori had opened up on this journey, now teasing Kimura like a pestering little sibling. Moori, on Yoshiko's left side, eagerly chatted away and shared stories with her. On her other side, Gora contented himself with eating and watching his crew, occasionally joining in the conversation with Yoshiko, Moori, and Kimura, mostly when called or when Moori finally gave speaking room to someone else. Yoshiko laughed when Kimura and Moori chastised one another, and more so when the other crew joined in, or when Kimura and Ikeda bickered across the table. The young samurai had opened up a little more, Yoshiko thought as she watched, and saw him flushing again as she caught his gaze.

Her face heated up in response, and she tore her gaze away and looked instead at her food.

When the excitement of the meal had worn off and fatigue hit the room, Yoshiko asked the castle workers to guide her guests to their rooms to recover. The next morning, she told them, they would be tended to by the healers and medics again. After that, she wanted to meet with Gora and certain members of the crew to discuss more what had happened, to hear their story and plan the next actions. Miyoshi's mother, rightly, had been heartbroken when Tomioka and Gora had gone to tell her, and Tomioka had skipped dinner afterwards. Yoshiko frowned, wondering how to ease both of their hearts and reassure them they'd find the boy. But for that, they had to have a plan.

'Gora, choose some of the crew you wish to be in the meeting, or any who wish to join. Some may rather rest. Let me know.'

Gora turned to look at her. His eyes were drooping and his thoughts seemed elsewhere, but he nodded. 'Aye, I can do that.' He addressed Ikeda and Daiki on his other side. 'Both or one of you good to join?'

Daiki declined, saying he wished to find out what was happening in the palace from the guards, but Ikeda accepted. Yoshiko left it for them to discuss, and with her own eyes fluttering shut, she rose from the table and excused herself to bed.

'Ah,' Gora called after her, jumping up. 'I was wondering, how long are these meetings goin' to be, now? I wanted to go back to Yamamoto for a few days—visit home and see the villagers. That okay? Just need some time to myself, ye know. Been a while since I've seen a forest. Hard to have space on a ship.'

A pang of loneliness gripped Yoshiko, and she struggled to keep her face neutral. Gora had returned only hours ago, and he already wanted to leave? Yoshiko blinked, begging her exhausted brain to think of something positive to say. Deep down, she knew his restlessness had nothing to do with her; it was about him needing to catch up with himself, and of course he'd want to visit home. Gora had always liked the calm and quiet of the forest. And he'd said it would only be for a few days. Nonetheless, Yoshiko's heart sank, and anxiety gnawed at her as she nibbled on her nail, desperately seeking the right words to say. Struggling for words, she nodded before turning and retreating for her room.

36

Find the Witch, Save the Boy

'I want to look for the sea witch,' Gora said, taking a sip of the green leaf tea as he knelt in the tea rooms in the *tenshu* keep of Hié the next day.

Yoshiko, sitting to Gora's left on another side of the large square table, caught Moori's expression, and she looked equally clueless.

'The sea witch? Why? What does that have to do with Pirate Queen Mammie taking the children?' Yoshiko frowned, turning back to Gora, trying to keep up with everything they'd told her since arriving back in Hié.

'Mammie mentioned going to the far north to speak with the old sea witch, one of the few magical beings left in the world. She must have made an agreement with her. If she did, perhaps we can find out more, or even find a way to stop it.' Gora remembered all the times he'd seen children being killed by the pirates. How they'd said that same thing each time, that he'd just thought was them being cautious. *Another soul for the great sea witch.* It all made sense now, why they never said it when they killed adults.

'But how can such a person really exist if magic was lost hundreds of years ago? Wouldn't the sea witch have disappeared then, too? What if she's just a myth or a superstition?'

'It's like the dragon spirit, perhaps,' Gora said. 'Generational. When I was still a lad, shortly after I was taken, a group of pirates got scared and killed the last sea witch, hoping it would be the end of her powers and influence over the sea. But, when one sea witch dies, their powers are transferred to another of their tribe in spirit, and another sea witch is born.'

'I still don't understand how that links to the pirate queen.' Yonemura frowned. She shuffled where she knelt, not used to wearing traditional Hizen clothing anymore.

'If the pirates are giving the souls of the children to the sea witch, then she must have to do something at the next step. Mammie won't be able to do it all by herself. She'll need some form of spiritual being to harvest the souls. Magic just doesn't appear out of nowhere. It needs an origin. That'll be one of the few remaining beings of power left.'

He looked over at Yoshiko, who was nervously fingering a brooch she'd put on that day—the one from the old farmer lady who'd helped her the year before. He sighed. She still fiddled when she was worried about something.

'If she'd known where you were, she'd have come to get you, too.' He looked into her dark eyes now as he spoke, remembering Mammie demanding he give her Yoshiko, his voice lowering with the severity of it. 'I can only say I'm glad they didn't know.'

She nodded and let go of the brooch. Gora looked to Yoshiko's side to Ikeda, who already looked ready to give his life for her as if the pirate queen was about to step into the room and steal his daimyō for some nefarious purpose.

'Well, not that I mind magic coming back,' Yoshiko said. 'In some way, it may benefit the world. But using the souls of children to do it … I can't accept that. If that's the cost of magic, I don't want it.' She looked down at the scales on her hands. 'Even if it means magical beings dying out one day. It's a shame, but if magic started dying out of its own accord, perhaps it's time for the world to head into a new age, without magic and magical beings.'

Everyone around the table nodded, expressions sombre.

'What do you propose, my lady?' Moori said, her voice strong and confident with perfect polite speech. She was the image of nobility—speech, dress, sitting, courteous behaviour. Here, her position meant she spoke ahead of the others in front of Yoshiko. She looked fairly at her captain and crewmates. 'I'm sure I speak on behalf of us all when I say that we'll do what we can to make your wishes come to fruition.'

Yoshiko nodded and sat up tall, a fiery energy lighting up her face. 'Captain, Hizen has taken great strides since you left, and we can spare more crew and warriors to aid you in this mission. I, too, will come. Take us to this sea witch you speak of. Let's see if she can shed some light on the matter. If she is, indeed, the one collecting the souls this pirate queen wishes to use to bring back magic, she will be the one we can go to put an end to it all. Even if it means killing the sea witch and ending another magical being.'

'My lady, you can't seriously put yourself in such danger!' Chisaka lurched forwards from where she knelt behind Yoshiko. Yoshiko twisted her body to look back at her guard and smiled. Beside her, Ikeda's face flashed with an emotion Gora instantly recognised—envy.

Yoshiko grinned. 'You know I can handle myself. If I can't go forth and protect others, even those beyond our empire, I'll never be able to look my mother in the face when I meet her in the spirit world. Besides, this has affected citizens of Hizen. Remember when they tried taking those three Hién kids in the distraction of our battle against Acrein? I won't take it lying down. I'll take full force.' Gora saw the sheen of light scaling on her face flash and a flame in her eyes flare, and her usually peaceful and cheerful face darken. To Yoshiko, her people were everything, the reason she became daimyō.

'But you know what happens if you use that power too much.' Chisaka panicked, edging forwards and kneeling on one knee beside her warlord.

Yoshiko's face became unreadable. Some in the room didn't know the curse that came with her powers, or what would happen to her if she used it. Not that it wasn't becoming visible. The room fell silent, and Gora felt immediately uncomfortable. He wasn't made for places like this, where the wind didn't pick up in the leaves or the waves with a constant lull of natural noise. Here, you could hear the beat of the fan Moori flicked in front of her slightly bored face. She snapped it shut, the sound deafening in this small space, likely feeling the same anxiety with the disturbance it made to use.

Despite this, Chisaka looked unfazed and held her daimyō's gaze.

Impressive woman. No wonder Yoshiko chose her. Gora thought. *Likely, though, she's there to keep Yoshiko from getting into trouble, not just to stop trouble coming to her.* He grinned.

'I must say, your *dragonness*,' he started. 'You seem to be handling that curse quite well. Much better since we last fought alongside one another. What's your secret for managing it?'

Yoshiko still hid the majority of the scaling from using the spirit powers of the dragons several times previously. She often wore long sleeves and traditional jackets to cover her arms, but one could still see the scaling that reached more subtly up her hands and fingers. The light scaling on her shoulder was often covered too, but her neck and face glistened in the light. She wasn't hiding that anymore. Now that he'd not seen her for a while, he noticed her eyes often looked different to when he first met her. Less dark brown in colour, more golden.

'Meditation,' Yoshiko replied simply, returning his stare. 'Local monks and priestesses have been visiting me with breathing techniques that expand my personal spiritual power source. Or so they say. I was a little uncertain at first. But, as I regularly visit that little shrine you and I often visited, I figured I may as well try it. I combine it with paying my respects. It feels more right there, anyway.' She slouched forward again, resting her elbow on the low table, then her chin in her hand. Moori smirked at her for her manners, but it was a sign that others in the room could relax a little more, too.

'You see, Chisaka,' Yoshiko continued, 'I'll be fine. I intend not to use my powers unless I can help it, anyway. If I can't lead my samurai to fight for the good of Hizen and the world, then what kind of leader can I call myself? And I can still fight with weapons without need of my birth powers. I have at least what that traitor Chinen taught me, and my mother.'

Chisaka bowed and returned to her place behind Yoshiko.

'Then,' Gora chipped in before any further trouble could get in the way, 'Miyoshi has nothing to fear. We'll find the sea witch and be on our way to save him and stop Mammie with the best force our great warlord can offer.' He flashed Yoshiko his best grin, and she rolled her eyes. 'My thanks, daimyō.'

'But where would we find a sea witch?' Shingo piped up, having stayed quiet, thoughtful, throughout the meeting so far. 'And will there be enough time before Yūki is sacrificed?'

The room fell quiet at those finishing words, and all turned to Gora.

'Do you know when it will happen, captain? Did the pirate queen say anything?'

Gora shook his head and looked down at his cup. 'All I know is he'll be the last. We'll need to act as quickly as we can, either way.

'As for the sea witch, we'll find her in the far north of the world, where the world turns to ice and she can watch over the world from its far top.'

'Who would live in such a place?' Yonemura gave an involuntary shiver.

'An ancient tribe, one that goes back to the days the world was covered in ice, I hear.' Gora thought about the stories he'd heard of the powers of the sea witch and why she was most feared. She was a being whose power had switched from generation to generation since the old days, so powerful was she, and she resided in the lands of ice, where very few could live.

'If she resides in such a place, how do you propose we get there?' Shingo asked, his voice low and cutting through the low murmur from the others. 'Can a ship get there?'

'Good point,' Yonemura said with a sigh, reaching forward for her cup and taking a sip, eyes watching Gora again.

'We can take a ship to where the ice meets the sea. From there, we'll need sleds, preferably, for speed, or thick boots and clothes for walking. The people there used sleds pulled by dogs, but I don't know whether our dogs could handle such a trip.'

'What if our lady transformed and pulled it?' Moori smirked, breaking her demeanour for a moment to return to the playful self that Gora knew from the ship.

Yoshiko's lips tugged and her eyes lit with amusement, but it was Chisaka behind her who chipped in, stern-voiced and with unamused eyes, before the daimyō could speak. 'My lady cannot transform again, for risk of her own life, unless the need is absolutely dire. Pulling a sled does not measure up to need.'

With that, Yoshiko sighed and slumped forward onto the table on her elbow again, resting her chin in her hands. 'Well, you heard her. I'd have been too fast for you anyway.' She smirked back at Moori, and Gora couldn't help but smile too.

From the days he'd known her outside the castle, she'd been playful and likely would have pulled the sled—and would have had fun teasing Moori for falling off it, too. But, with her guard watching her and monitoring her, it wouldn't be likely she'd get to let loose like the last time he'd gone on a mission with her. *I bet it's less meditation and more Chisaka that's helping her control her powers,* he thought to himself, meeting Yoshiko's eyes and raising his eyebrows in a mutual *well, you heard it* expression.

'Back to business, then,' Yoshiko said firmly, sitting up straight again. 'I will organise ships to get us there and something to use when we get to the lands of ice. I'm sure our craftsfolk will be able to come up with something.' Then Yoshiko turned to her side to look at Ikeda beside her, who straightened and met her gaze strongly this time, no hint of blushing, Gora noted to his amusement. Ikeda looked like he was determined to impress and win the heart of his daimyō and become a favourite before Chisaka. 'Can you help me pull together a plan for samurai? We'll need to organise people to help us fight the pirates to bring Miyoshi back.'

Ikeda bowed his head, letting out a soft confirmation, and when he returned to face the table and Yoshiko kept talking to them of their plan for the next few days to prepare, Ikeda's eyes were that little bit brighter.

'Well,' Gora said eventually. 'Sounds like we got all we need. We're gunna save the lad, stop this mess, and come back again.' He regarded Yoshiko as she nodded beside him. 'How long do you think it will take to prepare?'

Yoshiko's face fell to a frown as she thought. 'Maybe a week?' she guessed. 'Let me investigate it tomorrow, and from there I'll be able to make a more informed decision. In the meantime, everyone can see family and friends, and we'll let you know if we need people to come back to help.'

To Gora's surprise, Moori raised her hand to request to stay at the castle to help Yoshiko. Yoshiko's face broke into a smile, and she bowed her head lightly to say she'd happily accept, if Moori wasn't worried about not being able to see her family.

'Their estate is too far away for such a short trip. I'm sure they would understand, and I would rather be of help to you, my lady. Unlike last time, when I couldn't.'

Even watching on from the side, Gora could see the firm look passed from Moori to Yoshiko.

'We will save Miyoshi and stop this,' Yoshiko affirmed, ending the meeting.

When the others sifted out of the room, Gora stayed behind and leant back casually on the tatami mats, watching Yoshiko carefully. She held herself more officially and carefully than when he'd last seen her—back when she'd started to act more casually around him. But, this time, in the castle grounds and with her guard Chisaka ever watching her carefully, she likely felt she couldn't relax. *At least*, he thought, *she looks surer of herself now.*

He recalled the times she always tried to do or think of what her parents would do. Today, she'd thought of her own decisions and been sure of them. Gora was proud of her for that. She'd come a long way from when he'd met her.

'You all good for me to head out to the village today?' he asked her, laying his head back on the tatami. He felt exhausted now, and he knew going back to the village would give him the rest he needed.

Her face became unreadable, and he felt a twang of discomfort that she had to use such a face with him, not her usual expressive self. He didn't understand why she had to control her emotions around him now. Only Chisaka was here, and surely she knew her daimyō's true personality?

'What's wrong?' Gora dared ask.

This time, the formality fell from her face, and she sighed, eyes softening.

'I guess I just wanted you around more when you came back, but I know you have to go, so that's all.'

Gora paused, understanding. 'Aye, I getcha. You could come with, if you want, or visit for a day.'

Yoshiko looked like she was considering it, but it was some time before she answered. 'Unfortunately, though I would agree, I am needed here. There is much to do before we leave. Not only do we have to organise a trip for you while you're away, I need to make sure the region will run without me. It's not much notice.'

Gora felt a pang of guilt. 'Alright. Well, the offer still holds, if you find yourself with a day.'

Yoshiko let a smile cross her face. 'I'll remember it, thank you.' Then she stood, and Chisaka stood with her. 'Safe trip. Enjoy your visit home, and I hope we have something to surprise you by when you return, with ships prepared to sail and stop this madness!'

Gora grinned and rose too. 'Aye, I'll leave it to you.'

37

The Pirates' Message

Three days later, Yoshiko raced down the hill from the castle grounds to the port, heart thundering and breath coming in staccato gasps. Her veins flooded with panic, and she wished Gora had returned.

As it were, he was still in Yamamoto, and a messenger had just been dispatched to send for him. For now, she'd have to handle it alone.

That morning, a guard had raced to her training court, where she'd been training with Ikeda and Daiki once more, and Eshnaa and Simrita had joined at their request. With Ikeda translating, she was having fun training with the two Ishillian warrior women. But the guard's news had dampened all their spirits: a ship had been seen in the distance.

'For how long? What kind of ship?'

'Foreign, definitely, with a black flag. How long … it was spotted yesterday before sundown, some port workers said, but they thought it was leaving so thought nothing of it. Only when it was still there this morning did they tell anyone, and it's still there.'

Yoshiko saw the other four give each other wary glances as Ikeda and Daiki translated it for the two Ishillians. Their faces darkened.

'Pirates?' Daiki asked.

'Where is it?' Yoshiko added, turning once more to look at the samurai guard.

'Just off the coast to the south-west. Can we show you?' The guard looked at Daiki. 'And, sir, if you could come, too, to confirm …'

The man didn't need to finish his sentence. Daiki had already agreed, and the guard led them to a viewing point in one of the towers. From there, he said, they could see if they needed to do anything about it before going down to the port.

While Daiki peered through the spyglass in the watch tower, Yoshiko found a window and extended her vision to see down to the coast.

'It's leaving?' she asked, noticing a wake from the ship's stern side.

The others paused, and the guard looked over at her.

'So it is,' Daiki agreed, moving out of the way so Ikeda could look, directing the young man to the watch point. Ikeda hummed with agreement, but the guard froze.

'Why would it leave now?'

'Perhaps it just stopped for the night?' Daiki offered as a weak suggestion, his face showing even he didn't believe it.

'Black flag …' Yoshiko thought. 'You two would know more about pirate ships. Does it look like one?' She returned her gaze to the sea, trying to peer at the ship, stretching her vision more. She couldn't quite see enough from this far up. Perhaps at the coast …

'It does look like one,' Ikeda added, and then he moved out of the way and gestured for the two Ishillians to look, seeing their eager faces.

While the four were agreeing and discussing with the guards, Yoshiko noticed a growing crowd on the port below. The tiny figures of people were running to a point on the docks, and she fixed her vision there and frowned. 'What's happening down there? Can you see it?'

She could feel the others watching her but kept looking at the port. 'People are gathering on the docks.'

Simrita jumped down from the platform by the window and Ikeda jumped up again, looking through the spyglass at the docks. He couldn't answer, but Yoshiko felt a warning flush through her body, and she blinked back her vision a few times, her eyes straining at the change, and she turned to catch his eye.

'I'm going down there.' She ran out of the watchtower, ignoring their shouts behind as they tried to catch up.

Something's wrong, she thought, forcing herself to run faster. The people looked in a panic, nothing like when they ran to greet an incoming fishing boat. Yoshiko knew the others would follow, but she couldn't wait for them. She had to get there as soon as she could.

Guards yelled after her as she ran to the lower levels and through the *karaméte-mon* gate and over the bridge, asking if she was alright. But she tore past like a wind spirit, and she heard poor Daiki having to stop to explain when they followed. She stretched out her hearing even further, wondering if she could hear down to the docks. But she couldn't. There was, however, a strange hush over Hié town, as if word was spreading of whatever was happening down at the docks.

Yoshiko rushed down the main town street, the most direct path down the hill towards the harbour. As she got closer, she started to pick up the murmurs of disbelief and shock, even hearing whispers creep through it all. 'Where did it come from?'

'How horrifying.'

'*Funayūrei*?'

Funayūrei? Boat spirits of vengeful ghosts of people who died at sea? What would spirits be doing here? She'd never heard reports of *funayūrei* sightings before, but with what she'd been seeing lately, she'd believe almost anything now.

Yoshiko cried out to the people gathered at the port as she got there, seeing the crowd gathering, and they pulled apart for their daimyō, letting her through.

She came to a stop right in front of a small pale corpse lying on the wooden dock, and Yoshiko fought hard to keep her breath, feeling as if it had been punched out of her at the sight of the tiny body.

'It's a foreign child,' they said. 'The body washed up against the boats this morning.'

Yoshiko dared to peer closer. The body of the child wore only shorts, and on their stomach was a burnt branding mark like one she'd only seen on Gora. Not a slave mark like those she and her people and the people of Qecla had been given, but another. A pirate brand. As well as this, little handprints bruised the body as if it had been grabbed and pulled by other children, and the eyes were totally white. Its hair was just as pale.

Nausea spread through her.

'Some are saying it's a *funayūrei*, washed up here to curse us,' a guard who'd been posted down at the ports whispered in her ear, standing closely beside her, her hand ready at her katana. 'Daimyō, what should we do?'

Yoshiko was still reeling, her eyes burning as she stared at the child and the strange bruisings covering its pale skin.

'Not *funayūrei*. One of the sacrificed children?' she managed to mutter when she'd caught her breath, looking up to realise that no-one here knew about that. The looks of horror on their faces tugged at her heart, and she looked about at their faces, wondering what to tell them to ease the pain of what they'd seen.

She couldn't think of anything. This was horrifying.

'But who would sacrifice a child? What's wrong with just food or Hizen-shuu rice wine?' an old man croaked from behind her somewhere.

She shook her head, not knowing the answer.

More mutters of disbelief and shock at injustice echoed behind her.

Yoshiko crouched by the dead child and tried to look for more clues as to whether this really was one of the sacrificial children of the pirates, or whether it had just washed up by coincidence. She pouted as she thought, trying to recall what Gora had told her about it all. Of the dead children, not so much. Just that it happened. It had been like he'd blocked it out or silenced it in trauma. After seeing this and knowing clues about what he'd experienced on the ships, Yoshiko didn't blame him.

But where was Gora when he was needed? She knew he'd be coming soon with the messenger fetching him, but it wasn't soon enough. She wished she had his advice and knowledge now.

'Did it come from that ship?' someone around her asked.

Yoshiko nodded without looking around to see who had spoken. 'I think so.'

'Why?'

Now Yoshiko looked in the direction the ship was leaving. Tempted to transform and fly after them and burn them to ash, she pushed down the burning rage that threatened to engulf her heart like that day in Acrein. She knew if she transformed now, even to fly after them, she'd be lost in the flames again. So strong was the sickness she was feeling at what they'd done.

'Did anyone get a good look at the ship?' she asked, knowing details gave a good case to help find out what was happening.

There was an uncomfortable silence as people searched their memories. Then someone piped up. 'Jiro knows. He spotted it earlier and said something about it.'

People looked about for this so-called Jiro. No-one identified as him.

'Will Jiro be able to come and speak to us up at the castle later?' Yoshiko asked, sensing the person either wasn't there or was nervous to speak up.

'I'll ask him.'

There was a clattering again as Ikeda, Simrita, and Eshnaa ran up, breath gasping, searching the crowd for Yoshiko.

'Let them through,' Yoshiko said quietly.

The crowd parted, and Eshnaa tumbled forwards, tossing her green sari back around her shoulder. She stopped a few steps away from the crouching Yoshiko and the body on the docks and rushed her hands up to her face in disbelief, crying out and saying something in Ishillian that Yoshiko had no hopes of understanding. Ikeda walked up to them, calm, speaking to Eshnaa in what Yoshiko recognised as Traders', though again, she didn't understand. As Ikeda approached, he calmly took it all in, face cool as ever, but then a hint of anger washed over him as his eyes lit up with some form of recognition.

'Is it the pirates?' Yoshiko asked him.

He nodded. 'I think so. Though, we've never seen the bodies before.'

Eshnaa said something in Traders' to him, and he focused on translating. Behind them, Simrita stood stunned and disgusted, looking away from the body, jaw clenched, unable to bring herself closer. Yoshiko turned back to Ikeda as he finished speaking with Eshnaa.

'Gora's not told us much about this, but we need to ask him. Eshnaa says the boy looks like he's from the northern middling continent, about nine summers, and asks how long he's been dead for.'

Yoshiko froze. *How does one find out how long someone's been dead?* She turned back to the body and tried to think. 'How do you know?' she eventually whispered, and he heard her and crouched beside her, speaking in a low voice. Ikeda was so close his knee brushed against her, and she felt a tingle down her neck and spine as he bent his head close to the side of her face to speak quietly without others listening.

'Is there a way to take him back to the castle to examine there?' Ikeda asked. 'We need to take the body away from the people. It is shocking them.'

Yoshiko felt her cheeks flush at how close he was, and she stared down at the body to keep her grounded in what was happening. She nodded hastily. 'Let's do that. Thank you.'

There, they'd await Gora.

* * *

Gora arrived later that evening, the clattering hooves announcing the messenger's return with him. The autumn-haired man strode up the steps and into the *tenshu* keep, his green kimono pulling at his legs as he rushed up to meet Yoshiko, who stood at the entrance waiting for him.

His face flushed red with exertion, and his blue eyes pierced through in contrast, concerned. He grabbed her upper arms with both hands, and Yoshiko felt his grip tightening.

'What happened? Are you well?' His face was contorted with stress, his breath staggered and quick, eyes searching hers for any sign of unease.

Yoshiko let out a small huff of a laugh, relieved. 'I am well, but our situation is not. Come inside. What did they tell you?'

'Only that you needed me to return immediately.' He kept up with her as she led him to where the boy's body was.

'Oh,' was all Yoshiko said in return, and she realised that at the time she'd called for him, she hadn't realised what was wrong to be able to tell him why he was summoned. She frowned as she led him to the room, wondering what to tell him as a precursor. He couldn't just walk in there and see *that*. 'There was a ship hanging about the last day or so,' she started, 'likely a pirate ship. Then, this morning, the people discovered something that washed up.'

She stopped at the entrance to the room and turned to him, worried about how he'd react. He looked at her blankly, eyes still showing the same concern, clearly more worried about her at this point and confused about where she was going. He reached out again, and this time softer, he placed it on her head, just like always. Immediately, Yoshiko felt more at ease, and she let her shoulders drop and took a deep breath.

'You won't like it. But we need your help.'

His thick red brows furrowed, but he said nothing and gestured with his head for her to continue inside and show him. So she did.

The child was laid out on a blanket on the tatami mat in the middle of the room, and as expected, Gora's face flushed white the instant he saw it. His eyes widened, and he stopped where he stood in the doorway. Yoshiko waited in silence.

Is he swaying?

She frowned, wondering if she'd need to rush forward and catch him.

Gora's mouth opened and closed as if he was trying to speak but could find no words. Yoshiko understood. She looked once more at the child, thinking it looked almost impossibly pale now, and the little hand marks shone out all the brighter. When she turned back to Gora, he was scanning the body and then took an uncertain, heavy step to sit and slumped against the wall.

'Oh,' was all he said, looking now at her, eyes squinting, face scrunching up.

Yoshiko's heart fell to the pit of her stomach when she saw his eyes—haunted, broken.

'What is it?' she dared to whisper, feeling her lips go dry.

He didn't respond.

'The people think it's a *funayūrei*.' When he didn't seem to register what she'd said, she spelled it out for him. 'Spirits of vengeful ghosts of people who died at sea. They reckon it fell out of its boat and washed ashore.'

Gora remained silent, mouth a small line as if he were pressing it shut, and his eyes seemed dead.

Yoshiko heard movement outside and quickly dashed to the doorway, leaning out and asking the person outside to leave them be for a while. It was Suki, and she bowed and gracefully shuffled off. Yoshiko returned inside and slid to the floor beside Gora.

She waited. She would wait as long as he needed. Both stared at the body of the child.

Eventually, voice small and scratchy as if he was testing speaking for the first time, he said, 'Tiny hands …'

Yoshiko thought he looked almost green, and as he sat with his knees bent, he held his arms out in front of him and looked at his own hands, a look of fear and repulsion crossing his weather-beaten face.

'Tiny hands. That's how it happens … the sacrifice. All the time. Tiny hands reach out from the ocean and pull the child under, drowning them.' Gora paused again; then it spewed out like a stream. 'It was only a few hands at first, as if the ocean was pulling them towards it. I thought it was the sea witch. But then, over time, more hands, like the previous children were pulling others down to join them.

'More and more tiny hands. All pale. All dead.'

Yoshiko looked back at the marks on the child's body and imagined it, being a small child and thrown overboard, other small hands reaching up from the depths and grabbing at you, pulling you under. Terror rose through her, and the inner curse burned in response. *I should have gone after that ship.* She closed her eyes and focused on pushing the heat down, trying to think of why the pirates might have brought this boy here. 'Do you think it's a warning?'

'No doubt. We can't delay any longer, now. We have to go. Are the ships ready?'

'Soon. They need about half a day or so at least.'

'Please, make it happen. We have no more time to waste.' Gora frowned, leaning his head back against the wall, still staring at the child. 'And burn the kid. They deserve a respectful burial after …'

He didn't say the rest. Yoshiko nodded and passed him a *hyotan* gourd.

He took it gratefully, unquestioning, and his eyebrows rose as he sniffed at what was inside. Saké, just what she knew he needed. He took a great, noisy gulp and then rose it as if to toast, face pale and impossibly grave.

'Another soul for the great sea witch.'

38

Finding a Sea Witch

The washed-up child was news around Hié in hours, and Gora and his crew rushed to prepare the last needed items to set sail the next day, with the help of craftsfolk and townsfolk alike all pulling together at the last hurdle. Stores were stocked to beyond the point Kimura could be happy, and Yoshiko had provided extra guards for their safety. Now, near ready to sail, Gora stepped up onto the *Sea Guardian* and ran a hand along the freshly lacquered woodwork as he inspected his fixed ship, nodding near constantly as he judged the craftswork. He took the steps to the upper deck two at a time to check the figurehead, pleased that her arms and hands had been replaced and her face fixed, though he couldn't see much of her face from this angle.

Gora jumped at the sound of someone clearing their throat behind him, and whirled around, hair on end, hands rushing out to defend.

'Yoshiko?' he said in a low voice, barely believing it. He'd not heard her coming. 'Just like the old days, now, eh?'

She smiled and joined him in the last checks, gesturing to the figurehead's weapon systems. 'They've replaced the firing systems,' Yoshiko said in a calm, low voice, focused. 'It comes through the hands again, but the piping is tougher. Should you be attacked like that again, you'll still have something remaining to fire from, even if it won't be so aesthetic.'

'I don't want her ruined again,' Gora said gruffly, staring at the figure as it watched the waves. 'She reminded me of you, and it wasn't a good omen to have her destroyed.'

Yoshiko laughed. 'Don't say such foreboding things as I'm about to set sail with you!'

Gora turned once more to look at her amused face, and he felt the knot in his heart soften and untie enough for relief to flood back through his body. Feeling his jaw unclench, Gora ran a hand through his hair and let out a smile. 'Aye, I'll have the real one with me this time.' They continued strolling the ship. 'But is it really okay for you to join us?'

Yoshiko dipped her head in response. 'I've left a capable council and sent a message to the shogun. He already knows about the pirates trying to take the children the last time they came to Hié, and now with the drowned child ...' She took a breath, turning to look out at the sea. 'This has brought worry to all of Hizen. I don't know what's happening in other regions, but strange creatures are being sighted across the country, and the other leaders are worried. Something is happening. If I can join you and ease some of that— if the pirates are taking children from other regions, too—then it will be well worth the time and resources.'

'And you just want to join the adventure,' Gora teased, elbowing her arm gently.

Yoshiko laughed. '*And* I just want to join the adventure.'

Along with Yoshiko and additional Hién guards came Chisaka Reina, who Gora felt never let Yoshiko out of her sight. A larger, bulkier woman than Yoshiko and a stickler for wearing her full armour, Chisaka quickly became a great additional hand on ship when she wasn't supervising her reckless guard. Gora had been impressed. Few could keep up with Yoshiko—she whizzed about the place with an energy he was sure could only be in people whose hearts near literally burned with a constant fire—and yet Chisaka wasn't often far behind. 'Used to it,' were the words she'd given him, rather resigned, as he asked her upon passing one day.

'Aye, I'm sure,' he'd chuckled as he walked away, watching the guard dive after her daimyō once again.

He noticed, over the days since setting sail from Hizen, the difference with having Yoshiko on board. Several of his crew were more cheerful at having someone they admired so much around, and Gora himself embraced this extra time with the woman he thought of as his younger sister. Yoshiko joined in with the training, showing the crew new skills, picking up different fighting styles herself from the international crew members. Gora's heart sank as he realised how disheartened Miyoshi would be at missing out on the opportunity to have Yoshiko teach him how to use the knives she'd gifted him.

And Yoshiko had refused to have her own room. She and Chisaka took a hammock in the ladies' quarters just like the others, helping her quickly form friendships with the other women of the ship. Moori, she already knew, but it wasn't long before she'd bonded with the others as if she'd known them for life. Gora was amazed at how well she thrived in talking with people—a far cry from her uncertain energy back when he'd been the only one she'd really talk to daily as they hid. He'd never seen her able to talk so freely. Now, he heard clumsy conversations between Eshnaa, Simrita, and Yoshiko, with one of the others translating between languages for them, Yoshiko often trying to learn Traders' to join in more on her own. She regularly padded up to him to ask questions about the languages—endless questions, as always—and Gora felt the smile wipe from his face when he thought about how good Miyoshi would have been to help her learn.

'The lad was getting real good at Traders',' he mumbled to her one day to explain his low mood as they leant against the gunwale overlooking the bow and the sea that churned below the hull. 'Surprised me. Surprised us all.'

Yoshiko leant next to him, her dark indigo *haori* billowing in the wind and black hair pulled up in a knot to prevent it from getting too sea-tangled. She frowned, and Gora noticed how her eyes had become even lighter, like gold was melting into the deep brown-black, though nothing as golden as her eyes were when she was transformed. She turned to watch him, wary for a moment at seeing him watching her too, and he saw the flash of blue-silver scales curving around the edge of her face and down her neck, suddenly feeling a strange urge to touch it and discover how the scales felt.

'We'll find him,' Yoshiko said, interrupting his thoughts. 'We've already made good headway to the north.' She fell silent again, looking at the sea and sky, still, almost sniffing the air. 'The air and water are already turning colder.'

That it is, now, Gora thought, shrugging his jacket closer as if the mere mention could make him feel colder. They'd sailed east out of Hié and up the side of Hizen, past Iezo, the final island and holdings of Hizen. Now, they churned the Taiheyō Ocean to the wild north, the Ice Lands. The crew already had to wear warmer clothes for the night rotation. Any colder than this, and they may as well walk around with futons wrapped about their bodies.

'Shame there's no *kotatsu* on board,' Yoshiko grumbled, slouching against the wooden gunwale and staring down into the sea.

'Aren't you meant to be alright in the cold, Miss Has-Her-Own-Furnace-In-Her-Belly?'

Yoshiko narrowed her black eyes to glare at him, and Gora grinned. Her expression softened as she stared back out to the horizon dreamily. 'Aye,' she said with weight, openly copying him. 'But nothing beats feeling cosy.'

Gora rested his chin in his hand, elbow on the gunwale, also staring at the beyond. He thought back to the warm fire in his small village hut, and how everyone in Yamamoto loved gathering around the fireplaces of their *daidokoro* or under their *kotatsu* or burying themselves into their futons. Nights when he'd visited neighbours for a warm *nabé* meal in the winter, the whole family gathered in the *daidokoro*—no matter how late it was—even the children resting peacefully beside their parents as saké and nabé and sweetmeats were shared with stories until the moon was high. *Aye, nothing beats being cosy.* And when he thought back to his time on the pirate ships, where he'd never felt comfortable, he wondered how he could create the warm feel of a village *daidokoro* on his ship as the days grew increasingly colder and the nights more so.

* * *

The following days were much the same, the crew noticing the creeping cold more, more of them grumbling about wanting a fire or kotatsu to gather around. On a ship, that meant huddling in the galley, and the playful Kimura only egged them on by making them more green leaf teas and hearty salty broths. It was as they travelled further north that Gora found his time with Yoshiko dwindling. Her natural constitution made her perfect for the night rotation. She could handle the cold better than anyone else, and her cursed vision meant she could see at night—perfect for the night's watch. It was after a few days of this that Gora managed to catch Yoshiko in the morning between shifts and ask how the night was going. It was an isolated time, not something he wished her to experience.

'Somehow, I still feel safer when I think no-one can see me,' she said quietly, staring at her hands and clearly avoiding eye contact.

Gora felt numb at the thought. Back then, when Hié was in trouble, the goal to bring Yoshiko back into the sunlight where she could live in her castle home and see other people had been a key driver for him. To hear she still felt that way made his head spin. And while he fumbled on the spot for a response, Gora knew there was no other solution just yet. With times as they were, her body could handle what his crew could not, and even Ikeda and Chisaka, who joined her regularly on her night rotation, and Eshnaa, who had found herself attached to Yoshiko, found themselves wishing more and more that they were back in their hammocks, enviable of their young daimyō who still padded about simply in her *haori*, *hakama,* and kimono.

'Better fucking get there soon,' Gora muttered to himself as he breathed on his hands and rubbed them together for warmth. Even in the daylight, now, the air froze, and the crew wore their thickest clothes. He was thankful the Hién castle had stocked them up well, and many of the crew seemed to be walking linen cupboards; that or they ran about, refusing to stop. He found his moods dropping again with only limited time each day to chat to Yoshiko between shifts.

Better than before, though, now. Least she's here, you ungrateful sod. Or so he tried to tell himself. He tried to focus on their purpose—reaching the far cold of the north and finding the sea witch.

Gora's wish was granted when, not a couple of days later, Kyo called out from where he huddled on watch in the crow's nest.

'Ice ahead! What's that?'

Ahead, fields of white ice reflected the sun, the lapping water rippling and glinting. Beyond that, a towering wall of harsh blue ice seemingly blocked their way, and upon weaving through the sporadic patches of ice, the ship found itself at the entrance to a towering corridor etched into a glacier.

His crew were gobsmacked, standing silent in awe as they stared at the passage carved into the icy cliffs.

'Can it hurt or crush us?'

'Can we go through?'

'Aye, it could crush us,' Gora said, barely above a whisper.

Taro shuffled closer. 'I think I've heard of these. We can go through, can we not?'

'Aye—glacier gates. The way into the deep cold north, the top of the world.' Then he turned to face his crew, who were staring either at him or at the glacier gates. 'We have to go through.'

He looked around, noticing half the crew still below. They would need to be here for this.

'Go wake the others and bring them here. You have three minutes.'

Simrita and Rijul dashed off to wake the night rotation, who came back with shock upon their faces at such a drastic change in the scenery. Yoshiko rushed up beside Gora, leaning her hands on the gunwale to peer up at the towering ice cliffs.

'Ice?'

Gora nodded. 'Glacier gates.'

Her golden-brown eyes had lit up with the same enthusiasm as any time she discovered or learned something new, and Gora braced himself for all the questions he knew were to come, as always. She wouldn't unleash them in front of the crew—she'd learned, from her position of authority, not to do so. Instead, next time they were alone or just with a few they felt comfortable around, she'd be ready with them all.

'We're going in,' Gora told the others, and started explaining what he hoped would be on the other side.

In the places furthest away from humanity, the wild magic reigned. Here, among the ice, a cold magic dwelled, and he had already heard the stories.

'Keep yer eyes out for anything unusual. Report it immediately. Nothing stirs, not even a fish, without your telling someone. This ain't the place to be brave. We need to know. Nothing lives here without it being something strange.'

The crew looked about uncertainly, and Gora called for Yonemura to take over on the helm. Tomioka would be leading the watch, and Shingo leading the sailing team. Then, with the large blue ice cliffs towering over them, they sailed into the gap and through the glacial gates.

'There's a strange smell suddenly,' Yoshiko muttered to him later as she returned from standing at the bow railing, her favoured place on the ship.

Gora looked about them, making sure no-one else was close or listening until they figured out more. Even Chisaka was on the other side of the ship, talking to Daiki. 'Could it be a problem?'

She nodded. 'I think so. There is a heaviness to it.'

Gora ran a hand through the back of his hair and stared into the distance. 'Could be anything here. Keep looking.'

But Yoshiko didn't even need to return to her spot before Quinni, taking his turn up in the crow's nest, called out that there was something ahead after the glacial gates opened back up again.

'Clever monsters.' Gora raised his eyebrows to Yoshiko as they both ran to the bow to see where Quinni was pointing. 'Setting a trap after the gates.'

The tall walls of ice still crowded the ship either side, but ahead, it opened back up again to open sea and drifting ice. There, monsters lay in waiting for unsuspecting ships to sail with relief into the open, unable to see what lay at the opening of the ice sea.

'Be prepared,' Gora said lowly to Yoshiko before turning to warn his crew. Her face turned serious and dark, the eyes melting even more golden, and he knew a fire burned if needed, even if Chisaka tried to stop her.

'I wonder what sorts of creatures they are, to hide in icy places such as this.' Then Yoshiko's eyes flickered brown again, and a peaceful expression he knew from the year before returned to her face. 'Perhaps like the *yuki-onna*?'

Gora shrugged. 'Could be anything.'

Yoshiko fell quiet and narrowed her eyes at the glacier gates, Gora knowing she was trying to see ahead. Then she sighed.

'Winter's icy grip,
Yuki-Onna's deadly breath,
Frozen death awaits.'

Yoshiko's voice came low. Wary.

'What was that?' Gora asked, hoping it wasn't a premonition of what was to come.

'One of my father's haiku. Wrote it at some winter festival, if I recall.'

Father's poem or premonition, Gora didn't want to chance it. Yoshiko could sense things others couldn't, and he'd heard stories of the *yuki-onna*. If what they were to face was anything like that, the crew were in great danger. Before the *Sea Guardian* sailed into the open ice sea, they were ready for whatever might come. Daiki and his fighting team, Chisaka included, were ready with weapons, and Tomioka and Shingo prepared the crew to sail straight through to flee the danger as soon as they could. But, as the ship peeped out of the last of the glacial gates, what they saw didn't at first appear frightening. Strange half-human-half-creatures like those told in stories sat atop floats of ice, dipping elegant white tails into the freezing water and fluffing great grey-white feathered wings. Their upper human-like bodies were light blue-grey, and an almost human-like face peered at them with purple or grey eyes as they tossed long, white, silken-looking hair over their shoulders.

'Ice sirens.' Taro's face flushed pale, and he looked fearfully to his son, who stood beside him. 'Cover your ears, son!'

Kyo rushed to comply but remained watching, nonetheless.

Yoshiko looked at Gora, eyebrows raised, before regarding the creatures again. 'You've told me about these. It seems our fate is different to my father's haiku. How about this:'

> *'Ice siren's song calls,*
> *Shards of ice, a deadly lure,*
> *Frozen death awaits.'*

'You nobles like your pretty poetry.' Yonemura padded up behind them, smiling at Yoshiko as she was relieved of the helm by Nishimura, taking out her spyglass to inspect the creatures further. 'I often wished I could do that.'

'Either way, icy death awaits,' Gora grumbled, thinking they were all missing the point. Of all the things they might have met, he'd hoped it wouldn't be ice sirens. But, if he remembered the stories well, the ice sirens loved to cause chaos to any ship sailing in the ice seas—north or south of the world. They'd sit pretty, distract the crew, then scream deafening ice-shard screeches that would stun everyone on a ship before clambering aboard with wings and sharp talons and dragging their victims to the icy depths before ripping into their flesh for a meal. Now, it was his crew peering at the creatures curiously, as if there was no harm to the world, and he knew what came next. Gora rolled his eyes at his crew's ignorance and bellowed with all the air in his lungs. 'You heard Taro. Cover yer ears!'

One of the creatures lazily raised its arm and ran it through long, straight, beautiful hair, and the human-like face revealed a toothy smile. Thin rows of teeth more suited to an eel flashed the crew before the mouth opened wider.

'I said cover your ears!' Gora yelled again, this time in Traders'.

Simrita and Eshnaa immediately followed his orders, sheathing their blades and watching the creatures with their ears covered. More followed suit, but those slowest suffered a shock unlike anything they'd yet known.

More creatures opened their mouths, and a horrifying sound hit their ears. Even with his ears covered by his hands, Gora still grit his teeth with the sound of it.

A noise like shards of ice pulsing and grinding through his body overtook the sounds of anything else, drowning out the air, the sea, the sounds of the ship and the voices of his crew. Ice scraping on ice chipped through his ears and into his head, and Gora tried to squeeze his hands closer to his ears as he peered about at his crew doing the same. The accursed sound wormed an unwanted memory into his head. Blades clashing against blades, the war last year, and an image of bloated and bloody bodies piling on the ground beneath their feet, tripping them. He grimaced. The sounds were too similar, too overwhelming, too violent. Gora felt his breath coming in uncontrolled gasps, and he looked up to check on his crew. What did they hear in this madness?

Yoshiko, with her dragon-blood-curse hearing, had crashed to the deck onto her knees and keeled over with her hands against her ears, and Shingo had run to the railing, looking out and towards the creatures that screamed piercing ice-shard-like pain. Shingo looked to Gora, brow furrowed, mouth moving. But Gora couldn't hear him.

'What?' Gora tried to call back, but he couldn't even hear himself. Shingo had no hope.

Gora strode to the railing too, right beside Shingo, and dared to take his hands away from his ears for a moment to lean closer to Shingo to hear what he was trying to say, but the screaming of the sirens hurt his ears too much, and Gora pushed his hands back to cover his ears with the pain pulsating through his head. Almost immediately, his forehead throbbed with pain.

Even covering my ears, I can still hear the damned things! Gora growled.

He looked over the railing, looking into the black hole where the ice siren's mouth opened in the icy scream.

It's worse than they said. I can't think of anything.

Gora tried to reason what would happen next, but he saw Rijul crashing about, mouth open and eye squeezed together, presumably crying out. But Gora couldn't hear. With his eyes squeezed shut, Rijul stumbled about on the deck and nearly bumped into the railing and would have toppled over if not for Ikeda rushing towards him and tackling from the side, both young men tumbling to the deck. Throwing their hands out to catch themselves, both curled up and roared with the pain, Ikeda soon getting back onto his knee and peering over the gunwale, eyes squinting with the pain.

The sounds melded with his consciousness, and totally discombobulated, Gora felt himself swaying where he stood, eyes clouded and brain like mush.

This is how they do it. They'll attack next and eat us or something, he managed to think back to what he knew, squeezing his eyes shut to focus.

'Make it stop!' Gora heard faintly over the sounds of crushing ice filling his brain, and he turned to his other side to see Moori rushing across the deck, crashing into the side of Kyo as she made a beeline towards one of the guns. She cried out as she picked it up, not that Gora could hear, and rushed to the railing, biting her lip from the pain of the sirens' screams.

Gora watched in horror as he saw a trail of blood oozing down the side of her face from her ear, and he rushed to cover her ears, losing his own.

The pain from the sound was torturous, and he grit his teeth. There had to be a way to make it stop without them letting go of their ears.

Moori aimed the gun, but a flash of heat pulsed on the air, and Gora turned in horror. He knew that pulsing heat.

'Yoshiko, no!'

Yoshiko looked up at him from where she knelt on the floor, her face grimaced in pain, but her eyes flashed that same burning orange as the day she'd lost control in Acrein.

Gora shook his head, and a flame powder explosion right next to him numbed his ears all the more, its ring contending with the sounds of scraping ice.

The shot missed, and the small Moori stomped her foot and cursed, reloading another round.

By then, the scraping ice shard sounds became too much for Gora to bear, and he instinctively took his hands away from Moori's ears and covered his own. The young woman crunched to the deck with shock at the sound suddenly returning.

There was another flush of heat, and then a low, rumbling buzz overtook the sound of the ice shards, almost offering relief to the crew, who gingerly tested taking their hands from their ears. The buzz overwhelmed the scratching that had etched into their brain, their eyes, their bones. Most seemed pleased that this mysterious sound had taken over, but Gora's heart thudded into his stomach. What had felt cold and cut to pieces by the ice sirens' shards now turned to stone, and he warily looked towards Yoshiko again, her eyes still burning orange. She had removed her hands from her ears, and Gora could see they were covered in blood that oozed down either side of her ashen, shocked face. Another flash of heat hit him.

There was a splash, and Taro looked over the edge of the ship and cried out as loud as he could over the noise.

'They're coming closer!'

Gora's heart leapt, and the sound of crushing, scraping ice grew louder, overcoming the buzzing again.

A figure flickered past him, and still feeling sluggish, by the time Gora turned, Yoshiko was already standing at the gunwale, leaning over the edge and looking below, her black hair flying wildly about her. Chisaka and Ikeda rushed to her side, reaching out to pull her back, crying out as they removed their hands from their ears.

Yoshiko yelled, and it came out like a roar, overcoming all other sound, echoing around the icy chambers behind them.

The ice sirens' scratching ice cries stopped.

The buzzing stopped.

Everything fell so quiet that the people on the *Sea Guardian* could barely hear the faint lapping of the ocean on the hull of the ship and on the ice over the remaining ringing in their ears.

Gora clapped his hands on his ears to make it stop and strode to the edge, peeking at Yoshiko glaring down at the creatures and the shock on Ikeda and Chisaka's faces, and then down at the ice creatures.

Four were still sitting on the ice sheets, shock on their once again beautiful faces now their ugly mouths were closed. Two more were closer: one in the sea, the other hanging on to the hull just below Yoshiko, long, claw-like nails digging into the wood just inches from the daimyō, an ugly mix of fear and anger glaring back at them.

Gora took in a shaky breath.

'How did you know it was there, now?' he whispered, barely able to formulate words.

Yoshiko didn't answer. She kept her glare locked on the creature.

The crew stayed quiet, barely letting themselves breathe. Moori adjusted her position and aimed the gun down towards the creature on the hull, waiting, eyes focused.

Suddenly, a great splash came from ahead, and a huge black-and-white whale-like creature reared up from the ocean, crashing through the thin edge of the ice. Its great maw opened wide, countless needle-like teeth revealing themselves just as it launched through the air, ploughed into one of the sitting ice sirens, and snapped its mouth shut before the magical creature could even move. With a pale, elegant arm and part of a wing and a tail sticking out from its mouth, the whale crashed back down through the ice into the ocean below. Human and ice siren eyes hovered over the place it had disappeared below, dark blood oozing on white ice. Then, in a moment of chaos, the ice sirens darted about, and Gora saw the reason for their alarm. More black fins and smooth nubbed noses cut through the icy water, marking more of the black-and-white whales, and with one final piercing, disorienting scream, the ice sirens dived from the ice shelves into the water or rose up on their wings and darted off, leaving the human onlookers dazed.

'Fucking missed!' Moori cried out, stomping her foot again and unloading the gun.

'Language around the daimyo.' Chisaka looked at the young noble girl with a disapproving glare.

'Damn it!' Yoshiko pouted, staring at her bloody hands. 'Should've burnt them all. Creepy buggers. Did you see it climbing up the side with its *nails*?' She turned to catch their eyes, pausing when she saw Chisaka's look of exasperation. 'What?'

The tension wore off, and Gora couldn't help but let out a roar of a laugh. He ran a hand through his hair in relief and stepped forward, clapping the two young noble girls on their shoulders. Then he cast his eye about the ship, meeting one by one everyone else's stunned gazes.

'Well, that's how you get welcomed to the far icy north. And that's only the start. Who's ready for more?'

39

Aboard the Pirate Queen's Ship

Miyoshi was woken by the door to his tiny storeroom crashing open, and he squinted into the flame light, the brightness, though just a small flame, piercing his eyes after who knew how long of darkness. Beyond the flame, the pirate queen watched him.

'You speak Traders', boy?' she asked. Her voice seemed calmer than the last time he'd heard her speak.

He nodded. 'A little.'

'Good enough,' she said briefly, then gestured him to follow her. 'Come. We're eating.'

When he didn't move immediately, she snapped at him, and he rushed to his feet, following quickly down the corridors. He couldn't see any guards about her this time and pouted at the realisation that she saw him as so little a threat. He could fight! Miyoshi thought back to how they'd taken Yoshiko's daggers off him, and his shoulders slumped as he padded after her. Perhaps he couldn't.

A smell made his empty stomach churn and gurgle, and the boy looked up from the wooden plank floors and watched ahead hopefully.

The galley?

The pirate queen stopped. 'In here,' she said, and she walked ahead into the room, leaving Miyoshi standing alone in the walkway, suddenly nervous to enter.

Would they really let him eat? Wasn't he a prisoner here?

'Boy!' her voice snapped again, and he hurriedly followed, letting the wooden doors swing behind him.

'Ma'am!' he said habitually, and then blushed as a room full of strangers watched him, mostly women.

The captain's crew was all women save for two, the husbands of her two daughters, he learned, who worked as chefs and caretakers. Miyoshi was amazed to see how large the room was—much bigger than the galley on *Sea Guardian*—and he could see it had been specially made large to fit most of the crew at one time. A large table took up most of the space, and many of the captain's crew and guards sat conversing with one another, watching him, and pots boiled where the two men worked and dished up the meal.

The boy glanced at the small round window at the other end of the wooden dining area. The light beyond was dim, and he reasoned it must be twilight.

'Sit down, boy,' the pirate queen said, and she plonked herself at the head of the table. 'You're a guest today. Eat. Don't want you wasting away.'

A hand grabbed at his arm and pulled him to sit on the bench beside a lady with incredibly curly hair. He looked into the face of a woman he'd seen on the deck. She was introduced as Francesca, the pirate queen's second-in-command. 'He already looks skinny enough,' the woman said, passing him a plate and piling what Miyoshi recognised as potatoes on top. The boy watched it steaming.

His stomach gave a growl so audible it was heard even over the chatter, and the woman beside him let out a laugh. He flushed and looked around for a way to eat it.

No chopsticks. He looked for anything else to use, but the options stumped him. Metal sticks with spiky tops were clumped in a pile in the middle of the table. He saw the others using them, wielding them in one hand and stabbing at their food with them. He reached cautiously for one and sat back down, staring at it before looking about again to check how people were holding it to make it work.

'What's up, boy?'

He looked up to see the curly-haired woman beside him looking down at him oddly. Miyoshi had missed what she meant, but she pointed again. 'Not gunna eat?'

Their accent was heavy, and his Traders' was little, and the boy panicked, feeling his body overheat and the back of his throat burn as tears of overwhelm threatened. He looked back at his meal and stared at it before she noticed. The woman must've noticed, though, because a hand rested on his shoulder and she didn't look away.

The noise of the room became a din that overwhelmed his hearing, the loud chatter and strange accents ringing in his ears as the metal tableware clattered on the pottery. The edges of Miyoshi's eyesight went black, and he blinked it back, staring still at the bowl. His stomach churned again, and he desperately wanted to eat. With a sudden cry, he crashed the metal to the table and reached in with his hand, grabbing the first food item he saw and smushing it into his mouth, regardless of not knowing what it was.

It tasted good, and the tears escaped with a muffled, stuffed-mouth bawl.

The room went quiet, but the boy sniffled on, gulping down the food before reaching in with another hand. He felt all the women watching him, the pirate's queen's stare the strongest, but he didn't care. The boy wiped his nose with the back of his other hand and carried on.

A heavy hand rested on his shoulder, and Miyoshi turned to see who it was standing behind him. The back of his throat still hurt as he sniffled, making it hard to swallow the food. He gulped it down and stared into eyes so light they looked like gold. It was one of the two husbands, the one he'd seen earlier pouring red liquid into the pirate queen's cup.

'Do you not like the food?' His voice was thick with accent too, but he said it slowly, gently, and he had a warm smile. Miyoshi stared at this gentle face and felt the tears well more. He thought the man looked about the same age as his own captain, and wondered if they were from a similar country, though this man had thick, dark, wavy hair and golden eyes.

The boy shook his head and tried to speak. It came out like a squeak amongst bubbling tears. The room was still silent. 'No, it's good.'

The man smiled. 'Good. So, what's wrong?' He gestured his head to the plate, showing he meant the meal. The fact the boy had been stolen, he couldn't help with much.

Some of the women had returned to their meal, conversation light in the background, but some still watched. Miyoshi looked at them warily for a moment and then turned back to the table and picked up the metal stick. 'I don't know this.'

'Ahh.' And under the watchful eye of the pirate queen, the man held out the metal item, showing Miyoshi how to hold and use it. 'We call it *"forchetta"*. Did you know?'

The boy shook his head as the man showed him how to stab or scoop his meal and then reached for another metal stick. It looked different to the other one. The man showed the boy how to hold each in different hands, and how to wield them differently.

'A baby sword?' the boy asked as the man sawed at a piece of meat to cut it, pinning it down with the forchetta.

He earned a chuckle from the others around him, and calmer now, he looked up at the rest of the room, people eating but still watching him, this time eyes softer. The other man leaned casually against the cooking cupboards, supping from his own cup. This one was heavier set than the golden-eyed one but seemed just as gentle. Miyoshi felt himself relax. Even the women sitting at the table didn't seem too bad, though he'd seen them attack his friends and knew them to be dangerous.

'*Il coltello,*' the man said, and Miyoshi presumed he was telling him the name for the small food sword.

It was as Miyoshi was trying to saw at his food that the door swung open again, and a slim pirate woman with sandy hair and light straw-coloured eyes guided a young girl about Miyoshi's own age in by the shoulder. The girl didn't look scared, far from it, and she lit up and bounded into the room, her own sandy hair curling lightly and bouncing about her shoulders as she ran.

'Nonna!' she cried, rushing to the pirate queen and launching herself around the woman's shoulders.

Miyoshi watched, mouth wide, whatever he'd speared with his forchetta dropping back onto the plate with a subtle thud. The pirate queen's face lit up and she grinned jovially, crying out what Miyoshi guessed was the girl's name. Felicity. The conversation in the room returned happily, and plates clattered as the golden-eyed man put another two plates out in front of the new people, giving them hugs and looking at them fondly. Miyoshi thought they looked like family, with how they looked at each other so warmly and chatted so comfortably. Unable to tear his eyes away from this scene, his heart panged for his mother, and he wondered whether he should have stayed back home with her after all.

'My daughter, and granddaughter,' the pirate queen said as she noticed Miyoshi still staring.

He quickly looked down at his plate, trying to avoid being noticed again, but looked up again curiously. 'Not like me?'

The eating paused again, and people refused to meet his gaze this time. Even the pirate queen seemed uncertain, the smile on her face freezing for a moment. 'No, not like you.'

His heart sank.

'There are others, though,' she continued, sawing away at her own meat like a professional and deftly popping it in her mouth. 'Though finally this will be the last.' The pirate queen stared, her light brown eyes—matching her daughter's and granddaughter's—staring into an unseen distance.

'Why?' the boy dared to ask. He felt his heart pounding as if they'd rise up and strike him down all at once with their tiny food swords. He'd already forgotten the word for that.

Miyoshi never expected the woman to really tell him, but she watched him as she chewed, and the others all looked between them. Eventually, she must have decided telling him would lose nothing at this point.

'Because something bad will happen if we don't.' She saw he didn't understand and continued. 'We made a promise, but it comes at a bad price. That's why.'

The meal resumed, and the happy environment and chatter picked up again, and the boy slowly chewed at his food, thinking about what the queen had said. Something bad happening? What could be so bad that you sacrifice however many children as an alternative?

After the pirate queen finished her meal, she took Miyoshi by the arm and guided him to the deck, striding with clicking heels on the wood to the storerooms.

'You're our third guest here, the last.'

'Who are the others?'

'Look.' She took him to a room where two children were stored in the dark, scared. 'One, two,' she counted them, pointing at each of them and then back at Miyoshi, 'three. The perfect number.'

'What will you do with us?'

'Finish this.' She rested her hands on his shoulders and smiled, her voice becoming soft as if trying to win a young child over. If anything, the softer tone only frightened Miyoshi more, and he clenched his teeth together as he made himself meet her honey gaze. 'Saving you for last because you're special. You've been around recent magic; it's lingering on you. Do you know someone special, who has powers unlike others?'

Miyoshi immediately thought of Lady Yoshiko and how she'd transformed into a dragon spirit. Then he looked at the pirate queen and tried to shut Yoshiko out of his mind. The queen's eyes were boring into his, and he felt once more she could read his mind. She smiled more, and he realised she'd somehow seen what he'd thought. Even if not in detail, she knew he knew someone like she said.

'Wonderful, I knew it. You shall be the special one.' She spoke in almost a whisper at this point, turning behind her to the pirate woman with curly hair—Miyoshi thought her name was something like 'Furan—', but he couldn't remember the rest. 'That one,' Mammie said, pointing to a young girl in the storeroom. 'Take her now. Let's show our young friend the legacy he's a part of.'

The pirate woman stomped into the room, reaching down and pulling the young girl roughly from the floor. The child reached out for the young boy she'd been stored with, and they both held on to one another, crying out. The woman pulled at the girl harder, and she yelled in pain, the two children letting go and the young boy backing away to cower alone in the corner, crying. Miyoshi's heart dropped. That boy was only a few years younger than him— likely barely eight turns of the year—and had been stolen from his home just like Gora had been.

So this is how the captain was trapped until they'd made him a slave. Waiting like them, like me.

Miyoshi's blood boiled, but he had no time to do or say anything before the curly-haired pirate carried her crying prey from the room and slammed the door on the lonely boy, turning to follow Mammie down the corridor.

'Come!' the pirate queen commanded Miyoshi, not even turning to see if he'd follow.

Miyoshi did. He knew what would happen if he didn't.

Mammie led them up towards the deck and strolled towards the gunwale. There, she looked down into the ocean and smiled. She took a deep breath, resting her hands on her hips, and nodded to herself before turning to observe the pirate and the crying girl. Miyoshi looked around. More of Mammie's crew were watching now, and he realised they truly were all women, except the two men below in the kitchen. The surrounding women paused their chores and routines and duties to watch their queen on a momentous occasion they knew had been coming.

'My pirate ships, such as Foy's, you know, have been doing this for me for years. But now, the final three are mine to finish the job. The pact shall soon be paid.' Then she turned to the pirate and commanded, 'Do it!'

Furan, or whatever her name was, stepped towards the edge of the railing, and Mammie grabbed at Miyoshi's sleeve, pulling him to the gunwale, too. His heart leapt into his mouth, and he worried she'd be pushing him over. Instead, she held firm her grasp on his sleeve—so tight he could feel it pinching into the skin of his upper arm—and he clenched his teeth to stop from crying out. He'd not give her that satisfaction.

The girl wriggled and cried in the pirate's grasp, and she locked her green eyes on Miyoshi's—he'd never seen eyes that colour before. She paused crying for a moment, opening her mouth as if to say something to him, but before she could, the curly-haired pirate woman gave a short cry of effort as she simply tossed the little girl into the open sea, and the girl screamed.

Mammie moved her hand up to Miyoshi's head and forced him to look down, grabbing at his hair. Not that she'd needed to. He'd been watching the terrified girl as it was. As if he couldn't.

They're just going to let her drown? He panicked, trying to move his head and look at the women around him, trying to be sure, to ask someone if they were really just going to leave her there. Mammie held fast his head. Instead, he was forced to just stare as the girl flailed in the waves. She was so small as he watched from up here.

'Another soul for the sea witch,' Mammie said, as if reciting a spell, and the pirates all about the ship mumbled it with her.

The girl went under for a moment as a great wave crashed over her before slamming into the hull. Miyoshi wondered if she'd been pushed into the vessel too, body crushed with the force. Instead, Miyoshi stared open-mouthed as the girl broke water once more, looking up at the people on the ship and reaching up to them with her tiny arm, green eyes begging. Then Miyoshi's breath escaped him as watery arms reached up from the ocean and gathered all around the girl. The girl must have felt something touch her from behind and turned her head, seeing the arms. She shrieked and tried to swim and jump out of the way, not knowing whether to look up and beg for those on the ship to help her or look behind at those grabbing her. The arms followed her, as did Miyoshi's terrified eyes. He couldn't breathe. He felt like he was down there with her, feeling her fear, losing her breath, feeling the hands.

The hands grabbed at her hair and clawed at her face and her arms, pulling on her, dragging her down. The last thing Miyoshi saw of the girl were her terrified green eyes and the tears streaming down her face before the water washed over her, the watery hands pulling her down.

'Captain,' Miyoshi whispered, staring at the place the girl had been swallowed. A single tear fell down his cheek, and his legs buckled beneath him. 'Help.'

40

The New Sea Witch

'We can go no further. We'll have to leave the ship here,' Nishimura said airily as he weaved the ship through the last of the open ice fields and then met a great land of ice ahead. 'This is as close as we'll get.'

Gora nodded and strode from the helm to the bow, where Yoshiko was crouching up on the gunwale by the bowsprit. Gora's heart leapt a moment in fear of her falling, but Chisaka was beside her as usual, and Gora knew Yoshiko to be well balanced. All the same, the ship lurched as it drifted closer to the ice shelf, and Gora rushed towards his friend and grabbed and held her arm.

She looked around at him, face serious. 'Are we here?'

He nodded again, silent, looking around at the ice.

'Can you not melt it so we can get closer to that bit over there? It looks like firmer land.' Moori came up to their other side and leaned on the gunwale.

'I cannot, and I would not. There is life that relies on this ice, and there is no guarantee what melting this ice would do. If it were to start a chain reaction and melt all the ice, that would be a problem.' Yoshiko looked back down at the frozen sea. 'There is a reason there is ice here.'

'Yeah, the reason is it's bloody cold,' Gora mumbled, tugging at his friend's arm in the hopes she'd get the hint to come down.

She didn't, but she did turn and raise her eyebrow at his remark, which he was certain only she'd heard. He shrugged at her.

Moori sighed and mused aloud as to what they were to do next, brushing her short hair behind her ear and shivering.

'We have no choice but to leave the ship here and go by sled.' Gora turned and looked about the ship for his crew, readying the instructions in his head. The sleds were below. He'd have to get them brought up with supplies. Just as he was opening his mouth to call out, Nishimura padded up to them and spoke, face as peaceful as ever, but brow pinched slightly. Despite the icy winds, he pulled down his hood and looked around calmly.

'My concern is if the water around us freezes, how do we get the ship away?'

Gora faltered. 'You think it will happen?' Nishimura knew strange things like this. *If he thinks so …*

Nishimura untied his long hair from its knot, and it tumbled down his back as he shook it out. 'So close to the ice shelf, it would not surprise me. We don't know places like this. It could. Or it might not.' His deep eyes turned from scanning the view to look deep into Gora's eyes. 'The question is, is it worth the risk?'

'It's absolutely not,' Gora said certainly, and he rubbed his chin in thought with his loose hand. He tugged again at Yoshiko's arm to bring her down, and this time she listened and stepped onto the deck beside him. His heart relaxed a little knowing at least she wouldn't fall into freezing water should something knock the ship too hard. With the creatures they'd seen recently, who knew what lurked below? 'Okay. Nishimura, when we drop part of the crew below with resources, can you guide the ship back further out and anchor where you feel it would be safe? We'll signal you when we're ready to come back to the ship. Keep a watch on the ice shelf for when we're ready. Keep another watch out for strange creatures or danger.'

He looked at the young navigator. 'Does that sound safer to you, now?'

The young man cocked his head to the side and seemed almost in a daydream for a moment, but his eyes met Gora's again, and a slight smile crossed his face. 'We will be safe like that, no doubt.'

'Well, I'm not sure about no doubt,' Gora muttered as the young man turned to walk back to the helm where Shingo held it steady, the two gesturing to one another as they talked beyond Gora's hearing, and Yoshiko dug her elbow into Gora's side.

'Don't say such things,' she chastised quietly. 'You don't want to doom his word.'

'No tempting fate, eh?'

'Exactly.' Yoshiko turned to look over the gunwale again at the ice shelf ahead. 'So, what do we need to do to be safe down there? It looks desolate; it's too cold, dangerous. Who would live here?'

'Those who are tougher than anyone anywhere else,' Gora said, and he turned to Chisaka. 'You'll come with us, no doubt, if she goes?'

The guard straightened up, and her dark eyes were serious as ever as she bowed ever so slightly. *Always the formalities.* 'Of course. That is to be expected.' Then the woman's eyes flicked to Yoshiko sharply. 'There'd be chaos if I didn't.'

For leaving her, or because of her? Gora smirked to himself, earning a sharp glare back from the guard in return, and he hastily continued his plans.

He'd need a small group to go onto the ice, and plenty to look after the ship. They wouldn't be able to sustain a large group out there. 'Moori, will you stay here and help defend the ship?'

She eagerly agreed. 'It's cold enough here! And at least there are blankets to keep warm. I have no desire to step out there where it's even colder.' She looked to Yoshiko for a moment, and Gora could tell where her thoughts went next. She wanted to be around the one she'd looked up to since childhood and to be noticed by her, but she didn't want to step further into the cold. Gora wished he could reassure her that this wouldn't provoke any difference in how Yoshiko would think of her, but such things couldn't come from him. It had to come from Yoshiko herself, who was currently looking out over the ice and likely had no idea where Moori's thoughts lay.

Gora nodded. 'Good. You'll stay.'

Only a core group of six will go, he thought, stomping down below the deck with Tomioka and Shingo behind him, the trio heading for the storage hold to review the equipment they had for going onto the ice shelf. 'It's more ice than I thought, but we should be good with what we brought. Can you both stay with the ship and look after the crew? If anything goes wrong, I need both of you to guide the remaining crew safely back home.'

Gora turned to look at their faces in the dim lamp light, and both looked brooding.

'We hope that won't be the case,' Tomioka said when he and Shingo had met one another's gaze.

Shingo nodded. 'In fact,' he added, 'you'd better ensure it's not.'

'I'll certainly do my best, now,' Gora said as he turned back to continue looking about the hold, seeing what they needed. He nodded. There was enough for six, but no more.

'Tomioka, can you guide the crew in preparing these to go to land? I want them up on the deck with resources for several days, just in case, and plenty of things to keep us warm. Shingo, help guide the rest of the crew in keeping the ship steady. We don't want to suddenly lurch into the ice. Now, you both know what to do if we don't return, remember?'

Both nodded, professional as always, but sullen all the same. Gora shrugged to himself. That's all he could guarantee now. To at least ensure those who survived could return. He had no idea what stepping out onto the ice would hold.

'There's something ahead,' Yoshiko said as he returned to the bowsprit to ask her about joining them. 'There: smoke rises ahead.'

Gora had to squint and follow her finger, and even then, he couldn't see what she was seeing. 'You got your dragon eyes on?'

'Probably.' She sighed and turned to him.

'Aye, they never used to look like that unless you were transformed.' Then he nodded back into the distance. 'So, you think we should start there?'

Yoshiko nodded. 'It is a sign there is life there. People at a camp of some sort. It is the only sign of life I have seen thus far.'

Gora ran a hand through the back of his auburn hair. Then he too nodded.

Sleds were lowered on ropes down to the ice platform, and Yoshiko followed, climbing down a rope ladder and gingerly testing the ice. For the duration of her testing whether the ice was safe to walk on, Gora's stomach had tied itself in knots. If he lost her now, he'd never forgive himself. But he knew she was the best one to go down there: she was light but also had a higher chance of surviving should the ice break and she fall under. Her familial curse helped there, and no-one else had a body that could handle it.

As it happened, he could relax. She tested the ice carefully and surely and told them where it was safe. He, Chisaka, and Ikeda soon followed, with Yonemura and Jelani close behind. Everyone else would stay on the ship. Gora huddled in the thick furs they'd donned for the journey and shrugged as he looked up from the ice at the great hull of the ship. The icy water gently lapped over the ice shelf as Shingo yelled out for Nishimura and the crew to guide it back away from the ice.

'Well, we'd better get goin' too,' Gora said, stomping past. 'We gotta get to that smoke before it dies off and we lose it.'

'How will we find our way back here?' Jelani asked, in Hizen to fit with the others, sniffing as he looked back at the ship. 'It's not exactly a place with good landmarks.'

Gora pouted as he thought. 'Yoshiko, can you sniff the ship out?'

'What is she, a hound?' Yonemura chastised from slightly behind as she stomped about in snow boots that were too large for her and pulled her fur hood closer to her face. Gora turned and threw his arms out in an innocent shrug, and she clicked her tongue in response.

'I might be able to. The smells are strange but clear here. If the ship doesn't get too far away, it's possible. We'll have more luck just seeing it though, I think,' Yoshiko said, sniffing the air lightly as a tester.

'See,' Gora said, turning to Yonemura once again with a look of triumph on his face. 'It's fine.'

But Yonemura's face—or what of it he could see past the furs—was not convinced.

The walk over the ice and snowy rock was exhausting, and as expected in unknown flatlands like this, the smoke was much further away than they'd anticipated. Worse still was the lengthening days this far north, making it near impossible to tell how long they'd been walking for, so it felt like many hours or even half a day had passed. Their stomachs rumbled, but when they stopped to eat, their bodies froze and their skin ached, so they kept going, trying to cover up to stop any harm coming to their bodies. They ate as they moved, and Gora longed to have the curse like Yoshiko, where her body kept itself warm from an internal furnace. She, he wondered, didn't seem to be suffering too badly. Instead, she kept the crew going, and when they suffered most, she would look into the distance, spot the smoke, and tell them the best bearing. They'd be there soon.

That's what you say every time, Gora found himself thinking the fourth time she said it, and even the good-natured Jelani groaned in exhaustion and despair.

'I am too tired for another break,' he said. 'I will never start again. I will not stop.' He gestured wildly with his arms and sniffed, turning his nose up as he looked at Gora and nodded. 'Let's keep going. If the Lady Yoshiko says we are close, we should not stop.'

Yonemura looked exhausted, but she too agreed. 'It's true that I feel I'll not stand again if I rest now.'

Gora sighed, and he looked to where the smoke curled up into the light sky in the distance, considering how much ice was left. 'Aye, alright now. Let's keep going.'

Yoshiko nodded and kept them going, Ikeda stomping quietly at her side, not saying anything for how cold it was, even to complain about the distance. From all appearances, Gora would even believe the young man seemed content.

The group continued in silence, trying not to expend too much energy and pushing that last stretch. The wide, open plains of ice made it look deceivingly close, and yet it felt so far to walk. And only when they saw the base of the smoke pillar rising from within a huddle of small buildings did the group cry out with glee and bring themselves to a desperate trot.

'Those buildings are strange,' Yonemura said as the village came into view, panting at the strain of the jog in the icy air. 'Am I right they are made of ice? Am I seeing right?'

Gora squinted and nodded. 'Seems so.'

He looked to Yoshiko for confirmation, but she merely nodded and kept quiet, looking ahead again.

'Not far now,' she muttered, shivering a little, huddling the thick jackets closer.

The ice buildings became clearer, and the group looked in amazement at the low, round buildings carved out of ice blocks.

Smoke rose from individual buildings from a small hole in the centre of the dome of ice, and a few people plodded between the buildings, looking to the group with round faces furrowed with suspicion.

Gora hailed them with a cry and a wave.

The people looked concerned to see a group of unknown others walking their way, some even rushing inside, beckoning playing children into the icy huts.

Nonetheless, Gora acted unfazed, greeting the native ice people as they got closer, wondering now he was here if they'd even be able to speak a mutual language. He went for Traders'. If people had been here before to speak with the witch, they must know Traders', surely?

Gora frowned and tried to find something simple to say beyond hello.

'We are looking for the sea witch,' he said, jumping straight to business after receiving a distrustful glare from one of the two people they spoke to. He looked about at his group. 'We need her help. We came a long way.' He opened out his hands to reveal they were empty of weapons, showing that was free of ill intent. The others followed his lead, keeping back a little way.

The two villagers looked at one another silently, a conversation seemingly happening from just their gazes meeting. Gora's heart thudded and a shiver pricked at his back. *What do we do if they don't understand me? Can the witch even understand me?*

He waited, feeling time drag on, until one spoke in a deep, reverberating voice. 'Witch?'

Gora felt an easy smile creep across his face. He nodded. 'Witch,' he confirmed.

The two looked at each other again, and it was hard to see their expressions with their hoods covering their profile.

Then they looked back at Gora, black eyes seeming lighter in emotion than before, and one even softly smiled. They turned, pointed down between the buildings, then disappeared inside their ice domes, leaving the village quiet and the foreigners alone.

Gora heard a breath from behind that could have been a sigh. Yonemura caught his gaze. 'Did that help? Do we keep going?'

She seemed tired, and Gora understood her worry about keeping going. His legs wobbled so much that he, too, wished to rest.

'Seems they are wary of unknown people,' Ikeda said gently. 'We should leave so they can come out and resume their life.'

'They are hiding in their huts?' Yonemura asked.

Ikeda and Yoshiko nodded. 'I can hear them inside,' she said. 'They seem worried.'

'Well, they don't know what kind of people we are yet, so I don't blame them. Let's keep going.' Gora shrugged, understanding the reluctance the others might have to keep going. His feet ached, and the cold bit at him. He wondered whether it was warm inside the ice buildings.

'Come, my lady,' Chisaka said, her voice strained with fatigue as much as the others, but still she strode forward, taking Yoshiko's arm and bringing the group firmly into a walk again, and they continued the way the ice people had pointed.

Eventually, they came to a place the ice slipped down again into the sea—an estuary of sorts fairly near the village where clean water turned in to form a small lake or river. Rocks dotted about the edge, and Gora imagined children playing here, if they could, huddled in their furs and jumping from one rock to the other while adults gathered water or hunted for food. As he looked about, imagining this scene, wondering if it was their coming here that stopped people from gathering for their worry of the strangers, his heart leapt to see someone in the water.

'There's someone in the water. Hurry!' Jelani cried out, rushing forward. 'They must be half-dead in there.'

If not dead already, Gora couldn't help but add.

The group pushed their tired legs once again into a trot towards the edge where the rocks and ice met the cold water. Sure enough, bare shoulders poked out from the clear water, but the head was like nothing they'd seen.

A mottled, red-peach, leathery head blended in with honey-brown shoulders, like a creature of the deep seas, with tendrils reaching out and curling down a human-like torso. An elongated skull stretched high above the shoulders, and something undulated, like a heartbeat in the head.

'What—' Chisaka cried out in alarm, taking a step back and holding her arm out in front of Yoshiko to protect her.

The witch? Is this what a sea witch looks like? A creature of both earth and sea? Gora felt unable to speak, and his thoughts flicked back through everything he'd heard about this woman. No-one had told him before that she was a combination of creatures. Yet here she was, a human body with the head of a sea creature. Not too unlike those ice sirens or even the merpeople they'd seen months ago.

The body in the water turned upon hearing Chisaka cry out, and the head turned their way a little, large, watery eyes meeting their gazes. Another pair of eyes rested below that, and a human face peered up at them from beneath the larger eyes of the creature.

The group behind him gasped, but Gora paused for merely a moment and then let out a roar of laughter. He laughed so hard he felt his belly ache, and he held his hand to his stomach.

'There's an octopus sitting on her head!' he gasped, explaining it to the others.

As if in answer, the woman cocked her head, and the octopus shifted. The legs curled upwards, and dark hair appeared beneath. The woman looked up at the octopus and raised her arms to shift it, moving one of the legs that curled and tendrilled by her face so she could see the newcomers better.

She peered up at them beneath the raised leg, curiosity in the dark eyes.

This time, Gora looked properly at the young woman's face. She was about his age, if not a little older, he guessed. Ice dappled like snow about her smooth face, and her eyelids were so blue, likely from the cold, that they almost looked like she'd dusted on some kind of blue snow makeup like the women from the entertainment districts back in Hizen. Her lips were a deep pink, contrasting the pale sepia tone of her skin in the cold.

'Are you the sea witch?' Gora asked, coming out directly in Traders'.

The woman smirked. She moved forward in the water and brought herself to the edge, pulling up alongside a pile of clothes. She pulled at the octopus on her head, though it seemed to complain about budging, a grumpy look coming along its face and skin rippling with a slight difference colour.

Can octopuses even look grumpy? Gora wondered as that thought ran through his mind.

Eventually, the octopus allowed itself to be brought free, and it slid back into the water. The woman raised herself up onto the rock and ice bank, and Gora looked awkwardly away while she patted herself dry and dressed quickly in the thick furs left by the water's edge.

'Do you think anyone else could survive being in the water here?' A rich, warm voice said from behind them in excellent Traders', with a thick accent. 'The Inue are tough, but even they can't go in the water without dying.'

When they turned back, she was dressed, shrugging on a thick coat with a furry hood. She just looked like any other ice person. Nothing about her told them she was a witch at all.

The group looked at her, stunned, and Gora was sure his expression must have matched.

'How could you go in the water and not freeze?'

'Would water really kill a sea witch?'

Gora had no answer. He really didn't know.

'My name is Aqutak, and yes, I am the one you are seeking. So, you are here for my help, are you not? That, or it's to kill me?'

Aqutak looked their way as she walked past them, seemingly unfazed at the guests, gesturing with her head that they should follow her. She walked ahead as she talked, and Gora caught up quickly.

'For help, not to kill you. Someone we love is about to die because of an agreement made with the previous sea witch.'

She paused and turned her face to look at his. Her dark eyes narrowed, and her mouth fell into a frown.

'There is only one ongoing wish from the days of the old sea witch.' She paused, frown settling deeper. 'Your friend is a child?'

The group nodded, and before anyone could open their mouth to add anything else, Aqutak nodded, too. 'I know which pact you mean. Come with me. Let's talk somewhere you can warm up.'

Aqutak trundled through the snow and over the icy rocks towards the village. Once again, smoke rose from the little ice domes, and the witch led them to one on the edge of the group. This time, a few more people poked their faces out, and when Aqutak smiled to them and called out in their local language, their faces fell relieved, and they came out more confidently.

'Telling them we're safe, perhaps?' Gora overheard Yonemura mutter to Jelani, who seemed to nod in agreement.

Suddenly, a burst of activity erupted from one of the huts as two children ran out into the opening, calling out gleefully at being able to run about in the open again. Yonemura laughed and watched the children run about giggling, and an adult somewhere called out for them, chastising them lightly.

Aqutak ducked through the small ice entrance and down some steps into a dome, and the group followed. To their amusement, so did one of the children, running up to Aqutak with their arms out wide, and Aqutak's smile grew large. She called out to the person outside, and the child stayed in the hut.

To Gora's surprise, the ice dug lower into the ground, and the room inside was much bigger than he'd anticipated. A platform of ice ran around the circumference of the room as a seating place, with fur rugs and blankets laying about, and the sea witch gestured for them to sit and get warm. She fiddled with a small seal-oil lamp in the centre of the room, melting ice and boiling it for tea. The child followed Aqutak's every move, asking questions, trying to help, passing the sea witch cups between thick, padded gloves.

'How does the fire not melt the building?' Yoshiko hissed over at Gora. 'I want to know. Can you ask her?'

Gora looked at her face and saw the characteristic expression of the young woman wanting to ask many questions. He knew that face too well, and he smirked, allowing a small laugh as he remembered their time in the caves and the woods of Hié as she had drilled him, too, on his culture and old life. For now, it seemed she'd limited herself to one question. She really was holding back.

'Alright.'

He in turn asked Aqutak in Traders', and as the witch made the tea and passed it around, she explained how the walls of the dome were made from packed snow, which was good at keeping the warmer temperatures in and the cold out, and the wall was constantly kept cold from the outside.

'As you can see, it's not "warm" in here by perhaps your standards. You would still need to wear your furs, but out of the wind and the really cold temperatures, you can agree it is better in here.'

Yoshiko nodded as Gora relayed the message, face open and interested, eyes glinting. The sea witch looked at Yoshiko's awe and smiled too.

Good start, Gora thought, pleased that his friend's eagerness to learn about other cultures seemed to have helped them find an opening. People always loved speaking about their own culture, and loved when people showed an interest. Likely, Aqutak just had people coming here asking her to solve their problems. He would happily bet his whole ship that very few asked about her own way of life. Perhaps he'd suggest to Yoshiko she ask more questions later. For now, it seemed the sea witch happily went straight to business once the tea was passed around. Aqutak and the child settled cuddled together on the platform, the child happily sipping and blowing on the hot tea, large, dark eyes watching the group eagerly. Here, Aqutak looked comfortable, and she patted the child's hooded head lightly as she talked and listened.

The group listened to her speaking in her rich, low voice, happily sipping on the strange, slightly salted hot tea, feeling the hot water refresh them. She paused now and then as they translated for one another, mostly for Yoshiko and Chisaka who had no knowledge of Traders', though some of the others were still learning and needed help keeping up.

'Is there any way to stop it?' Gora asked, finally, when all the pieces of the puzzle between her story and his matched.

'I'm sorry, I can't undo any spell or agreement made by my predecessors,' Aqutak said. She raised the small child a little, who was sitting between her crossed legs, looking content, and smiled at it. Gora was amazed at how this woman seemed far from the way he'd imagined her, resting peacefully with children. Wasn't she getting them killed and collecting their souls?

'But there must be some way you can make this stop!' Gora felt close to begging.

The sea witch's face loosened with sympathy. 'I won't deny that the harvesting of children's souls causes me great displeasure. I feel it each time a child dies and is sent to me by the sea. But I can't undo this spell. What's done is done and can't be undone. That is the law of magic. It is wild and has its own desires. We can't shape that.'

Her gloved hand ruffled the child's black hair fondly, and she smiled sadly down at the child. 'The request was to help bring magic back, make it stronger. Of course the wild magics would want that. It has been tumbling more and more out of control and growing stronger with each death of each child, and it is thriving. It is almost irreversible now. No matter what I think of their deaths. No matter how it hurts me to do it.'

'You feel it?' Yonemura whispered.

The young sea witch nodded, leaning down to kiss the child's head. The two women caught each other's eyes. Gora knew what was running through Yonemura's head. Yonemura then leaned over to Yoshiko and translated. Yoshiko gasped, eyes wide. The daimyō leaned back and whispered to Yonemura, who shook her head sadly.

'But,' Aqutak continued, 'once a previous agreement is up, you can then make a separate request to have it how you want it.'

Those in front of her looked confused. The child, on the other hand, had fallen asleep in Aqutak's lap.

'The woman, Mammie, asked for magic to be brought back. My predecessor gave her the terms to make it so. Once magic is back, you can request that it is withdrawn once more from the world.'

'But what good does that make? Then the children will still have died.' Gora's voice raised and the child stirred. Yonemura rested a hand on his shoulder to calm him.

The witch closed her eyes. 'Forgive my bluntness. But they are already dead. Only a few children remain to fulfil that end of the agreement. Then the number of souls needed will have been met.'

'But we can make it so that *they* don't have to die. Yūki won't need to die!'

'You know one of the children?' The sea witch's dark eyes bore into Gora's light ones. He felt like he was sinking to the depths. 'I see.'

She stroked the dark hair of the child in her lap to send it to sleep once more. 'I don't mean to disrespect those who passed. It hurt each time one was sent to me. My powers came when I was young. I've lived with the deaths of these other children since I was only a child myself. I know the weight of this. And I do not wish for the children to die. But I don't know how else to explain how the ways of magic work. I cannot control this. I am simply a guide, or messenger, of the wild magics.'

Gora thought for a moment, then translated for Yoshiko. Beside her, Ikeda stiffened at the news. His young face darkened with a rage that mirrored Yoshiko's. The sea witch saw them and nodded gravely.

'So, what can we do to stop it?' Yoshiko asked Gora, nodding for him to ask Aqutak.

The young sea witch thought. She stared at the walls of the hut and then into the small lamp. 'Soon will be the time my predecessor told the pirate queen to be ready for the ceremony. Only putting a stop to it can save the last victims.'

'How do we stop it?'

Aqutak shrugged. 'There are many ways.'

'Kill you?' Yonemura sounded horrified at her own words, but it was the question in everyone's minds. The four of them watched Aqutak carefully, readying themselves for the notorious burst of unpredictable power Gora had told them was known of the sea witches.

The power of the oceans never came. Instead, Aqutak laughed.

'The last sea witch was killed, and yet the agreement continued over to me. If I die, it will just go to the next witch. The agreements made between this heritage power cannot be stopped by something so simple as one holder of the power dying. As I said, I just relay the wishes of the wild magics. I do not control it myself.'

Somehow, that answer made them feel better. Neither of them seemed to want to kill this woman. She wasn't the one killing the children and causing mayhem on the seas. She, like Gora, had got wrapped up in it from childhood, through no will of her own.

'But, if you were to happen to follow me to the meeting place and stop the pirate queen from achieving her end of the deal, that's another matter.' Aqutak smiled slyly.

41

The Cold North

They returned to the ship the next morning, with no desire or need to stay in the cold. Well, Yoshiko could only guess it was morning. That high up in the world, apparently, was known for having different day and night cycles. It could stay light for months on end then have long periods of dark. And, with the current constant light, Yoshiko had no real way of knowing whether it was day or not. Eventually, the group who had come to land grew weary, and Aqutak gave them a place to rest. When they awoke, they joined her and a group of her Inue for a meal around the central village fire, huddled in warm furs, and wondered at the meal of purely meat. After Yoshiko quizzing Gora on the meat, and the red-haired man giving in and translating her questions, they made their way back to the ship after an unusual but welcome meal.

Yoshiko felt she could have eaten several times the amount, but her body told her the inner beast was rebelling against the cold and burning up whatever she was using much faster. For her human side, it would do.

As they finally got close to the place the ship floated in the distance, Gora gave Yoshiko a gentle nudge on the upper arm with his elbow.

'Signal them, will you? They'll sail before we reach the edge, and we'll not have to wait long.'

Chisaka looked over at Gora disapprovingly, but Yoshiko nodded.

'It's not like we have any other way of identifying ourselves to them, anyway,' she told her careful guard. 'We discussed this before we left. It's something I can do, at least.'

Yoshiko took a breath, focusing on sending a course of burning flame down through her veins in her right arm and towards her fingertips, just like when she'd burnt a hole through that blond pirate Kipp on the ship when they stole the children. Since then, she'd practised using this power, more able to use it on demand. She was now almost certain her mother had been able to do this, leaving the scorch marks at the site of her death nearly two years ago.

The heat burst towards her hand, and Yoshiko raised her arm into the air and fired the signalling beams of flame into the sky, where they shot straight up in two beams, coming from her two leading fingers—index and middle. She held the beam for a count of five before letting it stop, feeling it hotter against her fingertips the longer she fired.

Oh, a welcome heat.

The group stopped walking to wait and listen for a response before continuing, lightly joking about having Yoshiko do it again just so they could gather around and keep warm.

Yoshiko held her breath, feeling her heart rate rise. Would they answer?

'Come on, Moori,' she breathed, knowing Moori would be one of the ones to answer if she saw Yoshiko's flame.

Sure enough, two gunshots in quick succession answered, the sound echoing over the ice planes, and the *Sea Guardian* flag raised in the distance, one that only Yoshiko's cursed eyes could see.

Ryoukai—understood.

Yoshiko grinned, and Gora and Ikeda commented cheerfully to one another beside her, Gora clapping Ikeda on the shoulder as they rejoiced. The group padded on, back towards the edge, Aqutak padding quietly beside them, watching the group and the ship with interest.

At the water's edge, the hull of the ship towered over them, daunting and huge. Yoshiko furrowed her brow as Aqutak bent down at the edge of the ice and dipped her bare hand into the water, and a creature climbed up her arm, tendrils and tentacles wrapping around the young sea witch.

The octopus. But why does it cling to her?

Yoshiko wished she could ask, but feeling mute with lack of understanding of the language, she sighed and grabbed onto the rope ladder that was lowered to let them up, climbing up the ship.

As expected, the young sea witch caused a stir. The crew curiously eyed up the Inue woman and her octopus friend, wondering aloud about the octopus.

'Why don't you ask?' Taro whispered to Kyo.

'I am anxious to ask. What if it offends her?'

Taro nodded as if that was logical. No-one had met a sea witch or an Inue before. How could they know what was culturally acceptable?

Yoshiko sighed and looked back towards Aqutak. *I'm sure it will be fine to ask.* She looked around for Gora, wondering if he would ask for her. *But he's busy. Maybe later.*

'I'll ask for you,' a low voice said beside her. Yoshiko startled and turned to see Ikeda waiting patiently, hood still up, but she could see a light smile on his smooth face. She felt her cheeks burn at how close he was standing. 'You wanted to ask, right? I don't know much Traders', but I'm sure I know enough to ask that for you.'

'Can you?'

'Of course. Come.' Ikeda pulled down his hood and took her hand, leading Yoshiko across the deck towards Aqutak, who stood at the front bow, looking over the sea, octopus resting on her shoulder. For a moment, Yoshiko was too distracted staring at his hand and wondering at how warm it was in this cold. It was when the octopus turned to watch them as they got close that she shook herself back to attention, watching the young woman turning peacefully when the sea creature's tentacle lightly tapped her on the other shoulder to get her attention.

Ikeda spoke to Aqutak, Traders' slow but clear, Yoshiko guessed by the sea witch's nodding of understanding, and Ikeda gestured his head to the creature on her shoulder.

Aqutak looked at the octopus' large, round head and then back up at the pair, smiling. When Aqutak replied, Ikeda quickly translated to Yoshiko. 'Because the octopus is lonely.'

'Oh, how cute!' Yoshiko said, smiling too and looking closer now at the sea creature. It waved a tentacle warily, and Yoshiko was certain she saw its eyes narrow.

Beside her, Aqutak said something else to Ikeda, and he paused before replying carefully. Yoshiko listened carefully to their conversation, not understanding, but finding the interaction interesting. Ikeda answered slowly at times, but the sea witch seemed to understand him, and him her. Yoshiko wondered at how quickly the crew had learned enough of this new language to communicate, and she marvelled at how much Ikeda had grown since she met him in the gardens on that fateful day for her family. He stood more certain, spoke more certainly, but still blushed a little.

His hair's longer, too, she thought, watching him now. *Even his fringe now ties up into his ponytail.* Her eyes drifted over to Gora on the other side of the deck. *Even his hair is longer, and he's grown his facial hair again. Do they not cut it aboard ship?* She wondered at how Kimura and Moori looked now and how different they might look. *Daiki's still bald, though,* she thought, heart dropping at the memory of being told he'd shaved his hair in shame. *Does he keep it shaven out of shame, still, or is it now habit?* she wondered.

Ikeda rested his hand on her shoulder to get her attention, and Yoshiko returned her attention to Aqutak and Ikeda.

'She was asking about who you were, as she noticed how the group treated you, and she was curious about your powers. She has never met someone who can shoot fire from their body before.' Ikeda's dark brown eyes looked gently into hers.

Yoshiko let out a small chuckle. 'Nor have I,' she joked.

A smile crossed Ikeda's face and his eyes shone, lighting up. 'What would you like me to tell her?'

'The truth is fine. She is here to help us and is someone of magic too.'

Ikeda nodded and looked back to Aqutak, explaining, a little clumsily by the sound of it, Yoshiko's powers. Aqutak focused to understand, but she nodded, interested, and looked again at Yoshiko.

His hand's still there, she thought, unable to focus on anything else now but the warmth seeping into her shoulder.

Her cheeks and ears burned.

* * *

Yoshiko loved watching the water slip past as the ship cut through the ocean. Even when the weather was wild and she felt like she'd be tossed straight out of the ship into the abyss below, she'd stand at the bow or hold on tight to the shrouds and watch the ocean rush by below.

I wonder how deep it is and what creatures lurk where we can't see.

She thought most about the creatures that could be there— living things they had no idea about. That huge black-and-white whale they'd seen at the top of the world in the cold lands had made her wonder. She'd never seen anything so big up close—though Gora had said that her dragon form easily outsized the whale they'd seen—but now Yoshiko was eager to know what else might lurk in the hidden or far-reaching places of the world, like the *umibōzu* she and Gora had discussed, or the other stories she'd heard from the crew. Of *funayūrei*, of sea serpents, of mermaids that clung to the ship and clawed their way up to kill those aboard.

Yoshiko gripped the shrouds tight as the ship lurched on a wave, and she turned to look at the figure ahead, squinting her eyes against the spray to push her dragon curse sight on. Her eyes fell on the sea witch.

The sea witch had only stayed on the ship for a few hours. After talking a little with the crew and then pacing about as if bored, Aqutak had leant over the gunwale, stared into the water for a while, and then suddenly leapt over, causing an alarm on the deck. Not a moment later, when Taro had rushed to the side and called out to Quinni and Daiki to help him and other members of the crew watched in horror, they saw the great black-and-white whale break through the water again, droplets sparkling against the light and the ice, and Aqutak was astride the whale's back, holding on to the dorsal fin.

The whale's face stretched out what seemed a large, playful grin, and it spurted out cold water in a rainbow of waterdrops. The crew had laughed at the time, but Yoshiko felt an uncertainty about whether Aqutak would really be okay.

As it happened, she had. She'd returned only to accept food from the crew now and then, and even then, she seemed to prefer fetching her own, sticking to fish meats the whale and other predator sea creatures brought her.

All manner of sea life had visited at some point with the sea witch about, and the octopus became a regular sight, often clinging to his human friend. But it wasn't that which intrigued Yoshiko most. She'd loved watching the whale the sea witch rode. Now and then, her friends came to join her in a small pod, and they played. Or sometimes, they left the sea witch with the ship and went to hunt in a fury of bubbling ocean, writhing fish, and spills of red blood in the distance.

Yoshiko cringed. She'd never expected whales to be vicious like that.

'Only really that sort,' Taro had said to her at the time as he saw the horror on her face. 'They're known as *killer whales* in Traders' and known for it for a reason. Others, like blue whales or humpbacks, are very peaceful and friendly—shepherd giants of the sea.'

Yoshiko watched how the sea witch interacted with the killer whale. It seemed friendly enough with her, and Aqutak looked more comfortable around ocean life than around the humans on the ship.

The witch turned her head to the side as she rode atop the whale, and something caught Yoshiko's eye ahead. She clambered down the shroud in a hurry and rushed to the bow, peering into the distance. Yoshiko strained her eyes, bringing on the enhanced effects of the curse, and saw ahead a flurry of activity in the ocean. Aqutak looked up at Yoshiko and called out.

Yoshiko pointed into the distance, still unable to reply to the young Inue woman. The woman turned, and she too squinted into the distance.

'What is it?' Chisaka asked as she ran up behind Yoshiko. Her long hair was loose, and her face was fresh. She'd only woken up not long ago and was preparing for her rotation. Yoshiko, on the other hand, was starting to feel the strain of being awake throughout the night shift, and she looked forward to being able to crash into her hammock. Chisaka running up behind her meant she could soon head below, spend time chatting with Kimura in the galley about the next food item he'd invented, and then sleep.

'I'm not sure, but something strange lurks below. It feels stranger than normal sea life. Of something ancient and magical. I felt its will pull at me, and I think Aqutak feels the same.' Yoshiko turned from the bright-eyed guard towards where the sea witch had been with the whale. 'Look, she's gone now.'

The smell and the footsteps Yoshiko had been waiting for drew closer, and Yoshiko ran to meet Gora before he had even stepped fully on the deck. His dark eyebrows raised in surprise, and Yoshiko was certain she heard a short, sharp intake of breath, just a little, at the surprise of suddenly seeing her run up to him.

'You need to see this.' Yoshiko immediately turned and padded back across the deck, not waiting for him to follow. She knew he would. Behind him, a yawning Moori and a calm, newly awake Ikeda followed.

By now, it was easy to see what was in the water with a spyglass. Gora frowned, passing his spyglass to Moori.

'What is it?' she asked, uncertain, pushing a strand of her short black hair from her face as the wind pushed it back again. She looked back through the spyglass.

'Not sure,' Yoshiko started, but was then interrupted by a great crash in the water beside them, and Aqutak appeared in her icy glory from below the ocean waves, skin slightly blued and frost covering her lips and dark hair.

The sea witch called up at them from atop the whale, and Quinni threw down a rope ladder for her to climb up on and join them.

'It is a sea battle. A giant squid against a creature like I've never seen before. Both are creatures from the deep, and it is said they originate from magic. We should stay clear.'

Gora listened deeply to the sea witch. Yoshiko saw him run a hand over his stubbled chin as he stared ahead at where the ocean bubbled, his brow furrowed.

'They must be huge to cause that.' He gestured with his hand. Then Gora looked back at Nishimura, who had come up behind them. 'Nishimura, you and Yonemura are to guide the ship safely around. I'll trust you both to organise the navigation. Keep your eyes on their movement. If it looks like the battle is coming our way, I need you to let us know.'

'Wouldn't it be wiser to head away?'

'We will. Take a wide berth.'

Nishimura eyed the bubbling ocean in the distance, and then the small group at the bow of the ship gasped as a great crash of water sprayed in the air, and a huge lizard-like head rose in the distance before a tentacle rose up, wrapped around the lizard's head, and brough it crashing back down into the waves.

The group fell silent, and Yoshiko turned to see how Gora would deal with it. Her eyes were heavy now, but she had a niggling feeling they might need her up on deck. She opened her mouth to suggest such a thing when Gora's eyes met hers. The concern washed from his face and he smiled softly, stepping closer to her, red hair ruffled in the breeze. He rested his hand on her shoulder, and she felt it, warm and heavy but gentle.

'Rest. Get some sleep. Gather your strength. We'll get you if we need your help. Let us handle this.'

'How did you know—'

'Everything's written all over your face, always,' he said with a grin, and Moori let out a scoff of amusement, agreeing.

Yoshiko pouted but nodded. She was too weary to protest either way. Instead: 'Will you be able to handle the magic?'

Ikeda, Nishimura, Quinni, and Moori looked to Gora now, and Chisaka looked out to the disturbed ocean ahead. Gora too looked into the distance, and then to the sea witch. He said something in Traders', and Aqutak seemed to respond in an uncertain tone. Yoshiko frowned.

'If Aqutak is of magic blood, can she keep you safe against the ocean?' Then Yoshiko paused. She looked at the sea witch, her heart freezing over for a moment, pausing. '*Will* she?' *Do we have to make an agreement with her like the pirate queen did?* Yoshiko wasn't comfortable making strange agreements with the sea witch if the last one meant thousands of children were murdered. A feeling like a warning speared her heart. 'On second thoughts, I'll stay up here. At least until we're safely past them.'

Everyone looked to her now, concern giving Gora, Ikeda, and Chisaka frown lines. But, it was Moori who stepped in. The young noble stepped forward, taking one of Yoshiko's hands in both of hers. 'Do you not trust us to look after the ship without you? We have kept the ship so far, let us prove to you we can do it again. Sleep. You can't look after anyone else if you don't look after yourself first. We will call for you if we need you.'

Nishimura added, 'And if all goes to plan, we can go around and will not get disturbed. But it does trouble me that such creatures, should they really be magical creatures from the deep, have risen.' He looked to Aqutak, asking her a question in Traders'.

Aqutak nodded and replied.

'It's the spell,' Gora translated for Yoshiko and Chisaka. 'Magic is rising again. Time is getting closer. Before, it was just the wild places of the world where those of magic hid and escaped from the increasing human population. But now, with magic teetering on the edge of disappearance and rebirth, magical creatures are restless.'

Aqutak said something else, her dark eyes now meeting Yoshiko's, her gaze burning into her brain. Yoshiko felt she didn't need Gora's translation to understand what she was asking.

'You are of magic. Do you feel it?'

Yet there was a discomfort to this question that made Yoshiko wish not to answer. Instead, she played innocent, looking blankly at Gora, trying to get him to move the conversation on. He did, grilling the sea witch on what she meant, asking for more on the creatures and location, what her role would be in the agreement now if her predecessor who made it was dead.

Aqutak watched Yoshiko for a moment, ignoring Gora's questions, and Yoshiko noticed Ikeda and Chisaka step closer to her either side, as if protecting her from the unusual witch.

'There's something else about this agreement my predecessor made that makes me uneasy,' Aqutak said airily, as if buried in thought. She turned now to finally look at Gora and frowned. 'But I can't quite remember it.'

'You mean it's not that it involves killing thousands of innocent children?' Ikeda said icily in broken Traders', looking sidelong past Yoshiko at the witch.

'Took the words right outta my mouth, ye did,' Gora muttered in agreement in Hizen, and then translated the earlier comments to a confused and enquiring Yoshiko. Then he paused. 'What d'you mean you don't remember? Don't you remember everything magical from your predecessor? Isn't that how the cycle works?'

Aqutak nodded and continued staring out at the sea. The ice field to their starboard side was closing in again, and a frigid wind blew up, whipping her black hair about. She, to her credit, ignored the sudden chill. 'For some reason, some things are lost to me. The tribe has wondered much over it. Usually, the sea witch passes peacefully with her tribe. But my predecessor was murdered, and her body lost deep in the southern Ice Lands and oceans. Where, we have no idea.' Aqutak turned and looked at them now, her eyes fierce, but Gora reckoned more in memory or anger than at them. 'The cycle was interrupted. She should be at rest at home with her tribe, her memories and magic close at hand for the next generations. But it is not. And my memories are like snowstorms.'

A silence so confused and uncertain overcame the group, and Yoshiko dismissed herself to bed thankfully but struggled to rest with Aqutak's words echoing in her mind. For once, her questions were drawn inwards, and she reflected for days as she stared into the ocean night, watching the stars, listening to the ocean rush past, the wind flapping in the sails, feeling her heart rate rise more each time she thought she saw strange creatures in the water—almost kidding herself that she saw ghostly figures of children in the ocean waves, their hands clawing above the surface.

Let this dark magic be done with, she thought to herself on one such night as she leapt back from the gunwale, heart thudding in her chest, stomping towards the galley and seeking the reassuring face of someone in the crew to tell her she was seeing things. *The meeting place cannot come soon enough.*

42

A Friend in Dark Times

Miyoshi had joined the pirate queen and her crew for at least one meal each day, with the rest of his rations being brought to the little storeroom they were keeping him in. Set apart from the other living captive child, Miyoshi spent most of his time staring at the small flame lamp they'd left him to keep the dark at bay. The long hours he had alone made him restless, and he longed for the company of the *Sea Guardian* crew. While the pirates fed him and some made small talk during meals, he missed being able to joke around and talk to people he knew well and trusted.

Ever did he pace and roll around in his small space, grumbling to himself about being bored or cold as the freezing winds seeped even this far into the hold. They'd given him blankets to hide under from the chill, but blankets couldn't curb the dull idleness that drove him to frustration in the dark. That time Gora hadn't let him go to the pirate isles was nothing. At least he'd not been locked alone in a cupboard back then.

Besides, the quiet hours and the longing made him remember the fight on the ship, the blood on his friends, Sakai's death.

Miyoshi sniffed and rolled over onto his stomach, trying to stretch out in the small space. It was big enough for him to lie down, but that was all. He rubbed his face against the hard wood floor, trying to banish the image of Sakai's death.

There was a light tap on the door.

His heart flared, and the boy looked up, breath catching. Had he imagined it?

There was a tap again.

Nothing like the determined bangs as the pirates knocked then barged in, demanding attention.

The door handle gently pushed down, and light seeped in through a small crack. Miyoshi knelt up, mouth agape, staring and not knowing how to respond. Was someone coming to secretly kill him?

He shook his head. Why would they? They were openly going to kill him any day now.

The gap got larger, and a small, pale face poked through. Light sandy hair tumbled in curls, and Miyoshi remembered the face of the pirate queen's granddaughter.

Ferichity?

He couldn't quite remember. While the girl had been at each of the meals with her family, happily chatting away, he'd not been able to talk with her. Of course, they were keeping him a prisoner. But they'd caught gazes now and then, and she'd smiled each time.

His heart gave a little flip as he saw her face again, and she smiled as her head poked in the doorway.

'Can I come in?'

He nodded mutely, and the girl quickly flashed through the gap, shutting the door gently behind her, placing her own lamp on the floor.

The room hadn't been so bright, and Miyoshi wasn't sure if it was the extra lamp or the company of this young, bright girl.

Her teeth flashed brightly as she grinned at him, and she plonked herself cross-legged on the floor in front of him.

She wore a smart dark jacket, white blouse, and dark slacks, but he couldn't really see the colour in the dark. Neat boots were laced well and shone, and her hair was pinned up with a bow.

Miyoshi felt like a beggar in comparison.

He fumbled awkwardly, but the girl kept her gaze and smile.

'I'm Felicity,' she said cheerfully. 'What's your name? Nonna never told me.'

'*Ferishity?*' he repeated, then smiled back. 'Yūki,' he said, remembering what his captain had said about everyone in countries like this giving out their given names first.

She laughed and tried to correct his pronunciation, but he only got a little closer. 'Nice to meet you, Yuukie.' Her own accent made him giggle too, and he tried to correct her.

Both fumbled and giggled quietly over names, and then she fell silent and looked at him sadly.

'Sorry, Yuukie.' When he asked why, she looked away. 'I know what Nonna and her crew are doing. They think I don't, but … I listen to things.'

She looked down.

'Did you see the girl?' Miyoshi fidgeted with his ragged trouser legs as he sat cross-legged, looking uncertainly up at the smart young girl. He could still remember the ocean's hands grabbing at her, clawing, dragging her down, and the terrified green eyes. Her eyes had carved into his soul, and he had a feeling it would be that way the rest of his life.

Felicity's eyes widened, and she too fidgeted, playing with a button on her jacket, nodding. 'I wasn't meant to see, but … I snuck after you all.'

'The hands?'

She nodded again, her soft curls waving over her shoulders, and she sniffed.

'Will it be the same for me, do you know?' He held his breath, not really wanting to hear.

Felicity paused. 'I think'—she looked up at him nervously— 'it will be different.'

When he asked how, she didn't know. All she knew was that they were going north, to the ice country, where it was either day or night all the time and nothing but ice beneath your feet. Miyoshi's mouth opened wide as she described it, and how she'd heard people lived deep in the ice, in houses made of ice, and ate animal fat.

In any other circumstance, this would have been an adventure that excited him. But to know he was going to die clouded the awe.

'You know, they're not bad,' Felicity said after a pause as Miyoshi tried to picture a land of ice.

He looked up at her and she was staring right at him, her small face serious.

'My nonna and Mama, and everyone.'

Miyoshi raised his eyebrows in surprise. 'But they're pirates,' he said.

Felicity shrugged and looked at the small flames sitting between them. 'Pirates are just people, like everyone else. Doing what they have to do to survive.'

'But they're hurting people,' Miyoshi said, thinking of the girl who had been dragged under the water. *Killing* them.'

'I know,' Felicity said in a whisper. 'But when I asked Nonna why, she said she saw something really bad happen, and she's trying to stop it.' She looked at Miyoshi and saw he didn't understand. 'Nonna's a seer,' Felicity explained. 'That means she can see the future sometimes. The disaster she saw, probably it happened all over the world. Evil creatures tore everything apart, and everyone died. She couldn't let that happen. Said the lives taken now would save thousands times more.'

A heavy silence followed as Miyoshi tried to catch up, and the two children sat listening to their own soft breathing and the creaking of the ship as it lurched gently through the waves. Miyoshi stared at the girl in disbelief.

'Something's going to kill everyone?' he asked her. She nodded, golden curls bouncing. 'So your nonna is killing children now to stop it?' Felicity nodded again. He scrunched up his face. 'How is killing them now going to stop it?'

Felicity frowned. 'Some kind of spell. An agreement with the sea witch.'

'The sea witch.' Miyoshi paused. He'd heard the captain whisper things about her under his breath, and the pirate queen had said it when she'd thrown the girl over into the water. '*Another one for the great sea witch,*' he repeated in a whisper.

Felicity nodded again. 'That's it. I heard it too.'

'But what does the spell do?' the boy insisted, leaning forward.

'I don't know.' The girl sounded miserable.

Miyoshi's heart sank. He was going to die, and apparently it was for some great unusual cause to save everyone, but it didn't make him feel any better. Didn't make him hate the pirates or their queen any less. So she thought she was helping people, but she was hurting more people too. Hurting those children and hurting everyone around them, too.

'But I don't want to die,' he admitted out loud, hearing his voice break.

When Felicity didn't answer, he looked back up at her, and Miyoshi saw her lip quivering and her light eyes watering. 'I don't want you to die either. I didn't want any of them to die. When I found out all that—' She sniffled and took a great gulp. 'I asked them to stop. Surely there was another way.'

Miyoshi nodded mutely, feeling his own eyes watering. Surely there was another way.

'You know,' Felicity said, changing the subject after another heavy silence followed. 'I brought you something.'

She reached into her smart little jacket pocket and pulled something out. Then she reached for Miyoshi's hand and pressed something into it. A small seashell. In the dim light, he couldn't see the colour, no matter how closely he peered. 'It's from the beach where we docked last week. In our home country.' She leaned in closer with a grin, holding her hand to her face as if covering a secret. 'You know, sometimes I like to sneak off the ship on my own to explore. When we dock, the crew leaves. Sometimes I take a boat on my own, too. I saw this when I was exploring and thought you might like it. Don't tell anyone!'

Miyoshi curled his hand around the seashell, feeling a warmth in his chest for the first time since he'd been taken and brought onto this ship. 'Thank you,' he whispered.

'You're welcome,' Felicity said, smiling at him. She wiped her eyes and stood up, taking her lamp with her. 'I have to go now. Can I come back and talk to you again?'

Tears stung his eyes again, and he didn't want her to hear the crack in his voice. Instead, he just nodded. And with a small smile, the brightness left the room, and he was left alone again in the dark, clutching the little sea shell.

43
Growing Tensions

Gora leaned over the edge of the ship and frowned at the waves. *Somethin' just moved down there ...* He eyed the ocean warily, expecting more foul creatures to suddenly leap up and claw their way up his ship, and then he felt the hairs on the back of his neck tingle, and his skin prickled. Someone was behind him.

'Fuckin' announce yourself if yer there.' He curled his lip at hearing his own shaking voice. 'Times are too creepy for that kind of nonsense.'

The person behind him excused themself, and he turned to see Yonemura, arms akimbo. She smirked.

'Crew's on edge too, now, aren't they?' Gora sighed, instinctively leaning his back against the gunwale as he spoke to her, and then feeling that prickling feeling behind him again. He jumped forward and disguised it as wanting to stroll about the deck. 'Strange things in the water.'

'Magical creatures again? Merfolk? Shall we increase patrol?'

Yonemura looked calm as ever, but her hair was more unkempt and her eyes looked tired, and for someone as neat as her, that was unusual.

'Might be a good idea,' Gora muttered, rubbing at his facial hair. 'It'll only get worse. We're nearly there.' When Yonemura asked how he knew, he gestured his head. 'Things seem to be gathering around *her*.'

He gestured with his eyes to the figure ahead of the ship. Yonemura looked past him at Aqutak, still riding the whale. She'd not stopped to talk to them or set foot on the ship since this last leg of their journey had begun. The sea witch had said they were meeting the pirate queen at the top of the world, so they were sailing west to meet the pirate queen on a tiny island in the middle north. As the days slipped past with no change in the light, time stretched out beyond measure, and the crew grew restless, on edge. Gora knew all worried about getting closer to the meeting place, wondering what it would be like to fight the pirate queen and her entourage, and whether they'd be able to rescue Miyoshi and any remaining children with minimal damage or loss on their part. But it was one ship against who knew how many, and they still didn't know if Miyoshi was alive.

Gora frowned. *I know he is. Magic still ain't fully back yet, and she said she wanted to save him for last. Spiteful bitch.*

And the crew only grew more restless as they closed in on the island where the pirate queen was heading to meet the sea witch. Each day they got closer, the more creatures they found in and around the water—both normal sea creatures and magical.

'I'm surprised to see this many magical creatures. I thought they'd be mostly gone,' Yoshiko admitted to Gora one morning as they dared lean over the edge of the ship between her rotation and his. Chisaka was standing closer to her than usual, looking warily at something in the ocean. Gora followed the samurai guard's gaze. A strange creature that looked like a white-and-grey goat on the front with huge horns and long tendrils like a shrimp reared up from the ocean and then slammed down a lengthy eel-like tail. Gora saw Yoshiko lean closer in that direction and turned to see her face—eyes wide with wonder. 'Yet over these past few months, more and more just keep revealing themselves from seemingly endless resources. Where do you think they were hiding? Or are they coming through the tears in the sky from the spirit world?'

Gora thought carefully. 'Probably. Though there are lots of unexplored places in the world still where they could hide. Either way, can't say I've seen one of *them* before.'

The goat-fish creature crashed down below the waves and then reared up again by the sea witch, who reached up and gently touched the creature's bowed head.

'While I have to admit seeing magic gathering again is an incredible sight, I don't like how it's been done,' Gora said, leaning his chin on his hand with his elbow resting on the gunwale. He narrowed his eyes and watched the sea witch, wondering what her true goal might be. He wasn't sure he believed the level of helplessness she had in the past agreements. Why would her ancestor even agree to such a thing?

Yoshiko and Chisaka hummed in agreement, and then they watched as the sea witch closed in on an island with huge rocky outcrops piercing the surrounding ice.

'In we go,' Gora sighed, standing up straight again. 'Looks like we're here. Gather the crew.'

The *Sea Guardian* crew followed the sea witch through harsh outcrops of rock and glacial ice, Yonemura and Nishimura straining together against the helm with Quinni yelling out dangers from the crow's nest. As they rounded a cliff that strutted out from the ocean, a safe harbour came into view. Safe from the wind and sea, not safe for Gora's crew. Several pirate ships of all sizes and styles gathered in the harbour, all rocking gently against their mooring.

Gora frowned. *That many came?*

His heart felt like it would ooze right on out of his mouth and vanish.

Well, we'll have to deal with those sea slimes either way, he thought, looking around at his crew and trying to be pragmatic. That's what the whole mission was, after all. Trying to make the seas safer. But were his crew ready?

Ready or not, Gora didn't need to be a being of magic to feel tension in the area. The night was drawing in, and he knew as soon as that sun set, the twilight hour—the notorious hour for the veil to be at its thinnest—would be upon them.

As soon as the veil was at its thinnest and magic tension at its highest, Miyoshi would die. That's when the wild magics operated.

Gora swallowed uncomfortably and eyed the sun in the distance. Could they dock and prepare in time? Up here, he could never tell when the night would draw in, if it did at all.

He strode over to Yoshiko, who was helping prepare the weapons and getting the flame powder and rounds ready for the guns and cannons. Her cursed strength helped them prepare quicker, and her brow was furrowed in a single-minded focus. She'd twisted her hair up with a pin to keep it out of the way, and Gora was reminded once again of the times they'd fought together before.

But not today.

Today, he couldn't let her follow him. She would stay out here, where she had room to use whatever powers she might need, away from pirates trying to do odd things with magic. He'd make sure of that. Gora quickly looked about for Ikeda. It would be him he'd have to talk to about keeping Yoshiko safe. Clocking eyes on Ikeda, Gora nodded to himself and then strode the rest of the way to Yoshiko's side. She looked up before he arrived, hearing his boots thud nearer.

'I knew those were your footsteps,' she said simply with a grin as she pulled herself up to stand.

'I need you to tell me when you think the magic is increasing. Can you feel it?'

Yoshiko frowned more, looking down at the weapons in her hands. 'I can feel something. There's a faint buzzing feeling, like air vibrating at high speed. It irritates my ears and makes my heart feel like it's vibrating too, and heat builds up within. It's hard to keep down. As if something's trying to force me to transform.'

She looks worried. Gora rested his hand on her head and let himself smile. At times like this, his crew and his friends needed to see him certain. Her dark eyes met his uncertainty, and then she let a small smile cross her face too.

'Well, we can make it. There is still time.'

'You'll let me know?'

'Of course.'

He nodded and left, feeling nausea at what would come. By now, Aqutak was walking up from the ocean and onto the rock, looking at the ships with a grave expression, and Gora knew she'd be heading into the island's caverns to meet the pirate queen.

There's no damned time to prepare at all!

He wanted to be on that island as soon as possible to follow. Who knew how quickly things would happen from here?

What if they kill him and bring back magic as soon as she steps in there?

He bellowed for his crew to work faster, watching the sea witch disappearing into the dark of the island's cave. But he needn't have stressed for long, as in no time, the ship was moored alongside the pirate ships, and his crew had dropped anchor.

Somethin' ain't right here, Gora thought, glaring at the pirate ships around them and grabbing his spyglass. *Why ain't they firing, or yellin', or anythin'?*

Through the spyglass, he could see a skeleton crew on each of the ships, some standing at their own gunwales and glaring reluctantly at the *Sea Guardian.* Gora didn't like it.

'It's like they're letting us moor here,' he spoke aloud to no-one, and scanned the rest of the island, or what he could see of it amongst the ice and rocks. Running a shaking hand through his dark red hair, feeling it tangled and knotted as his fingers caught, Gora stuffed the spyglass back in his pockets and stepped away from the gunwale. Watching would do no good. Very likely the pirate queen had known he'd follow and wanted to prove a point. Clearly, the pirates were letting them come, whether they liked it or not.

After all, I bet old Foy wants to kill me himself. He furrowed his brow but grinned as he stomped down the steps to the main deck. *Well, aye, the feelin's mutual.*

From the minute his foot stepped onto the main deck, he was ready. He clapped Tomioka on the shoulder as he walked past the man, pale with stress and worry and quieter since the boy had left. 'Today, we'll save Miyoshi,' Gora told him as he passed. The man nodded grimly, standing taller, determined. And then Gora felt more certain. They *would* save the boy. And not only that, but all the ships here other than his were going to be left here, in any condition, unable to leave. 'There's going to be no-one to sail them back,' he told himself.

That was the promise he'd made when he set out on this spirits-forsaken mission.

He rallied the crew on deck—even Kimura was up from the galley, looking like he'd take on anyone, cooking knife in his hands.

'This is it,' Gora said as he looked at each crew member, meeting their gaze. 'This is where we get Miyoshi back and stop the pirates. Finally. They're all in one place.' Then he swung his arm wide at all the ships moored on the island. 'Practically did us a favour! You know your positions. You know what you're doing. I won't tell you we're all going to get out of here alive. Just do your best to make sure you do. Protect yourself. Protect each other. Let's stop this madness.'

Gora saw Eshnaa and Simrita look to each other firmly. This was a big moment for them—the moment they could get revenge for their friend, who was also taken. They nodded. He knew they were some of the first who would be with him. He almost felt guilty for splitting them up: Simrita coming with him and Eshnaa defending the ship and helping to destroy others. But then, Eshnaa had asked to defend Yoshiko. The young woman had become strangely devoted to the young Hién daimyō since they'd met, and she'd wanted to fight alongside her.

His eyes landed finally on his friend.

'Fuck,' he muttered, Yoshiko's eyes a blending mix of gold and black, the only sign of the curse trying to well up within her so close to the rising wild magics. He'd not told her she was staying here yet—the only one he'd not told of their position in all this. He knew if he told her before, she'd find a way to persuade him otherwise or rebel against him to come with him.

Gora looked for Moori, hoping she would be able to persuade Yoshiko to stay on the ship. The two would fight together well, and Yoshiko's powers and fighting style were more suited to out in the open. If any two could defend the ships and destroy the others, it was the one who could shoot best and use the figurehead's fire, and the one who could naturally fight with fire. She was best suited out here. But now, to tell her all that.

Gora dismissed the crew, watching them scatter to their places and give each other courage and departing embraces. Then he turned to see that Yoshiko was standing right beside him.

'What's "fuck" for?' she asked calmly, though he could see she was fiddling with the handle of her katana. She always fidgeted when she was anxious.

He sighed. 'Just everything. I hope this goes to plan.'

'Things never go to plan. But you can still do your best to make something work.'

Her eyes were watching the entrance to the cave on the island the sea witch had disappeared into, and he knew she expected to come with them.

'I need you to defend the ships with Moori and the others,' he said, knowing the simple way was the best. 'Make sure we have a ship to come back to, now. It's the only way we'll be sailing home.'

Give her responsibility. It's what she thrives for, he thought, convincing himself more than anything, resting both his hands on her shoulders and looking at her firmly. Then he smiled and ruffled her hair while she paused in a moment of shock, face visibly confused. 'Don't worry. You'll have Eshnaa, and Ikeda, and plenty of others to help you. Bonus if you can make those unable to sail.' He gave a nod of his head to the other ships beside them. 'See you in no time. Make sure you stay alive.'

Gora turned, guiltily occupying himself with shrugging his jacket closer to avoid a chill, trying to leave before she spoke. His heart thudded in his chest at having to leave her behind like this, but he couldn't think of any other way to do it. She'd want to come with him, but he couldn't let her. He thought back to when they'd fought off the Acreins and discovered the traitor in her council. They'd fought separately then, but he also remembered the fear that she might have died. That wouldn't happen again.

Just protect the ship and look after yourself. He grimaced.

'Gora, wait!' He heard her footsteps thundering over the short distance, and she grabbed at his arm. He grimaced at how much it hurt. 'I'm coming too. I can't let you go alone again.'

Gora spun on the spot and grabbed her arm. She winced too but stared defiantly at him. 'No, you stay here. I can't let you go in there. Besides, you'll fight better out here.' He gestured about them with his eyes, raising his eyebrows slightly.

She said nothing, a sullen look of defiance setting her jaw.

'Some leader you are now, princess.' He let out a huff of a laugh and shook his head. He looked into her eyes. 'Seriously, we need you out here. You can cover more range. Look after the ship. We need it to get home.'

He let go of her wrist, and Yoshiko huffed reluctantly, but he knew she'd listen. Gora shrugged his shoulders, knowing he couldn't do anything else, and turned, not looking back until he'd stepped off the ship and onto the gangway. This wasn't like the last time he parted with his family. This time, he'd be back.

Ikeda was waiting for him at the bottom with Daiki, both looking past Gora at their daimyō. Gora stopped in front of Ikeda and looked square into the young man's face.

In a moment of desperation, Gora's heart lurched, and he grabbed at the young warrior's kimono collar. 'Go back up there. Look after her. She *must* live. No matter what happens today, no matter what happens to me, take her home.'

Ikeda's mouth opened for a moment, and then he glanced behind Gora and up at the woman on the ship. 'You know, she said the same to me of you.' He closed his eyes for a moment and then smiled before looking at Gora again. 'You know you're like a brother to her, don't you? What do you think she'll be like if you die?'

'And what about if she dies?'

Ikeda sighed. Gora tightened his grip.

'I know you're loyal to her; I know you care, and I thank you for that. I never want that to change. But right now, you're on my ship, and you're my crew. Not in Hié. You know my orders.' Then Gora moved his hand from the young man's collar and rested it instead on his shoulder and added, 'Please.'

The young man glanced once more up the ship and took a breath and then, after a short thought, met Gora's eyes once more and bowed. He gripped the handle of his blade and took a step to the side. Gora let go, turning aside to see who the conflicted young man would listen to—his captain, or the warlord he was clearly in love with. The young man stepped up onto the gangway and looked sidelong at Gora through his fringe, nodding faintly with a slight smile creeping on the corner of his lips. Gora let his anxious breath free as he watched the samurai step onto the ship, *haori* flicking about him as he turned suddenly and bowed to a confused-looking Yoshiko.

The young samurai looked down at her and said a short word before directing his gaze to Gora. Yoshiko looked on in horror as Gora turned and stepped onto the stone that led into the cave, running a hand through his hair to distract himself from the stress of forcing himself not to look back at her.

'Did I do the right thing?' Gora asked, half to himself, as Tomioka and Daiki fell in beside him.

Tomioka's face looked fierce, but the soft man inside him turned back and answered. 'She will not hate you. Our daimyō needs to stay alive, for Hié is still regrowing after what happened last year.'

'We know he will keep her safe,' Daiki added. 'How could he not? If she died, I feel a piece of him would too, he has been that devoted to her since before the takeover. Remember how much we said he fought to prove she was still alive?'

Gora nodded, and though he wanted to believe them and know he did the right thing, he knew how much she hated people acting as if she couldn't look after herself.

'Now we'll just have to make sure you come back!' Daiki said, clapping Gora on the back. 'And young Miyoshi, and if anything has happened to him, it will be more than Tomioka that the pirates will need to be wary of, but you, me, our whole crew, and our warlord. I believe, for him, she would use her powers once again to bury them all in ash, do you not?'

Gora let out a harsh laugh. 'Yes, but pray to the spirits that you never see such a thing. The last time she sought revenge in that form, half a stone city burned. I was not sure we'd ever get her back; she was so far gone. Her eyes alone could have melted me with fright, and they say her mother was more fearsome! I can't believe it.'

'Dragon warlord, devil's child—what a pair you are. I'm glad I'm following you and not against you,' Daiki muttered, squinting about the rocky ruins on the island, hands rested on the hilt of his katana.

Gora didn't need to be born of magic to feel the powers rising. The sun was sinking in the sky, and the shadows lengthening. A rush of wind gushed past, making the group pause as the ships rocked and strained against their moorings and the ropes clattered against the masts. A chill flashed down Gora's spine, and something made his head feel as if it was vibrating.

This is what she spoke about, he said, recalling what Yoshiko had said about the growing magical tension. *Now even we can feel it?* He looked about at the others, wondering if they'd felt it too. No-one's expressions seemed to have changed. *Am I just imagining it?*

Certain he could feel the pulsing energy, Gora looked about the rocky crags on the island, eyes drawn to the sky above the cliffs. In the growing darkness, something stirred above, almost rippling.

Gora squinted, looking to the night sky, and then swore. He'd seen that sky before, the day Yoshiko had transformed in Acrein. It was the veil, the tearing of the sky when the wild magics overcame a weakening area of the boundary between this world and the next. The spirit world.

He looked away, heart pounding, before he saw an eye or something, like last time. The spirits from beyond.

Don't need to see that kind of omen right now.

Gora's hands felt sweaty, and he gripped the handles of the dual blades hung at the belt on his hip. Then, glancing between each of Tomioka and Daiki, the three steeled themselves to enter. But, it was Simrita and Rijul who entered the entrance to the stone caverns first, pushing past the static three at the front, faces set, weapons born—Rijul with his *talwar* drawn, Simrita with her *chakrams* ready to throw and slice the head off anyone who stepped in her way. They turned and looked silently at Gora, wondering if he would follow. Resisting the urge to look around at the ship, he forced his legs forward.

'Miyoshi better be alive,' he growled, raising his dual blades.

* * *

The walls were cold and dark and dripped with what Gora could only hope was damp, not the blood of thousands of children meeting their untimely end. With Rijul and Simrita just ahead, Daiki and Tomioka at either side, and Yonemura, Quinni, Jelani, Shingo, and Satou dotted about behind him, Gora felt they had the best chance they could at going after Miyoshi and knowing the remaining crew would look after the ship.

Still, I wish we had more, Gora thought to himself as he thought back to how many pirate ships had been there.

This late in the game, though, this small group was all they had, and so they quickly followed Aqutak as she seemingly walked through the ruins unfazed, somehow knowing where to go like an ancient memory or instinct.

The night'll be soon. He cursed himself at his slowness and tried to listen out. A gaggle of pirates trying to perform some strange ceremony would surely draw noise.

There was a hum in the distance, as if voices spoke all at once.

'I can hear them,' Quinni suddenly said in a loud whisper, 'a din. As if many people are conversing.'

Rijul jogged ahead, but he suddenly ducked back behind the wall, staring at Gora and the crew with dark, wide eyes. 'They're there!'

Gora nodded, half to himself, accepting what was to come. Behind him, Yonemura cursed, and Shingo asked Gora a muffled question that he just couldn't seem to register.

'What?'

Shingo repeated himself. 'How are we going to do this now we're here?'

'Is the boy still alive?' Tomioka stepped forward towards Rijul, sounding impatient. He leaned around the bend and narrowed his eyes as he peeked ahead. 'He is!' he hissed. 'They've got him tied up, the bastards.'

No matter the situation, Gora let out a laugh. 'Never heard you curse before, my friend.' Gora sauntered forward, feeling a little lighter. 'If the boy is alive, we still have a chance. What is the witch doing?'

Tomioka and Rijul both peered around the edge again.

'She is just talking to the pirate queen,' Rijul said in Traders', 'but I can't hear her.'

Gora looked at Quinni. 'You go. You can hear best.'

The silent giant nodded, and Rijul made way for Quinni to look around the corner. The Qeclan's face fell serious, and he peered into the room above Tomioka.

'The pirate queen is saying she is glad the sea witch came and thanking her. The witch says not to thank her. She's doesn't support them. She just followed her ancestor.'

'What does that mean?' Shingo's face twisted up in confusion. 'Is she with us or not?'

'I don't think she is with anyone. But she told the pirates to let the last two children go.'

'Just two?'

Yonemura's words echoed Gora's own, and they both looked at one another, shocked.

'I thought there would be more. That the ceremony you said she mentioned would be much grander.' Yonemura looked distraught. 'I thought we could save more. It is already this close to the end.'

'We *must* stop those last two children from dying.' Daiki's voice was low and dangerous, and his face screwed up with anger. He finally drew his katana. 'Captain, we need to go now.'

'Wait!' Gora hissed. 'Quinni, how many others are in there?'

But by the time Gora had turned back to the Qeclan and spoken, Tomioka had disappeared, and Quinni was staring open-mouthed into the room.

A cry of Miyoshi's name bellowed from around the bend.

'Did he just—'

'He just rushed in!' Quinni spun around and stared at Gora, eyes wide, long arms gesturing wildly towards Tomioka, voice hitched high in shock.

'What now?' Rijul asked, on the balls of his feet to rush in.

'We go after that fool, of course!' Yonemura cried out, running forward.

Gora ran a hand through the back of his hair and gaped. *Tomioka, you idiot!* He sprinted after them, rounding the corridor and skidding into an open area as large as a great hall in a ruined castle, and he had to pause to take in what he was seeing.

A complex circle of red had been painted on the damp stone, and Aqutak and Mammie stood at the centre with the two children bound in the middle, the boy next to Miyoshi slumped like a rag on the floor, covered in blood. Miyoshi was looking wide-eyed at Tomioka and Gora, and then his expression eased into relief as he saw the others run into the room behind them.

Gora halted. Hundreds of pirates crowded about the room, their expressions shifting from boredom to excitement as they eyed up the incomers. But it was not the circle of bored or tense pirates around the room that bothered him most. As Gora looked closer, he could see the slumped child in the centre of the circle was ghostly pale.

'Dead,' he said aloud, his eyes resting on the child's body. 'May as well be completely drained.'

'What do you mean?' Tomioka asked from beside him with gritted teeth, glaring now at the pirate queen.

'What do you think made the circle of blood?' Gora prompted, looking now at Miyoshi to check he was sound.

Tomioka snarled, and for a moment, Gora would have believed Yoshiko was standing beside him, so animalistic did the noise sound. 'And our lad?'

'Safe for now, I think.'

'You think?'

The pirate queen's two daughters stepped into the circle beside their mother, drawing their weapons and glaring at Gora. The short-haired, boyish one walked up to Miyoshi, grabbing him by his collar and pulling him up. The boy cried out. Tomioka leaned forwards and yelled out in Traders' for them to stop.

'I knew you'd hate to miss the show. After all this time, you had to see what you saw begin.' Mammie smirked. 'Sad you can't get involved? Sorry, you're a bit old to replace him now. You should have died at the start.'

'Glad I didn't. I'd not have been able to stop you then.'

Mammie grinned. 'You can't stop me. You actually helped. You brought me the witch, and you brought me the girl, just like I asked.'

Around them, the pirates cracked their knuckles and drew their swords, waiting for the orders they needed to attack. Gora was amazed such a woman had control over them. Though, the way they leered and stepped closer showed it was barely much control. His eyes fell on silver-white hair and sharp grey eyes ahead of him.

'Foy,' he muttered, then returned his eyes to the queen. 'Don't know what you mean.'

'Blood of thousands of children's sacrifice, blood of a last pure child to mix in with blood of the old magic. I was going to use myself, being one of the last seers in the world. But the spell will work better with older magic, and more of it, and I'd rather live if I can help it. This way they can die and I can live.'

'What?' Gora said slowly, looking at his group. No-one here had magic.

Mammie's smile pulled higher. She looked at Foy. 'Go to the ships. Your little pup's brought us a gift. There's a girl with more of the old magic than me. I can feel it from here. Her power's just calling out to me. Like a buzzing heat. I need her in this cave. Go get her.' Then she turned back to Gora, light eyes boring into his with a smirk on her face. 'A witch *and* a dragon. You did very well. It *is* my lucky day.'

Gora's heart dropped quicker than an anchor out of water. His eyes slid to Foy, who looked at Gora with the look of won vengeance before he stormed back towards the entrance.

No.

'Are they talking about the daimyō?' Shingo muttered to Yonemura behind him.

No.

Mammie winked at him. 'I knew you would be helpful to us and listen to me in the end.'

'I don't understand. You said you were to come here.' He hated the panic in his voice as he looked at Aqutak.

She looked hesitant, confused. 'I don't remember everything well. Seems I was wrong. I now have a feeling that the previous sea witch never thought they'd find another being of magic if the previous sea witch hid from her, and never thought the pirate woman would sacrifice herself. Now ...' She looked about the cavern for a way out. But in that short time, the pirates had blocked it off, and their drawn weapons looked primed to kill.

'Can't you use your powers?' Gora's heart rose as he saw Foy slipping out of the caverns, taking a group of pirates with him. *They're going to the ships.*

The sea witch blinked; then her eyes clouded over and strange lines and swirled markings appeared on her face, and cold ice patterns glittered like frost on her cheeks and in her hair.

'Then fucking do it already if you can,' Gora growled, turning to run after Foy. But as he looked back at the young sea witch, he saw she still hadn't moved. Instead, she watched him strangely, as if lost in a memory.

'We watch the seas. Rarely do we join the fights of humans,' Aqutak muttered, looking at Gora as if it were obvious.

With a click of his tongue, Gora let her be to decide on her own. *Here's me, no magic at all, at it again ...*

'Gora, Miyoshi!' Tomioka cried out, panicked, and Gora turned to look back at the boy.

Gora swore. First things first—save the boy.

Ikeda, you'd better hold to your promise, 'cause they're coming for her, Gora thought as the pirates crowded in around them, and the short-haired woman drew her blade towards the boy.

'The night is here,' Mammie called out as she gazed through a gap in the rocks. 'It's been twenty years of hell to get here. Don't let them get in my way.'

44

Foy

Quinni hailed them from above, and Yoshiko, Ikeda, Moori, and Eshnaa ran to the ship's edge.

'Well, they came quickly,' Moori said, lifting the gun in her hands. 'Reckon they split up, too?'

'Must've,' Ikeda replied, narrowing his eyes. 'That was too quick for a fight. We'll have more chance with a bow from this distance.'

Moori nodded, so she propped the gun against the side for later and reached for her bow alongside Ikeda and Yoshiko.

'That's something the foreigners seem to be missing lately. The bow is still better for long distance aim,' Ikeda muttered as he nocked the arrow and shifted his stance, feet diagonal from one another, body side on. 'Loose at will?'

His eyes slid to look at Yoshiko for a moment.

'Of course,' she said, feeling the muscles on her back squeeze together as she loosed an arrow and didn't even wait to watch it bury in a pirate's shoulder before nocking another.

Eshnaa cried out with glee, though, so something must have hit.

'Can you ask Eshnaa to grab Kimura? He went back below. We'll need him.'

'Even with his kitchen knives?' Moori smirked.

Yoshiko chuckled. 'Even then. I heard he's getting skilled with them!'

A white-haired pirate strode through the pack, eyeing up Gora's ship and meeting Yoshiko's eyes. A shiver sparked down her spine. *His eyes …* she thought to herself, thinking the steely grey looked cold and soulless.

'That's him,' Moori growled. 'The one who took the captain. We hunted him into the wandering sea. So he got through it, of course.'

Yoshiko's heart flared, and the heat inside rose. 'It's him?' She felt herself snarl. The image of how Gora had looked that time back in the caverns in Hié as he told her his story flashed to mind—the look on his face, tortured and regretful.

'The dragon-wing-sailed ship is here, too,' Ikeda said dryly, letting another arrow loose. Yoshiko felt pleased this time when it buried itself into a pirate.

Something's different to the last time we went to battle, she thought, recognising the vindictive feeling spike through her. In her battle with Acrein, she'd felt sorry for having to kill people. It had been hard. This time, she felt like the time she'd finally gone up against Chinen—when she'd seen for herself what he was really like and fought alongside Masa and Ikeda to bring him down. She wasn't sure she liked how she felt this time. Nubia's words from the Acrein battle rang in her head.

'Who truly wants to be here? They fight because they're told to.'

'But do they?' she muttered, wondering about the pirates this time. Everything she'd been told about them, everything she knew about them, led to the belief that they chose this life and made things hard for other people. Pillaging, raping, stealing, killing. A lawless life. A hellish life, and one they'd chosen.

Hadn't they?

Gora didn't … She wondered how many others had no choice but to be here. She paused her arrows, reflecting as she watched the pirates' movement below.

It was in doing this that she saw what they were doing, and she strained her ears to listen. There was a scraping of heavy cast iron on wooden planks from the ships, and the wind catching the sails of another as the ship was released from its mooring, rope tossed onto the deck.

'They're sailing! Readying the cannons,' she cried out, turning to run down the deck towards the ship with the sound of scraping iron. 'Quinni, the ships!'

'Are they running?' Moori called out to her.

'No, fighting. They will pin us here and destroy us. We need to sail, too!'

'But the captain …' Ikeda protested, lowering his bow and turning as if to follow her.

Nishimura stepped in this time, stepping beside Yoshiko, watching the ships. He spoke calmly. 'The captain will be fine if we act to save the ship and fight. Do you need me to rally the others who can sail?' Yoshiko affirmed, and Nishimura nodded. 'We'll sail. You can fight better if we sail.' He gestured to the figurehead's fire at the bow of the ship.

Quinni was already climbing down the shrouds like a spider dropping from a web. He rushed to raise the anchor.

'How will we release the ropes with that crowd down there?' Taro asked, stepping in beside Yoshiko as she walked up the deck again towards the port side.

She paused for a moment. 'I'll burn them.'

'Burn them?' Taro's voice hitched with his shock. 'But then how will we moor again?'

'We can think about that after the battle. Take some rope from another ship. When all this is over and we can act safely.

We cannot risk someone going down there right now and being killed. From down there, they can shoot you. I will not risk that. And I don't think Gora would either.'

Taro met her gaze, and Yoshiko could tell he knew Gora would do something rash like this, too. 'You two,' he said, shaking his head. 'Okay, burn it. We'll raise anchor.'

He bowed and walked away, gesturing and calling out to the other two. Kyo met him at the spokes to raise anchor, and Yoshiko ran to the ropes that moored them.

'Will you use your powers that freely?' Chisaka asked, disapproving, her stern face reminding Yoshiko of a chastising parent.

'You knew I'd have to use them.'

'But to burn a rope?'

'I can burn something else at the same time if I do,' Yoshiko said, hopping up to stand on the thick wooden gunwale. Chisaka stood close, there if needed. Yoshiko looked down at a group of pirates scurrying on the docks towards Gora's ship, including the silver-eyed man. *Trying to sneak on board, no doubt.* 'Did they raise the gangplank?' Yoshiko muttered to Chisaka, feeling a rush of concern.

Chisaka moved for a moment and then returned. 'Yes.'

Relief flushed through her. *Of course they would. They know this ship.* Then, taking a deep breath, Yoshiko focused on the burning that had grown since she saw the white-haired pirate. The ship lurched as the anchor raised, straining on the ropes which creaked and tugged at the docks. The pirates cried out below and ran towards them. Ikeda yelled across the ship, running towards her as if he was worried she'd fall with the rocking ship. Chisaka even grabbed at her ankle, the woman's grip within the gloves firm. She ignored it all, feeling the flames rise. *As if I'd fall.* Her eyes flickered clearer, and she raised her hands to her lips, linking her fingers and cupping them to create a funnel to direct the flames. She'd tried to breathe fire as a human before. A human's smaller face didn't direct the flames enough, and it had blazed in a great mass before dissipating. This time, she'd funnel it. When the flames rose high enough, Yoshiko breathed out long and slow from her stomach, feeling her soul light up with that uncontrolled beast curse as it watched with joy and pride as the flames burst free and melted through the rope and rained down on the unsuspecting pirates below, setting the docks aflame.

She ignored their cries.

She straightened as the ship pulled away from the docks, away from the fire, watching the flames burn below. Her eyes lit up with the burning light, and that spark of flame deep inside flared brighter.

I controlled it better this time.

For the sake of Gora and her friends, both aboard this ship and inside the ruins, she would control it.

As she turned to hop down onto the deck, her eyes met Ikeda's. He'd got here quicker than she'd expected, and for once she felt she couldn't read the expression on his face.

Does he think I'm a monster now?

Yoshiko held her breath as she waited for a response. For something. Instead, Ikeda raised his hand, offering it to help her, and her heart lurched. She took it, though she felt she could have hopped down with ease, knowing he did it from politeness and not the expectation that she couldn't manage. But as she landed on the deck, she expected Ikeda to say something. The look in his eyes said he had something to say, but he didn't.

Say something, she thought, still watching him, worry gnawing at her insides.

He didn't. In a short moment, his gaze was pulled to something off to their side and he ran to Eshnaa, waving for her to follow him up the other side of the deck.

'My lady?' Chisaka questioned as she stood there a little too long and watched.

Yoshiko took a deep breath.

'Ever fought aboard a ship, Chisaka?' She turned and grinned at the samurai woman beside her. She almost looked shocked, not expecting Yoshiko to respond like that. Then the woman shook her head. 'Well, you're in for a bit of fun.'

The wind caught in the sails, and the small crew called out to one another, voices straining, as they guided the ship out of the harbour. Nishimura's face was surprisingly calm, Yoshiko thought as she watched how he took the ship out with seemingly easy effort. Her heart lurched as she watched two pirate ships follow.

'What of the cannons?' she asked Moori. 'Can we fire them? Gora said that Taro, Kyo, Tomioka, and the late Sakai would fire them most, with Miyoshi to run flame powder.'

'We prepared for that,' Moori said, striding to the starboardside on-deck cannon. She heaved it about and looked up at Yoshiko. 'Ikeda is heading down there now.'

'On his own?' Yoshiko had always thought it to be a multiple-person job.

'Others will help him.' The younger girl referred to the new crew and guards from Hié. 'He can show them what's needed. They'll manage.'

Yoshiko frowned and looked at Chisaka, wondering if she'd be able to run below to help. As if reading her mind, Chisaka nodded and headed below. Yoshiko looked back to Moori. 'Can I do anything to help you here?'

Moori grinned. 'By all means. Fancy a hunting competition like the good old days?'

Yoshiko snorted. 'Prey's a little different this time.'

Moori shrugged as she rose again and glanced at the pirates as she loaded a gun. 'Not really.'

* * *

The small crew managed to bring the ship past the shoals before the cannons began firing into them. With the rocks out of the way, Nishimura yelled across at the others on deck, and Yoshiko glanced up from where she passed a heavy iron ball to Moori. Three ships were following them. From the distance, she caught the sound of scraping iron and then saw a flash of fire on deck. An explosion echoed, and then an iron ball rushed past them.

'They're attacking us with their bow chaser,' Moori grunted as she too loaded an on-deck cannon. 'Looks like they have more fighting power on ship. Dammit!'

Yoshiko lit the rope with the tip of her finger, and their own cannon answered, scraping across the incoming hull.

'Missed the chasers.' Moori clicked her tongue.

Below, another cannon answered and hit an incoming ship, but it was above the waterline and wouldn't bring it down.

'We need more,' Moori sighed, and she eyed up the figure-head's fire.

'You can use that more if I'm here, right?'

The young girl nodded at her, short hair bobbing. 'But they have to be closer.'

Yoshiko smiled. 'That's fine. I'm sure Nishimura will oblige if we ask him nicely.'

The young girl nodded, and she dashed off to the navigator, gesturing towards the incoming ship. From here, Yoshiko could see the young man nod, and she turned back to watch the ship more closely. There was a man standing at the edge—white hair, steely eyes.

Foy.

Yoshiko felt heat erupt within and wanted that very moment to transform and burn the ship to nothing. But she'd promised to be sparse with her powers now. That was why the figurehead's flame would be used, after all. And Yoshiko had heard of Moori's skill with the great weapon. There would be no need for her to transform, at least for the moment.

I need to remember to rely on those around me. Yoshiko clenched her hands until the message sank in.

The two ships edged closer, and Yoshiko heard the warning cry of someone up in the crow's nest bellowing down. 'They're trying to board!'

Of course they are, she thought, readying her bow once more. *Not that it'll help them.*

Besides, the closer the ship got, the easier Moori could smother them with fire.

But upon Moori's return to the front deck where Yoshiko waited, the two women stared in shock as the pirate ship swung around, refusing the *Sea Guardian* the manoeuvrability to fire their greatest asset. Another cannon scraped past, crashing into the rock of the island, and Foy's ship lurched closer on a wave, crashing into the *Sea Guardian* with an engulfing shudder. Pirates flooded aboard, Yoshiko watching, nauseated, as even the white-haired man stepped aboard, making a beeline right for her. His eyes locked on.

'Quick!' Moori yelled, grabbing Yoshiko's arm and pulling her out of whatever strange magic held her to the spot under the old pirate's glare. The young woman grabbed a pair of guns and fired one straight into the crowd, dashing down the steps to the main deck to defend Nishimura from the onslaught.

Eshnaa appeared beside them, swinging from the shrouds and landing deftly beside the navigator, smiling at Yoshiko sweetly. But her smile froze as she looked behind them at the pirates still clambering onto their ship.

'That's too many, surely?' Moori muttered, aiming a gun once more and firing into the crowd.

Yoshiko was pleased to see that it had hit, but with the sheer mass of the crowd, it barely made a dent.

'We need to do more!' she growled, wishing she could transform and be done with it. But that would destroy each ship here, including their own. But what if she climbed on the other boats and sunk them, using her weight?

Gunshots echoed as pirates answered Moori with shots of their own, and Eshnaa rushed off, driving her blades into limbs. Yoshiko searched the deck for Ikeda and Chisaka, who she had no doubt would come upon hearing the commotion on deck, leaving the cannon deck to others.

As expected, they had, and both in full Hizen blue layered armour, diving forward to join Eshnaa in warding off the attack.

And still, the white-haired pirate stalked on, eyes still on Yoshiko alone, ignoring the fighting around him. She startled to see him so close.

'Girl,' he growled, lunging forward to grab her arm.

Yoshiko grabbed her katana and stepped backwards, slicing upwards towards his reaching hand. He pulled it back and spat.

'None of that nonsense now. You're needed inside. Don't want the lad Gora to worry now, do ye?'

Yoshiko stared blankly, clueless, blade ready to cut down if needed. But she wondered why he'd said Gora's name. She knew this man to be the one to have caught him, so it had to have been something bad.

Foy said something else, and Yoshiko snarled and leapt forward, swinging her blade down and then following with a sweeping kick.

Somehow, the man dodged both, and Yoshiko watched wide-eyed as he simply stepped backwards, as if it had been no effort at all. Even against her. As if he had powers of his own. She lunged again, and again he stepped back. The old pirate didn't even draw his sword.

It continued this way, with Yoshiko growing increasingly frustrated and crying out in anger, the others fighting all around her when she wished to be helping them, and yet still Foy didn't draw his weapon. Instead, he simply stepped aside. It was only when they reached the gangplank that Yoshiko wondered what the old man was doing.

It's like he's leading me off the ship, she thought, looking at him curiously as she paused her blade and glanced around them.

But with no way of asking him, she simply growled and kicked out at him, trying to kick him off the plank and down into the sea or onto the island below. Either would be fine. He'd be hurt or dead either way.

Instead, he leapt deftly down with a smirk that made Yoshiko want to burn him right there.

After all, why don't I? A darker part of her burned up like leftover embers on a midsummer day. *It would be easy.*

No. To succumb to that now would burn their ship too.

Instead, she turned her back to him and stormed back up to the deck, slicing through the stomach of a pirate that dared run her way. She scanned the scene for her friends. They were alive, still, but tiring.

Her ears twitched as a faint click of a gun came from behind her, back on the gangplank, where a waiting Foy grew impatient. She dropped to the floor as the shot blurred past, burying itself into a pirate ahead. Then, rolling instantly aside, she dashed back to the gangplank and rested her fingers on the wood of the ramp, looking up at the white-haired man as he aimed the barrel of the gun once more at her, this time aiming at her face.

This close, he wouldn't miss.

Heart racing, Yoshiko willed herself to act first. Heat shot through her veins and to her fingers, springing fire from her fingertips and burning holes in the wood. The gun's latch clicked again, and she knew the shot would follow any moment.

The steely eyed man must have realised what she was trying to do, as he gave a roar and stormed forwards, trying to reach the safety of the ship. But the movement gave Yoshiko exactly what she needed, and his weight caused the gangplank to buckle, snapping where holes had burnt through at her fingertips.

She dived behind the gunwale instantly, not daring to watch as the man fell, another shot racing past as another crack echoed from his gun.

Of course he'd try to take me down with him.

She dashed to the edge. There Foy was in the water, swearing up at her, steely eyes locked on hers. She shuddered. It was the face of a madman—one who had killed many people. She reached for her bow, knowing that if the man was to live, he'd be back. But a bow wasn't needed. The water bubbled and shifted, and from somewhere deep below, great tentacles burst from the waves and reached up, wrapping around the man and pulling him down before he could even cry out.

But not before Yoshiko could see the look of anger and shock in his icy steel eyes.

'And that's the end of Foy,' she muttered, knowing Gora would be relieved. But it felt almost unreal, as if he was the sort of man who could somehow survive anything and be back at any moment.

She shuddered and ran back from the edge, desperate to find the others. But as she did, she saw how desperate their situation still was. Their small crew was overrun and exhausted, and no matter how skilled she knew some of them were, it wasn't enough.

Yoshiko clenched her hands, feeling the long nails digging into the flesh of her palms. She said she wouldn't, but she had to. Beyond this were more ships, each with their own crews ready to fight for their queen and kill her friends. Kill others. This, of anything, must be reason enough to justify using her powers.

The words of the shrine maiden at the burial place of her ancestor returned to her. *When you die, bury yourself deep in rock so none can get to you. They will do anything to take your powers.* If the pirate queen was trying to bring back magic, she was sure the woman would do anything to get her powers, if she knew Yoshiko was here.

She shook her head. *Well, I'll just do anything to make sure I can leave here.*

The heat welled up, and she let it. The spirit burned with the golden light, and she felt her body growing, the snapping and stretching of limbs that followed. It hurt, but the growing spirit soared, and before she could sink her own ship, Yoshiko leapt and caught the wind, spiralling into the icy water below.

She saw the tentacled creature that had caught Foy, and the icy-eyed pirate was nowhere to be seen.

Eaten? Good.

Satisfied, she spun upwards, crashing from the waves and launching at the pirate ship that joined theirs, grabbing at it with her great claws and clambering up it, tugging her great serpentine weight back to the ocean and giving a growl of approval as the ship toppled over with her.

Her tail lashing against the ocean, Yoshiko leapt out of the way before such a heavy ship could fall onto her, masts and shrouds pinning and trapping her below to drown in this dark, icy abyss. Instead, she swam back into the air, catching an air current that lifted her skyward, before diving again and launching with a great roar at another ship that was turning to fire cannons at her crew. Yoshiko crashed through the main mast and grabbed at the mizzenmast, tugging it free and launching it at a third ship like a spear. It hit.

A light voice called to her from the *Sea Guardian,* and Yoshiko returned, hovering on the wind nearby and focusing on transforming above deck, trying to land safely as a human.

It was a longer way to the deck than she thought. Distance in her dragon form seemed so much shorter. The air whipped past her, and Yoshiko landed back on deck with a crash and a roll, trying to break her fall, landing with a grunt in a crumpled heap next to Moori, who fired a gun with a laugh ahead.

'This is just like when we hunted back home in Hié!' Moori cackled.

Yoshiko, still wincing at her landing, frowned and squinted up at the young woman. 'How is this anything like that?'

The short-haired woman shrugged and turned to offer Yoshiko a hand to stand up. 'Good job you took them down. I don't think we'd have survived if any more came aboard.'

Yoshiko's heart washed with relief as she followed Moori's gaze. The deck was finally quietening, and they watched as Eshnaa pierced another pirate through and kicked him to the floor, leaping away athletically to dispatch another. Her face was flushed red, and her hair hung limply beside her face, but that was all that would show of her fatigue. Though red staining her green silks brown alarmed Yoshiko, the woman still moved as if there was nothing to worry about, smiling gratefully as an ever-sturdy Chisaka helped her push another pirate overboard.

Next, Yoshiko looked for Ikeda, his beautiful, cream skin contrasted with blood—hopefully not his own, she thought—as he snarled and slashed at a final pirate in the area he'd blocked as his defence, keeping Nishimura from harm. He turned and caught her eye and frowned, marching over.

Her heart lurched, and without knowing why, Yoshiko took an uncertain step back.

The young samurai stopped right in front of her, so close Yoshiko felt nervous, and he cupped her face in his hands, searching her face. She felt her cheeks burn hotter than the fire in her spirit, but she could barely let out a word.

'Your face—there are more scales,' Ikeda said, his eyes finally meeting hers. 'You need to be careful. We are here. You don't need to use those powers.'

Her face flooded with so much heat she thought her head would explode. Jittery and unable to respond, as he was so close, Yoshiko simply stared, overwhelmed.

But we defeated them, didn't we?

45

The Last Child

The boy looked around the ruins at the pirates surrounding his friends. Only some had come, so the others must have been protecting the ship. But a group of pirates had marched out to kill them too, and the boy knew he and all his friends were in trouble.

They've gone to get Lady Yoshiko? He thought he could understand that much. They said they'd use her blood …

Miyoshi gasped and looked around at the red circle in fear. The last time they'd used someone's blood, they'd used it all to make this circle. Would they do this to Lady Yoshiko and that witchy lady too?

But she's powerful, so she'll stop them, right?

A crash of metal made the boy jump up and look up from the red circle. Rijul had pushed in front of Gora and Tomioka and met a pirate blade on blade, a snarl on his face. Miyoshi's heart pounded.

He pulled at the ropes that bound his hands and tried to stand up, but his legs burned from sitting here for so long, and the short-haired pirate woman, Adline, he thought her name was, nudged him with her foot, frowning. He toppled back over and crashed onto his shoulder on the floor.

'You'll stay still,' the young woman hissed in Traders', and Miyoshi was too frightened not to obey.

He felt helpless as he watched more of the pirates launch onto the small group of his crew. Even Tomioka, known to be a pacifist, roared out with fierce eyes as he sliced his katana through a man's stomach.

More than blood fell out, and Tomioka turned in almost slow motion as the man crashed to the floor, and instantly raised his blade again to slash at another. Tomioka was so different to before. He'd grown his facial hair longer, and his hair flopped more messily now than neatly, and he had a darker look in his eyes.

Miyoshi remembered how Tomioka had looked the day he'd been taken. *Like he'd failed.* A tear slid down the boy's face. He wanted to help. He wanted to make them happy.

If only I was a few years older. If only I was bigger and stronger.

They'd even taken the daggers Yoshiko had given him. He sniffed.

If only I could break free and help. Then we can run out of here before anyone gets hurt.

The boy looked up at Adline and Mammie, both watching on as if they expected the fight to end soon and not get in their way. Then, as if she knew he was looking at her, Mammie turned to face him and met his eyes with a smile.

'Shall we continue? Let's give your friends a show. They're too busy to bother us.'

She smiled, and two of her crew stormed forwards to grab the witch. But Miyoshi's eyes went wide when he looked at her. She looked different.

Her eyes … he thought. They'd gone white, and it was like snow had fallen only around her—her face glistened with frost dust, and a wildness had come over her.

The witch came peacefully, not fighting back, and Miyoshi thought for a moment she wouldn't. Instead, horror replaced confusion as he realised she *was* fighting back, in her own way.

Water pooled in through the entrance, slowly oozing across the stone ground. The ground began to shake.

'She's going to drown us!' he cried out, and he saw Gora stop and quickly look at the water lapping at their feet before shoulder-barging a pirate away and trying to run closer to the boy, growling as another pirate ran in his way.

'I remember now why this pact made me uneasy.' Aqutak turned to address his captain, and Miyoshi strained to see her skin frosting, lips blue like the ocean, and lashes turning white. 'It means going against you, and it means my death.' Her voice deepened, like hundreds of women speaking as one. 'But we are quite happy to have magic return, even if it means for this incarnation to die.'

Gora's mouth dropped open as the water bubbled around him, as if masses of creatures swarmed beneath.

'Captain!' Miyoshi screamed out, terrified as the water rose, searching the waves for unseen monsters.

'Mother, you need to be quick,' the pirate queen's other daughter, the elder one with shoulder-length hair, Dena, said. Her face wasn't soft anymore. She was looking anxiously between the water and the sea witch. 'Just kill her. Spill all her blood. Let's not risk anything.'

Mammie looked too peaceful, and Miyoshi hoped that didn't mean she'd seen this coming and knew how it ended. Instead, she simply drew her dagger, grabbed at Miyoshi's collar, and dragged the boy across the floor towards the centre of the circle. The pirate queen crouched in front of him, her light green-brown eyes lighting up as she smiled, like a grandparent would to a grandchild, but the dagger in her hand spoilt the aesthetic. Miyoshi shivered, trying to keep eye contact and be brave, trying to wriggle his hands free.

'And so it's finally the last child. After twenty years, the moon on the twentieth-year anniversary has risen. That's what your predecessor told me.' The pirate queen's eyes slid to look sidelong at the sea witch, who was kicked to the ground beside him into the icy waves. Adline grabbed the witch by her thick, dark hair and pulled her up so her face was close to hers.

'Where's that damn Foy when you need him?' Mammie growled, searching the cave. 'It shouldn't take this long to grab a girl!'

'He's getting old,' Dena said, smiling. 'Start. He'll be here soon, and then you can add Gora's friend's blood to the mix.'

Frowning, Mammie raised the dagger over the witch's stomach, but before she could stab it downwards, Miyoshi startled as Adline leapt past her mother and crashed her blade into someone else, who pushed the young pirate back and then lunged forwards again to slice upwards through the young woman's body. Adline cried out as she barely managed to deflect it.

'Daiki!' Miyoshi cried out thankfully, knowing if Daiki was here, he would soon be free. The boy struggled with the ropes at his wrists again, desperately trying to ease his hands out.

Daiki nodded to the young boy, eyes kind, and then rushed Adline again, pushing her back before quickly turning to run at the pirate queen. But in that small distraction, the queen had plunged the dagger into the sea witch's stomach.

Miyoshi winced at the piercing scream, and the sound of countless tiny footsteps beneath the water and on the cave walls drew Miyoshi's gaze to the doorway, and an army of crabs and lobsters and one octopus raced through the doorway, crawling over the pirates and snapping with their claws. The stone walls echoed with fear-filled screams as pirates tried to flee the sea creatures. They fell instead.

Blood spread in the water around the witch's waist, and Miyoshi was sure he saw the circle below the water glow red. The pirate queen laughed, raising the dagger once more, eyes maniacally thrilled.

Fear once again flooded through Miyoshi, quicker than the ocean flooded the room. The boy wondered why the sea witch didn't just drown them all.

But she'd said they wanted this? Why would she want to die? He couldn't understand it.

The pirate queen looked at him, straightening up where she stood. And while Daiki fought off Adline and two other pirate brutes, calling out for the boy to get away if he could, the boy could only look up at Mammie as she stepped closer.

Like I can run tied like this!

Desperate, the boy threw himself to the side, crashing into the rising water and panicking as it lapped around his face. He lunged upwards and took a great gulp of air before crashing down again, shuddering as icy water covered his body.

Floundering any way he could, Miyoshi was desperate to clear the circle and make it back to his friends. But the circle was bigger than the boy anticipated, and tied as he was and with the sea water rising about him, the boy struggled, and the pirate queen grabbed at his arm, fingers clawing into his flesh until he screamed.

He searched the chaos about him, trying to find his friends to cry for help. But they needed help of their own. Yonemura was wrestling with a hairless man to his right, both trying to dodge the incoming sea creatures in the waves. Quinni was leaping from a pirate in fright as crabs coated the man and pulled him under the waves. Gora was grabbing Tomioka, defending the both of them, seemingly one blade down. The boy's heart sank. No-one was close enough for him to call for aid.

Or so he thought. The pirate queen was wrestled off him, and Miyoshi cried out in relief to see Daiki crashing down into the sea water with her. The old samurai rolled and landed on top of the pirate woman, bringing a great fist down to land squarely on her face. The boy pulled himself up to standing and called out Daiki's name happily, but froze when a gunshot echoed nearby, and the samurai spasmed as the shot came straight through his head.

The boy screamed.

Grunting, the pirate queen wrestled her way up, heaving the slumped man off her and carelessly into the waves. Miyoshi watched hopelessly, begging the man to get up. He didn't. The pirate queen stood as her daughters ran up beside her, one with a gun in her hand, talking in low voices to one another.

'You!' Miyoshi yelled, and all three women turned to face him, all traces of friendliness gone. Tears streamed down his face and his throat felt raw and stung, but he didn't care. 'We'll kill you. You'll see.'

The pirate queen huffed, looking exhausted for the first time since she'd seen her. 'No. You'll be the one to die. There is no future for you.' She nodded to her daughters. 'We can wait for Foy no longer. It's finally time. Quick'—she gestured at the collapsed sea witch nearby—'before her blood washes away.'

And before Miyoshi could protest or try to run again, Dena lunged and grabbed him, pulling him back to the centre of the circle, drawing a dagger. Her hands clenched at his shirt, and the boy strained to look past her, searching desperately for Gora, pleading for help. But his captain was too far away now, and Dena dumped the lad harshly on the floor before turning to her mother.

The pirate queen nodded, and the knife rose.

46

The Pact, Complete

The young woman's blade rose above Miyoshi, an empty look on the young pirate girl's face. Gora roared and strained to reach, pulling on the arms that held him and slashing out with his blade. Miyoshi's face was defiant, resigned, but a trembling of his lips showed his fear.

No! We came all this way!

Gora sought out the pirate queen, seeing her victorious smile as she watched her daughter with the boy who would end her twenty-year hunt. He growled, wanting to wipe that smile right off her face.

He plunged his last sword into the guts of the pirate grabbing at him and wrestled aside, rushing for the boy. Tomioka was right beside him, and together the two pushed anyone in their way.

It's no good. Any moment now that knife will—

A screech from somewhere to the right of Miyoshi pulled Gora's attention away from the boy. From seemingly out of nowhere, a young girl with light wavy hair, a smart red jacket, and black trousers ran to Miyoshi's side.

'Mama, no! D—'

The area was silenced by the wet thud of a body being run through by a blade.

Gora's heart shattered.

The fair-haired girl stared up at her mother, eyes wide with disbelief, mouth parted mid-speech and in pain. Her mother froze too, and though Gora couldn't see the woman's face from where he stood, her now stone-like posture said it all. And behind the pair was Miyoshi's stricken face, unable to tear his eyes away from the young girl standing with her arms spread out protectively in front of him.

'Felicity?' Miyoshi's voice shook.

The girl's arms rushed in to cover her pierced stomach, slumping forwards, and her knees buckled. The woman was yet to even move when the girl collapsed to the floor at Miyoshi's feet.

'Felicity?' Miyoshi's cry was louder this time, and the look on his face tore at Gora's soul. The young boy let out a yell, and he struggled against his bonds, straining to reach the girl. Gora strained with him, and with a yell cut down the final sea scum holding him back and darted towards the boy, calling Miyoshi's name over and over to try to bring the boy back. He dared a look at the young girl, golden curls spiralling in the ocean water around her, eyes blank and staring.

Scarlet spilt, and the circle glowed red again. The wind dropped, the water stilled, and Gora felt all his hairs stand on end. He saw a shimmering on the air, the twisting and pulling of light and darkness, knowing the veil was tearing more, stretching from above the cliffs to down here, and braced for something strange.

'Miyoshi!' he cried once more, skidding towards the circle.

Gora's eyes widened; Mammie had disappeared.

Before he could halt and scan for the pirate queen, a green light emanated from the girl's corpse. The air picked up, whistling and screaming through the rocks, and a loud scraping noise—like two ships crashing past each other—echoed on the wind. All around them, people of all sides covered their ears and bent against the wind.

But not Gora. Eyes back on the shaking boy, squinting against the growing green light, he lunged and sliced his blade up the queen's daughter's back. She yelled and tried to turn, hazel eyes piercing his with hatred. With another swish of his arm, Gora sliced across her neck and kicked her aside, away from the small body of her daughter. The woman died, collapsed into a heap and unable to reach the girl who lay still beside her in a ball of dark-green light.

Gora yelled out Miyoshi's name and grabbed him, pulling the boy into a tight hug. The bellowing of the wind increased, and Miyoshi bawled into Gora's chest. Stroking the boy's head, Gora turned to face the girl and the light.

'What is it?' Yonemura yelled, striding towards them with difficulty against the storm-like winds. Her face was pale, blood seeped through her clothes, and her black eyes stared at the girl with uncertainty.

'I'm not sure. I've never seen anything like it before!'

Yonemura's lips pursed, and she dropped onto her knees beside Miyoshi and rested a hand on the boy's shoulder. She stared into Gora's eyes and nodded. Gora released the boy from his embrace and guided him to Yonemura. Then, standing, he scanned the area for the pirate queen and her cronies. All around them, the pirates were dissipating and doing whatever they could to escape the green light and roaring winds, yelling about the coming end.

'There!'

Gora followed Tomioka's arm as he pointed to the edge of the circle. The pirate queen had paused mid-flight, a wind pulling her back.

Towards what?

The green light expanded, pushing to the boundaries of the circle, swallowing even Gora and his crew, meeting where the veil rippled above. When the light touched the veil, the air tore open, and a great eye on the other side peered through.

Gora froze, certain his soul had left his body, and Yonemura and Miyoshi were screaming beside him, grabbing onto him. But the eye ignored them, landing on the small body of the girl at the centre and then disappearing. Ghostly figures on the other side moved in shadows, beckoning. The sea witch's body lifted from the waves and was pulled into the veil by unseen hands, and Gora tore his eyes from the scene to look over to the pirate queen still desperately trying to escape the circle.

To no avail. Gora watched in horror as the woman was swept up and dragged, crying out in her home language, reaching for anyone and anything that could save her. No-one did. No-one could. The great tear swallowed her up and snapped shut, leaving the caverns in petrified silence.

'Captain,' the shaken voice of Miyoshi whispered over to him. 'What happened?'

Gora sat for a moment, feeling his legs numb in the cold ocean water but unable to move. 'I think,' he said, carefully thinking, ignoring the shaking in his own voice. 'I think the spirits just took their final sacrifices: the beings of magic.'

Does this mean Yoshiko's safe?

He startled to remember there had been a tear outside, too.

'No!'

What if it got her?

Gora pushed himself up to standing and hauled up Yonemura and Miyoshi, who were still staring at him and waiting for explanation. But he couldn't give it. 'We have to go,' he said, rushing them, trying to get away.

Around him, others were trying to filter out, and Tomioka had rushed to Daiki's body, lifting the man from the waves. 'Captain?' The man's eyes searched his, and Gora nodded.

But they didn't get far before the green light from the girl grew, forgotten when the air rent open, but now exploding in a giant pillar of green that burst through the rocky roof, boring a hole to the sky. The green light blinded them, and forcing his eyes to look away, Gora grimaced.

'Quick, get out. It's coming down!' he bellowed, rushing his crew.

He wanted to take the girl, give her a proper burial, but as the rocks rained down upon them, his duty was to his crew. Gritting his teeth, he hated himself for looking away.

But as quickly as the light burst, it finished. Completely.

'Felicity!'

A strangled cry came from the cave edge, and Gora boggled to see a man rushing in, barging past everyone else on their way to escape. With dark hair and rich golden eyes, the man was strong, healthy, and the opposite of what Gora knew to be of pirate crew. Stunned, Gora and his crew stopped to watch as the man sprinted to the circle and the crumpled bodies of the girl and the young woman beside her. 'Felicity, Dena!'

He crashed into the waves on his knees, urgently grabbing for his daughter, her wet golden hair tumbling behind her as he dragged her into his arms and yelled, burying his face into her body and bawling.

Then, desperate, he searched the room, golden eyes hunting, yelling, 'Mammie! Show yourself!' The man snarled at the silence that followed. 'Mammie!'

'She's gone,' Gora said in Traders', watching the man. 'I'm sorry, we couldn't stop her.'

The dark-haired man looked at the stranger with an expression that Gora could forgive of a grieving father and husband. He stepped closer to the man, back into the circle, desperate to go above and see if Yoshiko and the rest of his crew were still safe but unable to leave this man behind on his own.

'Gone?' The man's face fell, crestfallen, as it sank in. 'Run away?'

Gora shook his head. 'Completely gone. She was taken too, like them.'

'Dead?'

This time, Gora nodded, but said nothing. 'I can tell you the rest later if you'd like. But come with us. We'll take you, and them, back.'

'Gone?' the man quavered. 'She dares disappear after what she let happen to them!' he was yelling again, face flushing with anger. Hugging his daughter's body closer to him, the man cried again. 'No! Curse you, Mammie! You said they'd be safe!'

And he continued to cry, cursing Mammie and those who helped her over and over until his throat felt hoarse and he crumpled into a bawling heap. But from his words and from his daughter's body crept thin tendrils of green light, stretching out and reaching like unfurling tentacles for the escaping pirates.

Yonemura cried out, drawing Gora's attention off the man. They saw watery hands reaching up from the icy waves and clawing at the pirates' feet, legs, whatever they could grab to pull them down. The green tendrils of light wrapped around limbs and flicked the terrified people up into the air and into cavern walls, and still the lonely man wept over his family.

'It's not coming after us?' Quinni gasped as he bound to Gora's side.

Humming in thought, Gora held fast to young Miyoshi and looked about the place. 'For now. Perhaps it knows we weren't involved.' Then he watched as a pirate was crushed into the cliff and flinched. 'Still, I don't fancy waiting around to find out. Come on. Run. Back to the ship. We're getting out of here.'

He crouched down and grabbed the boy's shoulders, looking him squarely in the face. The boy was shuddering, weeping, but Gora was impressed at how he still met Gora's gaze firmly. 'Boy, you're going to run to the ship. Don't stop, don't look back.

Got it?' The boy nodded, and Gora looked up to Tomioka. 'You're up. Make sure he gets there. Neither of you stop until your feet are firmly on deck. When there, head straight for the galley. Get Kimura to knock up something for the lad. For us all.'

The dark-haired man nodded and reached to grab for Miyoshi's hand. Gora gave a final nod to them and Yonemura, then called over to Rijul and Simrita, who were hovering, weapons drawn, watching in horror. He was relieved to finally see them alive and well—well, mostly. Injured, but alive—now the crowds had disappeared. 'Sim as well. Back to the ship. No stoppin'.'

'And us, captain?' Quinni asked, turning with Gora and clapping Rijul on the shoulder as he caught up, the trio striding through the sprawling green lines of light towards the grieving man.

'I need you both to help me with him. Will you?'

They nodded, and Gora gently shook the man. 'Come now, you can't stay here. Let's get them away from here.'

The man didn't look, but he rose, still cradling his daughter in his arms. He looked down at his wife, seemingly struck that he couldn't carry them both. 'Dena,' he said, a bawl spilling from his lips.

'S'alright. We got her.' Gora nodded to Quinni, who bent and picked up the young pirate woman with ease, holding her kindly despite her involvement in this mess. 'Rijul, I need you to watch the perimeter. Keep us safe. I'm going to make sure he can walk alright.'

The light followed them from the room, keeping with the young girl until they were out into the night. The man had fallen silent, walking as if in a daze. Gora couldn't fault him. Instead, he guided the man gently by his shoulders towards the *Sea Guardian* and relished in the fresh ocean air, crisp as it was, as they left the overbearing cavern.

'Gora!'

He turned as someone dashed over rocks towards him and yelped in joy to see Yoshiko unharmed as she bound for him. She stopped, flushed, and he swore he saw more scales dashed across her relieved face.

'You're still here, alive,' he whispered, his knees buckling as his heart dropped back into place. 'They didn't get you.'

Yoshiko nodded and grinned, but her face fell as she looked around at the tendrils of light leaving the girl and the man.

'What is all this? We just saw it crush one of those ships!'

Gora finally took in the scene, horrified at the destruction, with only one ship left. The *Sea Guardian*.

'We failed,' he finally replied. 'The pact was complete. Magic is back.'

47

A New World

'I thought you were gone,' Gora growled as he sat at his deck in the captain's quarters, glaring at Yoshiko, but not really angry at her. 'We nearly walked right into her trap. I should never have let you come.'

Yoshiko rose an eyebrow at him and sighed, sitting opposite him. 'But you did, and I'm still here, so can you drop this already?' He'd said this to her over and over since they finally set sail from that spirits-forsaken island, and Gora knew Yoshiko was fed up with him, but still, he wouldn't be able to drop the feeling of frustration in himself if she'd been swallowed by the veil like the others had. 'It just needed two people, you said. It got them.'

'But what if it noticed you and thought, *Ahh, another one would be perfect! The more, the better?*'

Yoshiko rolled her eyes, a flicker of annoyance crossing her face. 'We got Miyoshi back. He's alive. We achieved that.'

Gora's voice softened as he replied, 'Aye, but we lost Daiki and Eshnaa.'

Silence fell between them, heavy with the weight of their losses. Gora knew how deeply the deaths of Daiki and Eshnaa had affected Yoshiko and the entire crew. He had listened as Yoshiko recounted the harrowing tale of Eshnaa's sacrifice, dying to save her.

Yoshiko's gaze dropped to her hands in her lap, her fingers restless. 'I wish she hadn't,' she whispered, her voice barely audible. 'Then she'd still be here.'

Yoshiko's words echoed in Gora's mind from when she'd vividly recounted what had happened aboard the ship. The crew had fought with their full might to clear the vessel, driving the pirates back. Just when victory seemed within reach, a figure had slipped below deck, their intentions unknown. Yoshiko had bolted after the intruder, with Eshnaa and Ikeda close behind.

The agile Eshnaa had reached the stairs leading down to the cramped passageways to the hold just after Yoshiko, with Ikeda not long afterwards. The pirate had turned to see them and, desperate to protect himself, had brandished a gun and aimed it at Yoshiko. Eshnaa had acted selflessly. She'd thrusted Yoshiko away, shielding their leader with her own body, and took the bullet in her side.

Yoshiko, fuelled by a burning surge, had retaliated instantly, rushing past Eshnaa and clawing at the pirate's face, using every ounce of her cursed strength to smash his head against the wall. The impact had been devastating, leaving a huge dent in the wall, ending his life in an instant.

As Yoshiko had turned her attention to aid Eshnaa, her heart sank. The young warrior lay motionless on the steps, her head bearing the mark of a fatal fall on the steps. Gora still recalled how Simrita had screamed when she returned to the ship from the caves and found out.

Yoshiko sniffed. While it had been hard for her to talk to the young Ishillians due to the language barrier, Gora had always seen her happily in their company, pestering others to help them translate. He sighed then returned his attention to the map on the table in front of them.

'We're headin' home,' he said. 'Away from all this. I agreed to drop that man back in Ita at a port near his hometown, so we're heading south. Finally away from this damned cold.' He paused and looked up to make sure she was listening. She was, eyes pinned to a spot on the map.

'South? You think we can stop by Qecla on the way? See Nubia?'

Her eyes met his, dark once more with the curse under control, eager.

Gora looked away, not wanting to disappoint her. 'Not sure. We'll see. For now, I want us to focus on getting here.' He thrust a finger on the map. 'The ship needs patching, the crew needs a rest, and we need to stock up on supplies. And besides, since the pact was, you know, more creatures are abound. Not sure how we'll sail in new conditions.'

The pair hesitated, and wary, dark eyes met exhausted blue ones. The green light had faded, and the tear in the sky had disappeared, but the creatures that had gathered around the sea witch at the end were still about, and in greater numbers. In just the single day they'd been sailing, they'd come across many strange creatures they'd never seen before, and Gora had a feeling this would be life as they knew it now.

'Feelin' any different?' he prompted her.

She nodded. 'A little. Like the air is still buzzing. But always. Not just around the island.' Then, 'Do you think there will be more people like me, in the future?'

Gora stood, stretching his back. 'Who knows, now? Might be. Let's hope, whoever they are, they're not as much of a glutton for food as you are. There'd be no food left in the world.' She glared at him, but he laughed. And then he paused. 'The lad said the pirate queen was doing this because something dangerous was coming. Something that could tear apart a country and kill everyone living in it. Said we needed magic to fight it. That's why she did this. What d'ye think?'

Yoshiko rose her brows and thought for a moment. 'If something that bad was to come, I'm not sure anything could stop it.'

'Not even you?'

'If it can tear apart a country … You told me off just for destroying one town!' She then she slumped forward, resting her elbows on the table. 'I do not think I could stop that. Unless …' She thought back to what the shrine maiden had said about people using her bones if she died as a dragon and didn't hide well. She'd told Gora about it, of course, but he'd insisted that she simply stay as a human, not using her powers, so she didn't have to worry about it. 'Never mind.'

He frowned and waited for her to explain, but she shook her head. 'I'm just tired and worrying over nothing. Now I just want to get home.'

Gora smiled, revealing a flash of white against his sun-kissed skin, and ran his fingers through his unruly dark red hair. Then he beckoned her to follow him. 'Aye, I can agree with that. Come now, Kimura's said he made up some new dessert for us. Some kind of bread stuffed with that sweet *anko* paste you like. Let's grab the crew and have a feast. I think we all need it. It'll be a long way home from here. We can chat about something as grave as a disaster swallowing countries after that, when we're home and dry and not bringing wild fate upon us.'

Yoshiko regarded him with a mixture of amusement and curiosity as they strolled through the winding passageways, their footsteps echoing softly against the polished wooden floor. The glow of lanterns lining the walls cast a warm glow, and she narrowed her eyes at him with a playful scepticism. 'Hanging around pirates made you superstitious again?'

Gora shrugged, a smirk on his lips and a twinkle in his eyes. 'Well, who's to say, now? It's a new world, after all.'

Epilogue
And Beyond

Gora ruled the waves as captain of the *Sea Guardian* for three decades after this story ends. Many ships gathered under his banner to drive piracy and slave traders from the waters, also guiding merchants and travellers for safe passage through the new magical waters, safe from creatures. He became a venerated ocean-faring hero, known throughout history.

Yonemura Emiko remained on his ship, becoming promoted to first mate when Shingo retired. Ever since the events on the island, Gora would have sworn that something about her had changed. She could see further, clearer, almost seeing through the waves and looking at dangers they would soon face. In her time as helmswoman, the ship never ran foul of the shore or any rocks, no matter the route they took. She, too, became known as a respected ocean hero, helping him keep people safe on the oceans until she died in her sleep two decades later.

Miyoshi stayed with Gora for many years, continuing to learn all he could, becoming almost like a son. When Gora tried to promote him, Miyoshi asked him a favour instead: to visit Felicity's home country. He'd never been able to shake the guilt from her dying for him. Sailing to the place Felicity told him about, Miyoshi gathered a sack of mysterious things that not even Gora and Yonemura could get him to explain. He left Gora's crew on their next return to Hizen, when Miyoshi turned twenty-one, years after he first joined Gora's crew. He moved into Gora's old hut with his precious haul and planted seeds and fruits Felicity had told him about, growing grapes, olives, and citrus fruits like nothing Hizen had ever seen. His mother was able to live out the rest of her days in a comfortable life, where both used the fruits to move on and start a business. He even developed the first grape wine in Hizen.

Moori rose through the ranks and was gifted a ship of her own by Yoshiko, on Gora and Yonemura's recommendation. She captained her own ship until she was an 'old hag', as she liked to say, and was a fierce leader with no sympathy for anyone or anything that made life unsafe for people. She defended the eastern oceans and regularly visited home to enjoy herbal tea and sweetmeats with Yoshiko, followed by an afternoon of hunting. When she died a peaceful death in her old age, her crew gave her a northern burial: they hopped ship to a fellow *Sea Guardian* unit and set Moori and her entire ship ablaze. Many financiers at the time and in the future wondered why they'd waste such a good ship. The crew, on the other hand, said it was barely enough for such a captain.

Simrita stayed on Gora's ship for a few years but left to open a training school for women in Ishil. She faced many hardships and political onslaught for allowing women to be trained, but she imagined what Eshnaa would have done and beat them all off. If any man could beat her in one-on-one combat, she had said, she'd stop running the school. None could. Her school expanded, her students going on to open schools all over the country.

Quinni finally returned to his homeland, returning to discover a land rich with magic and rejuvenated health. He told his story to all those who came to meet him, and he was given a place on the new circle that ran the country—run by Nubia, her husband,

and some of her closest allies—to bring it back to its proper state.

Jelani remained with the *Sea Guardian* before transferring to Moori's ship to help her establish a good crew. Since meeting, they'd become like family, and he considered the wild, gun-loving noble girl from Hizen a daughter.

Rijul gave up fighting and travelled with Kimura across the continents to explore new foods and to experiment with making mixed cuisine. After several years of joint travel, Rijul returned to Ishil and opened a restaurant in the main port of Ishil, cooking fusion food where he could easily have ingredients shipped in. He eventually married and had three children, two of whom loved cooking and continued his food work. The other, a girl, joined Simrita's fighting school.

After Kimura and Rijul parted ways, Kimura continued travelling the world in search of new foods, flirting with anyone beautiful as he went. He became known as the famous wandering chef, making beautiful meals out of anything for anyone who let him stay the night. He never returned to Hizen. In his older age, he got caught up in a war, dying when an ill-developed magical weapon blew up.

Shingo stayed with the *Sea Guardian* for many years. When he eventually retired, he gave his position to Yonemura and returned to Hizen, living happily with Miyoshi and his mother in Gora's old hut, helping the lad tend to the land.

Satou went back to Hié to continue developing craftsmanship, combining magic and crafts he'd seen from overseas to create the first magical tools seen in centuries. He was well respected by many, and Yoshiko brought his skills to the attention of Kazuhito, the shogun, and Satou was given position in the shogun's court as a highly lauded craftsman. He led the development of defence and weapons for Gora's and Moori's ships, ensuring they were set no matter the creatures they faced.

Nishimura Gin also remained with the *Sea Guardian,* studying the energy of magic to guide the ship safely through infested waters or magical storms. Aqutak's octopus remained with Nishimura, becoming, to Gora's discomfort, a member of the crew.

Kyo and Taro returned to Hié, reopening their family shop. Kyo regained his former health quickly, comfortable that they'd both done what they could in their time on the *Sea Guardian* but ready to try living their old life again, with a renewed bond.

After the resurgence of magic, Yoshiko's dragon-blood grew stronger after years of waning in her family line. She led Hié for many years, longer than any daimyō in the past, the dragon-blood drawing out her age. Throughout her fifty-year period, she worked to bringing the citizens of her country into its ruling, beginning with small councils and representatives, to having a government rule beneath her. Yoshiko joined forces with many of the neighbouring domains, helping the shogun bring each region into joined peace. In her fiftieth year of leading Hié, Yoshiko left it to the government and disappeared, never to be seen again. She travelled with Ikeda—her last remaining friend from the old days—to countries overseas, finally trying to make the visit to Qecla that had never happened in her youth.

Yoshiko's first private guard, Chisaka Reina, married a neighbouring lord in a diplomatic marriage. Due to Yoshiko's lack of desire to marry, and her closeness with Chisaka, Chisaka was considered a highly recommended candidate for marriage in her stead. She moved out of the domain and regularly wrote to and visited Yoshiko, and ever remained a stickler, pestering her warlord in each letter.

Ikeda Hiroki remained Yoshiko's private guard to the end. As ever, he took his position seriously and never left her side. They fought beside one another many times and grew a closeness he, as a young man, could never have imagined. When she left

Hié to travel the world, he was the only one she took with her, knowing Ikeda would grieve should she leave without him. He accompanied and protected her until the day he died from old age. She burned him herself, the only other person she used her dragon fire to bury, beside Haruki—the time all those years ago when she first discovered her power.

What happened of Yoshiko from there, and her death, though, is yet unknown.

Noble Blood Teaser

Humans were never meant to live in the sky.

The wind clawed through the edge barrier and bit at Nia's neck as she gripped the ancient metal railing and stared into the clouds below.

A footstep behind her scuffed over stony soil, and then a heavy weight crashed over her shoulders.

'I told you you'd need this today,' a man's low voice grumbled.

Nia pulled the thick coat on with a grateful smile to Issam, one of her personal guardians, who now stood smartly at the railing to her right.

'Issam,' a woman's voice to her left chipped in, and Nia turned to see her other guardian, Faiza, leaning nonchalantly with her back against the railing, her cream headscarf billowing in the wind, still somehow pinned in place. 'You're such a mother with your nagging.'

The two glared at one another behind Nia. She rolled her eyes and cut in before the bickering could start.

'The wind feels stronger than usual,' she said. 'Shouldn't the barriers filter more than this? Or am I imagining it?'

Her distraction worked, and Faiza turned to peer over the edge, frowning as she inspected the edge, headscarf whipping behind her.

'No,' she said, raising her voice over the gusts. 'You're right. Look over there.'

She pointed at one of the circumference towers to their right, holding magic that held the edge barrier strong. The towers were meant to let out a constant blue-white glow at their core. But this one …

'The tower's a little dim, don't you think?' Faiza continued.

Nia and Issam both looked back at Faiza in horror, and Nia's hands tightened on the cold metal railing, the knuckles on her left hand whitening.

Not that this ancient rail could keep her from tumbling over the edge if the barrier magic failed. Humans had learnt long ago that the railings had not been built to stop people from falling. They had been built to remind them they could.

Nia glanced back at the edge tower. The dull blue light shrank and grew as she watched it, so she added it to a long mental list of other things she had to organise to be fixed. Then she curled her lip and looked away, staring at the field of clouds ahead and slumping against the railing.

'Just another sign we can't hold here much longer,' she grumbled as her two guards leant down with her. 'Our resources are dwindling, and our magic weakens by the day.' She nodded vaguely below. 'We have to return the mountain to the surface.'

'It is the sky mother's will,' Faiza said, her voice reverent. 'The sky citadel was a sanctuary – a haven from the creatures that ravaged the earth. But it was not meant to be our eternal home.'

Nia looked to Issam, both unable to help the small amused smile at Fazia's recitals of the texts.

'What?' Fazia burst out, giving them both a light smack on their arms. 'You know the surface was built for us, not the skies. Beautiful and powerful as they are.'

Nia could only shrug. She didn't disagree.

But Issam scoffed. 'Try telling the military that.' Then he glanced over at them, staring at him with tilted eyebrows. 'We all know how they think. We've lasted her generations, they'll tell you. Conquered the impossible. It's a sign, they'll say. That we're never meant to go back.' His eyes dropped to Nia's right arm. 'You know what happened the last time we tried going there. Even for a short time.'

His dark eyes flickered back up to meet hers, and burned when she held his gaze.

'They'll never stop using that against you if you try to talk to them about returning.'

Nia released a long, soft exhale from her nose as she looked down at her two arms, letting Faiza and Issam bicker about depressing motivational support speeches behind her. The cold metal bit into her left hand. But her right?

Nothing.

Metal from just above the elbow and down, her right arm felt nothing of the biting cold railing.

Issam was right, of course. A decade ago, she'd persuaded them to let a science and defence team run a short mission to the surface. See if the creatures were still there or if the earth was still inhabitable. Collect samples to use for testing. Scientifically, it had been a success. But they'd been spotted by a creature and had to run from a rampage. Nia had lost her arm, and her father, Amaechi, king of the sky citadel, had labelled the whole mission a failure and banned any further surface missions.

Except, back then, they'd not had the pressing knowledge of a resource issue. Now, she was hoping to persuade the council of elders and her father to retract that ban.

They needed to go back.

'The ground has been out of our reach for centuries ...' Nia stared into the abyss, trying to test her speech to persuade the elders of the council. She wanted it to sound inspiring, but it felt melancholy.

To her left, Faiza returned to leaning back against the railing, staring up at the sky as if she had no worry in the world. Nia envied this woman who could take things as the world gave them to her, rather than running things over in her head countless times.

'It's a delicate issue,' Issam said. 'Our ancestors made a big decision to raise the mountain up here to escape what was below. It'll be a big decision for the elders to lower it again, knowing the creatures are still down there.'

Nia supposed he was trying to be encouraging. Her face scrunched up as she tried to wipe out all worrying thoughts in her head and focus on her speech.

This was why it was good here at the edge. The harsh winds filtering through the edge barrier battered the worried thoughts right out of her head. It was oddly cleansing.

'I will find a way,' she said through gritted teeth, trying to persuade herself more than them. They had annoyingly good faith in her. 'I lost my arm last time we tried, but that shouldn't mean a whole civilisation is put to risk! The danger is real, but so are we, and so our need is real. We weren't meant to be up here for hundreds of years.'

Faiza shrugged. Rose from where she slouched on the railing and took a few steps and rounded on them, smirking. 'Well, sounds like you're ready.'

Nia turned back to watch the clouds scudding past them for a moment, and then stepped back from the railing too and grinned back at her guardian. 'I am,' she said. 'And I will be ready to tell the elders too. I just need to take a few more notes—'

Faiza let out a burst of laughter, and even the steadfast Issam chuckled.

'What?' Nia protested, following Faiza as she led them away.

'Always more reading,' Faiza cried, flailing her arms dramatically. 'Always more notes! Sky mother help us, this woman will never be ready to present at the meeting.'

Nia's mouth dropped open to protest, but Issam caught up and nudged her gently with his elbow. 'You do realise you only have one more night, right?'

The wind whipped up once more as they walked away, swallowing up Nia's protests and pushing them back to the safety of the hulking stone mountain where an entire city was carved into the rock. She laughed at their teasing, but somewhere in the sky citadel, an evening bell tolled, urging the city towards night.

Time was running out.

Faiza and Issam encouraged her their whole way back, walking quickly through the winding, rising streets and steps up through the stone city on this side of the mountain. They paused often to rest, hearts pounding and Nia's legs burning at the constant incline.

'How can you both do this so much easier than me?' she cried when they reached a rest stop only halfway back. 'You spend most of your time stuck with me.'

They both looked back and smirked.

'You sit down too much,' Faiza grinned. 'Too much reading.'

Nia groaned and stared up at the winding city yet above them. The central castle was further still, and her body suddenly regretted her decision to spend her final day of preparation for the council of the elders down at the edge.

'Come on,' Issam said, holding his hand out to pull her up from the bench she'd flopped onto. 'Not long before dark.'

The city lanterns flickered on as the light levels dropped, and Nia distracted herself by looking around at the bustling action of her people as they returned to their homes or went out to bars for an evening meal and a drink. Their buzz of energy encouraged her. It was for them she needed to succeed tomorrow. The last desperate measure to raise the mountain from the earth had cost the lives of many mages, but it had offered sanctuary to many. And they'd had a few hundred years of safety and progress.

But now, though the mountain still floated, the magic that held it amongst the clouds was failing.

The bells rang again, closer this time.

She glanced down towards the bottom of the mountain, where the edge tower's blue light wavered against the backdrop of darkening clouds. With it, the mountain groaned softly around them, stone settling against magical wards.

Nia clenched her metal fingers.

She'd already paid once to reach the surface. She wouldn't let that be for nothing.

Glossary

List of non-English terms

anko—A sweet red bean paste commonly used in Japanese desserts. I highly recommend it.

chakram—A circular, sharp-edged throwing weapon originating from South Asia.

daidokoro—The traditional Japanese term for a kitchen or a cooking area in a home.

daimyō—A powerful feudal lord in Japan during the pre-modern era.

dango—Japanese sweet dumplings made from rice flour and served on skewers. Also highly recommend!

funayūrei—Ghostly spirits of those who died at sea, often depicted as floating lanterns or humanoid creatures who try to use buckets to sink other ships.

Gaean—Language spoken in Eire.

hakama—Traditional Japanese wide-legged trousers often worn for formal occasions or martial arts. They were worn more commonly in history, particularly by the higher classes.

haori—A traditional Japanese hip- or thigh-length kimono-style jacket.

Hizen-shuu—A rice wine native to Hizen.

hyotan—A gourd-shaped fruit used in Japan as a container or decoration when dried.

Inari Jinja—Shinto shrines dedicated to the deity Inari, known as the god of rice, agriculture, and foxes.

kanzashi—Traditional Japanese hair ornaments often worn by geisha and maiko and noble ladies in history. These days, anyone can buy and wear them.

karamété mon—The rear entrance gate to Hié castle compound.

katar—A type of short, double-edged dagger used in India.

Kioto—Capital city of Hizen.

kitsuné—A mythical fox creature in Japanese folklore, often associated with shape-shifting and intelligence. They've also been known to trick unsuspecting people.

kiyohimé (also used as Kiyohimé, a name, with no italics)—A tragic figure from Japanese folklore who transformed into a dragon due to unrequited love and burned their love interest. It is used more as a magical creature in general in this series.

kodama*—Spirits or deities believed to inhabit trees in Japanese folklore. There are many interpretations of these, from giant trees that haunt or kill people, to cute tiny creatures as shown in Studio Ghibli movies.

komainu—Guardian lion-dog statues commonly found at Shinto shrines and Buddhist temples in Japan.

kotatsu—A low, heated table covered with a blanket, used in Japan during the colder months.

nabé—A type of Japanese hot pot dish typically cooked at the table.

noppera-bō—A ghostly creature in Japanese mythology that appears as a featureless human face or even a person without a face.

oté-mon—A large, decorative gate leading into Hié castle compound.

ryoukai—A Japanese term meaning 'understood' or 'acknowledged'.

saké—The word in Japanese for 'alcohol' in general, though typically in Western cultures it has become mixed up with 'nihon-shuu', the traditional Japanese wine made from fermented rice.

talwar—A type of curved, single-edged sword originating from South Asia.

tenshu—The central tower of a Japanese castle, often serving as the highest and most fortified point.

umibōzu—A giant sea monster or spirit said to appear and capsize ships in Japanese folklore.

yōkai—A class of supernatural creatures or monsters in Japanese folklore.

Acknowledgements

I've got a double Acknowledgements this time. Unfortunately, it was missed in Book 1, so I'll be sharing my greatest thanks to everyone who has helped me with both books thus far, or my husband will keep teasing me forever.

It'll be long—two books' worth—but worth it.

I'll start with **my dad**. He got me into reading early, encouraged random storytelling and role-play, and is such a nerd that of course I had no hope to be anything but, too. He's a fantasy and sci-fi reader and went with all the magical stories, so of course I am, too. He's a right softie, and I'm glad for that. Thanks for getting me down this epic nerdy path, Papa.

Miyuki: on our lunchbreaks in Sakuragichou, you sat and heard my ideas for the growth of these stories and gave me wonderful thoughts and advice, particularly as I wanted to write about the new world that had opened up to me: Japan. Writing about a culture that's not your own is a challenge, as you always want to do it well to give it the best, and it was you who really helped me get this right. I miss being able to chat to you every day at work, and I hope I get to work with you again one day. We're a great team!

Fran D: your energy inspires me, and you were a perfect *gaijin* friend for me in Japan, both of us wanting to make our lives there and having all kinds of weird and lofty goals. I moved away, but one day I'll be back. With tonnes of new puns to annoy you with.

And I promise I'll still write your book. The ideas are brewing, and it's going to be so much fun.

To my wonderful editors: **Chloe Cran and Kristy and Jason Martin**. I've loved your input and encouragement the whole way. You've never asked me to change the story or force it to fit a stencil, and never asked me to put romance in. That means a lot. It was a fear of mine, as every book seems to have it! But you've helped me keep the best, and I love how it's grown with you all. PS: Chloe, thanks for having nerdy jokes with me as we edit, too!

Jason Smith: Thanks for being you and a great book nerd and writing friend to talk with. It's always fun talking about ideas and plans, and I can't wait to see your books too.

To the artists. **Florianne and Giulia.** The reason it took me so long to get this story into the world was because I was so stumped to find the right artists to work with. Nothing I saw seemed to fit the bill. I think it was fate. With the delay in publishing, I found you both, and you've really brought visual life to the world I've written about.

Kristine, your formatting is always so neat, so clean. I wanted a simple design that matched the book but wouldn't be that it stole too much attention from the reading that it interrupted readers. You got it just right.

Mikayla: I'm glad this was the first fantasy book you read and that you chanced a new genre for me. I'm even more glad you loved it. Now you've challenged me to a book a year. Challenge accepted. Hold me to it.

Makoto, my son and new inspiration. For a long time, we joked about what would come first, Book 1 or baby. It was you. You're funny and a go-getter, and your resilience and persistence are incredible—and you're only seven months old right now! You've inspired me, and I love seeing your personality come out more and more each day.

And **my husband, Keita**. I put you last because you teased me about forgetting my Acknowledgements last time, so I made you wait! But in reality, also I don't know who else I would end on. You've put up with 4 am alarms when I used to get up to write, taken pictures of me asleep at my desk and teased me about them, made breakfast or dinner when I was stuck in the zone, attended events and signings with me even if they went on for hours, helped me think up ideas and plans of what I could do more of for marketing and events, and encouraged me the whole way. You're not a fiction reader, and have no clue half the time when I ramble about it all, but give me the best support of all. I'm so glad you're here to walk the world with me, and I can't wait for all our adventures in life, whatever they are.

About Sarah Caelan

I write and draw early in the morning (at stupid o'clock, as my dad says), before the day and all its demands crowd in. I make stories, art, and books around a full life (work, family, responsibility), and I don't want to pretend that balance is neat or easy. It's something I fight for (with deeply etched purple shadows under my eyes included) because making things is not optional for me. It's how I breathe and actually feel like myself.

My stories are rooted in the wilds: dark forests, long roads, weathered people, and the quiet hope of warmth at the end of the day. I'm drawn to characters with grit and tenderness in equal measure. Women with muddied boots, who endure and act. Men who aren't afraid to show they care. People who are allowed to be whole. Real. Because, in my head, the people are always the heart of the story.

I hope you felt this way about Yoshiko, Gora, and all the characters in this story.

See you in the next book.

Welcome to The Wilds.
We'll keep the fire lit.

Also by Sarah Caelan

For adults
Dynasty Codes 1: Origin Curse
Iron Angels
The Feather and the Fall

For children
Haru & Yuka and the Missing Kitsuné Guard